MW01004404

ANCESTORS AND OTHERS

ALSO BY FRED CHAPPELL

POETRY

The World Between the Eyes, 1971
River, 1975
Bloodfire, 1978
Wind Mountain, 1979
Earthsleep, 1980
Midquest, 1981
Castle Tzingal, 1984
Source, 1985
First and Last Words, 1989
C: 100 Poems, 1993
Spring Garden: New and Selected Poems, 1995
Family Gathering, 1995
Companion Volume, 2002
Backsass, 2003
Shadow Box, 2009

FICTION

It Is Time, Lord, 1963
The Inkling, 1965
Dagon, 1968
The Gaudy Place, 1972
Moments of Light, 1980
I Am One of You Forever, 1985
Brighten the Corner Where You Are, 1989
More Shapes Than One, 1991
Farewell, I'm Bound to Leave You, 1996
Look Back All the Green Valley, 1999
Ancestors and Others, 2009

COLLECTION

The Fred Chappell Reader, 1987

ESSAYS

Plow Naked: Selected Writings on Poetry, 1993
A Way of Happening: Observations of Contemporary Poetry, 1998

Ancestors and Others

FRED CHAPPELL

ST. MARTIN'S PRESS NEW YORK

This is a work of fiction. All of the characters, organizations, and events portrayed in these stories are either products of the author's imagination or are used fictitiously.

 For information, address St. Martin's Press, 175 Fifth Avenue, New York, N.Y. 10010.

www.stmartins.com

Library of Congress Cataloging-in-Publication Data

Chappell, Fred, 1936–
Ancestors and others : new and selected stories / Fred Chappell.—1st ed.
p. cm.
ISBN 978-0-312-56167-3
I. Title.
PS3553.H298A84 2009
813'.54—dc22

2009024034

First Edition: November 2009

10 9 8 7 6 5 4 3 2 1

For Leslie A. Phillabaum

CONTENTS

ACKNOWLEDGMENTS

"Broken Blossoms," "Children of Strikers," "The Three Boxes," "Judas," and "Moments of Light" were collected in *Moments of Light* (New South Co., 1980). "Linnaeus Forgets," "Alma," "The Somewhere Doors," "Ladies from Lapland," and "Mankind Journeys Through Forests of Symbols" were published in *More Shapes Than One* (St. Martin's Press, 1991). "Crèche" (under the title "Peaceful Was the Night") was published in *A Very Southern Christmas,* eds. Charline R. McCord and Judy H. Tucker (Algonquin, 2003). "The Lodger" appeared as a chapbook (Necronomicon Press, 1993).

"Christmas Gift!" appeared in *Appalachian Heritage,* "Gift of Roses" in *North Carolina Literary Review,* "Bon Ton" in *Five Points,* "Ancestors" in *Chronicles,* and "Tradition" in *Shenandoah.*

ANCESTORS AND OTHERS

THE OVERSPILL

Then there was one brief time when we didn't live in the big brick house with my grandmother, but in a neat two-story green-roofed white house in the hollow below. It was two stories if you stood at the front door; on the other side it was three stories, the ground floor a tall basement garage.

The house was surrounded by hills to the north and east and south. Directly above us lay the family farm and my grandmother's house. Two miles behind the south hill was the town of Tipton, where the Challenger Paper and Fiber Corporation smoked eternally, smudging the Carolina mountain landscape for miles. A small creek ran through our side yard, out of the eastern hills. The volume of the creek flow was controlled by Challenger; they had placed a reservoir up there, and the creek water was regulated by means of a spillway.

At this time my mother was visiting her brother in California. Uncle Luden was in trouble again, with a whole different woman this time. Maybe my mother could help; it was only five thousand miles round-trip by train.

So my father and I had to fumble along as best we could.

Despite the extra chores, I found it exciting. Our friendship took a new and stronger turn, became something of a mild conspiracy. New sets of signals evolved between us. We met now on freshly neutral ground somewhere between my boyhood and his boyishness, and for me it was a heady rise in status. We were clumsy housekeepers, there were lots of minor mishaps, and the tag line we formulated soonest was "Let's just not tell Mama about this one." I adored that thought.

He was always dreaming up new projects to please her and, during her absence, came up with one of masterly ambition.

Across the little creek, with its rows of tall willows, was a half acre of fallow ground considered unusable because of marshiness and the impenetrable clot of blackberry vines in the south corner. My father now planned it as a garden, already planted before she returned.

We struggled heroically. I remember pleasantly the destruction of the vines and the cutting of the drainage ditch neat and straight into the field. The ground was so soft that we could slice down with our spades and bring up squares of dark blue mud and lay them along side by side. They gleamed like tile. Three long afternoons completed the ditch, and then my father brought out the big awkward shoulder scythe and whetted the blade until I could hear it sing on his thumb ball when he tested it. And then he waded into the thicket of thorny vine and began slashing. For a long time nothing happened, but finally the vines began to fall back, rolling up in tangles like barbarous handwriting. With a pitchfork, I worried these tangles into a heap. Best of all was the firing, the clear yellow flame and the sizzle and snap of the vine ribs and thorns, and the thin black smoke rising above the new-green willows. The delicious smell of it.

After this, we prepared the ground in the usual way and planted. Then we stood at the edge of our garden, admiring with a full, tired pride the clean furrows and mounded rows of earth.

But this was only a part of the project. It was merely a vegetable garden, however arduously achieved, and we planted a garden every year. My father wanted something else, decorative, elegant in design, something guaranteed to please a lady.

The weather held good and we started next day, hauling two loads of scrap lumber from one of the barns. He measured and we sawed and planed. He hummed and whistled as he worked and I mostly stared at him when not scurrying to and fro, fetching and carrying. He wouldn't, of course, tell me what we were building.

On the second day it became clear. We were constructing a bridge. We were building a small but elaborate bridge across the little creek that divided the yard and the garden, a stream that even I could step over without lengthening my stride. It was ambitious: an arched bridge with handrails and a latticework arch on the garden side enclosing a little picket gate.

He must have been a handy carpenter. To me, the completed bridge appeared marvelous. We had dug deep on both sides to sink the locust piers, and the arch above the stream, though not high, was unmistakably a rainbow. When I walked back and forth across the bridge, I heard and felt a satisfactory drumming. The gate latch made a solid cluck and the gate arch, pinned together of old plaster lathe, made me feel that in crossing the bridge I was entering a different world, not simply going into the garden.

He had further plans for the latticework. "Right here," he said, "and over here. I'll plant some roses to climb up the trellis. Then you'll see."

We whitewashed it three times. The raw lumber sparkled. We walked upstream to the road above the yard and looked at it, then walked downstream to the edge of the garden and looked at it. We saw nothing we weren't prideful about.

He went off in our old Pontiac and returned in a half hour. He parked in the driveway and got out. "Come here," he said. We sat in the grass on the shoulder of the culvert at the edge of the road. "I've been to the store," he said. He pulled a brown paper sack from his pocket. I found ten thimble-shaped chocolate mints inside, my favorite. From another pocket he pulled a rolled band of bright red silk.

"Thank you," I said. "What's that?"

"We want her to know it's a present, don't we? So we've got to tie a ribbon on it. We'll put it right there in the middle of the handrail." He spooled off two yards of ribbon and cut it with his pocketknife. "Have to make a big one so she can see it from the road."

I chewed a mint and observed his thick, horny fingers with the red silk.

It was not to be. Though I was convinced that my father could design and build whatever he wanted—the Brooklyn Bridge, the Taj Mahal—he could not tie a bow in this broad ribbon. The silk crinkled and knotted and slipped loose; it simply would not behave. He growled in low tones, like a bear trying to dislodge a groundhog from its hole. "I don't know what's the matter with this stuff," he said.

Over the low mumble of his words I heard a different rumble, a gurgle as of pebbles pouring into a broad, still pool. "What's that?" I asked.

"What's what?"

"What's that noise?"

He stopped ruining the ribbon and sat still as the sound grew louder.

Then his face darkened and veins stood out in his neck and forehead. His voice was quiet and level now. "Those bastards."

"Who?"

"The Challenger Paper guys. They've opened the floodgates."

We scrambled up the shoulder into the road.

As the sound got louder, it discomposed into many sounds: lappings, bubblings, rippings, undersucks, and splashovers. Almost as soon as we saw the gray-brown thrust of water emerge from beneath the overhanging plum tree, we felt the tremor as it slammed against the culvert, leaping up the shoulder and rolling back. On the yard side it shot out of the culvert as out of a hose. In a few seconds it had overflowed the low creek banks and streamed gray-green along the edge of the yard, furling white around the willow trunks. Debris—black sticks and leaves and grasses—spun on top of the water, and the gullet of the culvert rattled with rolling pebbles.

Our sparkling white bridge was soiled with mud and slimy grasses. The water driving into it reached a gray arm high into the air and slapped down. My father and I watched the hateful battering of our work, our hands in our pockets. He still held the red ribbon, and it trickled out of his pocket down his trouser leg. The little bridge trembled and began to shake. There was one moment when it sat quite still, as if it had gathered resolve and was fighting back.

And then on the yard side it wrenched away from the log piers, and when that side headed downstream, the other side tore away, too, and we had a brief glimpse of the bridge parallel in the stream like a strange boat and saw the farthest advance of the flood framed in the quaint lattice arch. The bridge twirled about and the corners caught against both banks and it went over on its side, throwing up the naked underside of the planks like a barn door blown shut. Water piled up behind this damming and finally poured over and around it, eating at the borders of the garden and lawn.

My father kept saying over and over, "Bastards bastards bastards. It's against the law for them to do that."

Then he fell silent.

I don't know how long we stared downstream before we were aware that my mother had arrived. When we first saw her, she had already gotten out of the taxi, which sat idling in the road. She looked odd to me, wearing a dress I had never seen, and a strange expression—half amused, half vexed—crossed her face. She looked at us as if she'd caught us doing something naughty.

My father turned to her and tried to speak. Bastards *was the only word he got out. He choked and his face and neck went dark again. He gestured toward the swamped bridge, and the red ribbon fluttered in his fingers.*

She looked where he pointed and, as I watched, understanding came into her face, little by little. When she turned again to face us, she looked as if she were in pain. A single tear glistened on her cheek, silver in the cheerful light of midafternoon.

My father dropped his hand and the ribbon fluttered and trailed in the mud.

The tear on my mother's face got larger and larger. It detached from her face and became a shiny globe, widening outward like an inflating balloon. At first the tear floated in the air between them, but as it expanded, it took my mother and father into itself. I saw them suspended, separate but beginning to drift slowly toward each other. Then my mother looked past my father's shoulder, looked through the bright skin of the tear, at me. The tear enlarged until at last it took me in, too. It was warm and salty. As soon as I got used to the strange light inside the tear, I began to swim clumsily toward my parents.

BROKEN BLOSSOMS

At first, brightly colored stones and oddly shaped leaves and bird nests and cicada husks, and perhaps it ought to end there, when one is seven or eight years old, attracted to the gathering of things by the eye's joy and by a reverence for something which the natural world—so shadowy mysterious—has seemed to cast aside. Whatever it later turns into will be mere pleasure in collecting for the sake of collecting, in pigeonholing, in aligning things in rows, in piecing out categories.

In my own case, this dark latter urge struck me hard when I was eleven and was manifested as stamp collecting. The stamp album from that time has long been lost, or maybe I traded it away as a teenager. I should like to see it now, though I would blush shamefully if I had to display it before a true philatelist. I recall the color, a matte chocolate-maroon, and the gold lettering across the front, STAMPS OF MANY COUNTRIES, and my name, too, in gold letters in the lower right-hand corner. The situation in which I most vividly recall it is lying cater-cornered on the beat-up coffee table which served me as a desk (I sat cross-legged on the floor) under the bronze-painted table lamp with its dusty yellow shade. When the big square book lay there unopened, it spoke my name to me again and again.

Inside, what a mess! The stamps were supposed to be attached to the album pages with little gummed paper hinges, and this required a minimal amount of dexterity, which I never acquired. The stamps were to be stuck to the smaller flap of the hinge, while the large flap was pressed against the page. Often as not I got the flaps reversed. And spit was disallowed by the experts as a dampening agent. A saucer of lukewarm water was advised, temperature tested with the back of the wrist. I eschewed all such frivolity and laid stamp and hinge on my tongue and mashed the gluey bit of paper onto the page with the heel of my hand. A typical finished page would look like a crazy quilt, each scrap of color at any angle to another, each stuck there forever or clinging tenuously as a butterfly to a leaf.

Yet I regarded such a filled page with a proud tenderness. I had collected the stamps; I had affixed them; I had already in my life accomplished something. Sometimes I would open the album to one such page and stare at it until I was overwhelmed, and then I would spring to my feet and twirl about in a circle, overcome with happiness, with the feeling that a bright and shining future lay in store and here gave a foretaste of itself. Or I would stare at it long and pensively, in melancholy reverie dreaming a blurred, half-imagined history of the universe.

But the true and fatal attraction in hoarding stamps was the lure of instant wealth and global fame. It seemed improbable that I should not discover a rare stamp equal in worth to the fabled British Guiana or one with a magnificent printing error like the twenty-five-cent airmail with the upside-down biplane. I did not deceive myself that the odds were against me, but I was sure I would beat the odds. For, look here, I had already filled in five pages of this huge book, cheating only a little by sticking seven or eight stamps in or near spaces where they did not belong.

So that even if I had been able to afford the expensive sets of stamps I saw advertised in *Boys' Life*—mint sets of new Nicaraguan issues, or Swiss first-day covers—it is doubtful I would have been deeply interested. For me, the great excitement was in those big envelopes given away as introductory enticements, thick wads of ordinary canceled stamps, rose two-pence British, French and Italian airmail, and even three-cent Jeffersons. When one of these envelopes arrived, my father handing it over with a half-amused smile, I would tear it open and pour under the bronze table lamp this useless clutter of paper and claw through it feverishly. There would be nothing I had not seen and rejected scores of times before, but that was merely the preliminary examination. After I stirred about in this heap till my initial fervor wore off, I would go downstairs to the bathroom medicine chest and borrow my mother's tweezers, take up each stamp, look at it on both sides, holding it against the light. Not that I knew what to look for. Watermarks I had read about and had seen sketches of, but I never glimpsed one in a stamp. There were ribbed lines running horizontally, but I knew they were not watermarks, because they were not exciting. I thought that if I could just once sight a watermark of any kind, I would be well on my way to making my famous, inevitable discovery, because I would be able to recognize one of the components of rarity. . . . But at the end I would have to look down sadly upon them and drift them by handfuls into the wastebasket.

Of how my parents regarded this outlandish enthusiasm, I can form but a vague notion. My father, though educated, was a farmer and a practical man. I think he may have been mildly concerned about my interest, for he would occasionally bring me toys of a different sort, miniature farms with barns and silos and brightly painted tractors. My mother, fastidious and vocal as always, would complain about disorder and the absence of her tweezers. But their objections could not be taken seriously, I reasoned, for they had given me the album and the first bulky envelope of stamps for my birthday. Anyway, once I had made my discovery, once my picture appeared in all the newspapers, once the renowned dealers began to telephone with their unheard-of offers, I would be vindicated a hundredfold. And it wasn't only the money and the worldwide recognition—I would have proved that my imagination was healthy and brilliantly practical and would make its way in the world. Then my activities, which were not limited to stamps but also included chemistry experiments and poetry writing, would have to be reckoned with seriously.

After my father, chief among my continual teasers was Harmon Cody. Mr. Cody was a spare, sandy-haired man with unyielding green eyes who lived down the narrow dirt road about a mile from our farmhouse. The arrangement by which he worked on our farm is obscure, for he worked neither entirely for shares nor for wages, but for some intermediate combination. He took other jobs, too, part-time farmwork or repairs. The vagueness showed in the way he and my father treated each other. He rose to suggestions with such ready deference and spoke in such respectful tones that most people must have supposed his position was that of a sharecropper. But he was independent, and my father never talked to him in any manner suggesting his dependence, and any hint of inequality came from his side.

Mr. Cody's attitude toward me was another matter. It was clear to him that I was a new kind of animal upon this earth and he would gaze at me in unabashed wonder as I drifted empty-eyed from one chore to another, so abstracted at times as actually to stumble over an object in my path. He would ply me with bland jokes. "What's the weather where you are?" "Don't forget your head is on the top and your tailbone on the bottom." And when I smiled back dreamily, his mouth would quiver in amazement. He kept joking and after awhile became more pointed, though his motive was never malice, but a kind of bemused experimentation. What *will* this creature ever react to? he must have wondered. And I, half-conscious of what went on in his mind, was pleased with any attention he gave me.

It would be hard for a boy of eleven not to be pleased with his attention. It seemed to me that Mr. Cody knew everything there was to know about the world out-of-doors and that he could perform miracles of craft and repair, upon which he looked with baleful skepticism. He resurrected an ancient mule harness, restrapping and rebradding, glanced at his handiwork, and remarked, "Wouldn't hold a pup from his supper dish." He held every man-made artifact in suspicion, and I once heard him say of a neighbor's gleaming new John Deere tractor, "Wouldn't pull a candy cane out of a mule's ass." Male Americans are born to be Boy Scouts and a young boy regards an adult of Mr. Cody's cut as a sort of super-Scout, one of the geniuses who wrote that handbook so full of thumb-mashers and knuckle-crushers. Of mammals, birds, and insects, he knew every secret: how to cure colic in newborn calves, names of birds by their nests, how to keep bees from swarming. His knowledge was so various and profound that I early despaired of attaining to anything like it. The natural world became a gulf between us—for him, so plain and easy; for me, so dim and bewildering.

For all this, we were good friends, because he was at last a boy at heart. This was perhaps the reason he held my father in clear respect; Mr. Cody must have felt that my father was a respectable adult, since he had schooling and owned property and kept a family together, no matter how odd his offspring might be. Mr. Cody was a bachelor and owned nothing but his house and small lot, his piecemeal old Ford, and five lugubrious hounds. He was a foxhunter, and many a morning he would come to work in the fields directly from a mountainside campfire, red-eyed and edgy from a night of black coffee, but still energetic and industrious enough that my father had to strain to keep up with him. Twice he invited me to go hunting, but the first time my father refused permission, and Mr. Cody nodded, accepting this reply as adult wisdom. The second time, I refused, thinking of some lamp-smelling project I had under way in my room, and he merely gazed at me. I had added another lump of fuel to the blaze of his astonishment.

My mother, too, was fond of Mr. Cody, but in a more distant way. Her mind was filled with priorities, matters ranked in order of importance, and Harmon Cody, being only an overgrown boy, was as useful and amusing as Archie, our collie trained to cattle. No more than that, but no less. He, on his side, regarded my mother as he did all women: They were here in the world like starlight and moonlight, but their purposes were finally incidental, since a man could do as well without them as with them.

Came a time when an evangelical impulse rose in Mr. Cody. He must have decided that he had learned about me all he was ever going to with his gentle jokes; now he must educate me before I blundered on in a numb haze without discovering how to handle the pragmatic imperatives of life. He took me walking in the woods on Sunday afternoons, making laconic observations on bird and beast and bush. He took me trout fishing and instructed me in the use of the fly rod. He requested my help in repairing his car, a machine he spent years tearing down and puzzling back together.

But I was a sorry pupil and once, when for the hundredth time I had entangled my fishing leader in the overhanging branches of a laurel, he laid down his rod and put his hands on his hips and said, "Just where in the world are you from?"

I grinned and shook my head.

"No," he said, "what I mean is, Where are you *from*?"

"Well, you know," I said.

"I reckon I don't. I reckon it's past me."

I had no answer. I indicated my line stretched across the swift stream. "Well," I said, "I guess I'd better wade into the old H_2O and get my line loose."

"Wade into the what?"

"H_2O. That's the chemical formula for water."

He nodded, but if I had then begun to speak Mandarin Chinese and flapped my arms and flown to roost in the top of the nearest sourwood, he would no longer have been surprised.

This incident marked a turn in our relationship. There was an order of things Mr. Cody had determined he would never comprehend, and now I went into it, along with women, cats, and foreign cars. We were still friendly, but there were no further attempts on his side to bring me along, to tear away my blindness. It was just as well. This happy man must at last have broken his heart if he had kept to his first resolution.

That was Mr. Cody. With my father, it was a different situation. If he was toiling to get a horse harnessed to the plow and asked me to go to the shed and bring him a small clevis, I would trot off and return after too long a time with a broken and useless scrap of iron. His face would grow scarlet and his eyes enlarge. "My God!" he would say. "A *clevis,* boy! Don't you know what a clevis is?" He would snatch my wrist and drag me, tumbling, across the lot to the shed. He would find it and thrust it in my face, shaking it. "This is a clevis, dammit. How can you grow up here and not know that? What are you thinking about?"

"I don't know, sir," I would say, telling the gospel truth.

Then when we got back to the plow, the horse would have stepped out of the traces and there would be a delay, enlivened by grunting and fiery profanity.

Once it happened—and, remembering, I hardly believe it myself—that I lost his drinking water. He had gone off to one of the farthest corners of the farm to break ground for new tobacco beds and had left me in the house with instructions to find him in an hour with water. I was pleased to be left alone with an incomprehensible volume called *Industrial Chemistry* and, for a wonder, did not forget what I was charged with. At the appointed time, I rose regretfully from my wing-back chair and went into the kitchen and dropped into a mason jar as many ice cubes as I could. Then I filled the jar with tap water and sealed it with the cap and the rubber and started out, the jar tucked under my arm. It was a gloriously hot August day and I went along the dusty road in oblivious reverie.

But when I arrived where my father was working, I had no water. He had seen me coming over the hill and had halted the plow at the end of a furrow. His face and arms were pouring sweat and his heavy cotton shirt was drowned.

"Where's the water?" he asked hoarsely.

I couldn't answer because I was so completely astonished at not having it with me. I think my impulse may have been to search my pockets.

"Well, didn't you bring it?"

"I don't know where it is." A sudden hopeless depression darkened me like a blanket thrown over.

"You mean you came all the way out here and forgot my drinking water?"

From his tone of voice, I could tell he didn't believe it. He was thinking that perhaps I was pranking him, that I had hidden it nearby and just wanted to give him a turn. I wished sorely that it could be that way, because the poor man needed water desperately.

"No, sir, I didn't forget."

"Where is it, then?"

"I don't know."

"How can you not know? Did you drop it on the road and break it?"

"No, sir. I don't think so." Certainly I must have noticed breaking a mason jar in the middle of the road.

"What is there to think about? If you started out with a jar of water, surely to God you know what happened to it."

"I had it when I left the house. I was carrying it under my arm."

"And now you don't know where it is?"

"No, sir."

"Boy, you beat anything, you know that?"

"Yes, sir, I guess so." I raised and dropped my hands.

He turned and surveyed how much ground he had plowed and how much was left to do. When he turned back, his face wore such an expression of trapped frustration that I could have wept. "By the time you got back with more, I'd be finished here," he said. "Not that I expect you *would* get back with any. . . . You just sit down over there and wait and we'll go back together. I've got some things I want to say to you."

"Yes, sir."

In another hour he had finished and I helped him unhitch and load the plow onto the sled and then we rehitched and started back. When we came to the road, he drove along slowly and began to lecture me vehemently, but now it was too late. I had drifted down into my placeless lethargy again, like a dry leaf floating down, down into a well.

Then he stopped the sled and pointed. “Look there,” he said.

I saw the mason jar in a clump of ragweed in the ditch, still intact and full of water, gleaming and dripping.

That wasn't what he pointed at. His trembling finger accused my footprints in the red dust, where they straggled aimlessly from one side of the road to the other.

“Just look,” he said. “You're walking like a crazy man. What in the world is the matter with you?”

I said nothing, and as the sled dragged on, cutting two stark, sensible lines through my tracks, it occurred to me that they looked like writing in an unknown language, transgressing the boundaries of the copybook lines the sled made. And I thought, too, that here was another matter that I must study, and that by mastering it I would have one more vital clue to the future life that awaited me, incandescent with promise.

So I began to pursue my odd interests with even more energy and persistence. The evidence of my freakishness had at last impressed itself upon me, and now it seemed my bounden duty to transform myself from ugly duckling to swan by force of willpower. The great good luck that was to come upon me was already long overdue; the impatience of my parents must soon be satisfied.

But the grand event did not happen soon. In a month, school began again and schoolwork coupled itself with farm chores, and the time for my personal projects dwindled until I had only a few hours, at twilight and again after supper. This constricted schedule made me more efficient and I blocked out several elaborate time plans. So many minutes would go for my chemistry experiments, so many for the writing of poetry, and so many for the study of cryptography, my newest interest, and so many would be allotted to the stamps.

None of these plans proved viable, because the lazy vein of dreaminess was enlarging, encroaching now upon the same activities it fed from.

My head swam with visions even in the middle of some rote chemistry experiment, until the solution of purple potassium permanganate boiled over onto the card table I had set up on the back porch. In fact, the whole chemical enterprise was proving disastrous. What stinks and ruin of glassware! What obscene noises! The worst of it were the holes eaten into my shirts and jeans by acids. And I was learning nothing at all about the science except that powdered magnesium gave off a wonderful swift brilliance when touched with a match. When my mother put a stop to this possibly dangerous foolery, I was more relieved than disappointed. I poured the liquids and powders into proper containers, labeled them pedantically, and stored them in boxes in a corner beside the coal bin in the basement.

Cryptography, too, was frustrating. I had been attracted to it by reading a Sherlock Holmes story, "The Adventure of the Dancing Men," a neat piece of work whose thread of simple logic I was able to follow. But there was little information on this study in the school library or in the books about the house. I was, of course, already familiar with the Superman code, in which the alphabet runs counter to itself. I learned the typewriter code where one row of letters as it appears on the keyboard is substituted for another, but that was as far as I could go unaided. I did put together a number of codes of my own, but what use were they? Since I knew the keys, I could read them, and I knew better than to trouble my parents' forbearance with puzzles. And anyway, I had as yet no message to send. So cryptography dwindled away, leaving in my mind a heap of jumbled letters, like a box of pi in a printer's office.

Now it was February, the harshest month of the year in the Carolina mountains. Snow and rain continually, the days short and overcast, the nights long and bitterly cold. My physical energy subsided to a dull murmur and my nerveless dreaminess increased even more. Everything was suffused with lethargy, even the poetry and the stamps. Still I kept on.

I dread trying to speak about the poetry. It goes without saying that it consisted of the most awful trash thinkable, but perhaps I ought to suggest the special weirdness of that junk. It was expectably romantic to the hilt, rife with apostrophes and highly partial to the first-person pronoun.

It was, in some respects, nature poetry, but the kind of nature it portrayed will never exist, because this poetry concerned itself with the planet Varn, millions of light-years from Earth, spinning in a figure-eight orbit around its double suns. I had attempted to imagine the whole of it: a landscape completely alien and painted in an entirely new spectrum of colors, the sentient, perambulatory plants which roamed the landscape and the immobile, insentient animals these plants preyed upon. I imagined the dominant race of Varn, a species of flying creature something like terrestrial butterflies, whose method of communication was a music composed of tones beyond the range of human hearing, and whose habitations were enormous crystal aeries lodged in the crests of craggy mountains. For these beings I set down nature sonnets as I supposed they would have written them and love poems and battle hymns and courtly addresses to their council of rulers. I even tried to imagine what their sciences would be like, considering their different organs of perception, and I endowed them with sophisticated machinery adapted to their bodies.

The manuscript of this poetry, "The Cycle of Varn," grew to be huge. It filled to overflowing a loose-leaf notebook, and the composition of new poems became a cumbersome task. Since I was improvising natural and physiognomic and cultural detail as I went along, in order to write any new poem in the series I had to reread almost everything I had already written. So it would require an hour or so before I could even begin to compose the long, wobbly, stilted lines that showed in my eyes more color and importance than anything published by my model, Walt Whitman. Nothing in the world could induce me to introduce a sample of this stuff, even if I were able. For all I know, it may still exist somewhere, fouling cardboard boxes in attic or basement, but I am not going to search it out. All that is gone from me, the steady opiate urge to spin about myself cocoons of incomprehensibility. This poetry was merely the overlapping of my usual dream state into a limited physical activity. I began to realize that it was monstrously self-indulgent.

But the ideal of the stamps stayed with me. I still kept my faith, though I was aware that my method of procedure was mistaken for the purposes I had in mind. I acquired a magnifying glass and I stopped spending money on the worthless bags of ordinary stamps. I began to send off for the new issues of Brazilian or Mauritanian stamps, printed in two or three colors and portraying, often as not, nude girls. I would scrutinize these stamps with the glass, comparing them minutely with the written descriptions of stamps which appeared in *Boys' Life*. I was searching for anomalies, for it had come to me that if I could find discrepancies between what I was looking at and its description, I might actually discover a true error, and my fortune would be made. I read up on the processes of printing and engraving, having come to realize that a figure printed upside down was highly unlikely, and that the kinds of things I was looking for would be subtle, even mundane, in appearance.

This new procedure was expensive. We were not poor, but we were by no means wealthy; and even if we had been, it was no part of my father's philosophy to deal out heaps of money to children. Where before I had bought bucketfuls of stamps for fifty cents, I now sent off two dollars and received eight stamps, royally mounted on cardboard and wrapped in sparkling cellophane. I enjoyed first opening an envelope of these, with the colors bright and pristine, the depicted scenes exotic, and the stamps oversized. But the examination of these new acquisitions could last, with the minutest scrutiny, two or three hours at longest. After that I could only stick them in the album, and then there would be a wait of maybe three months before I could save enough money to afford another set. Between times, I would go over and over again the crazy pages of my album, hoping that in my earlier ignorance I had missed something important.

During this period, our family life went on in its usual fashion, my parents worrying about my schoolwork and the state of my mental health and, of course, scolding me constantly. But I took no more notice of them than of the empty wind in its blank courses. Their anxieties were to me a piece of the weather, inevitable and ceaseless. I was still convinced that my eventual success would straighten everything out, the past as well as the future.

Once, though, something happened that did fix my attention. There appeared on the dining table one evening an old, bulky manila envelope. It was addressed not to my father but to his father, who had been dead now some seven years. It was paperwork about surveying deeded boundaries for tax purposes, I think. In the corner of this envelope stood a one-dollar special-delivery stamp, printed in red, white, and blue and displaying the American eagle. I had never before seen this stamp or even heard of it.

Naturally, I lusted for it, and my father, preoccupied, gave it to me with a minimum of haranguing. I took it, studied it with more than customary thoroughness, and finally interred it in the album.

This stamp started a whole new train of thought. In various places in our house were boxes and boxes of old letters, bales of business and personal correspondence. Why it had never occurred to me to examine the stamps on these letters, I could not now imagine, and I began to tremble at the prospect. I felt as someone must who has come into an unlooked-for, rich inheritance. It was among these documents, here always right under my nose, that I would discover the long-sought treasure, right here in the house of my family, among my father's own discarded belongings. I did not deceive myself that I would find it right away; but somewhere amidst all that paper, it reposed, waiting, like an emerald in a garbage dump.

I gave myself over to an evening of reverie, and the next afternoon I began, down there in the corner by the coal bin where we stored the things we could not bring ourselves to throw away. It was there that I had shoved my disused chemicals, and when I saw those boxes, I felt a pitying contempt for the person I used to be, not at all the same fellow who was on the verge of wealth and celebrity. . . .

There were plenty of envelopes, sure enough, but most of them were Christmas cards from my parents' friends, most of whom were unknown to me. There were scores of these, and each envelope bore only the blue Jefferson, but I looked over each dutifully, sneezing and wiping my nose on my sleeve. By the time I had to come away to supper, I was black with dust from fingertip to elbow and the front of my green plaid shirt was nigh unrecognizable. So far in one afternoon I had found only Adamses and Jeffersons, but I was not discouraged. My feeling about these letters was strong; I had to trust my intuition; and anyhow, I had a long way to go. So at supper I received my scolding with equanimity.

February became March and March April. The landscape brightened and thawed and warmed and I still plundered the grimy boxes and found nothing. In all of them there had been not even one unfamiliar stamp to place in the album, much less anything resembling the great prize.

On the main floor of the house were two closets containing letters, one in the hallway and one in my parents' bedroom, but it would be difficult to search them, with my parents spending almost all their house time there, so I put these off until later and moved to the upstairs. There was one small closet at the top of the stairs and another large room which served as a storage space for all sorts of odds and ends, for we had no proper attic. The small closet I went through in less than an hour, finding nothing, but not entirely discouraged, for I entertained shining hopes of the storage room.

This was a dark room about fourteen feet long, with its low ceiling following the sloping roof of the house. Illumination was one naked seventy-five-watt bulb hanging from a cord. This room was the true Aladdin's cave, if my interests could have been different, for here all sorts of family memorabilia had been laid up. There was a violin case, for example, and inside it on the patchy green velvet a fiddle and bow, out of tune and screechy as car brakes when I attempted to sound it. It belonged to my mother—as I later discovered—and once she had been proud of her playing and used to perform at square dances with my uncle, a famous caller. There were the boots and hat of a First World War uniform which had belonged to my grandfather's brother. There was an old icebox of heavy oak and a barrel butter churn made of hickory, its dasher handle worn thin at the end. There were all sorts of beautiful and amazing objects which preserved a history of the times of my family. But I did not know how to value them, my hopes lying in a distant star. Even so, the patina of human usage managed to impinge itself and I did examine them and feel their textures with some curiosity.

Once again, though, I was disappointed. There were three boxes of letters, many fewer than I had expected, and these sported no interesting stamps, only those Adamses and Jeffersons, the glimpse of which now began to make me ill with disgust, a cold crawling sensation in my stomach that shuddered upward into my chest. After such continual disappointment, hopelessness was at last beginning to take root and I was starting to feel a cloudy sense of shame, to see that I was childish beyond the limit. I could not bring myself to give up the search, not yet, but I decided that when I looked through the house, that would be the end. I would turn my attention to another scheme. The world was full of opportunities for money and glory, none of them contingent on dull little bits of paper.

In this room there was a large trunk of heavy black metal with rusty brass molding. It sat longwise on the floor and was locked. I knew that it was against every rule for me to open this trunk, but I knew as soon as I saw it that I was going to. Though the trunk was heavy, the lock was flimsy, a flat brass plate with a hasp and latch. I went downstairs for a claw hammer.

When I laid the hammer on the floor beside me and, kneeling, opened the lid, a strange heavy odor, camphor and mothballs and another bitter but unnameable smell, washed over me. It was such a dizzying sensation that I almost dropped the lid. Then I looked inside, and if the trunk had been mysterious when locked, it was no less so when opened. Nothing within it was what I could have expected.

There was, first of all, a football jersey, green, with the number 14. It must have been my father's, but he had never mentioned that he had played football. I lifted the jersey out and laid it on the floor, uncovering a cardboard box with a cellophane panel in the top which revealed a doll with exquisite features and an elaborate dress, a finely fashioned red crinoline skirt with a candy-stripe bodice. It looked expensive and I handled it gently as I read the legend: OFFICIAL SCARLETT O'HARA DOLL. Next was a small tin box without a lid, containing a number of small metal cylinders about three-quarters of an inch in diameter and with one end open. I looked at these for a while, shaking the box gently to make them rattle, but I could not think what they might be, and set the box down on the football jersey.

This trunk was filled with fascinating objects: medals, coins commemorating the Chicago World's Fair, dance programs with gold-thread tassels, belts and leather work, photographs of all sorts, some of them so old as to be backed with tinplate, a number of college newspapers, in some of which I found poems by my mother and pictures of my father, who, I discovered, had made All-Conference tackle at Carolina Christian College. A wave of tenderness came over me as I fumbled these things, and I determined, once again, that I would begin to be a better person, obeying my parents readily and taking hold of myself.

The trunk contained no letters, not a single paper bearing a stamp. This was the final letdown—but in a way I felt relieved, as if a misty but heavy weight had been removed from my body. Here was the end of it. I was never going to become rich and famous by finding a stamp. It rested in my mind with the certainty of a rifle muzzle that I had been wasting my time, staking my daydreams on a chance so slim, fantastic, and ephemeral that only a desperate person could have conceived it and only a dimwit could have persisted in it. But here was the end. I would look through no more closets; I could close this chapter.

I replaced all the things I had taken out, as nearly as I could in the order I had removed them. I closed the trunk and tried to snap the lock shut, but it wouldn't go. I wasn't trying to hide the evidence of my snooping; I wanted to undo the fact of it, to erase the deed entirely. An impossible wish to restore my balance.

Now I had become a different person. I still believed, though warily, that my near future was flaming with a glorious treasure. But the collecting of stamps had been a false lead; I must search out another path; I must plunge more deeply and thoroughly into the waters of my dreaming reverie. Somewhere at the bottom lay the gleaming key.

Three days later I returned home from school, books under my arm and one shoelace untied and dragging, to find Harmon Cody sitting on our porch steps. He was smoking a hand-rolled cigarette and a .22 rifle lay across his lap. When I greeted him, he grinned and waved his hand. "You better go on in the house," he said. "Your daddy's waiting to talk to you."

When I entered, I found him sitting there, and it was obvious that he was waiting for me, because he was dressed in his work clothes and had on the heavy brogans he never wore inside the house. He was sitting in the wing-back chair and he gestured for me to sit down opposite him on the sofa.

"How was school today?" His voice was gentle, tired.

"All right, I guess. It doesn't change much."

"That so?"

He didn't look directly at me, but into a space above my head. For a long time he said nothing, and then he leaned forward, resting his elbows on his knees. "You've been poking around in the stuff in the house, haven't you?"

"Yes, sir. I was looking for stamps for my—"

"You took a hammer or something and broke into the trunk up in the storage room."

"Yes, sir. Like I said, I was—"

"And you don't need me even having to say anything to know it's wrong to be busting into places that are locked."

"No, sir."

"Tie your shoe," he said, still not looking at me. "If something is locked, there's a reason for it. The first reason might be to keep people out. And there might be some other reason, too."

Bent to my shoelace, I craned to see him. "I'm sorry," I said. "It was only—"

"I want you to take a little walk with Mr. Cody," he said. "I've asked him to show you something. You go with him. After that, you can come back here and change clothes and meet me in the second barn. Some of that damp hay has been heating up and we've got to move it around."

"All right." I put my schoolbooks on the coffee table and went outside.

Mr. Cody rose as I came through the door and flipped his cigarette away. "Let's you and me go out in the pasture a ways," he said, and we set off, walking easily and deliberately.

It was a warm, bright, cheerful day, one of those days you might look about you, breathe deeply, and think, Yessir, this is springtime; this is the beginning. The landscape glowed a pale clear green and the waters in the ground seemed audibly to loosen underfoot. Near and far on all sides twinkled birdsong.

Mr. Cody looked not at me but kept his intent green gaze on the bushes and hilltops. He carried the .22 loosely in his left hand, half twirling it by the trigger guard, the way a man walking along will play carelessly with a stick he has picked up.

There had been something so grave in my father's manner of speaking and now something so studied in the way Mr. Cody avoided talking that I asked no questions. Whatever was to happen, it was obvious that the two of them attached importance to it, and I would spoil the drama by anticipating. So I walked along silently, swinging my arms and taking about half again as many steps as Mr. Cody. But as we came near to the far southeast corner of the pasture, my curiosity rose, for there was nothing here I knew of but a few easily sloping hills and grass and yellow broom sedge.

I had not thought of the apple tree. This was a little tree which stood halfway up the side of an otherwise-empty hill. Dwarfed and stunted, it had once been struck by lightning. The crown had flattened and what was left of the trunk twisted back until it looked as if it might fall over. Half was missing; the whole front side was a pith of weathered long splinters enclosed in a canal of bark so smooth and tough where it had grown over the fire scar that it looked like molded wax. Part of it yet struggled toward life. The other side, with its sheared-off platform of twiggy branches, was blooming, absolutely rife with blossom, pinkish white, already freckled now with bees. It was a wonder, this tree riven down half its life, one side shattered and barren as sand, the other a warm fountain of flowers.

Mr. Cody halted about twenty yards from it, and I halted, too. He handed me the rifle and from his shirt pocket took a cardboard prescription pillbox. He opened it and removed carefully a square of white cotton batting to reveal, lying on top of another square of cotton, one of the little copper cylinders which had been among the others in the tin box I had discovered when I broke into the trunk. "This is a blasting cap," he said. "You stay right here. Don't move."

He held the box before him and walked up the hill to the apple tree. When he got there, he took the cylinder from the box and fitted it carefully and securely into a crotch of the branches on the left-hand side. Then he tossed the box down and came back, and over his shoulder I could see the button of gleam among the leaves, a tiny spot of polished gold shining amid the green and white.

"Here," he said, and I handed him the rifle. He took a single bullet from his pants pocket and slid it into the chamber. Then he raised the rifle and, without seeming to aim, squeezed the trigger. The apple tree jerked and quivered and a big piece of it fell to the ground and a ladder of black smoke climbed the blue air. My ears buzzed, but I could still make out Mr. Cody's words: "You see, honey, you're going to have to take better care. Happened you hit one of these caps a lick up in your house, you'd have been blowed to pieces. Blowed half the roof off."

And that, I suppose, is the way it happened. But when I remember it, it takes place in a different time scale, much slower in duration. When I remember, the muzzle of the gun comes down slowly, then wavers to rest, and the trigger is squeezed, and the graphite-colored bullet leaves the muzzle, screwing forward steadily through the dark waves of air it displaces. When the bullet strikes the burnished dynamite cap, it touches it gently. Then there is an orange-white flash, jagged as in a comic-strip panel, and a heavy remnant of the tree tears away agonizingly with a sound like bones breaking and the white flesh of the wood shows clear and watery. The mass of limbs plummets to the damp earth and a sprinkle of white petals showers up and slowly settles like snow drifting windblown.

At this moment, invisible layers of clothing peel away from my body. My eyes perceive the objects around me as more colorful, more angular, more distinctly themselves than I have ever known them. My skin receives a shock, as if I had stepped from a warm bath into a freshet of icy wind. Every nerve opens its eyes. The world rushes in upon me violently.

And in this moment that someone who is myself is born, someone also dies. From this instant I date my awkward tumble into the world and here now I remain, alert and unready.

If I could return, I would undo it all. I would wrap myself in dream ever more thoroughly and would sink to the bottom of time, a stone uncaring, swaddled in moss. And when the Judgment Day trumpet shattered open this universe, and when I had to go sit across the desk from that harassed angel who sat there making out the endless dreary forms for everyone who ever lived, I would account for my life this way:

I slept and never woke. Even in my dreams I never harmed another, for no one else existed in those dreams. I am so innocent, I might never have existed.

But now I cannot say so.

THE THREE BOXES

Three men, naked but of indeterminate color, came at last to the edge of a river. Here they flung themselves down gratefully in the grass and lay waiting for strength to return to their bodies, for they had been marching a weary time through the wide savanna. Silence welled up about them, then subsided, and they began to hear the singing of birds and insects and the wind in the leaves and the purl of the swift, broad river. A cloudless sky arched above and they gazed deep into the coolness.

In awhile they stirred themselves, stretching knotted muscles. One by one they crept to the edge of the riverbank and scooped water and drank noisily from cupped palms. The water of the colorless and silver-glinting river was almost tasteless, but it refreshed them in body and spirit.

Then they sat up in the grass and thought.

"How far have we come?" one asked.

They looked at one another. They could not say. Now they could not remember where they had come from or why they had set out to begin with. Once they had started, the journey itself was sufficient to satisfy their minds; the steady striding over the ground, with the silky-topped grasses nibbling at their ribs, had taken up all thought. They had encountered few obstacles, and not even inclement weather.

"How long have we been walking?"

None could say. They examined their bodies, as if the journey had told itself upon their skins, but they seemed no different. Their limbs were tired but not sore; the soles of their feet had perhaps thickened slightly, but even of this fact they were not certain.

"Where have we come to?"

A foolish question, as they could not recall where or when they had started. But here was a practical answer plain before them. They had come to a river and for the time being they must halt.

They crept back away and started to take stock.

The river was about fifty meters wide, but how deep, they could not guess. The water was so clear that the large smooth stones in the riverbed looked only just out of reach. The men reasoned, however, that it must be much deeper than it appeared, because the water went by with great force and they could feel cool air pouring off its surface. One man dropped an alder leaf on the water and they watched it sweep away quickly, twirling round and round as various strands of current nudged it.

So now they concluded that it was a dangerous river and that they had no pressing cause to cross over. They would strike out downstream and search for a more hospitable place. They rose and gave a long, regretful look at the other side with its blossoms, flowers of a sort they had never seen before. But this time when they looked, new objects had appeared in that prospect.

Now on the other side were three boxes. Of a matte ivory color, they sat solidly in the grass; sunlight streaked the sides in broad patches. It was impossible to tell much about them, smooth and featureless and square. Waist-high, or a little taller. Was there a hasp or a hinge in the center at the top edge? The men shaded their eyes and stared but could not see.

The boxes made all the difference. Over here were three men and over there were three boxes. It was obvious that each man was intended to open one box.

They sat down again to consider.

The river had not abated its force and the cool air above the surface now felt chilly. One of the men leaned over the bank and plunged his arm in the water up to his elbow. He held his arm straight down, steady in the river rush, trying to judge the strength of the flow. He pulled his arm out, looked down at the water, and shook his head slowly. He leaned back and enfolded his knees in his arms.

The other men chewed grass blades, gazing on the river. Finally one spoke, and this was the thread of his thought: "This pure river is a powerful, mighty river, and I am a poor swimmer. Neither of you swims much better than I do. It is bad that this is so, for if one of us swam strongly, we could send that man to open all three boxes and tell us what they contain. Since we cannot do that, the chances for each of us are equal, and each of us must choose whether he wishes to brave the current. If any of us does, then one of the boxes—only one—is his."

The other two nodded gravely.

Still no one moved. Fear was too great in them. They had marched miles without having to make choices, and they would have preferred to continue, one foot before the other without impediment.

At last one man stood up. "I must try to cross over," he said. "For look, we have traveled so long that none of us can remember where he started from or when. But there must have been an hour in which we chose to set out, and when we chose that, we also chose to accept our chances in the world. If it happens that I am dragged away and drowned, then that is what my journey has come to. It is not a matter of choosing to die, but of choosing to accomplish the end of my travels in a logical manner."

With that, he approached the edge, stretched up on tiptoe, and plunged awkwardly into the water.

The other two men watched intently. Long moments passed before he came to the surface, and the men on dry ground trembled. But he emerged in a flurry of droplets and began making his way across, not swimming so much as thrashing forward. They could see what a terrible struggle it was. He could not keep his legs high and the current kept tugging away his lower body. Above the loud splashing they could hear him gasp and suck air.

Still, he made progress. His desperate churning carried him little by little away from them.

Their bodies were taut in sympathy with him.

It was easy to mark his distance. His battle with the river stirred the water heavily, so that where it had been air-clear before, it now ran a milky yellow color. They had supposed that the current was too strong and the river too deep for the milling of a single swimmer to make a difference; yet it was so. The muddied yellow stain followed where the swimmer swam.

Past midpoint of the river, his strength seemed to fail and he was carried some way downstream. But then he gathered himself and reached the other side. They watched as he dug his fingers into the earth and clung. He reached higher to secure a better hold and he rested a moment before pulling himself out.

Now all the river was yellow.

They watched him as he sat on the edge and shivered, his hands in his lap. Water streamed from him, and his body had been washed white, or, rather, pinkish gray, the color of some kinds of mushrooms, and his hair had turned blond. He rested a long time, but finally rose and went to the three boxes.

He wasted no time in choosing among them, but opened the first he came to, which was the one farthest downstream, because he had been carried pretty far. They saw the surprise in his body when he lifted the lid back. He stood looking for a while and then reached in and began taking out.

First he brought out four large leather sacks. He set them on the ground and untied one of them and dipped his hand in and brought it out flashing, gold coins spilling between his fingers, shining in the sunlight. The other two men imagined they could hear the clash of coin on gold coin, and they looked at each other and grinned.

Eagerly the whitened man reached back into the box and began taking out numbers. 1 2 3 4 5 6 7 8 9 0: They glowed red with their own light, and he laid them carefully aside in the grass. And now he was bringing out books, great leather-bound volumes, book after book after book; he stacked them as neatly as he could. He took out of the box a contraption they could not understand, an ungainly ugly thing with wheels and pipes and gears. It seemed that their friend could not understand it, either, for after he set it down, he stood pondering it for a long time. Then he reached and touched it in a certain place and it sprang into quivering motion. Smoke and steam rose from it and it uttered a loud savage cry and began vomiting forth floods of paper. Papers sailed up in the breeze and caught in the thicket of bushes that enclosed the flowery clearing where the boxes sat. The blond man hastily touched the machine again and it shut itself down with a regretful cough.

More and more things he brought out; it was simply not possible that the box could contain so much. He brought out glass and plutonium and theology and engineering, law and chemistry and moldboard plows and harpsichords. He brought out many things that the watchers did not comprehend.

He leaned over the box and stood looking down into it; he wagged his head slowly, and his friends understood that this box contained so many different things that he could never empty it. In their hearts they congratulated him on the grand treasure his courage had gained.

The blond man picked up the books and began placing them back into the box. He went round the little area where he had been standing and everything he had taken out he put back in. He closed the lid and latched it. Then he turned toward the river to face his comrades. They saw him turn his head from side to side and shade his eyes with both hands. They shouted and waved their arms, but he seemed unable to find them, though surely they were as visible on their side as he on his. But he gave no indication that he could discern their presence. He shrugged and turned his back toward them.

He bent down to pick up the box, and his friends could see what a burden it proved. But he planted his feet solidly, leg muscles and back muscles distended and shining like rivulets of water, and finally hoisted it up on his left shoulder. He walked away, struggling with the weight.

As they watched him cross the clearing and enter the green thicket, it appeared that his body had grown shorter. His figure was not so tall and manly as it had been before; the weight of the big box distorted his carriage grotesquely.

It took a few minutes for comprehension of what they had witnessed to come to the two men. They looked at each other, uncertainly calculating, and looked once again at the river. Except in color, it had not changed. The steady ferocity of current rolled on.

Finally one said, "What one man can do, so can another. We have seen how well our friend was rewarded because he was able to overcome his hesitation—though it is possible that his gallant fight with the river somewhat impaired his eyesight. Now it may be that because he was first among us, or because he made a lucky choice among the boxes, he has already taken away the best part of the treasure. Even so, much must remain, for, as we saw, he was unable to display all that even his one box contained."

The other said, "But maybe he was a stronger swimmer than we. I am still fearful of this river."

"So am I. But what opportunity remains to us here? Even if the box I choose contains nothing, if it is as empty as an old conch, I am determined to swim across. Maybe I can overtake our friend and hear his account of the box he opened up. Maybe he will share with us if we go luckless."

Having said this, he advanced to the edge, closed his eyes, and leapt gracelessly into the river.

Immediately at the point where he plunged, the water streamed away an inky black, black as charcoal or starless midnight. It seemed an age before he gained the surface, and his clawing in the water was painful to see. It was obvious that he had not the strength his other friend possessed, and the lone man on the bank turned his back on the river and covered his ears with his hands. He was incapable of saving his companion if he was drowning and he could not bear the horror of seeing him torn away.

But of course the suspense was too great for him and in a few minutes he had to turn and look. He discovered, to his joyful surprise, that his friend had made up over half the distance and was cutting unsteadily onward. When his friend reached the bank, he clapped his hands in delight. The other had drifted downstream some way, and it took him a longer time than the first man to regather his strength. After awhile he rose and began walking toward the boxes.

Now his hair was dark and his skin had turned the yellow color the river had been.

Between the two men, the river ran swift, cinder black.

Like the first, the second man did not choose, but merely opened the box he came to, the one farther downstream. He looked into it a long time, meditating. The lone man on this side guessed that the new treasure was nothing so splendid as the first.

His friend lifted out the money first of all. It was not gold, but only paper money, and there was a modest little pile of it. And the objects were not eye-filling, though they were solid and useful, necessary. He brought out loads of hand implements: hoes, spades, brooms, axes, planes, wedges, hammers, and so forth. He brought out fabrics of every sort: silks shining like silver, pristine cottons, linens, velvets, and burlap. There were delicacies: fragile ceramics, wines and liqueurs, little poems like snowflakes, carved gods in ivory, jade, and mahogany, and tenuous paper kites. He brought out animals, pony and ox, dog and cat and nightingale; and plants, the tea shrub and the mulberry and the scarlet poppy, wise and treacherous. Carefully he took out and laid in the grass civil order and respect and tradition, oil lamps and fertilizer and the game of chess. He brought out diplomacy and seafaring, cartography and hempen rope. Finally he brought out tranquillity of spirit; this was a large white robe of the softest texture; and he pulled it about himself and turned the hood over his head so that it left most of his face in shadow.

He sat down in the grass, crossing his legs so that his thighs rested on his feet. He seemed to be murmuring to himself or singing, but his friend on the other side could not tell, so much of the face was obscured by the hood.

He saw then happen what had happened before. His friend turned to face him; slowly and patiently he began scanning the landscape on this side of the river. The lone man shouted and waved and danced about, but his yellow-colored comrade could not seem to discern his presence, though he kept looking, looking more intently than had their first friend.

Reluctantly he turned away and packed into the box what he had taken out. He bent down to hoist up the box, but then straightened and turned and one last time searched this side of the river. Still the lone man could not make himself seen. The yellow man shouldered the box and stalked away through the greenery. Again, as with the first man, his stature appeared shortened by the weight of the box.

The lone man was alone. There were only the insects and birds and grasses and bushes and the quick river, black as basalt. The day had worn down and shadows were long and the atmosphere cool. Off the river rose an air that was truly cold.

The lone man began to curse and berate himself for his lack of confidence. Shortly he stopped. "No," he said. "I must not give over to vain recrimination. It is not because I lack courage that I am left behind alone. I know myself and my friends well enough to say that I have not less courage than they. The trouble is that I am tardy in understanding the situation. Only now that my friends have disappeared do I realize that I have nothing. But *they*—why, as soon as they set eyes on those damned boxes, they realized that there are things to have in the world, things which, once their existence is known, make all too obvious one's state of having-nothing. Seeing the boxes, my friends determined to acquire something, but I, I only remembered that I was already content. And so the best chance has passed me by."

Thinking these thoughts, he was mollified, no longer bitter and angry. But he was still all alone and lonely.

He said, "The box that is left is mine. If I don't cross to claim it, I may well have to stay here the rest of my days. So I will go, but I have no feeling that this final box will do me good."

He took a running start and dived into the humus black river.

The passage in the water was a kind of death. He toiled in an icy darkness that moved against him with the strength of tigers. How many eternities passed, how many times did his hope for life dim down to a red ember? He could not know, knew only that he must keep paddling forward, however feebly.

Against all his expectations, he succeeded in reaching the other bank. He gripped a rib of clay and held on tightly, the rest of his body washing in the stream. Inch by furious inch, he climbed the slick bank and collapsed on the grassy edge, his chest shrieking for air. He lay on his back and saw the sky swirl. It was deep twilight now, and two stars peeped out and scurried in circles around each other.

Strength seeped into him by little and little. After a long time he rose and tottered to the box.

The dull box in the twilight looked menacing and the man halted apart from it and sat down. Misgivings shadowed his mind. He began to weep. But the tears did not wash clean his stained skin. Crossing the river, he had become a black man, his skin all dusky black.

There was no choice. He went to the box and opened it and looked. It was like looking down into a hazy well. No light came from inside, and with the light growing dimmer he found it hard to make out anything at all. Then when the objects became sharper, he uttered a loud groan and slammed the lid shut.

He walked up and down the greensward in distress. In this box that was his he had seen nothing but misery and terror and agony.

He walked back and forth on the ground. Still—hadn't there been something else besides? . . . He shuddered as he recalled the things he had seen. But in a dusty corner of the box hadn't he glimpsed something of worth, of some least value?

Well, it was his box.

He reopened it and began taking out all the heartsick materials. Length after length of chain, first of all, great heavy chains with raw, cruel links; there seemed no end of these. And fresh scars and old wounds were piled here in plenty, and he took each of them out and laid them tenderly in the grass. Hang nooses, branding irons, iron hobbles; scorn, contumely, and hatred: All these he lifted out and set on the ground as gently as if they had been chalices of fragile crystal. He took out the diseases, the anemias and exotic fevers, and he brought out the pests, the rats and mosquitoes and tsetse flies. Patience and endurance were in the box and he took them out, but they were inextricably entangled with slavery and pain, so he had not much regard for them, feeling that they did him little honor. He brought out the bottomless cotton sack, the mule harness, and the hot rail spike.

At last he worked down to the thing he remembered seeing, and out of the box he brought music. It was something that few others would have recognized as music—just some rusty steel strings and hollow gourds and knobbly old bones—but he foresaw possibilities and momentarily his spirit brightened.

But when he saw them spread out on the ground all the other things that had fallen to him, the music seemed only a taste of nectar after a meal of shit. In profound sadness he continued to pace up and down.

He sat and rested his chin on his chest and wept. He knew he would never be able to bear the destiny the box laid out before him.

A white brightness fell upon his sight behind his closed lids and he heard a measured rustling in the leaves of the thicket. He opened his eyes and the inner thicket was suffused with a bright white glow; it was a strange fire, and the bushes screened the burning heart of it away from his sight. He felt the presence, and knew that it was God standing there among the green leaves.

"Is that You, Dominie?" he asked.

"It is I."

The worst that could happen had already come to the lone man and he felt no fear at all in the presence of God. "Was it You, Dominie, Who ranged these boxes on the riverbank?"

"It was I."

"Forgive me, then, my complaint. Is it fair that the first man should get so much from his box, and that the second man should get so much less than he, and that I, only because I came last, should have nothing but cruelty and misery and shame?"

"It is not fair," said God.

"Excuse me, Dominie, but I know, as everyone knows, how wise You are. Could You not find it in Your wisdom to distribute the treasures of the boxes equally? This terrible unfairness comes near to breaking my heart."

"The reason the distribution is not fair," God said, "is that the principle of justice is not yet established in the world. I—even *I*—cannot act justly until justice itself comes into being."

"When, then, will justice happen?"

"Justice will not happen," God said. "Justice must be created, and it is you who shall create it."

"How is that possible, Dominie? I have no tools to create justice with. To the first man You gave law and mathematics, to the second You gave civil order and respect. Surely these are the foundation blocks of justice, and my brothers have carried them away."

"No. These are not the foundations of justice, but only the means of preserving justice once it is established."

"But there have fallen to me only the means and emblems of injustice."

"Out of these justice shall be created. For it cannot come into being in the abstract, by fiat. It can inhabit only the human soul and the human body. You shall create justice in the ravaging of your spirit and in the torture of your blood."

"I think I shall not be able to bear it. Surely I am the most misfortunate creature that has ever lived."

"You are not. There are others less favored than you, and it is partly for their sakes that you have been given the task of creating justice."

Then God caused pictures and emotions to form in the mind of the lone man. He showed him first the long travail of women, and the lone man considered it. Next He showed him the unreasoning suffering of children, and the man writhed as if in fever. Finally He showed him the blind, helpless, eternal pain of the animals, and the man began to weep afresh and clutched his head in his hands.

"No more!" he cried.

God began somewhat to relent. "In the box," He said, "you found patience and endurance and courage, but these you threw aside because you thought them too much alloyed with evil and sorrow. Yet these shall sustain you in your struggle. . . . Now at this moment I am going to lighten the palms of your hands and the soles of your feet."

The lone man examined himself, and it was true that the black river stain had been taken from those parts of his body. But this act seemed a stupid joke to him, and his question to God was bitter: "Dominie, what possible good can this do anyone?"

"It is as a reminder to you," God said. "It is for you to remember when you are oppressed and beaten down by men of other color that it is themselves also they crush into the earth and grind against the stone. It is for them also that you labor in the creation of justice. For I tell you now, forever, that until oppression of you shall quit, not one step toward victory shall have been taken by a single person."

At these words the white light in the thicket disappeared and the rustling in the leaves hushed. The man was once more alone under the little stars of the night sky. He fumbled in the darkness, repacking his box. He closed the lid and secured it and lifted the box to his shoulder. It was dreadfully heavy, this box, but the man walked away tall and erect. He was going to search for his friends, and in his heart there was a small happiness like a warm candle flame. For he knew that although his comrades had no gift for him, he could give one to them. He was carrying to them the gift of justice, the one thing in the whole world worth knowing that can be learned in the world, and is not divinely revealed.

EMBER

When I came out of Paradise, they were shooting at me. Shotguns and pistols mostly, whatever they could grab hold of. I jumped into my old green pickup truck in the parking lot and drove off. I couldn't shoot back because I'd already pitched my .44 pistol away. I wouldn't have shot back anyway, so I stepped on the gas. Probably it was rocks thrown up against the undercarriage, but it might have been bullets hitting the truck, so I ducked my head down.

Scared, hell yes, I was scared. Couldn't breathe except in gulps and my hands were shaking and two drops of dead-cold sweat inched from my armpit down my left side. It wasn't so much getting shot at—though I hear tell you never get used to that—but the faces of the people, faces of them that used to be my friends and neighbors turned red and murderous. I couldn't stand up to that.

Ten minutes later I felt a little easier and stopped trembling so much, not seeing the headlights after me in my mirror. But I knew they'd be coming and I knew they'd already called the sheriff and the Highway Patrol. I was a wanted man now, the only time in my life. I didn't know what to think.

I had already made one big mistake. If I'd turned right coming out of the parking lot there at West End Tavern and Dance, I'd be traveling toward the broad highways, the ones that connected with Georgia and all the other states and all the nations of the world. But I'd turned left instead and there was nothing in front of me but the brushy mountains of western North Carolina, brier thickets and tear-britches rocks over the steep slopes. And especially there was Ember Mountain, where nobody went in the dark, nobody that would anyhow talk about it in the daylight.

But I started thinking maybe some things wouldn't be so bad. I had fished the streams around here and knew my way some, and the more the men that were trailing me didn't know Ember, the better. So I made a turnoff onto a little clay road that goes up Burning Creek and crosses it three times. At the third ford, the trail's no wider than a cow path, and I pulled the truck over into a stand of laurel and cut the motor and the lights and opened the door.

Then it was like stepping into another world, because the silence came down so sudden and the darkness. The world of Paradise Township, where I'd shot with my .44 my untrue sweetheart Phoebe Redd, was sure enough a world away, I was thinking, and then the silence let up a little and I could hear the hood of the truck ticking as the motor cooled and the feathery swishing of the wind in the treetops and the low mutter of Burning Creek off to my left. Those noises brought me back to myself and how I had to keep running.

I scrambled down to the edge of the creek and got down on all fours and drank like a dog, tasting the mountain in the water, the mossy rocks above me in the dark and the humus and the secret springs of Ember. When I stood up again, I could hear the night sounds of late August, the crickets and cicadas and somewhere a long way off to my right the long-drawn, empty call of a hoot owl.

But there was nowhere to go but up the mountain. The farther I got in the nighttime, the farther away I'd be come sunup. Let them try to find me in six hours, or eight. Carolina wouldn't hold me now, nor Georgia, either, once I got past Ember Mountain.

I dreaded to do it, though. It wasn't only what they say about the ridges and hollers of Ember, and I'd heard plenty of that and put stock in some of it. But just any old mountain in the dark of the night is a reckless time, and if there hadn't been so many certain dangers behind me, I wouldn't have been traveling on to meet new ones.

So I started up, my pants wet and my feet soaked in my shoes. My breath began to pound in my chest and my knees felt weak, but I climbed any way I could, tripping over tree roots and crawling on all fours and sliding down on the loose shale. It was a wonder I didn't just tumble to the bottom and lie at the end of the valley like a rag doll a little girl has lost on her picnic.

But I kept on going and the rocks and roots and bushes kept tearing at me. The left side of my face got laid open by a bramble or a twig and I could feel the blood oozing down my neck into my shirt. I had to stop and rest a lot of times, but I didn't like to, and it got worse the higher I climbed, because the silence got deeper and I began to remember more and more what folks said about Ember.

Oh Phoebe, I thought, oh Phoebe Redd. See what your faithless ways have brought on me.

I went on. I kept going till I thought I couldn't stand it anymore and then I came to the backbone of a stony ridge and struck south along it, still climbing and climbing till I came to a weedy clearing. Then I saw a point of orange light up the mountain to my left. The more I tried to make it out, the more I couldn't see it clear. That's the way it is in the dark silence with trees everywhere.

But when I climbed some more, not breathing as hard now, I saw it again, clean and shining but shadowed over by something every now and again so that it flickered. I figured it to be a hunter's campfire, even though I had not heard his dogs running. Not everybody was scared of the tales and there was aplenty of game varmints up here; I could tell that just by listening.

I started toward the light. Not a wise decision, maybe, but it wasn't like I decided. A picture in my mind drew me: I could see how there'd be a fellow there by his campfire and how he'd have coffee or a sip of whiskey and maybe both. I was hot and cold and sick of the rocks and the bruising. I'd make up some lie to tell him about what I was doing up here, any lie that would stick.

But then when I came to the edge of the clearing, I found it was no campfire. Here was a neat mountain cabin with a hearth fire inside and the clearing about me was a garden. I could make out the shape of the cabin pretty well. It was a clean place, the shingle roof mossed over, the little porch propped up on flat rocks. From the chinked rock chimney rose the ghost-colored smoke of the fire I'd spied so far away.

I waited at the edge, watching and listening. There were no dogs. I took it strange there were no dogs. A man at midnight walking up to a house in the solitary woods—he expects to hear the hounds begin to racket and come out to meet him.

Who was it lived here anyhow? Nobody I'd ever heard about.

I tried to walk quiet, but they'd have to be stone-deaf in there not to hear me rustling and crackling through the goldenrod and the cornstalks. But I came right to the side of the house without anybody raising a holler and saw that it was just a cabin like many another I know. Weathered oak boards and mud-chink rock foundations and on the porch flowers growing in lard buckets and a cane-bottom rocking chair empty but for starlight and shadow. There was silence all around.

On this side there was a little square window curtained with dotted swiss, just above eye level. I stretched up on tiptoe to see inside.

The room was neat and cheery in the firelight. There was a hooked rug on the floor and another bigger one hanging on the wall and two little tables and a couple of straight chairs. There was a tall, dark rocking chair beside the fire and in it sat a little old granny woman with iron-colored hair. She was wearing a washed-pale blue gingham dress and a blue-gray apron. She wasn't rocking in her chair, just sitting there as still as a tombstone, but she was not asleep. I could see the firelight glinting in her eyes like they were cat's eyes.

I let down flat to ease my legs. It was nothing strange to see, an old woman remembering in front of her fire, but I had to wonder. How could it be only her up here and no menfolk about to help her do? It looked all right, but when I thought, there was nothing right about it.

I decided to take another look, and this time it wasn't an old woman in her rocking chair, but another kind of thing hard to tell about. All gnarled and rooty like the bottom of a rotted oak stump turned up. Or all wattly, the way toadstools will grow on fallen timber. Maybe more like it looks at the bottom of a candle burnt halfway down, where the wax has gathered in smooth pulpy lumps.

I can't say exactly, because it was nothing exact to see. Something alive that nobody would ever think could live, something that knew about me out here by the window without seeing me, something that was an old woman in a chair and was no old woman any way in the world.

All right, Bill Puckett, I thought. This is what comes of your jealous murdering. You have landed in the hardest place a man can land.

I figured that maybe my third glimpse might be the true one, and when I peeped again, it was the same old woman as before, sitting just the way she was at first, with her eyes still shining yellow and not rocking in her rocking chair.

So maybe I'd imagined the rooty thing there, tired and scared as I was, and I was determined to get the good of her hearth fire, no matter. Ember Mountain with its ditches and brambles was too much for me this night; I was willing to take my chances with the old woman.

I went around to the front and up the five worn porch steps, trying to fix on a lie to tell her and whoever was with her here. I rapped three times and thought I heard a "Come in," but the door planks were mighty thick. Anyhow, I shot back the smooth-handled latch and entered.

When she craned her head to look, it came to my mind what a sorry marvel I must appear. I was all wet and muddy and my clothes were ripped and one side of my face and neck was probably still bleeding from a gash. Not a handsome sight to look on.

But she didn't show the least surprise. "Come in," she said. "Come to the fire, where it's warm."

I was grateful. I crossed over to the clean rock hearth and held my hands up to the fire, the way you can't help doing. I warmed one side of myself and turned to warm the other.

She was looking me up and down. "You appear to been a good while in the woods," she said.

"Yes, ma'am, I have been."

"Even on a summer night you can get cold and tore up on this mountain."

"Yes, ma'am."

She was just a nice old granny woman. Even with her sitting down, I could tell she was real short. Short and thick, I thought, before I observed she was a humpback woman. I couldn't place her age, the skin of her face being so smooth and ruddy. Apple cheeks, folks call that, but she was old.

Her hands were wrinkled and looked powdery and her voice was shrewd and trembly with her years.

"You got to be careful," she said. "There's many a good man been lost on Ember in the night."

"Yes, ma'am."

She turned her head sideways and the firelight caught in her eyes till they shone like pieces of gold. "Why are you up here, then, so late into the night?"

I hadn't made up my lie yet and now when I tried to, I couldn't do it. It stuck in the middle of my throat and I coughed and choked. I couldn't make sense in my head except just the truth and finally that was what I told her. "The law is after me," I said, "and some other people, too. They're wanting to hang me on a big hickory tree, I reckon."

"What for?"

"I shot a woman," I said.

"Did you kill her?"

"*I* don't know. But it was an awful big pistol I pulled the trigger on."

"Who was she?"

"She was just a woman that treated me wrong. There ain't no use to say her name."

"Sit down," she said. "Pull up a chair to the fire and sit you down. It's good you told me the straight of it and not some infernal lie."

I felt better leaning forward in the chair and soaking up the heat. My pants legs were steaming as the denim dried. "I didn't take no pleasure in it," I said. "It just came over me too powerful. When I went to the West End Tavern and Dance, I saw them both and I shot and threw down my pistol and fled away."

"Wasn't it Phoebe Redd, this woman?"

"How did you know that? How could you ever hear about it up on this mountain?"

Her voice dropped to a mumble and it was hard to hear her. I thought she said, "Because it's not the first time, never ever the first time."

"What did you say?" I asked.

She looked at me then with a look as straight as a broomstick. "How old a man would you be?"

“My name is Bill Puckett,” I told her. “I’m twenty-seven years old.”

“Ain’t you surely old enough to know better about women?”

“It came over me. I was in a fever when I couldn’t think.”

She nodded and got up and limped to the fire, showing she had a bad leg. She took up a big wrought-iron poker and shifted three logs. Red-and-orange sparks went up fantail and the wood snapped and sizzled. Her bunched-up shadow divided into three on the walls. “Well, what’s done is done,” she said. “What you’ll be doing next, that’s the question.”

“I don’t know anything to do but to just keep running,” I said. “Because all they’re going to do is just keep coming after me.”

“You could give up and hand yourself over.”

“I don’t know,” I said. “They’re riled pretty hot. No telling what they might do to me.”

“Sit you back,” she said, “and take your ease. I’ve got some herb tea already made that I can warm up for you. It’ll take some of the ache out of your bones.”

I didn’t say her no but began to rub my ankles and the calves of my legs. My skin was itching where my pants legs dried by the hearth fire.

With her heavy poker, she swung the iron crane out from the fireplace wall over the blaze and lifted down a black kettle from the adze-scarred mantelpiece beam. She hung the kettle on the crane hook. “Take off your shoes and your stockings,” she said, and when I did, she drew them to the hearth with the poker and arranged them to dry. “A good strong herb tea. Here now, move over into my rocking chair and rest a little easier.”

I did that, too, and began to unloosen a little in my muscles. I leaned back and looked into the fire, and then when I looked at her again, she blurred in front of me because of the firelight. I put it down to the firelight. “You’ll need you a cup and saucer,” she said. “I’ll go and get them from the kitchen.”

I tried to get up.

“You just stay here. You’ll be needing all the rest you can get.”

I listened to her shuffling about and I wondered again about her being lame and how she managed up here on the mountainside all alone by herself. I wondered, too, a great deal about how she heard of Phoebe, only I expected she had a radio back there in the kitchen that she would listen to anights, though I hadn’t seen any power lines when I found the house.

But the fact that she knew the name of Phoebe just showed how soon they'd be catching up with me.

I must have dozed a little, because next I remember her face close to mine, her apple cheeks smooth and reddish, and her eyes, away from the firelight, not yellow now but black-dark as two soot spots. And something I hadn't seen before: There were dents in her skin here and there, two in her forehead and one in her left cheek just below the eye and three dents in her throat, little pushed-in places like the thumbprints you'd leave in biscuit dough. The skin was smooth in the dents, smooth as isinglass. Wounds that have healed over, I thought, old wounds. Except for one in her throat just under her chin: That one looked healed but looked fresh, too, as red and rare as a scarlet flower.

She's had a bad time, too, I thought, and right then that was all I thought.

"Here now," she said. "Drink this all down." She offered me a china saucer with little blue painted flowers and a gilt edge and on it a blue enamel cup almost brimful of steaming tea. I remember the look of that cup and saucer as clear as the bluest sky. "It'll be good and strong for you," she said.

I knew I'd spill it if I tried to hold the saucer, my hands unsteady as they were. I set the saucer on the floor and held the cup in my thumb and first finger by its fragile little handle. When I sipped at it, the taste of its heat went right to my breastbone. It was strong and rank and bitter and it tasted of something that reminded me of *far away.* That is the best I know to tell: It tasted of *far away,* every bit as strong as she had said. Just the steam lifting out of the cup clambered in my head.

"There now," she said. "Can you feel anything from that?"

"It's mighty good," I said.

She was standing close over me again, her face almost touching mine and looking deep into my eyes. "Go on. Drink it down."

I didn't want to look into her eyes, so it was her throat I saw, the red new-healed smooth place beneath her chin. Right then I recognized that wound for the first time as the place on her body where my .44 bullet had struck my deceitful Phoebe back in Paradise. It was the exact same spot.

I wanted to understand that; I wanted to try to make some sense, but it was too late. The old woman's tea was too strong in me and the little china cup slipped out of my unnerved fingers onto the hearthstones. It didn't break into a hundred splinters; it stuck solid and quivering on the rock like an arrow shot into a tree trunk. I stared at it there unharmed.

I kept staring at the cup because I didn't want to look at the granny woman. It shivered my body to know if I looked at her, I'd see her again all ugly roots and lumps and with her fire-lit yellow eyes deformed.

But that's what I knew and not what I saw. All I saw was a heavy black roaring before my eyes and a sick shaking and I dropped then into a deep swoon, the deepest, I reckon, that a man can endure.

And when I came back to myself, I was not sitting in the rocking chair and there was no hearth before me and not even a cabin around me. I was lying flat on my back under the stars in the middle of a fair-sized grassy bald, a circle with edges so sharp against the trees and bushes, it looked like it was cut here with a knife.

It took a long time for me to get steady and sit up, and when at last I do, I find you-all here, all twelve of you men sitting cross-legged on the edge of the circle, all watching me with your wild eyes.

And when one of you, the tall, dark-complected man there in his ancient buckskins, asks me to tell my whole story, I don't hold back the least little crumb of it. Awful as it is, it's the truth and you know that.

Because you don't need to explain anything to me. I can see in your bitter faces and in the bitter shadows of your eyes how it is and how it is going to be, that we are the men who killed Phoebe Redd. Over the years and the generations and centuries it was us that left the marks of our pistol balls on her again and again. Mine was the freshest one just beneath her chin, as red as a scarlet rose. I know how her revenge on us is everlasting and how we are to be scattered howling to and fro on the mountain; and how there is no rest for us and no surcease, but only being driven miserable on the rocks and thorns until Ember Mountain perishes and time itself passes all away.

ALMA

I feel different about women than a lot of men do and I'll tell you why. It's because I had me my own woman one time. I lived real close with her and that has made me think thoughts apart.

The way it come about was there was a drover who told me he had journeyed up from the marshlands and he was pushing a string of twelve through the Suffering Mountain foothills. Headed for Fort Ox 1, the soldiers there, he said, and I tell you exactly what he said because I don't know better. But whatever he said is probably not in sight distance of the truth. If you know drovers, you know what I mean. I don't like them and never did.

Anyhow, they come to the edge of my campground there at Busted River about two hundred yards down from the big waterfall. He stopped them at the edge and I had to think it was the plumb sorriest string of women ever I laid eyes on. Most of them wouldn't make good buzzard bait when he got hold of them and he had took no pains to keep them up, never washing them down, and I could tell they had been fed scanty, their ribs sticking out. The rattiest bunch you could think of, mud and dust and scabs and their hair all ropy and their eyes wild. There was some of them sick, I could tell by looking.

He had them strung together with some old moldy leather tack and he tethered them to a big shagbark hickory and come on in toward me with his hands up and open. Which meant he was all alone except for his livestock but didn't know whether I was alone or not. I was because I didn't journey with gangs no longer. I was fed up with the squabbles and the knife fights and the pizen cooking and I had struck out on my lonesome to fish and hunt and trap and never regretted it, though you got to keep on your toes every minute when you do that, being your only own protection.

Come toward me hands open and careful like I say and says to me, "Stand easy now. My name is Dingo and I'd like to rest a spell with you and maybe use your cooking fire."

"You alone?" I asked him.

"Not exactly," he said, and grinned a sideways grin.

"I don't mean the women."

"It's just me and the shoat line," he says, shoats being what some drovers call women. "But they won't be no trouble. I can stake them out in the woods. I'll move them downwind if the smell bothers you. I've got kind of used to it myself."

I thought for a moment but was pretty sure he was alone. If he'd been trying to spring something on me, he wouldn't've put his livestock at risk.

"All right, then," I said. "Make you welcome. I've got my fire and there's a path to the river and that's all the camp I've struck here. If it will do you any good, make you welcome."

"A lot of good," he said, "and I thank you. First thing for me is to take care of these shoats. Where'd you say the path was?"

I showed where and he gave them a hand sign and the women unshucked the tote sacks from their shoulders and laid them on the ground and I could see how glad they was to do it. Then he herded them off the way I pointed, taking them down to the river to drink.

While they was gone, I slipped away from the fire and made me a quiet circuit of my ground, trying to find any sign of others. I was pretty well satisfied already that he wasn't with no gang, but you can't be too careful up there in the mountain territories.

By the time he got back from the river, I had some coffee going, parched oat coffee that was, and I was right tired of it after two months on the trail. He settled the women down by a blackberry thicket, downwind like he said, and staked them. They would have to be watered again after that meal, I thought, but right then they seemed pleased to get something to eat.

So then he came over to where I was and I pointed to the coffee and he took some in a little tin cup he'd fetched along. He offered me a crumb of chew tobacco, but I didn't take, not wanting to get too friendly in a hurry. You never know. But he was a free-talking jasper and said he was heading up to the fort to get shed of his women. Hoping to trade for firearms and ammunition or maybe for cutlery and if he couldn't get any of that, then just for canvas and cloth goods. "I don't much care what they bring, as long as I don't have to drive them no farther," he said.

I asked how long they'd been on the trail and he said ten days, which I judged a lie because those women had been marched a lot longer than that, easy to see. I just nodded, though, and figured to myself that this one was a raider. He had probably cut this string from one of the big herds heading south toward the Pleasure Cities. Snaked them away in dead of night and had to run them hard in the dark and that was why they looked so bad. Either that or he had come across some small outfit up on one of the tributary trails and killed them and took the women and made tracks out of there. Because he wouldn't be driving them all alone if he wasn't running scared.

I asked him if Fort Ox 1 was a pretty fair market for women and he said he hoped so. "If there hadn't been too many drovers before me," he says, and clawed in his beard for a flea and was disappointed. "It kind of depends on the weather. If it's good traveling, then a pretty many drovers will come through. But raining like it's been doing and not so many. They'll probably take them no matter because it's wonderful how many women the soldiers use up. Use them for domestics, you know, swabbing and scouring and whatnot, and the way they treat their women, they don't last all that long." He drawled out that word *whatnot* and slipped me a slow wink, but I gave no sign. None of my business what the soldiers do as long as they don't conscript me, which they'd tried twice.

So the time wore on like that, us jawing, him mostly. He asked me if I'd seen any other drovers in these parts and I told him I'd seen a string of horses and then five days ago a string of pigs, both headed south.

"No," he said, "I mean shoat lines. You see any drovers with women come along this way?"

"You're the first I know of," I said.

He nodded and it was plain he was relieved and he started talking again. "It ain't much of a business," he says, "and if I hadn't lit on such a long run of bad luck, I'd never be in it. Women, you couldn't dream what trouble, and them a glut on the market these days. They'll run a man crazy if he don't keep a tight rein, so I made up my mind right from the start I would. Dirty, you can see how dirty. And you can't teach them nothing; it's like they ain't got nothing to learn with. Dangerous, too."

"I heard that," I said, but they didn't look dangerous to me, only miserable as dug-up moles. They had pushed back the vines a little and huddled on the ground, picking twigs and trash out of each other's hair, picking off vermin. They were dog-weary and hollow-eyed and they would hug one another and croon and rock back and forth on their hams.

"Oh yeah. They'll jump a man in a minute if he was to get careless. And you wouldn't never want one of them to bite you, you know why?"

"Why is that?"

"Pizen," he said, and wagged his head slow. "A burning thirst comes over you and you swell up like a bullfrog."

I'd heard that and never believed it and didn't believe it now. Because a body pretty often bites hisself by accident, his lip or inside his cheek. If it was so, the women would've died out long ago. "I've heard tell there's some people that raise them for food," I said. "I wouldn't want to eat nothing that would pizen me."

He leaned back against a stump and sipped off the rest of his coffee. "I've et, I reckon, just about everything," he says. "Dog and snake and I don't know what all. But I can't think how starved I'd have to be before I'd eat a woman. They're my trade, you see, so I know how dirty they are. I wouldn't eat one, but I've heard that some do, like you say. You ever have much truck with women?"

"No," I said.

"Maybe you might want to learn a little. Come on over and I'll show you how a drover judges them to trade."

"I can see fine from where I'm at."

He stood up. "Come over and get you a good look so you'll see what I am talking about."

We went over and he made them stand up and we passed down the line. I couldn't see much difference up close because I ain't much judge. The truth is, I never did really hold with women trading. I know it's how things are and I suppose somebody will always be doing it, but not me, never. Something ugly about the whole thing, the way they look at you dog-eyed but also in a way so you know there is something going on in their heads and you'll never know what. And other reasons, too, I had no words for then.

He tried to explain me the finer points of his stock and I made like I understood what he was talking about. But there was one of them that stood out from the others. She was a redhead or would be if she was washed up, and she was a little bit smaller than the other women, but wiry, and looked to be quicker and maybe tougher. It was the way she carried herself, though, that made me take notice. She had been kicked and whipped, but she wasn't *beaten,* if you know what I mean. The way she held her chin up, the way her eyes were bright and no dog in them. She might just step up and spit in your eye and say, "Do your damn worst and I'll endure it." She wasn't no cleaner than the rest of them and she must have been just as tired, but she was different. One look at her and I knew and I wondered if Dingo knew.

"Well, what do you think of them?" he asked me.

"I guess they're fine," I said. "I ain't no hand at judging women."

"See any of them you might like to trade for?"

"In the first place I wouldn't know what to do with one and in the second place I ain't got nothing to trade with."

"You got your mule there and your cart. I'll make you a square deal. You won't find nobody fairer than me."

"No thanks," I said. "I got to have my mule and my cart. Especially this winter when I set up trapping. But I don't have no use for a woman."

He grinned that ugly little grin. "You would be surprised. Once you get a woman broke in good and get used to having her around, you'll wonder how you ever got along without."

All that meant to me was that I better not get accustomed. "Well, maybe next spring I might be interested," I says, "if I have a good season with my traps." Because I was set in my mind I'd never see him again.

"You don't know what you're missing, what a comfort and ease one of these shoats can be to a man. Don't go by the way you see them now. You get one of them cleaned and fattened up a little and it makes a difference you can't hardly picture."

"How could I get one fattened up? Here in these skinny old hills I can just barely feed myself." I turned away and went back to the fire. He come along with me and kept talking trade but must've known I was having none.

Twilight was in the woods now and I went down to the river and brought back some water and then fed my mule Warlock a double handful of grain. Dingo had already put more wood on the fire, so we commenced putting our grub together to boil up a stew. He had some cornmeal and seasonings and so he took some water and patted out johnnycakes and slapped them down on a sheet of tin by the fire. He made sixteen of them and said there would be one apiece for his shoats and two apiece for me and him.

"We could pass around some stew," I said. "We've got enough for all of them."

"No," he said. "They've had jerky and hardtack and now this johnnycake and in a little while I'll take them down and water them again. If you overfeed them, they get too feisty. They get treacherous and then there's no telling. The way I do is to keep their feed down during the drives and then right before I'm ready to trade I fatten them up real smart."

He went on about it, telling how he fixed them up to sell, scrubbing them down and grooming them. Every one of them carried her a dress in her tote sack, along with some other stuff they liked to have, and when she was ready to be sold, she would put on her dress and it fetched up her price something remarkable. No other time would she wear it, especially not on the drive to get tore up and dirty. They would comb out one another's hair and brighten their teeth with sassafras bark and wash up all shiny and put on the dresses and bring almost the same price as a good sound horse. You had to be careful, though, about the dresses because they got a little wild then. Many a time they'd kill for another's dress.

I was plumb sick of hearing about the woman trade.

It was night now and we ate the stew, which was better than I was used to, and set by the fire misinforming each other while trying to get some straight information, and I'd call it a draw. He was as stingy with the truth as a horse trader about the years on his animals, but I'd got the measure of him and matched him lie for lie.

In a little while I was ready to bed down, but he took one last turn to look after his shoats. He unhitched the women two by two and pegged them around the neck with rawhide cord and led them off into the woods to shit.

I bided my time, laying on my blanket and just resting till he got his business all took care of and laid hisself down. I wasn't fool enough to go to sleep first and I made sure my big knife was handy under my bedroll. I kept as still as a blacksnake in the noontime sun till I heard him breathing deep and easy and then my eyes got scratchy and I drifted off with the sound in my head of the women moaning in the dark.

I woke up with a jerk, thinking a long-legged bug had crawled into my ear, and it took me a minute to figure things out. Of course, I'd already reached and had my knife out and so I found that I was holding it pointed and ready to use under the chin of that redheaded, green-eyed woman who had been tickling in my ear with a grass blade.

She didn't flinch and didn't drop her eyes, so we stayed a long minute at stalemate, but I meant business. If she made a quick motion, I would've cut her throat.

Finally I let my hand drop back, though I still kept the knife ready, and then real slow she raised her hand to her mouth and signed for me to be quiet. Then she leaned toward me and scrooched down and put her face next to my ear, making sure I saw she kept her hands away, where she couldn't do me no harm.

"My name is Alma," she says to me, whispering.

I was thunderstruck. I didn't have the least idea that women could even talk, much less have names. And then the notion that they might know what their names were was queer. I didn't do nothing but gape for a while and Alma settled back to wait me out. Because she must have figured it was going to take me some little time to catch on.

I raised halfway up on my elbows and she motioned me to keep quiet and lay down again. She looked over to where Dingo was stretched out by the fire and he wasn't stirring.

"What is it you want?" I said, and I whispered, too.

"You can kill him," she said.

"Kill who?"

"Dingo," she said. "You can kill Dingo and then all of us would be yours. We would rather be your women than hisn."

"How come?"

"Because you're the better man. We would be your women and treat you sweet and act right. We wouldn't give you no trouble like we do Dingo."

"How did you get loose?"

"It ain't hard. I could get loose anytime, except there wasn't no reason to till you showed up."

"I can't kill him," I told her. "And I ain't got no use for women."

"You could trade."

"I wouldn't trade women. That ain't my way."

"Don't need to kill him, then," she said. "We can just tie him down. By the time he got loose, we'd be a long way gone."

"Then he'd track us down and do me in."

"Never," she said. "Not ever. He's ascared of you, you being the better man."

I kept glancing over at Dingo because the talk with Alma had got a little heated, but he didn't move except to wiggle for comfort now and again, which is a sign that a person is asleep good and sound.

And she kept on after me. "I believe you're going to do it," she says. "I can tell you want to."

"It's just that I ain't got no use for women," I said.

"When you say that, it means you never had one." She leaned her face next to mine and her eyes shone in the firelight and looked into me. Then she laid hold of me there for a minute where women do, though I didn't know that yet, and I looked away. "You're going to do it. I can tell you are." And she rubbed me a little and then I decided I would.

Maybe it was just her looking at me like that and then laying hold of me. But more likely it was her talking in the first place. I couldn't get used to it and was confused. A lot of new notions had come too fast. So I thought that maybe if I'd been wrong about a few things before now, I might be wrong about a lot of things.

But the truth is, I didn't think it out all that close. I just decided I would throw in with her rather than with Dingo because I didn't like him and I didn't like women traders in general. They were not his women anyhow, not till he'd robbed some other trader. So I figured he was only getting paid back even, if I figured on it at all.

The hardest part was crawling over to him without waking him up. You never notice how loud you breathe till you have to breathe quiet, and then you sound like you're heaving like a cantered horse. But I crawled on my belly the last few yards, moving pebbles out of the way so they wouldn't scrub and click.

I grabbed his blanket and rolled him over in a flash and felt under him for a knife or pistol. He was laying on his back, and when I saw his foot come halfway up, I pinned it with my knee and slipped the little dirk out of his boot and flung it into the fire. I didn't want Alma to get it and decide to do me after I'd done for Dingo. I didn't trust her; that would take a long time.

He was right strong, the twisty, wiry type, but I outweighed him by a good twenty pounds and about all he could soon do was thrash and swear. I took care to pin down his hands because I knew he'd have another weapon or two on him somewhere, so I knelt on his chest, moving up, and was surprised to see that Alma held down his ankles to help me out. That showed a lot of gumption.

"Just settle down," I said, but that only made him squirm harder and swear meaner. "No now, you settle," I told him again. "I wouldn't want to have to hit you with a stick or a rock."

So then he laid quiet but was still cussing in a low voice and I just let him work off his fury. Then when Alma handed me some rawhide thong she'd got from his gear, I tied his wrists first and then tied his feet to his neck with that Rag Mountain strangle knot the old-timers use. That one will take the fight out of anybody, but I couldn't let it stay on too long or he would straighten his legs out and choke hisself to death.

He looked a lightning bolt at me, spitting and groaning. "She's got you now, Fretlaw," he said. "You don't have the first notion what you've let yourself in for."

Alma got a handful of gravel and stuffed it in his mouth and then some dirt and leaves. She stepped on his cheekbone and ground her heel down.

"That's enough," I said.

"No," she says, "it ain't enough."

"Back off," I told her. "Unless you want to settle with me right now who'll be giving the orders."

She gave him a last kick but not so hard and said no settlement needed, I'd be the one giving the orders. "You don't never need to worry you won't be the boss," she said. Then she bent over him and fetched hold of a twine around his neck and jerked it loose and a little bone-handle double-edge knife come with it, which she handed over to me.

The women were all awake and they cowered back, mumbling and moaning and looking at us with eyes scared wild. When I made a step toward them, they all shifted back toward the blackberry thicket into the thorns.

"What about them?" I said.

"You ain't no trader. Why not turn them loose?"

"Is that what you want me to do?"

"Yes."

"They'll starve to death out here. Or worse."

"They've got their tote sacks," she says. "And anyhow, if it comes to that, they'd rather starve than be drove and sold."

"All right, then," I told her, "turn them loose. But if they start to come at me, I'll kill all I can."

"You've got everything all wrong. They wouldn't never hurt you. You the one that has saved them."

But Dingo spoke up to say, "If I was you, Fretlaw, I wouldn't sleep for a year. They're just waiting to cut your throat." It was hard to make out his words. Alma's dirt was still in his mouth.

But they earned him anyhow another kick from Alma as she went by on her way over to untie the women. Then she stood talking to them in a low voice and I couldn't hear her. They were happy, laughing and crying and hugging and kissing on the mouth. A few of them glanced at me and nodded while Alma was talking, but most wouldn't look my way. Then they detached into couples and struck off into the woods.

Dingo glared at me. "You got to turn me loose," he says. "Them shoats will come back to murder me the first minute you're gone."

"I'm going to undo the strangle knot and tie your feet kind of loose.

You'll be able to get free in just a little while. But if you come after me, I'll leave you to the tender mercies of my woman."

"That one woman will be your first thing to wish you never had."

I fixed his binding like I told him I would and he stretched out and eased a little. "You might be right," I said, "but if you come after us, she'll be the first thing you wish you never owned, either."

He swore some more and began struggling with his bonds.

"Wait now," I said. "Wait till we're out of sight or I'll have to tighten them up again."

Alma came back to where I was standing over him. "Go set down," she said, "and rest easy. I'll get us ready to move out. You don't need to raise a hand."

And so she done it, scouring out the cookware with sand and a bucket of water and piling that and the bedroll in the cart and packing Dingo's roll, too, without even a remark. I was dumbstruck again to see her hitch Warlock to the cart. Where could she have learned?

When we were all fixed to go, I climbed right up on the seat board and took the reins, but nothing would do for Dingo except to holler out that I'd be sorry, and I said, "I'll take my chances," and clucked Warlock up and we headed out toward the old Deer Salt Trail. I knew we'd better keep pointed toward the deeper mountains and put some rough distance between us and this campground.

When we had rolled and bobbed along about two miles, I told Alma that Dingo wouldn't starve, that I had tied him up in a way so he could work loose in a little while.

"No, he won't starve," she says. "That's one thing a dead man don't worry about."

"What do you mean?" I asked her.

"They went back and got him."

"The women?"

"Yes."

"What about me? Will they be coming after me now?"

"Not while you're with me," she said. "So you better stick by me for a good long time."

I didn't say nothing and she could see I was feeling gloomy about Dingo and wondering what I'd let myself in for, so she gave a little laugh and spoke soft. "Just wait till we come to a stream tomorrow. I'll clean up good and wash my hair and get nice and shiny. I'll put on my dress I've got in my tote sack. You won't believe your eyes to see me in my dress. And you won't never be sorry we throwed in together, you'll see." And she rubbed me there again where she rubbed before, where it was a pleasure, and we went on in the dark.

She was right about a lot of things, Alma was. We put in the winter trapping up on the Swagback and come spring we went down to Two River Post and traded our pelts, wild dog mostly and some fox and right much beaver and muskrat. She told me the kind of things to say when I traded with One-Eye Narbo there and played dumb herself and we come out all right.

That summer we just laid by the Upper Barrelhead and fished and loafed. Then with fall coming on she said we ought to head even farther north than the Swagback, all the way up to Frozenever, where hardly anybody had been. She said we'd do good there, and we did.

Five years we put in together like that and prospered. Maybe things got too easy for us and that made her restless, I don't know. Because one day she asked me if I'd ever thought we might want a child.

I said no, I had never gave it a thought.

"Well, think about it," she says. "One day you and me, we won't be so young anymore. It would be a big help to have us a youngun."

"Let me ponder," I told her, and I did. It's hard to picture yourself getting old and helpless and feeble, but that was what was coming if a flood or a rock slide or the rabies didn't carry us off first. Trouble was, I didn't know how to get hold of a youngun or what you did when you got one.

"That part's mostly up to me," she says. "The youngun is the woman's choice."

"What is it that you do?"

"Well, there's some things you and me do together." She chuckled and said, "You'll like that part. Then I have to go off by myself for a while and then if everything turns out all right, I come back with a child."

"Where do you go to," I asked, "that I can't go?"

"Where I go it's all women and they kill any man that tries to get close. There's an island in the middle of Weeping Lake and the women there ferry me over and after awhile I get to have a youngun to raise up and bring back to you."

"How long will you be gone?"

She frowned a little. "Hard to say. Maybe five years."

"No," I said in a hurry. "Five years. No."

"You don't know how chancy they are, little like that. If I was to bring back one that was too small, it might die up here in the woods. It's a hard way of life on a child."

"Bring back a big one," I said. "Get us a big old tough boy."

"All the ones you can get are only little."

"Well, I'll think," I said, "but I ain't much in favor."

That was only the beginning and the days went by and she kept talking, till finally she talked me into agreeing, as I halfway knew I would from the start. So we did the things we needed to do together and she was right about me liking that part of it. Then a few days after, we headed out to Weeping Lake and she got down from the cart there on the shore and we waited. In a little while we could see the ferryboat coming, the wind in its big black sails and the oars rowing, the black boat scuttering across the lake like a water beetle.

"Leave now," Alma told me. "Don't wait till the Guardian Women get here. They're well armed and they don't like men. So you go on and come back three springs from now at shadblow time. Like I said we'd do."

"I've changed my mind," I said. "We don't need no child. Let's go back to the mountains, where it's been good for us."

"No now," she says. "We've done decided, and you won't turn on your word, Fretlaw. I know you."

"You could change your mind, too."

"This is the chance we need to take. And if it turns out right, everything with us will be better than now and for a long time to come."

"Well, I won't turn on my word," I said. "But it don't feel right to me. My heart misgives me about this."

"It'll turn out fine," she says, and put her arms around me for a big warm hug. "Now go on."

So I did like she said. At the top of the sand ridge I stopped Warlock so I could square around and look at her standing there on the shore of the lake with the big black boat bearing down on her. I could see some of the Guardian Women on board in armor and with spears and pistols and cutlasses, but mostly I looked at Alma, how small she seemed all of a sudden with the big boat in front of her and all the width of Weeping Lake around. And it come to me then that she was scared, too, just as scared as I was, and I felt a little bit proud, too, as well as scared and sad.

And that was the last ever I saw of her, her alone like that, with the boat coming on. I went back the next spring, and every shadblow for five years now I go down to the shore of the lake and wait for as many weeks as I can stand it.

I'm not alone, neither. Every now and then there's another man or two will be there waiting, but the boat don't come for them no more than it comes for me. I suggested one time that we ought to get our own boat and head out to the island and bring our women back, and one of them, Benthook it was, says to me, "That's been tried before and the Guardians sink them every time. There's many a good man drownded in Weeping Lake."

I still might do it, though. I'm going to wait this springtime on the shore and maybe the next, but if Alma don't show up, I'm going out on the lake and search for that island.

Whenever I hear them talking in the whiskey sheds about women, going on about how dirty they are and how they're pizen and more murderous than bobcats and copperheads, I just feel weary in my bones. Because I had me a woman one time, my own woman, and I know different. And if I run across any traders in the mountains running shoat lines, I'm going to try to find out how to get those women away and turn them loose.

JUDAS

It wasn't the money; I never asked for money. The Department of Internal Security insisted that I accept thirty pieces of silver as a matter of convenience, so that they could keep their records neat. It was explained to me that the forms already had spaces for purchased information, whereas information got by other means and from other motives required pages and pages of complicated explanation.

So I took the money, even then thinking that thirty pieces of silver was too much reward for an unimportant sentimental socialist—or Communist? (What an ideological weasel he was!)—who had never been quite right in the head.

My motives were entirely personal and obsessive but not—I now realize—profound.

I had a number of separate grudges: his favoritism; his alternating periods of self-righteousness and humility; his pretensions to occult knowledge and power; the occasional fanaticism; that simpering, long-suffering attitude he struck when it came into his mind to "forgive" someone; his incessant prattle, mere strings of slogans and riddles; his neurotic wastage of Movement finances; his disregard of bathing or any personal sanitary practice. Add to these the utterly chaotic manner in which he conducted our business: wandering aimlessly about the settlements in the company of politically useless refuse—winos, thieves, con artists, pimps, whores, slaves, lepers, and a fatuous gaggle of over-the-hill society matrons. It became obvious that we had all been taken in.

When I realized all this, there began a most irksome period. I kept my conclusions to myself, never dropped a hint about what I was thinking. But I must have let slip some unconscious clue—an unguarded gesture, perhaps, or an unavoidable pun—for as soon as I had made up my mind, he knew, and I knew that he knew. After that, it was an unending game of cat and mouse. As he uttered some trivial nonsense, he would stare gloomily into the air above my head. Or he would glance at me sidelong, with a heavily ironic smile. Or he would refuse to serve my plate at meals, passing it off to Peter or Andrew or another of those idiots.

Of course, it came to a head at our final anniversary dinner when he announced flat out in his usual melodramatic fashion that someone present in the room would betray him and all those suck-ups began gabbling at once. *Not me. Who'd do a thing like that? You're kidding, aren't you?* Etc., etc. I could have taken the opportunity to throw suspicion off myself, but, frankly, I had too much pride to join with those sheep. I was disgusted by the whole scene, and at that moment I was glad I was taking the money.

I haven't got to the main reason, hardest to talk about, that I turned him in.

It was his character. He possessed an insufferable schizophrenic personality, trusting and suspicious at the same time, and these combined attitudes imposed upon me a feeling of responsibility no man's nerves could bear. He managed somehow to play the role of the wise and watchful father who, anxious for our well-being and amused by our infantile errors, would finally countenance no transgression of those vague, almost undefined, limits he knew to be absolute. Simultaneously with this posture, he put on a kind of doggishness—with those earnest myopic eyes—a blind animal trust; so that you felt that if you wronged him, he would drag off to starve to death in the bushes. As I say, he engendered an insupportable feeling of responsibility.

In short, he was simply goofy, a nut whose unfocused madness is harmless to the State but ruinously destructive of interpersonal relationships; and it was on the bases of these latter that I gave him over.

I feel bad now; my guilt feelings grow larger and darker. And though I have set down orderly on paper my motives, and though I can see that they make proper sense, I am deeply dissatisfied.

That was the whole trouble, you know. His kind of madness is contagious.

LINNAEUS FORGETS

The year 1758 was a comparatively happy one in the life of Carl Linnaeus. For although his second son, Johannes, had died the year before at the age of three, in that same year his daughter Sophia, the last child he was to have, was born. And in 1758, he purchased three small bordering estates in the country near Uppsala and on one of these, Hammarby, he established a retreat, to which he thereafter retired during the summer months, away from his wife and five children living; and having recently been made a Knight of the Polar Star, he now received certain intelligence that at the opportune moment he would be ennobled by King Adolf Fredrik.

The landscape about Hammarby was pleasant and interesting, though of course Linnaeus long ago had observed and classified every botanical specimen this region had to offer. Even so, he went almost daily on long walks into the countryside, usually accompanied by students. The students could not deny themselves his presence even during vacation periods; they were attracted to him as hummingbirds to trumpet vines by his geniality and humor and by his encyclopedic knowledge of every plant springing from the earth.

And he was happy, too, in overseeing the renovations of the buildings in Hammarby and the construction of the new orangery, in which he hoped to bring to fruition certain exotic plants that had never before flowered in Swedish soil. Linnaeus had become at last a famous man, a world figure in the same fashion that Samuel Johnson and Voltaire and Albrecht von Haller were world figures, and every post brought him sheaves of adulatory verse and requests for permission to dedicate books to him and inquiries about the details of his system of sexual classification and plant specimens of every sort. Most of the specimens were flowers quite commonly known, but dried and pressed and sent to him by young ladies who sometimes hoped that they had discovered a new species or who hoped merely to secure a token of the man's notice, an autograph letter. But he also received botanical samples from persons with quite reputable knowledge, from scientists persuaded that they had discovered some anomaly or exception that might cause him to think over again some part of his method. (For the ghost of Siegesbeck was even yet not completely laid.) Occasionally other specimens arrived that were indeed unfamiliar to him. These came from scientists and missionaries traveling in remote parts of the world, or the plants were sent by knowledgeable ship captains or now and then by some common sailor who had come to know, however vaguely and confusedly, something of Linnaeus's reputation.

His renown had come to him so belatedly and so tendentiously that the great botanist took a child's delight in all this attention. He read all the verses and all the letters and often would answer his unknown correspondents pretty much in their own manner; letters still remain to us in which he addressed one or another of his admirers in a silly and exaggerated prose style, admiring especially the charms of these young ladies upon whom he had never set eyes. Sweden was in those days regarded as a backward country, boasting only a few warriors and enlightened despots to offer as important cultural figures, and part of Linnaeus's pride in his own achievements evinced itself in nationalist terms, a habit that Frenchmen and Englishmen found endearing.

On June 12, 1758, a large box was delivered to Linnaeus, along with a brief letter, and both these objects were battered from much travel. He opened first the box and found inside it a plant in a wicker basket that had been lined with oilskin. The plant was rooted in a black sandy loam, now dry and crumbly, and Linnaeus immediately watered it from a sprinkling can, though he entertained little hope of saving—actually resuscitating—the plant. This plant was so wonderfully woebegone in appearance, so tattered by rough handling, that the scientist could not immediately say whether it was shrub, flower, or a tall grass. It seemed to have collapsed in upon itself, and its tough leaves and stems were the color of parchment and crackled like parchment when he tried to examine them. He desisted, hoping that the accompanying letter would answer some of his questions.

The letter bore no postmark. It was signed with a Dutch name, Gerhaert Oorts, though it was written in French. As he read the letter, Linnaeus deduced that the man who had signed it had dictated it to someone who translated his words as he spoke. The man who spoke the letter was a Dutch sailor, a common seaman, and it was probably one of his superior officers who had served as his amanuensis and translator. The letter was undated and began *"Cher maître Charles Linné, père de la science botanique; je ne sçay si . . ."*

"To the great Carl Linnaeus, father of botany; I know not whether the breadth of your interests still includes a wondering curiosity about strange plants which grow in many different parts of the world, or whether your ever-agile spirit has undertaken to possess new kingdoms of science entirely. But in case you are continuing in your botanical endeavors, I am taking liberty to send you a remarkable flower [*une fleur merveilleuse*] that my fellows and I have observed to have strange properties and characteristics. This flower grows in no great abundance on the small islands east of Guiana in the South Seas. With all worshipful respect, I am your obedient servant, Gerhaert Oorts."

Linnaeus smiled upon reading this letter, amused by the odd wording, but then frowned slightly. He still had no useful information. The fact that Mynheer Oorts called the plant a flower was no guarantee that it was indeed a flower. Few people in the world were truly interested in botany, and it was not expected that a sailor could have leisure for even the most rudimentary study of the subject. The most he could profitably surmise was that it bore blooms, which the sailor had seen.

He looked at it again, but it was so crumpled in upon itself that he was fearful of damaging it if he undertook a hasty inspection. It was good to know it was a tropical plant. Linnaeus lifted the basket out of the box and set the plant on the corner of a long table where the sunlight fell strongest. He noticed that the soil was already thirsty again, so he watered it liberally, still not having any expectation that his ministrations would take the least effect.

It was now quarter till two, and as he had arranged a two o'clock appointment with a troublesome student, Linnaeus hurried out of his museum—which he called "my little back room"—and went into the main house to prepare himself. His student arrived promptly but was so talkative and contentious and so involved in a number of personal problems that the rest of the afternoon was dissipated in conference with him. After this, it was time for dinner, over which Linnaeus and his family habitually sat for more than two hours, gossiping and teasing and laughing. And then there was music on the clavier in the small, rough dining room; the botanist was partial to Telemann, and he sat beaming in a corner of a divan, nodding in time to a sonata.

And so it was eight o'clock before he found opportunity to return to his little back room. He had decided to defer thorough investigation of his new specimen until the next day, preferring to examine his plants by natural sunlight than by lamplight. For though the undying summer twilight still held the western sky, in the museum it was gray and shadowy. But he wanted to take a final look at the plant before retiring and he needed to draw up an account of the day's activities for his journal.

He entered the little house and lit two oil lamps. The light they shed mingled with the twilight, giving a strange orange tint to the walls and furnishings.

Linnaeus was immediately aware that changes had taken place in the plant. It was no trick of the light; the plant had acquired more color. The leaves and stems were suffused with a bright lemonish yellow, a color much more vivid than the plant had shown at two o'clock. And in the room hung a pervasive scent, unmistakable but not oppressive, which could be accounted for only by the presence of the plant. This was a pleasant perfume and full of reminiscence—but he could not remember of what the scent reminded him. So many associations crowded into his mind that he could sort none of them out; but there was nothing unhappy in these confused sensations. He wagged his head in dreamy wonder.

He looked at it more closely and saw that the plant had lost its dry parchmentlike texture, that its surfaces had become pliable and lifelike in appearance. He began to speculate that this plant had the power of simply becoming dormant, and not dying, when deprived of proper moisture and nourishment. He took up a bucket of well water, replenishing the watering can, and watered it again, resolving that he would give up all his other projects now until he had properly examined this stranger and classified it.

He snuffed the lamps and went out again into the vast whitish yellow twilight. A huge full moon loomed in the east, just brushing the tree tips of a grove, and from within the grove sounded the harsh trills and staccato accents of a song sparrow and the calmly flowing recital of a thrush. The air was already cool enough that he could feel the warmth of the earth rising about his ankles. Now the botanist was entirely happy, and he felt within him the excitement he often had felt before when he came to know that he had found a new species and could enter another name and description into his grand catalogue.

He must have spent more time in his little back room than he had supposed, for when he reentered his dwelling house, all was silent and only enough lamps were burning for him to see to make his way. Linnaeus reflected that his household had become accustomed to his arduous hours and took it for granted that he could look after his own desires at bedtime. He took a lamp and went quietly up the stairs to the bedroom. He dressed himself for bed and got in beside Fru Linnaea, who had gathered herself into a warm huddle on the left-hand side. As he arranged the bedclothes, she murmured some sleep-blurred words that he could not quite hear, and he stroked her shoulder and then turned on his right side to go to sleep.

But sleep did not come. Instead, bad memories rose, memories of old academic quarrels, and memories especially of the attacks upon him by Johann Siegesbeck. For when Siegesbeck first attacked his system of sexual classification in that detestable book called *Short Outline of True Botanic Wisdom,* Linnaeus had almost no reputation to speak of and Siegesbeck represented—to Sweden at least—the authority of the academy. And what, Linnaeus asked, was the basis of this ignorant pedant's objections? Why, that his system of classifying plants was morally dissolute. In his book, Siegesbeck had asked, "Who would have thought that bluebells, lilies, and onions could be up to such immorality?" He went on for pages in this vein, not failing to point out that Sir Thomas Browne had listed the notion of the sexuality of plants as one of the vulgar errors. Finally, Siegesbeck had asked—anticipating an objection Goethe would voice eighty-three years later—how such a licentious method of classification could be taught to young students without corruption of minds and morals.

Linnaeus groaned involuntarily, helpless under the force of memory.

These attacks had not let up, had cost him a position at the university, so that he was forced to support himself as a medical practitioner and for two barren years had been exiled from his botanical studies. In truth, Linnaeus never understood the nature of these attacks; they seemed both foolish and irrelevant, and that is why he remembered them so bitterly. He could never understand how a man could write "To tell you that nothing could equal the gross prurience of Linnaeus's mind is perfectly needless. A literal translation of the first principles of Linneaen botany is enough to shock female modesty. It is possible that many virtuous students might not be able to make out the similitude of *Clitoria*."

It seemed to Linnaeus that to describe his system of classification as immoral was to describe nature as immoral, and nature could not be immoral. It seemed to him that the plants inhabited a different world than the fallen world of humankind, and that they lived in a sphere of perfect freedom and ease, unvexed by momentary and perverse jealousies. Any man with eyes could see that the stamens were masculine and the pistils feminine, and that if there was only one stamen to the female part (Monandria), this approximation to the Christian European family was only charmingly coincidental. It was more likely that the female would be attended by four husbands (Tetrandria) or by five (Pentandria) or by twelve or more (Dodecandria). When he placed the poppy in the class Polyandria and described its arrangement as "Twenty males or more in the same bed with the female," he meant to say of the flower no more than God had said of the flower when He created it. How had it happened that mere unfanciful description had caused him such unwarrantable hardship?

These thoughts and others toiled in his mind for an hour or so. When at last they subsided, Linnaeus had turned on his left side and fallen asleep, breathing unevenly.

He rose later than was his custom. His sleep had been shaken by dreams that now he could not remember, and he wished that he had awakened earlier. Now he got out of bed with uncertain movements and stiffly made his toilet and dressed himself. His head buzzed. He hurried downstairs as soon as he could.

It was much later than he had supposed. None of the family was about; everyone else had already breakfasted and set out in pursuit of the new day. Only Nils, the elderly bachelor manservant, waited to serve him in the dining room. He informed his master that Fru Linnaea had taken all the children, except the baby asleep in the nursery, on an excursion into town. Linnaeus nodded and wondered briefly whether the state of his accounts this quarter could support the good fru's passion for shopping. Then he forgot about it.

It was almost nine o'clock.

He ate a large breakfast of bread and cheese and butter and fruit, together with four cups of strong black tea. After eating, he felt both refreshed and dilatory and he thought for a long moment of taking advantage of the morning and the unnaturally quiet house to read in some of the new volumes of botanical studies that had arrived during the past few weeks.

But when he remembered the new specimen awaiting him in the museum, these impulses evaporated and he left the house quickly. It was another fine day. The sky was cloudless, a mild, mild blue. Where the east grove cast its shadow on the lawn, dew still remained, and he smelled its freshness as he passed. He fumbled the latch excitedly, and then he swung the museum door open.

His swift first impression was that something had caught fire and burned, the odor in the room was so strong. It wasn't an acrid smell, a smell of destruction, but it was overpowering, and in a moment he identified it as having an organic source. He closed the door and walked to the center of the room. It was not only the heavy damp odor that attacked his senses but also a high-pitched musical chirping, or twittering, scattered on the room's laden air. And the two sensations, smell and sound, were indistinguishably mixed; here was an example of that sensory confusion of which M. Diderot had written so engagingly. At first he could not discover the source of all this sensual hurly-burly. The morning sun entered the windows, shining aslant the north wall, so that between Linnaeus and his strange new plant there fell a tall rectangular corridor of sunshine, through which his gaze could not pierce clearly.

He stood stock-still, for what he could see of the plant beyond the light astonished him. It had opened out and grown monstrously; it was enormous, tier on tier of dark green reaching to a height of three feet or more above the table. No blooms that he could see, but differentiated levels of broad green leaves spread out in orderly fashion from bottom to top, so that the plant had an appearance of a flourishing green pyramid. And there was movement among and about the leaves, a shifting in the air all around it, and he supposed that an extensive tropical insect life had been transported into his little museum. Linnaeus smiled nervously, hardly able to contain his excitement, and stepped into the passage of sunlight.

As he advanced toward the plant, the twittering sound grew louder. The foliage, he thought, must be rife with living creatures. He came to the edge of the table but could not see clearly yet, his sight still dazzled from stepping into and out of the swath of sunshine.

Even when his eyes grew accustomed to shadow, he still could not make out exactly what he was looking at. There was a general confused movement about and within the plant, a continual settling and unsettling as around a beehive, but the small creatures that flitted there were so shining and iridescent, so gossamerlike, that he could fix no proper impression of them. Now, though, he heard them quite clearly and realized that what at first had seemed a confused mélange of twittering was, in fact, an orderly progression of sounds, a music as of flutes and piccolos in polyphony.

He could account for this impression in no way but to think of it as a product of his imagination. He had become aware that his senses were none so acute as they ordinarily were; or rather, that they were acute enough, but that he was having some difficulty in interpreting what his senses told him. It occurred to him that the perfume of the plant—which now cloaked him heavily, an invisible smoke—possessed perhaps some narcotic quality. When he reached past the corner of the table to a wall shelf for a magnifying glass, he noticed that his motions were sluggish and that an odd feeling of remoteness took power over his mind.

He leaned over the plant, training his glass and trying to breathe less deeply. The creature that swam into his sight, flitting through the magnification, so startled him that he dropped the glass and began to rub his eyes and temples and forehead. He wasn't sure what he had seen—that is, he could not believe what he thought he had seen—because it was no form of insect life at all.

He retrieved the glass and looked again, moving from one area of the plant to another like a man examining a map.

These were no insects, though many of the creatures inhabiting here were winged. They were of flesh, however diminutive they were in size. The whole animal family was represented here in miniature: horses, cows, dogs, serpents, lions and tigers and leopards, elephants, opossums and otters. . . . All the animals Linnaeus had seen or heard of surfaced here for a moment and then sped away on their ordinary amazing errands—and not only the animals he might have seen in the world but the fabulous animals, too: unicorns and dragons and gryphons and basilisks and the Arabian flying serpents of which Herodotus had written.

Tears streamed down the botanist's face, and he straightened and wiped his eyes with his palm. He looked all about him in the long room, but nothing else had changed. The floor was littered with potting soil and broken and empty pots, and on the shelves were jars of chemicals and dried leaves, and on the small table by the window his journal lay open, with two quill pens beside it and the inkpot and his pewter snuffbox. If he had indeed become insane all in a moment, the distortion of his perceptions did not extend to the daily objects of his existence, but was confined to this one strange plant.

He stepped to the little table and took two pinches of snuff, hoping that the tobacco might clear his head and that the dust in his nostrils might prevent to some degree the narcotic effect of the plant's perfume, if that was what had caused the appearance of these visions. He sneezed in the sunlight and dust motes rose golden around him. He bent to his journal and dipped his pen and thought, but finally he wrote nothing. What could he write that he would believe in a week's time?

He returned to the plant, determined to subject it to the most minute examination. He decided to limit his observation to the plant itself, disregarding the fantastic animal life. With the plant, his senses would be less likely to deceive him. But his resolve melted away when once again he employed the magnifying glass. There was too much movement; the distraction was too violent.

Now he observed that there were not only miniature animals, real and fabulous, but also a widespread colony, or nation, of homunculi. Here were little men and women, perfectly formed, and—like the other animals—sometimes having wings. He felt the mingled fear and astonishment that Mr. Swift's hapless Gulliver felt when he first encountered the Lilliputians. But he also felt an admiration, as he might have felt upon seeing some particularly well-fashioned example of the Swiss watchmaker's art. To see large animals in small, with their customary motions so accelerated, did give the impression of a mechanical exhibition.

Yet there was really nothing mechanical about them, if he put himself in their situation. They were self-determining; most of their actions had motives intelligible to him, however exotic were the means of carrying out intentions. Here, for example, a tiny rotund man in a green jerkin and saffron trousers talked—sang, rather—to a tiny slender man dressed all in brown. At the conclusion of this recitative, the man in brown raced away and leapt onto the back of a tiny winged camel, which bore him from this lower level of the plant to an upper one, where he dismounted and began singing to a young lady in a bright blue gown. Perfectly obvious that a message had been delivered . . . Here in another place a party of men and women mounted on unwinged great cats, lions and leopards and tigers, pursued over the otherwise-deserted broad plain of a leaf a fearful hydra, its nine heads snapping and spitting. At last they impaled it to the white leaf vein with the sharp black thorns they carried for lances and then they set the monster afire, its body writhing and shrieking, and they rode away together. A grayish waxy blister formed on the leaf where the hydra had burned. . . . And here in another area a formal ball was taking place, the tiny gentlemen leading out the ladies in time to the music of an orchestra sawing and pounding at the instruments. . . .

This plant, then, enfolded a little world, a miniature society in which the mundane and the fanciful commingled in matter-of-fact fashion but at a feverish rate of speed.

Linnaeus became aware that his legs were trembling from tiredness and that his back ached. He straightened, feeling a grateful release of muscle tension. He went round to the little table and sat, dipped his pen again, and began writing hurriedly, hardly stopping to think. He wrote until his hand almost cramped and then he flexed it several times and wrote more, covering page after page with his neat sharp script. Finally he laid the pen aside and leaned back in his chair and thought. Many different suppositions formed in his mind, but none of them made clear sense. He was still befuddled, and he felt he might be confused for years to come, that he had fallen victim to a dream or vision from which he might never recover.

In awhile he felt rested and he returned again to look at the plant.

By now a whole season, or a generation or more, had passed. The plant itself was a darker green than before, its shape had changed, and even more creatures now lived within it. The midsection of the plant had opened out into a large boxlike space thinly walled with hand-sized kidney-shaped leaves. This section formed a miniature theater or courtyard. Something was taking place here, but Linnaeus could not readily discern what it was.

Much elaborate construction had been undertaken. The smaller leaves of the plant in this space had been clipped and arranged into a grand formal garden. There were walls and arches of greenery and greenery shaped into obelisks topped with globes, and Greek columns and balconies and level paths. Wooden statues and busts were placed at intervals within this garden, and it seemed to Linnaeus that on some of the subjects he could make out the lineaments of the great classical botanists. Here, for example, was Pliny, and there was Theophrastus. Many of the personages so honored were unfamiliar to him, but then he found on one of the busts, occupying a position of great prominence, his own rounded cheerful features. Could this be true? He stared and stared, but his little glass lacked sufficient magnification for him to be finally certain.

Music was everywhere; chamber orchestras were stationed at various points along the outer walls of the garden and two large orchestras were set up at either end of the wide main path. There were a number of people calmly walking about, twittering to one another, but there were fewer than he had supposed at first. The air above them was dotted with cherubs flying about playfully, and much of the foliage was decorated with artfully hung tapestries. There was about the scene an attitude of expectancy, of waiting.

At this point the various orchestras began to sound in concert and gathered the music into recognizable shape. The sound was still thin and high-pitched, but Linnaeus discerned in it a long reiterative fanfare, which was followed by a slow, grave recessional march. All the little people turned from their casual attitudes and gave their attention to the wall of leaves standing at the end of the wide main pathway. There was a clipped narrow corridor in front of the wall and from it emerged a happy band of naked children. They advanced slowly and disorderly, strewing the path with tiny pink petals they lifted out in dripping handfuls from woven baskets slung over their shoulders. They were singing in unison, but Linnaeus could not make out the melody, their soprano voices pitched beyond his range of hearing. Following the children came another group of musicians, blowing and thumping, and then a train of comely maidens, dressed in airy long white dresses tied about the waists with broad ribbons, green and yellow. The maidens, too, were singing, and the botanist now began to hear the vocal music, a measured but joyous choral hymn. Linnaeus was smiling to himself, buoyed up on an ocean of happy fullness; his face and eyes were bright.

The beautiful maidens were followed by another troop of petal-scattering children, and after them came a large orderly group of animals of all sorts, domestic animals and wild animals and fabulous, stalking forward in their fine innate dignities, though not, of course, in step. The animals were unattended, moving in the procession as if conscious of their places and duties. There were more of these animals, male and female of each kind, than Linnaeus had expected to live within the plant. He attempted vainly to count the number of different species, but he gave over as they kept pouring forward smoothly, like sand grains twinkling into the bottom of an hourglass.

The spectators had gathered to the sides of the pathway and stood cheering and applauding.

The animals passed by, and now a train of carriages ranked in twos took their place. These carriages each were drawn by teams of four little horses, and both the horses and carriages were loaded down with great garlands of bright flowers, hung with blooms from end to end. Powdered ladies fluttered their fans in the windows. And after the carriages, another band of musicians marched.

Slowly now, little by little, a large company of strong young men appeared, scores of them. Each wore a stout leather harness, from which long reins of leather were attached to an enormous wheeled platform. The young men, their bodies shining, drew this platform down the pathway.

The platform itself supported another formal garden, within which was an interior arrangement suggesting a royal court. There was a throne on its dais, and numerous attendants before and behind the throne. Flaming braziers in each corner gave off thick grayish purple clouds of smoke, and around these braziers small children exhibited various instruments and implements connected with the science of botany: shovels, thermometers, barometers, potting spades, and so forth. Below the dais on the left-hand side, a savage, a New World Indian, adorned with feathers and gold, knelt in homage, and in front of him a beautiful woman in a Turkish dress proffered to the throne a tea shrub in a silver pot. Farther to the left, at the edge of the tableau, a sable Ethiopian stood, he also carrying a plant indigenous to his mysterious continent.

The throne itself was a living creature, a great tawny lion with sherry-colored eyes. The power and wildness of the animal were unmistakable in him, but now he lay placid and willing, with a sleepy smile on his face. And on this throne of the living lion, over whose back a covering of deep-plush green satin had been thrown, sat the goddess Flora.

This was she indeed, wearing a golden crown and holding in her left hand a gathering of peonies (*Paeonia officinalis*) and in her right hand a heavy golden key. Flora sat at ease, the goddess gowned in a carmine silk that shone silver where the light fell on it in broad planes, the gown tied over her right shoulder and arm to form a sleeve, and gathered lower on her left side to leave the breast bare. An expression of sublime dreaminess was on her face and she gazed off into the far distance, thinking thoughts unknowable even to her most intimate initiates. She was attended on her right-hand side by Apollo, splendidly naked except for the laurel bays round his forehead and his bow and quiver crossed on his chest. Behind her, Diana disposed herself, half-reclining, half-supporting herself on her bow, and wearing in her hair her crescent-moon fillet. Apollo devoted his attention to Flora, holding aloft a blazing torch, and looking down upon her with an expression of mingled tenderness and admiration. He stood astride the carcass of a loathsome slain dragon, signifying the demise of ignorance and superstitious unbelief.

The music rolled forth in loud hosannas, and the spectators on every side knelt in reverence to the goddess as she passed.

Linnaeus became dizzy. He closed his eyes for a moment and felt the floor twirling beneath his feet. He stumbled across the room to his chair by the writing table and sat. His chin dropped down on his chest; he fell into a deep swoon.

When he regained consciousness, the shaft of sunlight had reached the west wall. At least an hour had passed. When he stirred himself, there was an unaccustomed stiffness in his limbs and it seemed to him that over the past twenty-four hours or so his body had aged several years.

His first clear thoughts were of the plant, and he rose and went to his worktable to find out what changes had occurred. But the plant was no more; it had disappeared. Here was the wicker container lined with oilcloth, here was the earth inside it, but the wonderful plant no longer existed. All that remained was a greasy gray-green powder sifted over the soil. Linnaeus took up a pinch of it in his fingers and sniffed at it and even tasted it, but it had no sensory qualities at all except a neutral oiliness. Absentmindedly, he wiped his fingers on his coat sleeve.

A deep melancholy descended upon the man and he locked his hands behind his back and began walking about the room, striding up and down beside his worktable. A harsh welter of thoughts and impulses overcame his mind. At one point he halted in mid-stride, turned and crossed to his writing table, and snatched up his journal, anxious to determine what account he had written of his strange adventure.

His journal was no help at all, for he could not read it. He looked at the unfinished last page and then thumbed backward for seven pages and turned them all over again, staring and staring. He had written in a script unintelligible to him, a writing that seemed to bear some distant resemblance to Arabic perhaps, but which bore no resemblance at all to his usual exuberant mixture of Latin and Swedish. Not a word or a syllable on any page conveyed the least meaning to him.

As he gazed at these dots and squiggles, Linnaeus began to forget. He waved his hand before his face like a man brushing away cobwebs. The more he looked at his pages, the more he forgot, until finally he had forgotten the whole episode: the letter from the Dutch sailor, the receiving of the plant, and the discovery of the little world the plant contained—everything.

Like a man in a trance, and with entranced movements, he returned to his worktable and swept some scattered crumbs of soil into a broken pot and carted it away and deposited it in the dustbin.

It has been said that some great minds have the ability *to forget deeply.* That is what happened to Linnaeus; he forgot the plant and the bright vision that had been vouchsafed to him. But the profoundest levels of his life had been stirred, and some of the details of this thinking had changed.

His love for metaphor sharpened, for one thing. Writing in his *Deliciae naturae,* which appeared fourteen years after his encounter with the plant, he described a small pink-flowered ericaceous plant of Lapland growing on a rock by a pool, with a newt as "the blushing naked princess Andromeda, lovable and beautiful, chained to a sea rock and exposed to a horrible dragon." These kinds of conceits intrigued him, and more than ever metaphor began to inform the way he perceived and outlined the facts of his science.

Another happy change in his life was the cessation of his bad nights of sleeplessness and uneasy dreams. No longer was he troubled by memories of the attacks of Siegesbeck or any other of his old opponents. Linnaeus had acquired a new and resistless faith in his observations. He was finally certain that the plants of this Earth carry on their love affairs in uncaring merry freedom, making whatever sexual arrangements best suit them, and that they go to replenish the globe guiltlessly, in high and winsome delight.

LADIES FROM LAPLAND

Once fired, passion for the philosophy of Isaac Newton proved unquenchable in Europe. The celebrated Emilie du Châtelet provides an example of enthusiasm. She was so engrossed in writing her treatise of Newton that she would not leave off even to bear her child, and this daughter was born there in her study and laid in linen on a large-folio geometry text. Not many days afterward, Mme. du Châtelet was laid in the severer angles of her grave.

The famous savant had first heard of Newton from a quick-tempered and rather acid *virtuoso* named Pierre-Louis Moreau de Maupertuis. Maupertuis began as one of those child prodigies whom we may find either charming or detestable; at age six, he desired to know why the same wind that extinguishes a candle flame serves to make a fire grow roaring. It was during his leisure hours as an officer in the Gray Musketeers that he trained himself as a scientist-philosopher.

As much for his malicious wit as for intellectual achievement, he established such reputation that he was highly favored by the learned ladies of the 1720s, and Mme. du Châtelet employed him as her geometry tutor. Immediately, there was rumor they were lovers, and why should they not be? Maupertuis reserved his angry jests for his male rivals and was willing and complaisant among the females; Mme. du Châtelet had amorous desires to match the fierceness of her intellectual desires. In fact, it was the urgency of her physical need that led her from the cooling embraces of the preoccupied Voltaire to the comely but butterfly-minded Marquis de Saint-Lambert, who gave her the child that was her death.

But this was an age when honors could not long stand without a basis of solid accomplishment, and Maupertuis, who was as hungry for fame as Emilie for love, conceived the notion of establishing the first physical proof of Newton's theory of gravitation. It was thought that if any part of Newton could be demonstrated physically, the whole of the system, constructed with such rigorous consistency, must be taken as fact.

One of the corollaries of the theory of gravitation was that the Earth is not perfectly round but, rather, an oblate spheroid, larger around the tropic zones and slightly flattened at the poles. So that a Huygens clock sitting on the equator, and thus farther from the center of gravity, would have to shorten its pendulum in order to keep time with an identical clock in Paris. Maupertuis proposed to test this notion by taking measurement of the Earth. He would head an expedition to the polar circle and measure a degree of the meridian, while another expedition would journey to the equator for the same purpose. Gravitational experiments could be carried out that might corroborate the earlier findings of Jean Richer at Cayenne.

This is why we see, when we look at a contemporary engraved portrait of Maupertuis, in the predella below, the figure of a man, bundled in a sleigh like a baby in a cradle, and urging on a reindeer with a menacing bullwhip. This is Maupertuis, intrepid in the icy vastness, rushing to the end of the world, anxious to triangulate and compute.

The device is merely emblematic. His colleagues in the expedition—Clairaut, Othier, Camus, and Le Monnier—complained that they lumbered about in the snow with the bulky instruments, while Maupertuis did little of the work or none.

Yet he was not idle. There were women in Lapland, as there must be in every society upon the Earth, and when Maupertuis caught sight of these small round-faced ladies with their shiny black hair and their eyes dark and trusting, his thoughts ranged far from gnomons and clocks and Newton.

He looked at the Lapland women and thought that here, too, was a terra incognita from which he could learn things unknown in Europe. And it was a territory to which he could bring enlightenment, cultivating the civilized arts of love in an untutored land where the nighttime went on for months. Was ever such opportunity given a man? He thought of Ovid in exile, bringing the amatory practices of Rome to the rude provincials. He thought of many things.

He was utterly charmed by these women who gathered round him, marveling at the whiteness of his complexion and his strange clothing. They reached out to touch him, tugging like curious children at his hands and waistcoat and breeches. They murmured liquidly like quail; they looked at one another and giggled.

The Lapland men stood apart, smiling in friendly fashion, shier than the woman, but with a reserve of dignity.

Maupertuis wasted no time. As soon as lodgings were set up—large round reindeer-skin tents open at the top—and the other members of the expedition sent off to capture angles and degrees, the famous scientist invited two of the prettiest and shiest of the women (sisters, as it turned out) to take supper with him in the main tent. He spoke to them in French and accompanied his invitation with the full panoply of Continental gallantry, sweeping bows, bended knees, hand kissing, and so forth. The sisters, at first alarmed, became amused and burst into melodious laughter. Maupertuis felt confident that he had made himself understood, and he retired to prepare.

When the sisters arrived a little past the appointed time, an astonishing spectacle met their eyes. The air inside the geometrician's tent smelled not of burning tallow but sweetly, as of uncountable flowers. The round shell of cured hide was hung with gauzy drapery that stirred languorously as they opened the tent flap. Maupertuis had spared no expense. Two bound racks of reindeer antlers hung suspended from the tent poles and on each antler point was flaming a precious wax candle: a crude arrangement but still a chandelier. It was the most light these ladies had ever seen, except for the light of the summer sun. The geometrician had undergone a transformation, dressed now in stiff rich cloth with glittering yellow buttons and large stiff frills at his wrists. His face had grown even paler than before except for two large red spots on his cheeks.

The sisters were struck with wonder and gazed about as if they could never see enough of these strange sights. When Maupertuis motioned for them to seat themselves, they huddled together on a bench over which woolen lap robes had been thrown, and clutched each other's hands. They were numb with amazement; they could not speak.

The sisters seemed to have been transformed also, for their names had changed. Aimu found herself being addressed as Mademoiselle Choufleur and Tsalma as Mademoiselle Doucette, these titles accompanied by Maupertuis's exaggerated bowings and genuflections.

The ghostly-looking man drew up a bench and sat before them, chattering away in French and gesticulating languidly. He smiled continually. He looked first deep into the eyes of Mlle. Doucette and then into Mlle. Choufleur's eyes; then he looked away coyly, like a child with a naughty secret. He rose and went to the other side of the tent and brought two sparkling crystal glasses for the sisters and one for himself, and he filled the three glasses red from a bottle.

The sisters had never taken wine and at first did not like it. But in the interest of good manners they emptied their glasses a number of times, to find that Maupertuis always replenished them. They grew warm and exhilarated and by way of experiment attempted to imitate some of the sounds their host poured out in gushing profusion. These primitive tries at the French language delighted Maupertuis and he became more voluble than ever. Tsalma fumbled with her new name, "Mzelle Dooz't," and these words so excited Maupertuis that he leapt up and kissed her on both cheeks. His eyes were brighter now and his breath quickened. She was covered with confusion and clapped her hands over her eyes.

He then produced a platter of strange foods, biscuits and jellies and sweetmeats, and prevailed upon the ladies to experiment. They were wild as children for these delicacies, and Mlle. Choufleur's mouth and chin were colorfully smeared with jam, and her fingers, too, as she ate the sweets as a bear would eat honey. This gave Maupertuis reason to kiss her on the mouth and then, not content with this pleasantry, he began to lick her face. She laughed and her sister laughed and also began to lick her face.

An elaborate and exhilarating game developed, the three of them smearing and licking, smacking their lips and kissing one another repeatedly. All was proceeding now more smoothly than Maupertuis had anticipated. The tent was quite warm, the sisters heated with wine, and the scientist encountered little resistance in divesting them first of their long fur waistcoats and then of their sealskin trousers. Gravely and ceremoniously, Maupertuis bared himself to the waist, retaining for the moment his linen breeches. But the sisters were completely naked, except for Doucette's head, for she had found a wig in an open trunk. Maupertuis helped her to don it, and Choufleur and the Frenchman burst into hilarious laughter.

Doucette stood, this lovely women with skin the color of darkened bone and her round face merry and astonished and her small dark-nippled breasts bare, before them, the silver wig as incongruous on her brow as the golden helmet of Mambrino. She uttered some sounds, which she must have intended to sound like French, and attempted a low bow in the manner of her new friend. The wig fell at his feet, and then Doucette fell between the other two, who were now seated on the bench. She was laughing so heartily, she could hardly breathe, and Maupertuis began to pat and caress her bare shoulder. Doucette turned her head to peer up at him, and her face was full of impudent mischief.

The sisters once more became intrigued with the strange whiteness of his skin and began to examine closely his chest and back and arms, tugging at his flesh like puppies. Their curiosity was aroused and they pulled at his breeches, anxious to determine whether his nether parts were as snowily French as the rest of him. Nothing loath, Maupertuis joined them in nudity, and seemed to show as great an interest in their bodies as they in his.

In fact, he thought that he had never seen figures so perfectly formed, such charming dusky beauty. Their faces, shoulders, and hips were of a delectable symmetrical roundness. They were not all covered with savage hair as he had imagined; even the pubic hair was contained in a small neat triangle as delicate as Alençon lace. Very striking, too, was the gleaming whiteness of their perfect teeth, set against so much loveliness tinged with shadow.

By degree and degree, Maupertuis allowed his investigations to become less anthropological and more personal. The ladies, who had at first exhibited no special interest in his penis, now made it the focal point of their pullings and pokings.

He rose to his feet and with due gravity flung a large fur lap robe down beside the fire in the middle space. He took Mlle. Doucette's hand solemnly and led her to couch upon it. He knelt above her and parted her legs gently, but before beginning any part of his maneuvers, he turned to smile encouragingly at Mlle. Choufleur, and beckoned her to join them. She smiled but looked aside modestly.

Maupertuis from the first had intended by way of experiment *de faire minou* with a woman of Lapland, and when he crept between her legs and commenced those operations with mouth and tongue that were so widely appreciated in Paris, Mlle. Doucette burst into uncontrollable laughter, like a child being tickled along the ribs. This was rather disconcerting for Maupertuis, but he had expected resistance of some sort and was determined to carry out his project. He was possessed, after all, of the patience of the geometer, and, stretching his arms upward to clasp her breasts, continued in his delicate task. He was surprised to find that Doucette did not taste of rancid tallow and seal blubber, but was reminiscent of cool ferns and clear springwater.

Maupertuis persisted in the familiar practice until Doucette's resistance gave way and the power of Venus held sway over her blood. She gasped openmouthed in delight and after awhile found herself brought to that condition that eighteenth-century diction renders in such terms as *transports of joy, effusions of balm, heights of ecstasy,* and so forth. Afterward, when she had somewhat collected herself, she gazed at Maupertuis with an expression of submissive adoration.

But this episode hardly allayed Maupertuis's own fervor. Now he enticed—it took no special pleading, to be sure—Mlle. Choufleur to the selfsame trysting spot and they began to make love in more ordinary fashion, in ways recognizable even in Lapland. Highly satisfactory it was, too, to the representatives of both exotic cultures.

The ladies were astonished to learn, however, that this was not the end of their amorous merrymaking. The scientist was not content to be satisfied; he must be sated. And so the sportive pursuit began all over again, this time in a more tender and deliberate motion and at a slower tempo, involving all three of them. A sweet languor characterized their movements and they dallied thoughtfully, like figures in a reverie on a long summer afternoon.

Gradually the night's encounter came to an end. The sisters' warm dark eyes were dulled, as if they were under the influence of narcotics.

They warbled softly in Lapp and insisted in covering Maupertuis with kisses once more—his arms, chest, hands, even the knobbled knees. Doucette rubbed reflectively at the patches of red on her inner thigh where Maupertuis's face rouge had come off. Her finger came away painted with rouge and she put it into her mouth.

With drowsy lassitude, and regretfully, the three of them put on their clothes. They stroked one another and murmured endearments. Finally, with slow reluctance, the sisters took their leave. They had duties to attend, though Maupertuis did not know what these duties might be. In truth, he did not much care. His active spirits were in abeyance; he did not wish to think of the morrow. He stood for a long moment at the open tent flap as the sisters disappeared into the dimness.

When he came back to the fire, though, he began to revive a bit. He had met such degree of success as he had hardly dared to hope for, and how was there any way his researches should not continue? Why should they meet with any less success in the future? He sank tiredly onto a bench and looked into the orange heart of the sinking fire and smiled the smile of reason.

The fame of Maupertuis's pleasure tent spread rapidly. The number of his female visitants must have been prodigious; rumor imputes upward of a dozen at a time, but surely this number is unlikely. The numbers were undeterminable. Who can, or would, be accurate in these circumstances? But there must have been crowds of yielding ladies, for after some weeks even the most obliging of the Lapland men began to shows signs of restiveness.

Maupertuis's colleagues were thoroughly displeased. Their leader aided hardly at all in taking measurements, and contented himself with totting up columns of figures and with commenting sardonically upon the quality of their labors. Clairaut, especially, among the other scientists, was bent on painting Maupertuis in his true colors when once they returned to civilization.

Perhaps it was Clairaut's determination to expose Maupertuis that was as responsible as any other factor for the swift and triumphant completion of the project. All was finished on schedule, and the scientists were ready to return to Paris, there to await the arrival of La Condamine from

Peru, where he had gone to measure the equator. Word had reached them that the Peruvian expedition had been plagued with harsh and even tragic difficulty but that La Condamine would persist and overcome.

Here in Lapland, there was a different sort of difficulty regarding departure. The ladies of Lapland were heartbroken to hear that Maupertuis was on point of leaving. Individually and in hastily assembled groups, they invented every possible allurement to keep him here at the top of the world. The philosopher explained over and over again that his work here was ended, that he had a duty to science, that generations unborn would share his gratitude toward the Laplanders for their gracious hospitality.

It occurred to the ladies that if he would not stay, they would go with him, all the way to the wilderness of Paris; they could not bear to be without him. Even as Maupertuis was demonstrating to them that this fantasy was impossible of fulfillment, the memory of desire came over him and he relented so far as to agree to take four—only four—of the women to France. He would choose. There was to be no violence, no lamenting, no unseemly display; they were to abide compliantly by his decision. He went among them like a housewife selecting vegetables from the market and chose four comely companions to journey with him and taste the gratifications of silken hose and chocolate gâteaux. Incurably sentimental, he included among these four his old friends Mlle. Choufleur and Mlle. Doucette. He then, with awkward speed, made ready to embark.

Clairaut and the others at first were furiously angered by Maupertuis's decision to carry back these living specimens of polar fauna, but then they realized that their wayward leader was taking to Paris the very evidence that would damn him and justify their accusations of negligence and knavery. At the hour of departure they were so thoroughly reconciled to the venture that they applied themselves to assist the ladies in all possible ways.

As the ship pulled away from the icy shore, Maupertuis thought that he heard in the wind a wailing as of tribes of bereaved women. He shook his head to clear away this delusion.

The homeward journey was terrifying due to bad diet and foul weather. They endured shipwreck off the coast of Norway, an incident that

Maupertuis, in ensuing years, wrought out in such heroic terms that Voltaire felt constrained to make angry mock of it in his "Micromégas." The four Lapland ladies were continually frightened and bewildered and clung to Maupertuis as threatened children to their mother.

But the philosopher was in process of making a surprising and disappointing discovery. The farther the four women traveled from their snowy homeland, the more their beauties suffered diminishment. Their complexions, which by firelight and lamplight in the tent had appeared as the quality of old ivory, now seemed dun and dingy. The delicious small roundness that had made their figures so attractive had become a squat dumpiness. Their formerly amusing attempts at French sounded like the irritable chatter of apes. And even their teeth seemed to have lost dazzle.

By the time the ship made port at Le Havre, Maupertuis was thoroughly disillusioned. He now conceived that he might be seen as a laughingstock, and this, above all other things, he could not bear. There was danger, too, that the exotic presence of these females would draw attention away from the scientific value of the expedition, and that his merited reputation would be occluded by the atmosphere of the raree-show.

After an hour of restless and regretful cogitation, Maupertuis decided to abandon these ladies as soon as the company arrived in Paris. Or if he did not abandon them, he would find ways to keep them hidden away, at least until the time that his scientific endeavors had garnered due recognition.

He ended, of course, by abandoning them. It was left to Clairaut to minister after this further piece of reckless impertinence. He arranged a house for the four of them in one of the less frequented quarters of the city and gave them what assistance he could in adjusting to the rigors of civilization. At a later date he was able to obtain for them a small but sufficient royal pension.

Maupertuis had accomplished his grand scheme and had experienced no tarnishing. He leapt from glory to glory, recounting his adventures, explaining the importance of his newly proven theories, strutting like a young bravo with his first challenge to duel. He turned up at Café Gradot, that favorite haunt of astronomers and mathematicians, perspiring under the full bulk of his Lapland costume. His accomplishment was universally bruited, and his face was known everywhere, especially after the broad dissemination of the famous engraving taken after the painting by Tournières.

Mme. Graffigny, another celebrated savant, was excited to have come upon this engraving. She was slightly acquainted with Clairaut and wrote to congratulate him upon his close association with the great man. She described the engraving closely, the reindeer and sleigh in the predella, and the figure of Maupertuis above, pointing with his left hand toward the marvelous unknown future, while his right hand pressed down on a figure of the globe of the world, flattening it slightly at the poles. Globe-flattener had, in fact, become Maupertuis's fond public sobriquet.

In answering the letter, Clairaut, after tendering his affectionate respect, desired her to look more carefully at the representation of that globe, to make certain it was not a woman's breast beneath the hand of Maupertuis. He then went on to tell the whole story, assuring her that it could be verified by a visit to number 44, rue de l'Eplatisseur.

Mme. Graffigny wasted no time in making her visit, accompanied by an intellectual friend. She found the situation to be more or less as Clairaut had reported, though he had not indicated the full range of strangeness and contradiction. Here were the four Lapland ladies, lonely and dispirited, quarreling spitefully in a debased and raucous tongue. They were dressed in fashionable gowns that in no way could contain their capacious hips and upper arms. No shoemaker stocked a last to fit them, and they flopped about in soiled carpet slippers. Wigs they wore, too, monstrous high-piled wigs they were immoderately proud of; but these would not sit straight and kept sliding down over their eyes. By this time the splendid Lapland teeth were ruinous, as the ladies partook incessantly of cakes, confits, sweetmeats, and syrups. Mme. Graffigny visited with them for two hours, learning what she could, but she left the house with such feeling of relief that she was never to return.

She described in one of her many voluminous letters to M. "Panpan" Devaux some of the details of her visit. "You will not be sorry to hear, my dear friend," she began, "that our love-attracting Frenchmen please even in frozen climates, and that love is of every country." She went on in her usual way to make an entrancing narrative of the episode, telling of the many oddities and vanities, and of the general ridiculousness, of these strange women. Maupertuis's secret was abroad now, and Mme. Graffigny concluded her account by saying, "All Paris goes to that house to see the Lapp ladies. Ah, mon Dieu, how can one be a Laplander?"

MOMENTS OF LIGHT

1

During Haydn's first London sojourn, honors fell upon him like snowflakes settling upon a public statue. He was adored, worshiped, idolized. He was invited, or, rather, importuned, to fetes, balls, dinners, concerts, tours, to every sort of occasion. But though a naturally sanguine man, Haydn was then fifty-nine years old and long ago had learned to order his life. His pressing concerns were, as he put it, "first . . . my health, and second my work." He tried to take all things in stride, to accept some invitations deliberately and to refuse others delicately.

His first year in London passed and the attention paid him did not abate. It seemed that no amount of information concerning the maestro could sate the appetite of the newspapers; nor, spreading himself ever so widely, could he satisfy the eager expectations of polite society to see him. He grew tired sometimes, but—keeping close watch upon himself—never so exhausted that he was irritable or unable to compose.

He was long past the time when his head could be turned by flattery, and anyway, it was simply not in his nature to be affected by currents of social fashion. This, after all, was the man who, when asked at the Austrian border his profession, replied, "*Tonkunstler.*" The customs official, having not the faintest idea what a composer might be, wrote down "*Topfer*"—potter—for to this functionary, *Kunstler* (artist) always signified potter. Haydn, observing this error, was serenely amused, and he reflected that if his work could attain the solidity and shape of dishes and pots, he should consider himself successful. Franz Joseph Haydn was the man who exclaimed at the age of seventy-seven, “Am I to die so soon? I have just begun to understand the wind instruments!”

It must be a great advantage for an artist to have such a steady disposition, to have the kind of emotional balance that we most often imagine scientists to have. But then, in Haydn’s time the scientist and the artist were not thought of as antipodal creatures. In the eighteenth century, it seemed only inevitable that the advancement of learning and the refinement of the senses should go forward hand in hand. In fact, in England, Haydn’s music was praised as “pleasing to every scientific ear.” And the foremost astronomer of the time, William Herschel, had in his earliest youth been trained as an oboe player, and later had become organist at Bath, composing seven symphonies, which he finally consigned to a cheerful oblivion.

That Haydn and Herschel should meet was taken for granted. They were both amiably social creatures, they were Germans residing in England, and they were the preeminent geniuses of their respective endeavors. Eleven years earlier, in 1781, Herschel had discovered the planet Uranus. He had at first mistaken the new member of the solar family for a comet, and only arduous observation and painful computation had shown that it was indeed a planet. This was news of enormous scientific and theologic import, since it completed the mystical number of seven planets, and King George III rewarded the wide-browed astronomer with an annual stipend in order that he might pursue his researches without fret. Herschel pursued them assiduously, contributing important papers on the parallax of the fixed stars and on the motion of the sun, and beginning the notes for his grand treatise on the construction of the heavens.

It was thought that the two great men would take pleasure in each other’s acquaintance; Herschel’s musical background must count heavily in favor of a close friendship.

But Haydn procrastinated.

Week after week, the composer put off the historic encounter. There was first this pressing appointment to be kept and then another; he had promised to hear this violinist and that cellist; he must make an excursion to hear this cathedral organ and the other church choir. And finally and always, there was his work; he had accepted commissions he must deliver; and a lady had brought him some verses he thought promising for a cantata. There was, no doubt, truth in all that he said, but at last even his less intimate friends perceived that he was reluctant to meet his celebrated compatriot.

Why?

It was always easy for even those who knew him well to overlook a steadfast peasant strain in Haydn's character. He was descended of no very illustrious parentage, and the fame and fortune he enjoyed he had wrested by force of talent from a world sweetly indifferent to the success or failure of one *fiddler* or another. New discoveries in the supralunary heavens seemed to be reported almost daily in these years and they disturbed profoundly the four-square conservative fabric of Haydn's nature. It was a good thing to have moved up in society, but, having moved up, Haydn observed many things he disapproved of. He had met butchers with more gracious manners than shown by counts; he had known carters who had a broader knowledge of the world than princes. Here at the top of the social order and at the forefront of philosophic investigation, Joseph Haydn discovered an inconstancy of direction which quite dismayed him.

Herschel was one of the foremost disturbers. Those big glasses he had made sought out ever newer and farther objects in the sky, stars multiplying in the heavens so rapidly as to make the mind ill. Thinking of these discoveries, Haydn felt as if he were looking dizzily down from a great height, looking down upon a flimsy earth from the top of the Tower of Babel. Simply this: Haydn was a little frightened what such a man as Herschel might say to him.

Dr. Charles Burney brought them together. This officious musicologist wrote to Herschel to expect them, and to distract the composer's fears, Burney took him in the early afternoon to a horse race. At Ascot, Haydn fell in love with the English horses, with their lightness and grace, and he admired the English easiness with the animals. Smitten with colors, he observed the jockeys, "lean as greyhounds, and clad in silks of pink, green, blue, red." He came away from the horse race flushed with excitement.

They were received by Herschel's sister, Caroline, herself a famous discoverer of comets, and taken immediately into the library, where William awaited them. He greeted them with a smile and with hearty handshakes, not bowing. Seeing him, Haydn was obscurely relieved to find that he was taller than his host and for this reason began to feel quite gracious.

They took port, an English habit Haydn had learned to forbear.

Burney at once struck up a pompous political topic. The other two men appeared to listen attentively to this recital of unfamiliar names, but with sidelong glances they were taking the measure of each other.

What did they see?

Haydn, described in the newspapers as a "fiery angel of harmony" and so forth, was one of the most ordinary-appearing men God had ever fashioned. He was neatly dressed in a suit of dark gray velvet and his fastidiously powdered wig had not been in the least discomposed by the excitement of the afternoon. He had a musician's aristocratic long-fingered hands, which contrasted violently with the strong plain features of his face, with the heavy blunted nose and the thick weathered lips. But Haydn's eyes were remarkable. They expressed a highly intense life force, but at the same time those dark brown eyes overflowed with calm. A person looking into Haydn's eyes would be overcome with a feeling of deep certitude and serenity. What things are there in this world? What terror and joy, what agony and beauty, what order and disorder? In Haydn's eyes were the knowledge and foreknowledge of it all; a man felt flooded with a sense of the rightness of things. Not one furtive glimmer in those brown eyes betrayed the apprehension of Haydn's soul as it looked upon the queasy, humorless future.

When he looked at Herschel, Haydn saw a man alert, independent, and resolute. At the moment he formed no further opinion.

Dr. Burney leapt like a cricket from politics to letters. He spoke of Fenelon's *Entretiens sur la Pluralité des Mondes.* "Do you recall," he asked Herschel, "the passage in which he imagines the worlds of the Milky Way to be so close together that pigeons might carry lovers' messages from one world to another? Dr. Herschel, you have destroyed many a pretty fancy with your observation of the immeasurable distances between planets."

Herschel smiled. "I should be distressed to learn that I have interrupted any discourse of lovers," he said.

At this, his sister, Caroline, laughed and came to kiss her brother on the cheek. She then excused herself and took leave of the company. Dr.

Herschel explained that Caroline was engaged in a series of elaborate astronomical calculations and could spare little time during these weeks.

Haydn was delighted to discover that Herschel still spoke with a thick accent. He felt more and more at ease.

Burney pursued his notion. "But don't you think it at least possible, sir, that much of the poetry of our lives will be in retreat under the advance of science? Why, sir, even the symbol of poetry, the winged horse, no educated child can now countenance."

"Dr. Burney, that particular emblem, and many others with it, was never intended by the poets to be taken literally. It is merely a way to paint in one phrase both the power and the graceful lightness of the poetic art."

"Even so, Dr. Herschel—"

"And we must never forget how much our present state of scientific knowledge is indebted to the writings of the ancient poets." Herschel now spoke at length of the atomist theory as it was received from Lucretius, of the botanic wisdom to be found in Homer and in the *Georgics.* He began to grow quite impassioned, and Haydn noticed that a new energy interfused his body and animated his regular placid features. Herschel shifted to the new experiments of Joseph Priestley, experiments which demonstrated that air possessed weight and mass and hence offered resistance to objects in passage through it. "Well then, Dr. Burney, you will recall that in the fourth book of the *Aeneid,* at the funeral games dedicated to Anchises, an arrow is shot from the bow with such force that it bursts into flame. Mr. Priestley has shown us that if an arrow could be so constructed as not to break, and that if it could be driven with sufficient force, then it would indeed catch fire. To me, that is a near proof that the ancients possessed a great body of scientific knowledge that we are now in the process merely of rediscovering. I begin to have grave doubt that anything *very* new is to be known."

"But perhaps," said Burney, "the genius of the Roman was able to pierce the veil of Nature at this point, just as in the Fourth Eclogue he was able to see past his proper time into the future of our Western societies."

To this proposition, Herschel assented readily, but he maintained that the supposition would more reinforce his point than weaken it.

Haydn discovered that he was taking the liveliest interest in this topic, to which he could add nothing, not even an intelligent question. The little astronomer whom he had feared as a bugbear unruly and impatient was, in fact, charming company, whose enthusiasm only served to season his conversation.

Dr. Burney fastened once again upon his original contention. "And yet some ideas of great beauty have to be discarded. Surely according to the laws of your own discipline, we must now give over the venerable notion of the Music of the Spheres."

Haydn watched Herschel expectantly.

"Come now, Dr. Burney," Herschel said. "Simply because a young child has learned to fashion a toy cart and to pull it behind him, we do not expect the king to give up his carriages. I consider that astronomy is only in its early infancy and that many years must pass before we attain to a true appreciation of the Harmony of the Universe, which is surely the conception of the greatest grandeur that the ancient world could claim." Still speaking to Burney, he turned to face Haydn. "If we discard the Music of the Spheres, then we shall reduce our maestro's art to a series of pleasing noises. In the deepest part of our beings, we reject such a proposition, do we not?"

Burney was complaisant. "Sir, I will hold that I am well bested in the argument if we can vindicate the ways of Haydn to man."

Haydn made a sound of polite demurral, yet still he failed to speak.

It had now grown fairly dark and tapers were lit. The three gentlemen sat at their ease, talking of one thing and another until dinner was announced.

They dined without benefit of the fair sex. Herschel gave plausible explanations for the absence of each of his family, but Haydn received the impression that the Herschel clan was simply bored by a long procession of nobles, geniuses, and virtuosi breaking in upon their lives. He felt sympathy for their predicament, which was very like his own, but did not regret that he had come. . . . They devoured plaice and a chicken and an excellent venison.

Afterward, they returned to the library for port.

Haydn felt at last obliged to say something of Herschel's profession and celebrity. He complimented him effusively, mentioning various circumstances in which he had heard Herschel's name bruited on the Continent; and he congratulated him on the profession of stargazing, which, he said, he imagined to be one of the pleasantest in the world, thus always to be searching out new moments of light and volumes of new worlds.

Herschel was at immediate pains to disenchant his guest. "I doubt you would find it a happy profession upon close acquaintance," he said. "First, there are the computations, which are very fine and tedious, but without which any amount of gazing is fruitless. And then the observation itself must take place out-of-doors in every sort of weather. I am often racked with ague and stiffened with cold. Then there are the problems of constructing these big glasses and working around them in the dark. Many times my brother and I have suffered accidents which might well have proved fatal." And he went on to tell how once, stumbling in the night, he had imbedded a hook deep above his right knee. To free himself, he had had to give up a good two ounces of flesh to the iron. He added with some pride that the attending physician told him that a soldier with such a wound would be entitled to six full weeks in hospital.

Haydn was surprised. Nothing about astronomy was as he had pictured. He had imagined that an astronomer sat indoors at his ease, poked his tube out through a window, and there waited like a fisherman for something astounding to take place at the other end of the sky. All these mathematical details and physical hardships he could not have guessed at. Especially he was impressed by Herschel's suffering cold weather, for dearest of all things to the composer were his health and well-being.

Burney was seized by a sudden fancy. "Dr. Herschel," he cried, "if there are other worlds with men, may we not think they, too, are employing telescopes? Perhaps at this very moment they are searching out our world with their glasses."

"They must inhabit nearby to see us," Herschel replied, not at all excited by the notion. "They must live in the Moon or in Mars or Venus. Or they must have very powerful glasses indeed. For you must not imagine, Dr. Burney, that it is an easy matter to catch glimpse of a planet within all the shine and empty space of the heavens."

"Let us say that they live in Mars," Burney said. "I can imagine them scanning our own orb anxiously, looking for traces of men like themselves."

Herschel said placidly, "It is easier to imagine that than it is to imagine a race of men who would have no curiosity about the stars. If there are men in other worlds, we may suppose that they are looking somewhere, though perhaps not at us."

Burney was silent for some moments and then said, "See here, if there are such beings as Mars men, I would give anything to hear their music. Indeed, I would give whatever I have."

The other two men smiled, and Herschel then told of the two twelve-foot telescopes he had made for the king, who had paid one thousand guineas. He spoke of the twenty-two-foot telescope and finally of the new forty-foot telescope, which had so broadly opened the skies, showing star upon star without number. Even he, Herschel, could not have guessed at the depth of the local universe nor the extent to which it was populated with bodies.

"Is it so very full, then?" Haydn asked.

"No, maestro, it is in the main empty, the distance between star and star being so incalculably great. But there are so many more stars than anyone had suspected. It is just that it is all so much *larger* than we could have thought. . . ."

"May we not have a look at these wonders?" Burney asked. "For I consider it a gross breach of manners that a Mars man is looking down upon me and I am not looking back at him."

"By all means, let us go to the telescope," Herschel said.

He led them out into the June night, soft and purple and scented. Burney kept chattering ebulliently, but Haydn was downcast. His fears had returned.

2

It was the most beautiful of spring nights, velvety warm. Now that they were crossing the lawn under the shell of stars, even Dr. Burney fell silent. They had a wide view of the sky here, for all the bordering trees had been felled to give access of vision. Here and there a last glowworm drifted sparkling.

Against the purple horizon, the telescope presented a startling aspect. It was seated within a tall openwork pyramid of joists, crossbeams, and ladders, stark against the sky, like the skeleton of some monstrous insect. At the huge mouth of the instrument open to the stars were two platforms, a smaller above a larger. The other end rested upon or within a little hut situated within the base of the pyramid. The tube of the glass was larger in diameter than Haydn had expected. As they mounted the ladder to the first platform, Haydn—a little breathlessly—remarked upon this.

Herschel did not reply until they had reached the safety of the platform. Then he said, "The diameter often surprises those who have heard only of its length. Before the optical part was finished and the tube lay yonder on the grass, many visitors had the curiosity to walk through. Two of those so moved were King George and the Archbishop of Canterbury. In their passage, the archbishop happened to stumble slightly on one of the interior supports. The king then reached him his hand, saying, 'Come, my Lord Bishop, I will show you the way to heaven.'"

They ascended to the second platform, and here Herschel pointed out to them the complex and ingenious arrangement of pulleys which enabled the telescope to be brought into position by a single man, who need be no Goliath. He showed them the great lens and explained his strategy of polishing by means of a troop of men wearing numbers. He told of the hardship and frustration that accompanied so many of the smaller details of workmanship. Burney and Haydn expressed proper surprise and commiseration at the intricacies of construction.

They descended and stood on solid ground once more.

"Are we now to see into the skies?" Dr. Burney asked.

"Yes," said Herschel, and he led them into the hut and up onto the viewing platform.

This was the moment that Haydn had dreaded. He was overtaken by a misery so acute that he neither noticed his surroundings nor heard the dialogue that passed between Burney and Herschel. The depths of his mind cried out to the musician that he must not look into this instrument, that whatever he was to see beyond the pale of the moon would have only a disruptive influence upon his nature, that it was his task to think calmly upon the business of timbre and tempo, of chord progressions and tonal transitions. He could not tell himself what he thought, but he had a vague picture in his head of a score sheet, of the stave lines broken and lying loose like pieces of string.

Herschel had now finished the operations necessary for viewing, and he stood back from the aperture. "Sir?" he said, inviting Haydn to take his place.

Haydn refused.

The astronomer gave him a look full of astonishment, but his astonishment immediately changed to sympathetic alarm. "My dear sir!" he exclaimed, rushing to Haydn's side. He took the composer's hands. "Why, dear sir, you are all atremble. Here, you must sit down." There was a small straight chair at the edge of the platform and he drew it up.

Haydn sank into it gratefully.

"Maestro, are you ill?" Dr. Burney looked extremely anxious.

Haydn attempted to speak but could not.

Herschel hurried back to the telescope. Into a speaking tube that trailed down from the platform, he said, "Caroline, will you please bring wine and some cakes here? Our guest has taken a bad turn." Then he came back.

Burney was distracted by this machine. He ran to it and cried, "Ho! Miss Herschel, are you there?"

"Please don't shout, Dr. Burney," Herschel said. "You will deafen my poor sister. The tube is designed to carry a normal speaking voice." He turned to Haydn, who was now regaining his color and some of his composure. "Can you tell us what is the matter?"

"It is nothing; it will pass." He lied: "Now and again I am taken with a spell of dizziness."

"Are you certain? Our physician, Dr. Ormond, lives not far."

"No, please. It is nothing serious."

Caroline arrived, bearing a platter with a bottle of claret and some little apple cakes. She appeared sharply concerned about him, and proffering him a glass of wine, she murmured something he could not quite hear.

He drank off the wine greedily; a burning thirst had come upon him. He thanked her. She replenished the glass and offered him one of the little cakes, but he could not take it.

Burney looked upon him curiously and said with an air of bemusement, "You are well; you look entirely recovered now."

"Yes, it is nothing." He *had* recovered and there was nothing to be done, but still they fluttered around him, until he began to grow a little irritable. "Please, I am *gesund*. . . . I am sound, I am sound."

"Not mere sound," Burney said. "You are music itself."

This lame jest restored the equanimity of the company, and they now left Haydn in peace. Herschel and the eager Burney withdrew to the telescope, and Burney was instructed how to view. As soon as he looked into it, he became voluble, exclamations pouring out of him like steam from a teakettle. He waved one hand freely and Dr. Herschel hovered at his side, evidently a bit worried about danger to his machinery.

Caroline stayed by Haydn; and he was grateful, for he was always soothed by the presence of women. He asked her of her astronomical accomplishments and how she came to be so extraordinarily learned. She mentioned something of her father Isaac's instruction and of her brother's, then passed the subject off and began talking of the domestic arrangements of the household, of the special provisions that had to be taken for a house full of stargazers. Haydn was gratified by this topic and questioned her closely about servants, about the disposition of meals for the odd hours that astronomers must keep, and about the house itself, which he found was rather cramped, since the many thousands of pages of observed data had to be stored. He was amazed that the Herschels kept their pages of errors as well as the true pages; and she was surprised that when a passage went badly for the composer, he simply crumpled the sheet and discarded it.

Burney had, at length, glutted his eyes, and now he came away, still expostulating and querying.

Haydn heard only Herschel's reply to a final question: "You must believe," said the astronomer, "that in a strip of space fifteen degrees long and two degrees wide, I found there were fifty thousand fixed stars and four hundred and sixty-six nebulae."

These numbers struck a pang in Haydn's breast and his resolution almost failed once again. Yet when Dr. Herschel invited him to try the telescope, he marched to it steadily, like a soldier marching in rank. As instructed, he put his eyes to the aperture and found the metal still warm from the brow of Dr. Burney.

At first he could see nothing at all, not even darkness. There seemed to be a gauzy gray curtain that withheld his sight completely. Then at last this obstruction disarranged itself, and stars began to show themselves and the immense spaces to show themselves.

3

The spirit of Joseph Haydn went from his body through the telescope like liquid sucked up through a glass tube.

He was not where his body was, but his spirit was already in the sphere of the moon. The world beneath him was no longer dark; it shone with various colors, pleasantly, like an artist's watercolor. Presently his spirit was in motion again, faster and faster—or was it that the globe began to revolve faster?—and the colors melted all together and the world diminished in size until it was no larger than a washed jewel, and fell away below him, shrinking to a candescent blue jot and then vanishing entirely. After this it was total darkness and awesome silence for a long while; and then the blackness was punctuated with streaks and points of brilliant white light and there came a rushing sound of swift wind, though nothing touched his body. For he had no physical body.

He no longer felt fear or apprehension, not the slightest tinge. He felt, instead, expectant, felt that he was about to witness something of great importance. That feeling persisted through the whole adventure, and even later when he recalled, there seemed to be something—an event, an image—of moment just outside his line of sight, just beyond earshot. There was about it forever a feeling of *impendingness.*

Now came a sensation of slowing, though the smears of light, which he took to be star shapes stretched and tormented by the speed of his flight, began to appear more frequently, until the whole firmament was surfeited with blinding light. Here his flight paused and Haydn gazed into the light, the heart of it, which moiled and leapt and reached out arms of lacy fire. If there was heat, he was insensible to it and received only the spectacle of the light in its joyful agony, quaking and pulsing as it strove to manifest its being in the same moment that it strove to negate that being. He did not find it mindless. If music and poetry are not mindless, but instead the appreciable workings of personality, then this drama of light was intelligently assertive in the same way.

Franz Joseph Haydn passed through the center of that fire. It felt no more tangible than a cobweb. Beyond it was another absolute darkness, but the speed of his flight was not so terrific as formerly and the space about him no longer seemed boundless, but enclosing. He traveled now as if he were struggling against some odd physical property of this space. There was a half-smothering quality in this new area. At last he burst through this odd place. It had seemed a shoddy, unfinished plot of creation, and when he returned to pure customary space with the stars ranked before him like pearls in a coronet, he felt pleased and refreshed.

A destination became evident. He passed a blue-white sun and three inner planets and his spirit body began to settle tentatively as a butterfly in a fourth world, which rose below him like an immense red-yellow-and-black carpet lifting itself. He skimmed along the rim of the sky and came to rest in a city. He thought the city sleeping or dead. He walked, in quite ordinary fashion now, through streets and plazas. Each object, every building, was cyclopean, and some of the structures he gauged to tower at least a mile above the ground. The geometry was uncanny; angles were acute or obtuse—there were no right angles—and many of the buildings looked to fold back in upon themselves, so that their surfaces were both inside and outside at the same time. Every prospect was vertiginous and looked granular to the sight, as if even the minute particles which composed the building materials had been turned askew to one another. The breadth of the streets and alleys did not correspond to the immense heights of the city, being narrower than they ought. Yet there was no feeling of constriction.

Most strikingly, there was about it an impression of the primeval. The city looked not only the result of sophisticated handiwork, of accumulated architectural technique; it retained evidence of the firstness of things. When he inspected closely the wall of a building, he discovered that every inch of it had been chopped out with a rude tool from some mineral he could not recognize.

Haydn walked on.

He was touched by an urgent desire to see one of the inhabitants of this world. Looking about the city, he had experienced a feeling of outlandish kinship, and he wanted to meet a member of this ingenious race.

But for a long time there was no indication that the place was inhabited.

An easy silence hung over every plane and corner. Then there began what he at first took to be a tremor of the ground, a gentle regular quivering that grew gradually in intensity as he went forward. But it was not a movement of the earth; it was a deep, dark music. As soon as he recognized it as music, it took his mind as wholly as a gentle spring rain. This was a single slow bass line, sostenuto, of unrepeating tones, resonant and elating. He could not determine its source.

The huge city was widely various in terms of space and structure. He began to think that it was centerless, but as that music continually increased in intensity—though not in volume—it occurred to him that if he came to the source of the music, he would find the midpoint of the city.

Under the brilliant blue-white sun, colors burned with a hard vividness. Indeed, these colors, primaries, along with others that Haydn could not name, looked not really to be properties of the surfaces from which they emanated. They seemed to stand slightly away, so that when he touched any wall, he pushed his finger through the color, as through a film of oil. Curious phenomenon, considering that he cast no shadow, but multiple shadows all tinted with the strong colors that flamed about him.

At last he drew into a large parklike area and saw at once the source of the deep music he had been following. All about, in shapes as irregular as cloud formations, stood huge clumps of spongy fungoid-looking vegetation of different pastel colors. Wide, sinuous paths cut through this growth to arrive at a large paved circle of gray stone or metal. In the center of the circle stood a fountain. It rose tier upon tier high into the bright air. It jetted without surcease from the top a shining onyx black substance, but so steady and continuous was the impulse of the fountain that Haydn could not distinguish whether the substance were water or oil. In fact, it looked like cold black stone as it dropped from tier to tier in strait unwavering streams. It occurred to him then that it was some fantastically complex structure of two materials: the veined leaf green stone of the fountain, the sheeny black stone in descending arabesque. And from here the music issued; it was still no louder than before, but it was more resonant and permeated darkly his whole figure. When he glanced at his shadows, he saw them throb and dance like blown candle flames in helpless obedience to the music of the fountain.

He was finally able to turn his attention from the fountain and saw beyond the paved area a scarlet ramp, glowing scarlet. It was broad and exhibited the usual irregular angles. The ramp led to another of the irregular structures, this one a double pyramid with the upper section inverted, so that it looked like a strange hourglass. The building was dull orange in color, and Haydn thought that if we were going to see one of the constructors of this alien city, it would come forth from here. At this point, the wall peeled away upward at the ramp juncture and the creature appeared. It looked like nothing so much as a huge, coarse, dense tangle of hempen rope. It came down the ramp with a monumental slowness. He could see no means by which it propelled itself, nor could he discover the center of its intelligence or any organs of perception. But though there were no visible indications, the composer was certain that the creature was feminine in gender, and there rose in him a vehement wave of tenderness and awe. His heart went out to it entirely. In his spirit body, Haydn fell on his knees to worship.

But the ground did not receive him.

He did not stop tipping forward, somersaulting, and the landscape surged up before him and washed over his sight in a confused blur. When he regained his equilibrium, he found he was traveling once again; once again he was in the interstellar spaces. The stars and planets and the broad silence welled up about him and quickly disappeared. He was traveling even faster than before, in mere moments traversing vast tracts of the universe. Of a sudden he halted. Floating before him in the void, surrounded by emptiness and a sparse starlight, was a yellowish object no larger than a loaf of bread. He drew closer to inspect it and found that it was a dragonfly, a delicate four-winged dragonfly, made painfully of gold and worked finely to the last impossible detail. There it floated, absolutely apart from everything else that existed, like a tiny planet unto itself. He stretched out his hand to touch it, but before he could do so, it fluttered its wings in a delicately mechanical fashion and, after a soft whir, uttered a series of musical notes, silvery tinkling. Ah, it was a music box traveling along out here in the void. . . . Though he could not place it, the gossamer little tune that the music box played was dearly familiar to him. Dearly familiar and nostalgic and so rendingly nostalgic that the simple sound of it returned the spirit of

Haydn to his Mother Planet, to the nation of England and the village of Slough, where his three friends awaited him in anxious trepidation.

4

"So high, so far . . . So high . . . So far . . ." These were the words Haydn heard himself saying as he regained his body and his senses. (He was told later that he had muttered these same words for twenty minutes by the clock.) Once more he was shivering violently, for a heavy chill had come over his body, harsh cold piercing to the marrow.

He had been standing immovable, but now they were able to lead him back to the chair.

"Maestro, Maestro, we must take you in at once. We will send for the physician."

He waved his hand to brush the sentence away.

"Come, you must allow us to—"

"I am perfectly in health," Haydn said. His voice was clear and strong and seemed almost to abash his ministrants. "I feel strong and whole. These seizures of mine have sprung from nothing but force of imagination. They proceed from nothing but a childish fear, and now I find I am indebted to Dr. Herschel for presenting me the means to conquer this fear." He rose and gave Herschel a swift, almost comic bow.

Involuntarily, they reached out to steady him, but they withdrew their hands when the composer made a slight frown.

"You do appear remarkably recovered," said Herschel. "But you will not put my mind at ease until you have at least taken some tea."

Haydn nodded, smiling; he was beginning to be amused by so much solicitude.

They returned to the library and Caroline caused tea to be brought. They kept watching Haydn with kindly, calculating eyes, and the composer felt assured he was among fast friends.

As they enjoyed the tea, along with the little cakes Caroline had rescued from the observatory, Haydn told them all. He told them in detail of the spatial journey of his spirit and of the strange prospects he had glimpsed. As he spoke, they looked at one another in naked alarm, and then a happy comprehension spread over their faces. The maestro was simply telling them of a vision; it was a *flight of genius,* of the sort that must come not infrequently to an artist of Haydn's magnitude. . . . At several points, Dr. Herschel seemed to wish to interrupt with questions, but he held himself in check, hearing his guest's narrative to its conclusion.

When he finished talking, a sweet lassitude overtook him, and Haydn yawned and stretched his limbs languorously.

Even before he could apologize, Herschel and his daughter had rung for a servant and begun importuning Haydn to stay the night.

He agreed. It would be tedious to try to say them nay, and indeed he was feeling very tired, deliciously so. As he was allowing himself to be led up the stairs, Dr. Burney called to him: "Now I have solved the conundrum. That Mars man I felt was looking down upon me, that, sir, was you!"

Haydn woke later than usual the next morning. Full sunlight streamed through the little window, shining on the stacked volumes of astronomical figures shoved against the farther wall. When he sat up in bed, Haydn noticed a note addressed to him lying folded on the bedside table, beside the pitcher and basin. He opened it and read:

> *Ur, gleet edd gromius Orban! Lummities org Bok-Finlay thum smummute. Moery edd Carti er franpau losh. Freasly ik frammis ter bergey, edd anoot tur twillig Bonest ell.*
>
> *Meliesly tarse,*
> *Yenrub*
>
> —My dear Haydn, during the night I received this communication, which I am convinced is writ in the Mars man's dialect. If you will breakfast with me here at the New Genesis Inn, we will attempt to puzzle it out. The inn is not far. I have arranged with the Herschels.
>
> With affectionate esteem,
> Chas. Burney.

Haydn laughed and spoke aloud: "Ah, Dr. Burney, in your company one does not have to seek far for the Mars man." Then he rose from bed.

• • •

Some commentators are not content for the account to end here. Two scholars at least have declared that this acquaintance with the cosmos made Haydn's mind receptive to the music of the young composer Beethoven, who was then twenty-one. Less than a month later, Haydn, on his homeward passage, stopped in Bonn and there heard the *Cantata on the Death of the Emperor Joseph II.* He immediately accepted Beethoven as a composition pupil.

And Sir Donald Tovey, in his *Essays in Musical Analysis,* asseverates that it was on the platform of Herschel's observatory that *The Creation* was born. Some certain physical symptoms might seem to corroborate this view, for when Haydn came to conduct the premiere performance at the Schwarzenburg Palace on April 29, 1798, he reported his condition in these words: "One moment I was cold as ice, the next I seemed to be on fire. I thought I should have a fit."

The performance was received with an enthusiasm almost incredible. The audience sat transfixed during the musical description of Chaos. When at last came the lines "Let there be light—and there was light," they rose as one for a prolonged and deafening ovation. Haydn turned to face his admirers and pointed his baton upward, toward the ceiling. "Not from me," he said, "from thence comes everything."

THE SOMEWHERE DOORS

No true light yet showed in the window, but he could feel the dawn coming on, the softness of it brushing his neck hair like a whisper, and heard the stir of trees outside the screen of his open window. He sat staring at the paper before him, the Blue Horse page he had so painstakingly covered with his light slant strokes, and held his pen poised above it, ready to write the final line of his story.

Here was his keenest pleasure, writing down at last the sentence he had aimed at from the beginning. It was like drawing the lines under a column of numbers and setting in the sum, a feeling not only of winding up but of full completion. He waited, savoring the moment, then inscribed the words: "Lixor looked at the lights in the sky and wondered if one of them would begin to move toward him." And then, to prolong his satisfaction, he printed THE END below in tall, graceful letters embellished with curls of flourish. Reverting to his careful script, he put down his name: "*Arthur Strakl, Cherry Cove, North Carolina, September 12, 1936.*"

When he looked at his handiwork, his name seemed strange to him, out of place on this page full of exotic sights and notions, as homely alien as a worn tin thimble in a jeweler's fancy display case. So he set about inking the postscript out, producing a shiny black rectangle where each word had stood. The page looked better, he thought, without this reminder of our world of familiar impressions and of a dispiriting time in a place that was all too local. Anyhow, he would see his name enough times when "The Marooned Aldebaran" was published.

If it was published.

His luck was not good. Only about three of ten of the stories he wrote ever saw print, and then in so mutilated a fashion, so mangled by editorial obtuseness, that he felt a sad weariness when they did appear.

He went to his one bookcase and took up a copy of a recent *Astounding Stories* from an unread stack of similar pulp magazines. It was the August issue, and commenced with *The Incredible Invasion,* a serial novel by Murray Leinster. Names familiar to habitués of this kind of literature were displayed: Weinbaum, Fearn, Schachner, Gallun, and Williamson. The cover illustration showed grim hominoids in gleaming gray armor battling among themselves and menacing a brace of plucky young ladies in dapper short skirts. He supposed the armored men to be the Incredible Invaders. Arthur did not read invasion stories; he could not imagine that Earth, unfashionable and located far from its galactic center, would be a desirable prize.

We are, he reflected, a bunch of hicks. Why would anyone bother?

Opening the magazine, he flipped past the ads for self-education and self-medication, but his attention was drawn to the announcement for a new character pulp, *The Whisperer.* "The Whisperer!—NOT a Chinaman!—NOT a modern Robin Hood—NOT a myth or a ghost!—But—HE IS———a good two-fisted, hard-hitting AMERICAN cop who gets his man!"

Arthur sighed, thinking how he could never write a story about the Whisperer, how, in fact, he probably could never bring himself to read one. He had tried to write some of those stories about two-fisted cops, two-fisted cowboys, two-fisted orphans of the jungle, male and female, but that talent was not in him—nor for flying aces, nor scientific detectives, nor steel-armed quarterbacks or boxers. Again it was a question of belief. He did not believe that human beings came from so predictable a toy box and he could not engage himself in heroic fantasies. To him, those daydreams lacked imagination and verged upon braggatry. But he did not wish to condemn. Hard times now, and writers needed to stock groceries, and readers wished to enjoy the brief glimpses of triumph the pulp stories afforded.

But his own stories were not fashioned in that mode. He could write only these melancholy twilight visions of things distant in time and space, stories that seemed not entirely his, but gifts or visitations from a source at which he could not guess. His most difficult task was to find words for them; he was a shy man, naturally taciturn, and he considered himself unhandy with language. But when the stories came to him, the impulse to write them down was too strong to resist. The stories compelled him to write, to struggle with phrases in a way that felt incongruous to his personality. And so he wrote, stealing the hours from his bed, the strength from his body. Each stroke of the pen, every noun and comma and period, brought him closer to the beautiful release that he always felt, as he did now, upon completion of a tale.

That was the main thing, to finish, to tell the stories through to the end. He got little money for them and what he received was always late in arriving, and little acclaim came his way, for the readers who wrote to the letter columns preferred the loud, brawny stories of superscience, with their whirling rays and burning cities, colliding suns and flaming rocket ships, to his delicate accounts of loneliness under the stars, his elegies for dying worlds and soulful perishing species. Of course, his stories as they appeared were mutilated, so that readers could not form fair opinions about them, but Arthur suspected that even if they were published just as they came in their final drafts from his typewriter, with every nuance and adverb complete, readers would still prefer the yarns about genius engineers and iron-thewed swordsmen.

He replaced the magazine on top of the stack and paced the narrow strip of floor between his desk and the foot of his lumpy bed. He was too elated to sleep, and anyway, the night was nearly gone. A dim gray showed in the window. He would go to his job at the Red Man Café red-eyed and nervous and in the afternoon a dull lassitude would creep over him and he would drink cup after cup of acid coffee until closing time. He was "chief cook and bottle washer," as the owner, Farley Redmon, called him, and his hours were long and ill paid. But he earned his food and his rent for this little outbuilding that was formerly a toolshed—and he had a job, and in this year of our Lord 1936, he was grateful for it.

He would be grateful to light down anywhere he could find in order to write these stories that gave him no peace.

Arthur decided to walk out. The excitement of composition was still warm in him and the hour was inviting, cool and quiet. He pulled on his thinning blue wool sweater and peered out his window and, seeing no lights in any of the settlement windows, departed his room, taking care to turn off the little desk lamp with its green cardboard shade.

Cherry Cove was quiet, almost silent: no dogs barking, no radios in kitchens reporting farm prices, no clatter of breakfast cutlery. Everyone snug and warm and dreaming, and as he walked along the broad gravel road that led east, Arthur wondered whether any of their dreams might be as strange as the one he had just set down, in which the last survivor of a race of orchidaceous philosophers journeyed to the moon of its planet in order to send a signal to the cosmos, a message telling them that though the Kornori had died all but for Lixor, he had one valuable secret to share with every other species everywhere.

Arthur smiled, assuring himself that the dreams of his neighbors would be stranger and more exciting and more urgent than his little tale. Then he set out at an easy walking pace for the Little Tennessee River two miles distant, the river that ran counter to all the others.

He was headed toward the peeling iron bridge. He had no particular purpose in mind, drawn only by that obscure impulse that leads us to the sound of running water as a source of comfort and refreshment. When he stood there at the railing, listening to the water twenty feet below rush away over the rocks—going the wrong way, for the Little Tennessee is a backward river—his anxieties fell quiet and the utter lack of hope that characterized his days took on the aspect of courage rather than of fear. Arthur Strakl often felt that he stood on the abrupt edge of an ebony abyss, and that if he fell, he would fall without crying out, without making a sound, and that no one on earth would remark his passing or remember that he had sojourned here. These considerations sometimes made him gloomy; at other times they strengthened his resolve, and did so now, with the completion of "The Marooned Aldebaran" fresh in his mind. He listened to the water and smelled its clean smell and watched where the river drew away into the forest of oaks and firs. On his right-hand side, just at the bridgehead, was a stand of slender trees with flowers beneath, and he glanced at it without really seeing it.

Then he became aware that he was not alone on the bridge. A woman stood beside him. He had not heard her approach, but he was not startled; her aspect was calm and easy. He was surprised to see that she was dressed in a white silk party frock with a wide square collar. She wore white pumps of patent leather and her dark hair was tied back with a broad ribbon of shiny white silk.

She was a beautiful woman, and when she spoke, it was with a quiet musical accent that was stranger than any other he had ever heard. "Are you Arthur Strakl?" she asked.

"Yes, ma'am," he said, though she was not his elder. She looked rather younger than Arthur's thirty-five years.

"I'm glad," she said, and said no more for such a long time that he began to think that the conversation had ended. Then she added, "To meet you. I'm glad to meet you."

"I'm glad to meet you, too. You don't live in Cherry Cove, do you?"

"No," she said. "I've come a long way to find you."

"Me?" He laughed. "Well, that's a little hard to believe."

"Why is it hard to believe?"

Arthur noted that she spoke slowly and hesitantly, as if these words were foreign to her. "There's no good reason for anyone to look for me. I don't have a family or any close friends. No one knows who I am."

"Are you not Arthur Strakl, the author?"

"I write a few odd stories. I never thought of calling myself an author."

"But didn't you write 'In the Titanic Deeps,' the story about sea dwellers in another galaxy?"

"Yes. My title was 'Blind Oceans,' but they changed it. That one was about the great worms that lived on the bottom of an ocean. They were suffering because they had the power to foresee centuries into the future and saw that nothing would change, that their destiny was fixed. Then one of their mathematicians devised a theory that admitted the possibility of the end of time, and this idea brought solace to them."

"And then what happened?"

"Nothing," he said. "That was it. . . . Well, their music changed."

She turned upon him a superbly friendly smile. "Yes," she said. "Their music changed."

"I'm amazed," he said. "You can't imagine. This is the first time I ever met somebody who has read one of my stories."

"Oh, I've read many of your stories. I remember them all."

"Well, I haven't actually published all that many."

"I remember your story about the beings you called 'kindlers.' They were incandescent blue nervous systems that lived on the surface of a faraway sun. I remember the planet you called Zephlar, where the wind streaming over a continent of telepathic grasses produced an unending silent musical fugue. I remember your city Alphega, which was an enormous machine that was writing a book; each word of the book was a living human citizen. I remember your story about the language you called 'Spranza,' which communicated so efficiently that listeners experienced directly the objects and actions it spoke of. And the sentient river Luvulio that had become a religious zealot, and the single amber eye named Ull, which lay in a primordial sea waiting for the remainder of its organism to evolve, and the parasite that reproduced itself by causing allergies in its hosts. At the magnetic pole of a tropical planet grew a tree whose leaves were mirrors; there was a world where humanlike people communicated by differences in skin temperature. There was a plague virus that heightened the sense of taste to a painful degree."

"Good Lord," Arthur said.

"So you see," she said sweetly, "I have read your stories. They have afforded me"—she paused, as if waiting for the correct phrase to present itself—"a fine pleasure. Many fine pleasures."

"Thank you for saying so," Arthur said. "But I didn't write all those stories. Somebody else must have written about the religious river and the alphabet city. And none of the magazines would take my story about the telepathic grasses. I don't see how you could have heard about that one."

"You have more admirers than you're aware of," she said. She smiled and turned away to watch the early light smear tree shadows on the river surface. "Sometimes the editors talk about your stories even when they don't buy them. Sometimes they want to buy them and are afraid to. But word gets around."

"Well, you obviously know a great deal about this," he said. "What do you do for a living? I mean, are you a literary agent?"

"I'm a representative for a group of people who are interested in new ideas," she said. "They have great faith in the power of ideas to make the future better for everyone."

"Who are they?"

She turned to meet his gaze directly. Her brown eyes were serious. "They prefer to remain anonymous."

"Are they Communists, then?" he asked. "I met a Communist once who talked like that, sort of."

She laughed lightly. "I don't think they belong to any recognizable political group. . . . To tell the truth, I don't know all that much about them. They just pay me to deliver messages to people they think are important to their way of looking at things."

"And I'm important to them?"

"Oh yes," she said, and there was no mistaking the sincerity of her reply. "Extremely important. They're very pleased to discover you. That's why they sent me to trace you down."

"How did you find out where I live?"

"It wasn't that hard. You're a publishing author, after all." She laughed again, and the light sound reminded Arthur of a child's laughter.

He found himself smiling. "Only a few people know about that."

"But it's not how many," she said. "It's who they are."

"And these are important people?"

"I don't know anything about them," she said, "but they seem to have decided that they're important."

"So now you know who I am, but I don't know who you are."

"I'm not supposed to tell my real name. I was supposed to choose any name that I took a fancy to. Do I look like a Francesca?"

"I don't know," he said. "I've never seen any Francescas."

"So this must be exciting for you." She offered her hand. "It's nice to meet you, Arthur."

He held it for a moment. "I'm pleased to meet you, too. May I ask about the way you're dressed? Or is that against the rules?"

"Oh this," she said. "Of course. I came from a dinner party that went on till too late, so then I came straight here."

"Straight here to this bridge?"

"Yes."

Confused, he could not formulate the question he wanted to ask. "How did you get here?"

"My driver dropped me off," she said, and hurried on to add, "and the car will be returning for me very soon. So I'd better go ahead and deliver my message."

"From these unknown people?"

"Yes." She laughed again, and now there was something teasing in the sound—teasing but not mocking. "Yes, my message that I don't understand from a group of people I don't know . . . This doesn't really make sense, does it?"

"No," he said. "But I don't much care. A lot of things don't make sense to me."

"I'll bet you like it better that way."

"I do." His tone changed. "I sure do wish you lived around here. Are you married?"

She reached gently to touch his face with two fingers. "You're sweet. Truly. It's very sweet of you to say that. But I live far away and our time is short. I'd better tell you what I came to say."

"All right." He grinned. "Fire when ready."

She closed her eyes for a moment, then opened them. "Two doors will be brought to you. Don't be afraid. These doors open to other worlds, worlds different from our own. Behind the blue door is a world that has no people in it. The violet door is the entrance to a world of great cities. You can live in either world very pleasantly, but once you choose either door, you can never return. You will be gone from this planet forever."

"Wait. I don't understand."

"It's no good asking me," she said. "I don't understand, either. I can only tell you what I was told."

"Did they send a letter?" he asked. "I'd like to read it."

"It was a telephone message and the voice sounded like it came from a long way off. I couldn't even tell if it was a man or a woman speaking."

"Is that all, then? Two doors?"

She closed her eyes again, appearing to recollect, then went on: "The two doors will be brought to you at some future date. It may be soon, or it may be quite some time from now. And things may happen so that you think the doors never will arrive. But they will."

"Where will I find them?"

"I don't know," she said.

"All right. What else?"

"Nothing else."

"That's all?"

"As far as I can think, that's the end of the message. I hope I haven't forgotten anything. . . . Oh, don't look so alarmed. I'm sure I haven't."

"I honestly don't know what to make of all this."

"Neither do I," she replied, smiling her fine smile once more. "I'm just glad I don't have to make sense of it.— Wait. Now I remember. There was one other thing. You must keep on writing your wonderful stories. That is the most important thing. You must keep on imagining the kinds of things that only you can imagine."

"All right. I wish I could sell more of them, though. I could use the money."

"I'm sorry. The person I talked to didn't say anything about that. But I'm sure you'll do well.— Oh, here comes my ride." She raised her right arm and waved.

He turned, to see that the car was at the end of the bridge, by the stand of birches there, rolling very slowly toward them, almost silent on the gravel. That was strange, and the car was strange, too, with its darkened windows and its smooth, almost featureless sedan shape and its deep oxblood color. There was something dreamlike about its appearance as it approached so slowly.

When it drew abreast of them, it stopped and the passenger door opened—seemingly of its own accord—and the girl got in, showing neat ankles and pulling her skirt over her knees. He leaned down, trying to see the driver, but the car was in shadow on that side.

"Good-bye, Arthur," she said. Her tone was grave now and she didn't smile.

"I suppose I won't ever see you again."

"No," she said. "Never."

"I hate it," he said. "I wish—"

"No. Say good-bye."

"All right . . . Good-bye." He sighed.

And she closed the door and the strange smooth car pulled away, the sound of its motor no more than a warm hum and soon lost in the normal sounds of an autumn morning by the water, the birdcalls and squirrels frolicking and the wash and gurgle of the river. He watched the car till it floated out of sight around the tall bank of the road all yellow and red with locust and sassafras bushes.

Two years passed and Arthur Strakl waited patiently. He had a serene confidence that the two doors, the doors that opened upon different Somewheres, would be brought to him. He did not know why he was so secure in his faith; he was not introspective in that particular way. The fancies that his mind produced entranced him, but the workings of his mind held no interest for him.

Not much changed. His employer, Farley Redmon, had undertaken to make his hut a little more comfortable, paying to have it plumbed and rewired. But he explained that he could not increase Arthur's wage, and Arthur accepted the statement, his needs few. His heaviest expenses outside basic necessities were pulp magazines and typewriter ribbons and now and again some small fees for the repair of the ancient Underwood. He was healthy and lucky.

For he kept on writing his stories, just as he had promised, and he was beginning to have a brighter success with them. He was still no great favorite with readers, but their letters spoke now and again of his work with intrigued bemusement rather than with irritated incomprehension. He appeared more regularly in the magazines and now and then his name would be featured on the covers, tucked away in the corner of the pictured insane laboratory where the flimsily clothed girl stared in horror at some loathsome transformation.

His better satisfaction, though, was that editors began to do less violence to his sentences. His style of writing was still hobbledehoy, he thought, but it was better left alone than improved. At least something of the intensity of his visions flamed through, even if sensual nuance was lost. The essential strangeness of the tales did not diminish. He wrote, for instance, a story based on the idea that the positions of the stars in our galaxy had been designed by the immensely powerful science of an ancient superrace as a kind of wallpaper. In another story, the ghost of a dismantled robot visited its inventor and sat each night silent and reproachful at the foot of his bed. In "Black Receiver," an intelligent butterfly composed of a carbon gas picked up through its antennae the radio communications of a space fleet and thus formed a very surprising view of humankind.

So he was fairly content and hoped for better things to come, even though it was clear that the times were verging on catastrophe. Arthur was no great reader of newspapers, but no one could escape hearing about the events in Europe, and all the world was darkened by suspicion.

Arthur's own apprehension was deepened when he was visited by a man who claimed to be a government agent and asked whether he knew Sheila Weddell. "I don't think so," he said. "The name doesn't ring a bell."

The agent gave him a long stare. Then he said, "All right, sport. I'll have coffee."

When Arthur set the thick mug before him, the squat little man added cream and three spoons of sugar before saying, "You sure?"

"Sure of what?"

"About the woman. Sheila Weddell."

"I don't know her." He knew, however, that he didn't like this dumpy little man with his false smile that let the sneer show through and his slicked-back silver-blond hair. He had a firm impression of the fellow as one who took deep satisfaction in feeling contempt. His bored eyes and twisted mouth betrayed a jaded spirit.

"I got a picture." He reached into his inside jacket pocket and produced a crinkled photograph.

The picture, as Arthur had expected, was of the woman who called herself Francesca, and he had already decided to keep this agent—if that's what he was—at arm's length. "Pretty," he said, and handed it back.

The man laid it carefully on the Bakelite counter, then turned it around to face Arthur. "You've seen her before, haven't you? About two years ago?"

"Two years is a long time."

"It's longer inside the jailhouse than it is outside. Even in a fleabite place like this." He giggled. "What do you call it here? Cherry Cola?"

"Cherry Cove," Arthur said. "You're in Cherry Cove, North Carolina."

"And I want to know if you ain't seen this woman, Sheila Weddell, in Cherry Cove, North Carolina, about two years ago."

"You say you're some kind of an agent? I'd like to see your identification."

He drew a toothpick from an upper vest pocket and stuck it in the front of his mouth, so that it bobbed up and down as he spoke. "You know, sport, I don't think you'd be asking for identification unless you were trying to hide something. I got me an idea you're hiding something."

"And I have an idea you're no government agent of any kind," Arthur said. "I have an idea you're a lawyer or a Pinkerton who is meddling in a lady's private affairs."

"I see. You kinda like her, do you? Well, let me tell you, you don't know what's going on. You don't know the least little thing. If you did, you wouldn't be calling Sheila Weddell no lady. I guess she must have been real nice to you, am I right?"

"You'd better leave now," Arthur said. "Your coffee is cold and we are just now fresh out."

"Sure, I understand," the oily blond man said. "She let you have a piece and you think you're Sir Galahad or somebody. But, brother, if you knew what I know . . ."

"Since you're a government agent, you'll be glad to talk to Robbie Calkins. He is our sheriff here in Jackson County. Would you like to wait here for him? I'll give him a call right now."

"That's all right. I believe I've already found out what I needed to know. It's pretty clear she passed through here two years back." He laid a nickel on the counter and pushed it toward Arthur with one finger. "Here's what I owe."

Arthur pushed it back. "Keep it," he said. "I don't believe the coffee agreed with you."

The man smiled his twisted smile but did indeed rescue his nickel and made his surprisingly quick way to the door with an odd waddling stride. Arthur expected him to stop in the doorway to turn and make a final curdled remark, but he only pushed the screen open and stepped out into the late-September sunlight that streamed saffron through the leaves of the big poplar there.

Arthur sighed tiredly and looked up and down the long room with its empty tables covered with red oilcloth and the big iron coal stove in the center of the aisle and the long counter with the five stools before it. When he emptied the remains of the coffee into the zinc sink behind him, he saw that his hands were shaking. He washed them and dried them on his apron and headed toward the storeroom in back to sit down and collect himself for a moment.

But Farley Redmon opened the kitchen door and called him back. “Arthur,” he said, “could I talk to you just a minute?”

“Sure thing.” He retraced his steps, and when the older man held the door for him, he entered the kitchen.

“Sit down,” Redmon said, indicating a tall wooden stool by the chop block. When Arthur sat, Redmon leaned back against the wall counter and folded his arms. “What was that all about with that little stout feller that come in?”

“I don’t know,” Arthur said. “He was asking questions about a woman I met one time.”

“You got woman trouble, Arthur? Hard to believe.”

“I’ve got an outstanding lack of woman trouble,” he said. “It’s hard for me to add up how much woman trouble I don’t have.”

“Ain’t that kind of burdensome?”

“I just hope it’s not fatal.”

“Generally it ain’t,” Redmon said. “Not till some ornery husband stirs things up with a shotgun. You want to be careful now.”

“I am careful,” Arthur said. “I’m a careful man.”

“Yes, you are. That’s the truth.” Redmon produced a new package of Luckies from his shirt pocket, zipped it open, and tapped one out. He lit it with a kitchen match from a box on the counter. “I’ve been thinking about you,” he said, “and how careful you are. I don’t know what it was all about with that stout feller, but I thought you handled it okay.”

“I don’t usually drive away the customers.”

“You did fine. You would’ve had your reasons.” He looked into the cloud of smoke he exhaled toward the ceiling. “There’s something I’ve been meaning to talk to you about. You know how it’s been here at the café. Business is steady, what with the sawmill and the railroaders, but there ain’t much profit. I’ve been trying to figure out how to do better by you, but I don’t see no way I can come up with much more in terms of wages.”

“That’s all right,” Arthur said. “I know how it is.”

"Yeah. But you've been doing a good job. I don't know when I've seen a steadier man. I never could figure out why you stuck."

"The arrangement suits me fine. I get time to write my stories."

"Your stories, yeah." Redmon tapped his ash into a soiled plate and smiled. "You know, I read one of your stories one time. I went down to the news store and bought one of them magazines and read it. Just to see. Beginning to end, I couldn't make head nor tail of it. It was about some animals on another world—that was all I understood. Do you believe there are other worlds with animals on them?"

"I don't know."

"The Bible don't say nothing about it. So it must be something you just make up in your mind, is that right?"

"Yes."

"You ever thought about writing a cowboy story, or something that people like more to read?"

"I'm not cut out for it," Arthur said. "I write the only kind of stories I'm able."

Redmon nodded. "Okay. The reason I ask, I always figured you were staying here till you made some big money with your writing and then you'd move on. If you did, I wouldn't know what to do. My boy Cletus ain't interested in this café and he ain't settled enough in mind to run it. I figure Cletus is just about ready to join the armed service, only he don't know it yet."

"Cletus is a good boy. He'll straighten out."

"I thought maybe if he got married, but then I got to studying on these women he's been running with. Ain't none of them would be any help. The trouble was losing his mother when he was little. I didn't have the furthest notion how to raise a youngun. So I reckon it's going to have to be Uncle Sam finishes the job."

"You're probably worrying about it too much."

"Well, I've worried myself gray-headed. Unless it's just natural age." He crushed his butt out on the littered plate. "Which was the other thing I was going to bring up. I don't want this business to go down the rat hole. Someday, Cletus might grow into it. Right now he don't want it, but later on he might. I want you to stay with me and help keep it going. Since I can't pay you better wage money, I thought I'd offer you an interest in the place. That don't mean much now, but when times lighten up, it will. I can just about guarantee that."

"What do you have in mind?"

"Two percent to start with and then another percent every year till we get to ten. One of these days you'll find it was a good deal."

"But in order to get ten percent, I'd have to stay on another eight years."

"Yep."

"I'll have to think about it."

"That's all I want." Redmon offered Arthur his hand. "I just want your word you'll give me fair consideration."

"Sure I will. The offer means a lot to me." Arthur took Redmon's hard, dry hand and shook it twice gently. His own hand was soft and pulpy from washing dishes and he was beginning to grow flabby about the waist.

In fact, his health was none so sound as he had assumed. He learned from his army physical examination in 1942 that his teeth were in need of immediate repair and that one of the doctors thought he detected a heart murmur but wasn't sure. At any rate, Arthur Strakl was turned down for military service and rode in the bus back to Asheville with a group of other rejects, who were rowdy and gloomy by turns. Then he took a westbound milk-stop bus to Cherry Cove, trudged through the lonesome hamlet dark at ten in the evening, went into his little hut, and fell asleep without undressing, only dropping his scuffed brown shoes by the bed.

When he woke next morning, he was still tired and all his skin felt grimy. He took off his shirt and pants and stumbled blindly to the tiny sink and ran water into a porcelain basin and bathed as quickly and thoroughly as he could. Then he placed a blue spatterware pot on his hot plate and set about making coffee.

It was only when he sat at his writing desk, sipping at the strong unsugared coffee, that he noticed how the big armoire standing against the opposite wall had changed. It was an ancient piece of work, this dim armoire, heavy oak boards stained dark. Inside were Arthur's other three white shirts and two pairs of pants and various socks and handkerchiefs—the respectable wardrobe of a penurious orphan bachelor. He always kept it neat and orderly, the way he kept all his few possessions, the way he kept his life. His life, like his little hut, was always prepared for visitation.

But now the visitation had occurred while he was absent. The doors of the armoire, which had been stained almost chocolate, were now blue on the right side and violet on the left. His Somewhere Doors had arrived. Arthur was so profoundly gratified that tears trickled down his cheeks, and the back of his neck flushed red and warm.

They were not prepossessing. They were the same size and shape as the armoire doors had been; only the color had changed. The surfaces were matte and cool to the touch when he placed his hand flat against them. But the texture of the surfaces was strange; the material didn't feel like wood or metal or plastic. More like glass with a subtle grain. He placed his ear directly against the blue door and waited a long time but could hear nothing. Still the old chest seemed to breathe silently and steadily, like a great distant creature asleep.

He began to take stock. The room seemed otherwise unchanged, except that his clothing and other belongings had been removed from the armoire and carefully folded and laid out on his one other chair and on his bookcase. But there was a sheet of paper in the typewriter with a phrase cleanly typed in capitals:

THANK YOU FOR YOUR VALUABLE EFFORTS

It was unsigned.

"My valuable efforts," Arthur said. He rubbed his eyes, brushing away the wetness. "I wish I could see what was so valuable."

He knew already that the presence of the Somewhere Doors would make an enormous difference, but he could not foresee what different shapes his life might take.

Now, though, he would have to choose. Before the doors arrived, he had thought only vaguely about their contrasting possibilities; today the choice had become unavoidable. Would he like to inhabit the golden utopian world that philosophers and visionaries over the centuries had guessed at? To immerse himself in the grandest productions of religious thought, scientific ingenuity, governmental peace, and aesthetic achievement of which human beings were capable? Or would he not rather live on the Garden Planet, the world brimful of pristine creation, the way our own had been before Adam appeared? There, as nowhere else, he would be living in the very throb of the heart of existence, in the closest proximity to truth that his organism could endure.

He had been assured that neither world was noxious or dangerous, and he relied upon Francesca's word.

He knew, though, that the choice would haunt him, sleeping and waking, until it was actually made, and he knew, too, that he would have to watch himself closely so that the balance of his daily existence was not disturbed. He would need to go on about his ordinary business as calmly and orderly as possible; only in this fashion could he make a wisely considered preference.

At this moment it came to him that there was a third choice. A third door, in effect: his own. He could choose to stay on the earth he knew and to go on with his life in Cherry Cove. Where before this obscure cranny of the universe had been a necessity, the haphazard lighting-down place of a kinless and disconnected man, now it assumed the dignity of election. He could choose to live here; he could choose to leave. He turned to look at the flimsy pine door of his little shack, warped and showing morning light at the jamb, and it seemed as strange to him and almost as inviting as the blue door and the violet.

When Cletus died at Anzio, the spirit of his father flickered violently and burned low. He was a man who rarely drank liquor, but during the months of February, March, and April of 1944, he was drunk almost every day. Arthur didn't mind that; he knew the frenzy would wear off. But he worried about what would happen when Redmon came to himself again. He couldn't think how the man might change.

After he stopped, it took another three weeks for him to dry out. He was sick the whole time, weak and shaking. Arthur ministered to him and gradually he began to eat normal meals and to drive his old Chevrolet pickup about and to tramp in the woods. One day he came into the café with a tinted photograph of Cletus under his arm, the one he'd gotten made with the boy in his uniform and overseas cap. When he climbed on a ladder to drive a nail and hang the picture on the wall behind the counter, Arthur knew that the old man had recovered and was going to make it.

For an old man was what he had become. His gray hair had whitened and his shirt hung loosely over his sunken chest; he had lost weight these last three weeks. His eyes were watery behind his wire-rimmed bifocals and now and then Arthur detected a nervous tic new to him: Redmon's head would jerk suddenly to the left in response to some of the remarks he heard people make. But Arthur was unable to discern what kind of comment caused the reaction.

He took Arthur aside one evening in June when they had finished cleaning up after the supper trade. He spoke as plainly to his friend as he always did, telling him that he regretted his lapse from duty during the winter months. "I hated to let it go like that," he said. "But I knew it was either drink or die. And I figured you would either stand by me or you'd haul on down the line. My mind has got better now. It ain't never going to be well again, but it has got better. I probably wouldn't be here if you hadn't helped me out. So I'm having papers drawn up for you to take possession of one-third of the Red Man Café business. We have started to make a little money here now, and if we can keep going for a while longer, there will be real money in it. Not millions, you know that. But comfortable—you can live comfortable."

"You must have known I'd stick with you in the hard time. Didn't you know that?"

Redmon nodded. "I figured you would, but I didn't know how bad it was going to be. To tell the truth, I still don't know. I don't remember it real clear. But I expect I was pretty far gone."

"I was worried," Arthur said. "You came close to hurting yourself a couple of times."

"So I figured the best way to pay you back was to have these papers drawn up. And there's something else in the contract, too. It says that when I die, sole ownership of the business will come to you."

"Wait a minute," Arthur said. "Don't you have some relatives somewhere to take exception to that?"

"I got a sister I don't know where in California. I don't even know what her last name is these days. She'd have five or six of them by now, I reckon.

I got three cousins and an aunt who will do fine on their own. You're about the closest thing to real family I got left."

"I'm afraid I make a mighty scrawny family."

"Times is hard," Redmon said, and he actually smiled a small sad smile. "What do you say to my offer?"

"It's just like you for being generous, and a man would be a pure fool not to take you up on it. But this time again I'm going to ask you to let me think about it for a while."

"Sure. I'd expect you to."

"I'll tell you right now that I've got an opportunity that few people get. Nobody that I ever heard of, in fact. And it's more than likely that one of these first days I'll be gone from here. I don't know when. It depends on some decisions I need to make."

"You let me know about any offers you get. I'll do my best to match them."

"This is the kind of opportunity that can't be matched. And I won't be able to let you know beforehand. Once I'm ready to go, I'll just leave. You won't know where and you won't be able to find out. Don't worry, I'll be all right. I'll be exactly where I want to be. But you won't be able to get in touch."

Redmon's face darkened and his shoulders slumped. "Are you going to be leaving real soon? You could tell me that much at least."

"I don't know. I'd tell you if I could."

"Listen," Redmon said. "Why don't we dress up that ratty little shack you live in? Or why don't you move out of it for good? If you get set up nice and comfortable, you might change your mind about leaving."

"No." He spoke as calmly and firmly as he knew how. "I'm doing all right where I am. I've got everything fixed just the way I want."

Eighteen months later made it seven years since he had laid eyes on the man he had named in his mind Ugly Dick, but as soon as he pushed into the empty café at three in the afternoon, Arthur recognized him. Time had left the dumpy little man almost untouched. His silver-blond hair had thinned so that his mottled scalp showed through, and contempt had made the lines of his lips and eyebrows more deeply crooked. When he spoke, he showed teeth small and brown and yellow.

"Hello, sport," he said. "You remember me?"

"Yes," said Arthur, and reached behind him for a soiled rag and wiped the clean counter in front of the man. "Last time you were in here, our coffee didn't suit you. I don't know that it's changed much."

"I believe I'll try a cup anyhow. It couldn't've got no worse."

"Price went up," Arthur said. "Prices are up everywhere."

"Even in Cherry Cola, North Carolina, huh?"

"Even in Cherry Cove."

He poured in cream and added three precise spoons of sugar and stirred. Then he lifted his head to peer at Arthur and give him that wildly crooked smirk. "I bet you remember our mutual friend, too, don't you?"

"You say you've got a friend?"

"Oh sure, you remember. Sheila Weddell. You wouldn't be forgetting her." He gave Arthur a soiled, heavy wink.

"I recall you asking about a woman. But I figured you must do a lot of that, considering."

"Considering what?"

"Considering what a low-down son of a bitch you are."

The man's smile only grew more saturnine. "Still playing Sir Galahad, ain't you? But I got to tell you, sport, there ain't no use in it anymore. You might be interested to see this newspaper story." He took a white envelope from his shirt pocket and laid it on the counter. When Arthur stood unmoving, content to give the man a long stare, he tapped it with a pudgy finger. "Go ahead and read it. I guarantee you'll find it interesting."

He picked it up. The headline read WOMAN IN SPY SCANDAL COMMITS SUICIDE. The story was short and vague. A group of New York people was suspected of gathering information for "a foreign power." Arthur supposed that the foreign power would be Russia, but the story was hazy in all its details. Sheila Weddell, thirty-four, had been found with her head in the gas oven of her apartment on Amsterdam Avenue. There was no evidence of foul play. The police investigation was continuing.

The clipping did not reveal which newspaper had printed the story. A photograph of the woman was placed above the headline, and Arthur studied it intently. It was overexposed and the features were blurred. At first it looked a little like the woman he knew as Francesca, and then it didn't. Then it did again.

"So what do you think of your sweetheart now, huh?"

"I never saw this woman in my life," Arthur said. He took care in replacing the clipping in the envelope, then laid it on the counter. "I hate to be such a big disappointment to you."

The man produced a toothpick and put it between his front teeth. "We know she passed some information on to you. Something technical. We know you got brains. You don't fool us, hiding away in this little possum-turd settlement. We read them stories you write, and I'll go ahead and tell you, sport—we're right on the edge of busting your code. We've just about got it figured out."

"My code?"

"Yeah. The hidden messages in that crazy horseshit you write in them weird magazines. You don't think your buddies overseas are the only ones that can read, do you?"

"I don't know what you're talking about."

"Yeah. I was just real positive you wouldn't know what I was talking about."

"I'm going to ask you again, just like last time, to show me some identification," Arthur said. "If you're a government agent, I want to see what kind."

"What for? I ain't asking you for nothing. I'm telling you about your girlfriend. That's all I came in for. I'll leave this newspaper story with you, to maybe give you something to think about." He stood up. "And a dime for the coffee, right?"

"Keep your damn dime. We don't want your money."

"Well now, that's mighty neighborly of you. So long, sport. Next time we meet, it ain't going to be as pleasant as it has been."

"I'll bear that in mind," Arthur said. He watched the one enemy he ever knew he possessed waddle toward the door, his toothpick waggling up and down under his nose like a mechanical gadget. When he was gone, Arthur took fifteen cents from his pocket and rang the money into the cash register. He had just remembered he still owed the café a nickel for the coffee Ugly Dick had ordered seven years before.

• • •

The next dawn found Arthur before his typewriter, struggling with a tale that was not progressing satisfactorily. He could not say why this particular story about visible creatures who inhabited an invisible planet was so difficult, but he had pottered with it two months now, and it still didn't show signs of life. He sighed and stood up, arched his back and stretched his arms above his head. This mid-September morning, though still only pinkly lit by a pink sun, was full of life, cicadas and crickets sounding away and four roosters near and far voicing their victory over the nighttime.

He took up the envelope again for the dozenth time this morning, opened it, and took out the clipping. Peering at it closely under the lamplight, he still couldn't tell. Was the woman in the photograph his Francesca? He would never be certain about the picture, he knew, and had decided simply to trust his instinct. He felt that the news story was about someone he didn't know.

The truth was, he didn't know anything. He didn't know who Francesca was, or Ugly Dick, either. He would never understand what tangle of circumstance had bequeathed him the Somewhere Doors. He looked at them now, their colors still vivid, their surfaces still warm and lightly pulsing with promise. One thing was certain: Ugly Dick with maybe some ugly help would have gotten into his hut and would have tried to open the doors and they had failed. Neither door would open even for Arthur until he made his fateful decision. Nor could they be damaged in any way.

He was forty-four years old now; he had grown middle-aged in this pleasure of indecision. They had hired a teenager to help wait tables and wash up at the café, so his workload had lightened, and his financial situation was secure, compared to the bone-scraping poverty he always had endured. His little hut was still brutally cold in winter, but the Somewhere Doors were here and their nearness supported him, comforted him, and never failed to entice with the dilemma they presented.

He slipped the clipping back into the envelope and laid it by his typewriter. Then he tugged on a light denim jacket and went out walking, stalking the dusty gravel road to the bridge and the river. The light was brightening now and a breeze came by as fresh as a cool hand across his forehead.

At the bridge, he looked above the twisted waters into the swaying tops of the balsam trees and remembered meeting Francesca here in her white party frock and her white shoes. Maybe one of these days the smooth ox-blood car would come darkly humming along again; maybe Francesca would step out. He turned to look, but the road was empty in both directions. Once more he sighed and began to retrace his steps to the hamlet.

On the bank by the bridgehead was a stand of six young silver-birch trees and beneath them a clump of knee-high bright scarlet bee balm. He stopped for a moment to admire.

And then this scene—the little young trees with ragged bark fluttering, the brilliant red flowers nodding as the river purled—overwhelmed him. Almost every day he saw these things and did not see them, walking along absorbed. Anytime he liked he could remember this sight, and yet he would always mostly forget. He burst into tears and went down on the gritty gravel in the road on his hands and knees, realizing that he had made his decision.

The sadness of utopia was the same sadness as that of paradise. Utopia and paradise could not remember. They were eternal and unaging and had no history to come to nor any to leave behind. They were dreams that Arthur for a long time had been experiencing with all his senses except those of his body. He had already opened both doors and visited both Somewheres. He was ready to fling open the third door, the entrance to the world in which he already lived. Much had passed him by. Oh yes. Yet much awaited him still.

But right now and for five minutes longer, he had no strength to rise. He remained on his hands and knees in the hard gray dirt of the road, weeping aloud like a child deceived or undeceived.

GIFT OF ROSES

1

The winding two-lane asphalt was bordered by the cool-looking mint green hills of western North Carolina, but inside the cab of this dented Ford pickup the heat was oppressive. Joley drove fast, trying to whip a breeze through the windows. She was sweating a little, but her seatmate, Elizabeth Gentry, looked supremely cool in her white linen dress. Her hair was silver; her eyes were silver, reflective with the blindness that had been hers since birth. Her hands lay separate in her lap; her feet in the white button-over shoes were crossed on the dirty floorboard. If she thought Joley's speed excessive, no gesture betrayed her feeling. She was ever a figure of ivory and silver, calm and patient.

"Maybe Shady Hill Cemetery will live up to its name," Joley said.

"How did you hear of it?" Elizabeth's voice, too, was cool, flutelike.

"Can't remember exactly," Joley admitted. "I think it was last spring at a meeting of the Bennett County Rose Society. I asked an older lady there about the history of her plant and she told me her mother got one cutting from a woman named Ramsey or Ransom or something. She was real sure of the first name—Davida. But she couldn't recall the last and she didn't know where that woman might have lived."

"You had told me that this particular quest would require more detective work than usual."

"Not much to go on. I had to try to figure out when she might have lived, so I asked the Rose Society lady the age of her mother and tried to count backward. Bennett County wasn't heavily populated until the 1950s; that made it easier to go through the courthouse records. I would have found her sooner if I'd known how to spell Davida. I kept thinking D-e-v-i-t-a or D-i-v. When I finally realized she was a female David, I felt kind of silly."

"Those were reasonable spellings."

Joley pushed her red cowgirl hat back from her forehead and wiped at a film of sweat. She dried her forefinger on her blue bandanna shirt. "I should've thought about when she lived. Davida was in use before the turn of the century, but uncommon enough to be helpful with the records. We're looking for Davida Rathbone, born in 1837, died 1913. Lost her husband in the Civil War in 1862 and her son in the same war two years later. They owned—she owned—a small farm down on Slater Creek and passed it on to a cousin. He sold it off and left the county for who knows where. . . . And that's the best I've been able to do."

"I think you've done splendidly. I could never master such investigatory deducement."

Joley smiled. *Investigatory deducement.* This sort of phrase was a consequence of Elizabeth's gift. She spoke a language no longer in use and would employ terms as quaint as bustles: *pishery-pashery, lorn, gullaries.* Her sentences so disconcerted strangers that Joley was sometimes called upon to translate, as when she had to explain to the university botanist, Allard Noble, that when Elizabeth declared November roses "the sweetest because they were less exhaled by Sol," she meant only that late-opening roses were more fragrant than summer roses because they were newer to the air. When she spoke, people stared, but they would stare at Elizabeth anyway, so silver she was, so self-composed in her dark world.

"What I do requires patience and a lot of practice," Joley said. "What you do requires something I can't even guess at, something you can't describe yourself."

"But patience and practice are my helpmeets also."

"Sometimes I think I'm the blind woman. Or deaf, maybe. It's like when I smell a flower, I hear a single tone. C on the piano, maybe. Or with a musk rose, maybe two, C and E. But you hear a full chord, lots of notes played by different instruments."

"Gracious," Elizabeth said. "You have been long pondering this analogy, Joley."

"Yes. I have been trying to find a way to tell you how I feel, how much I admire your gift—"

"And?"

"And how I feel kind of left out. Like I was deprived of a sense at birth, the way you were deprived of sight."

"I was fortunate in my parentage," Elizabeth said. "If my father had not been wealthy, I probably would never have discovered or developed what you refer to as 'my gift.'"

That was true, Joley thought. Elizabeth's father, Harold Gentry, had heaped his hoard in the 1880s from railroad stock and real estate and mineral investments. He was an early sponsor of the telegraph. As a sometime crony of George Vanderbilt, he had come to North Carolina from St. Louis and had received from Vanderbilt invaluable advice about finances and architecture. The latter became one of his passions and, though he could never attain either to anything like Vanderbilt's fortune or to the sumptuousness of his Asheville residence, he had erected in the forest area south of the city a large, eccentric Tudor mansion with a spacious and elaborate garden. Elizabeth had inherited not only her father's money but his house and grounds and the duties thereunto.

The duties thereunto.

Joley smiled again, thinking, That is not my kind of talk. I am becoming more like Elizabeth every day.

"Lots of folks are born blind and a few are born rich," she said, "but nobody else can do what you do."

"I have thought sometimes that you have an immunity I don't have. That's closer to the truth than saying that I have a gift. 'Gift' sounds like a desirable thing, but if you were to receive this 'gift,' you might wish it away from you, far away."

"Is that possible? That someone else could receive this gift or talent or whatever you call it? How could that happen?"

"In only one way," she said, "and of that we shall not speak."

"If you say so."

In fact, Joley was content not to pursue the subject. Lately there had crept into Elizabeth's sentences hints and whispers that distressed her. She tried to push her apprehensions away by force of will; she would not think of the future. It was important, necessary, for things to remain forever between them just as they were now.

"Damn," Joley said. "I missed the cutoff. We'll have to turn around and go back."

Finally a graveled one-lane brought them to their destination. Joley pulled into the wide-out halfway up the hill, cut the motor, and looked crossly out. "There is not one iota of shade in Shady Hill Cemetery," she said.

She stepped down carefully, touching the toe of her boot to the yellowing grass as if she were testing the temperature of a lake. Then she scooted out decisively and the legs of her jeans slipped down, covering again the expensive cowgirl footwear with its intricately tooled rose pattern. She reached in behind the seat and withdrew the serviceable, dull Civil War saber. She turned to look at this disused burial ground that was almost exactly what she had expected, the dry grass patchy, weeds and bushes dotting the slopes, the tombstones lichenous and slanted and sometimes tumbled over. A scattering of Budweiser cans indicated the character of the vandals.

She asked Elizabeth if she cared to wait for her return outside the truck. "Might be a tiny bit cooler."

"I shall rest here content," Elizabeth said. The sunlight silvered her hair and eyes more brightly than before.

"I'll go searching, then. Shouldn't take too long. This is one of the smaller graveyards we've visited."

"Go explore. The sounds of the daylight shall pleasure me."

"Be back soon."

Joley set off up the hillside, headed directly toward a scrubby clump of crab apple. She harbored a superstition that the most unlikely-looking prospects hid the most precious treasure. If these runty bushes concealed the tombstone of Davida Rathbone, the effort to find it would be worthwhile. If this puny herbage disclosed a copperhead snake or timber rattler—well, that was what her trusty saber was for.

But this clot of thorny greenery yielded neither reptile nor grave marker—only a spurt of grasshoppers that sprang away when she poked among the twigs. Still, from here Joley could see most of the rest of the area and she waited to see if one of the visible stones would draw her to it. She believed she had a sixth sense for her searches, not a gift anything like Elizabeth's, but something she was willing to claim, even though it had many times played her false.

Coming down the hill toward a time-eaten stone that leaned in her direction, she worked up creditable sweat and took off her hat and scrubbed her forehead with her shirtsleeve. She was mannishly handsome—broad shoulders, a face full of tomboy freckles. She was proud of her strength and endurance and also in her stock of sturdy common sense. She liked to tell Elizabeth, "One of us has got to have some, and I guess it's up to me."

This time she was correct. Here was the gravestone of Davida Rathbone, born to this world of sorrow December 16, 1837, and relieved of its burden March 12, 1913. The records of stone and musty courthouse paper agreed. There were other things to find out, but these were for Elizabeth to discover, for they had not come for the stone, but for the flower.

In the old days the custom was to plant upon the grave of a woman deceased her favorite bloom, the flower upon which she had lavished her most caring attentions. The custom was so pervasive that even a male or two had been included. And here was Davida's rose. Luck visited Joley and Elizabeth.

Beside the stone that canted toward the summit grew a tough brownish vine with barbarous black thorns. Joley recognized *Rosa canina,* old-fashioned dog rose, the species that Shakespeare called the "canker-bloom." It arrived in Massachusetts in Colonial times and afterward was naturalized from Pennsylvania southward. The single blossoms were bland, only slightly more pink than white. For Joley, their perfume was pallid, hardly noticeable, but Elizabeth would experience it differently.

Here, too, were horse nettles and ragweed and a tall thistle just coming into bloom. She cut these away, hacking an uneven path for Elizabeth. Then she stood back to admire.

The vine had twice twined around the narrow granite marker, climbing both sides and depositing a perfect blossom just above the *D;* it was as if this dog rose had tried to memorialize Davida Rathbone in the most obvious ways. The vine was unkempt but sinewy, rugged, and Joley thought it must hardly have lengthened since it came here from the widow's dooryard. Maybe it had given its vigor to blossoms rather than to height; there was a spendthrift bounty of bloom. The gravestone was sheeted with roses, a delicate, profuse embroidery costly beyond the reach of mortal purse.

She wondered when Mrs. Rathbone had last looked upon these flowers and what she might have thought, standing within her doorsill and musing. What would she think if she could see it now, enwreathing, celebrating, the stubborn dates that counted her span?

Elizabeth would know. Joley turned away and went back down to the truck. She stood by the open door and began to speak, but her friend forestalled her: "It must be quite a comely flower—and stalwart."

"*Stalwart* is good," Joley said. "And *durable. Showy.* There are lots of blooms."

"Of what sort?"

"A very old strain of dog rose. Are you ready to go see it?"

Elizabeth nodded, unsmiling. She heard the verb *see* as natural and, in fact, in her mind she would see it, as visibly as did Joley, though her eyes had never yielded her a single image of any kind, not rose or star or tabby cat. Her eccentric gift extended in narrow directions; she could describe in quaint but accurate terms such hybrids as Gloire de Dijon, Harry Kirk, Anna Olivier, and the others, but she was unable to say what Joley Wilder looked like.

Joley shoved her saber behind the seat and helped Elizabeth down. They began the climb and she felt Elizabeth's hand trembling on her forearm. The slope caused Elizabeth to feel her seventy-nine years. A breeze wafted by but did little to allay the August heat. It played with Elizabeth's long white skirt and displayed the white shoes beneath and her slender calves in white hose.

Someone might see us in this graveyard, Joley thought, and think I was walking along with a ghost.

Elizabeth asked about the landscape and Joley obliged with an efficient account. In these past six years she had learned plants and gardening. Before she came to Elizabeth's employ, she had hardly known the name of a single flower.

All I knew, she thought, was that I would not commit murder.

Yet if she had remained in Chicago, shackled to her brutal husband, Max Plymell, she might have killed the bastard by now and be wasting away behind penitentiary razor wire. But she had been discovered in a homeless shelter by William Belson, Elizabeth's friend, her Episcopal minister. He recognized her intelligence and capacity for loyalty and willingness to learn. He had been seeking a companion for Elizabeth; his admiration for her amounted almost to reverence; he wanted a perfect helpmate. Joley's story checked out; she had fled her husband. Max Plymell had become her stalker, but it was hard to think he could trace her to Asheville, North Carolina. Ideally, she should know flowers—but she could learn. She did learn.

Maybe I knew some stuff from school and all, Joley thought. But I really didn't know anything of any use till I met Elizabeth.

She named off the trees bordering the graveyard—yellow locust, flame oak, sarvis, low dogwoods. She was not surprised when Elizabeth asked if a tall poplar stood nearby. Yes—a splendid one just at the ridgetop along the roadside. She understood that Elizabeth identified the particular sound of the breeze that fingered it.

But I am no longer surprised by her, she thought. I take for granted.

Here at the site, Elizabeth's features showed signs of excitement. Her lips parted and her eyelids fluttered. Joley guided her by her elbow around weedy hindrances and Elizabeth leaned in toward the vine-clasped stone. At first she did not inhale deeply, but seemed to allow the scents of weathered granite and dusty nettles and parched grass to filter away; then she centered upon the light, pink smell.

She stood up straight and licked her lips—as if tasting honey. Now she leaned forward again, Joley supporting arm and shoulders, and inhaled profoundly. She closed her silver eyes. When she opened them again, they shone more brightly than ever.

Her whole figure, face and hands and clothing, seemed to glow. Joley had observed this enlightening dozens of times but was mesmerized once again. Elizabeth, tall and white and slender, now seemed but the lightest of material garments ever to enclose a spiritual being. She was vibrant and cool, a figure of light in the bronze-hot patch of ground.

The intensity of her friend's concentration infected Joley and she tried, as she had done before, to see what Elizabeth was seeing. She closed her eyes and saw . . . what? Nothing she could put a name to: a buxom, short woman in a gray housedress, perhaps.

Or probably not. When she strained her imagination in this way, she was merely deceiving herself. I am only seeing what the name Davida suggests to me, she thought.

Elizabeth opened her eyes. She still inclined her figure toward the rose, still inhaled it, but she was more within herself now, less within the plant. They had already shared everything to the fullest, the elegant woman and the rose, but she remained as she was a little longer, embracing with memory as well as with her senses. Joley knew the transference was complete; the old dog rose had told Elizabeth all. The Davida Rathbone who died in 1913 lived now again in Elizabeth Gentry.

She trembled from the strain of leaning and Joley brought her upright. "Are you okay?"

"Right as the rain on corn shoots."

Joley understood that this would have been an expression customary with Davida.

"Aren't you tired out?"

"I fear I may be."

"We'll go home. I'll take a cutting, if you like."

"Thank you, Joley."

"Hold steady now while I let go."

She made sure Elizabeth was secure in her stance before slipping her fancy pruners from the tooled leather holster on her belt. She found a likely length of stem and squeezed it between thumb and forefinger. "Here?" She knew Elizabeth could feel in her body where Joley touched the plant.

"A little higher, perhaps."

"Right you are." She snipped the cutting free and tucked it into her shirt pocket, careful with the thorns. She clipped twice more, resheathed her shears, took Elizabeth's arm, and down they went toward the truck.

• • •

The heat had gotten worse during their half hour at Shady Hill and Elizabeth was perspiring, too, now. Joley's shirt was soaked at the armpits and she doffed her red hat and laid it on the seat between them. "I wish it would rain," she said.

"It would be a boon," Elizabeth said. "No matter how often we water the garden, it is never so healthful as rain."

"I'll put the cuttings in bud vases. We'll enjoy them this week."

"Yes, and when you return for the plant, it will be cool. You'll count that a blessing."

"*We*. When *we* come back in late November to dig up and transplant, you'll be coming with me."

"Davida Rathbone is the last guest I shall personally welcome. I believe she'll find herself in worthy company, don't you?"

"The last? May I ask why?"

"My strength is ebbing daily, more quickly than I had anticipated. We must have the Belsons in for sherry early next week."

"Do we have to?"

"Yes."

"I know what this is about," Joley said. "You are fixing up to die. I think it is a mean trick."

"Perhaps you could make some of those spicy little cheese biscuits that the reverend is so partial to."

"Cheese biscuits!"

"They are delightful."

"Maybe if you wouldn't decide it was going to happen, it wouldn't happen. It seems like you want it to."

"Not really. Not entirely."

"She told you something, didn't she? That wretched Rathbone woman told you something."

Elizabeth had closed her eyes and Joley could see that she was drained. Her color had darkened; her voice was but a sigh. "Five o'clock Tuesday would be choice, if they could come then."

"Yes," Joley said. "That woman told you something."

2

But, as she had known she would, Joley baked her special biscuits and set out slices of Smithfield ham, bread and butter pickles, Spanish olives—all the usual. Elizabeth had mostly kept to her room since the graveyard visit. Her fatigue had dissipated only a little. Joley had to go alone to the west wall and mark out a place where the transplanted rose would be set.

As she tamped in the short green rod and tied a rag to it, she reflected that Elizabeth knew at this moment exactly what she was doing, exactly where the rose would be placed. The garden had been part of her since it was left in her tendance when her father died. That was almost forty years ago, and her mother, the first Elizabeth, had predeceased him by three years, victim of a boating accident. Harold Gentry liked to refer to her as "Elizabeth the First" or "Good Queen Bess." After her death, he had made the garden a memorial, patterning it after the border of a Persian carpet his wife had been fond of. So love and piety worked in Elizabeth to maintain, with a few minor improvements, the original design. If she had felt the garden to be wholly hers, she might have favored a less formal approach. But she had made herself its living memory and could not change it.

And if the rose of Davida was to be the last addition, then Joley and Elizabeth would go searching no more. Their adventures in tracing down ruined gardens, brambly sites where houses had burned, old graveyards, and abandoned farms were over and done with. No more would they wander the countryside, querying strangers and inching the pickup through the narrow thicket passages and over rock-ribbed mountain roads. No more would they sit by a river and wash down Joley's spicy egg-salad sandwiches with cold beer. Never again would Joley watch Elizabeth transfigure to a creature of light in the scent of a discovered rose.

She thought that she had only just begun to understand the meaning of the life she enjoyed with her friend, and now it was to be snatched away. This garden was filled with women's voices present in the roses they had rescued. Joley could not hear them, but they spoke to Elizabeth. That was something to revere.

And so she was not in the comeliest of moods when the Reverend

Belson and his young wife, Penny, arrived for drinks at five on Tuesday. She would not even put on a dress, but only clean jeans and a denim blouse embroidered with rodeo motifs. She would not show disrespect, only discontent.

Once she had brought the reverend and his merry little wife back to the library, she did not join them in the customary sherry, nor with Elizabeth in her light Riesling. She plumped down in a cavernous red leather armchair in the corner, tossing back two fingers, then three, of sour mash bourbon.

I will not be a party to this, she thought.

The conversation set off in the dullest way with obvious notes on the weather. It had rained at last and Elizabeth expressed gratitude but pleaded for more. The Reverend Belson made no promises but started an account of a flower show he and his Penny had recently attended in Blowing Rock. They both professed chagrin at some horrors of new hybrids. These remarks gave easy entry into praise of Elizabeth's enterprise of saving the old strains with their forgotten fragrances. They pursued the subject for a while and Elizabeth recounted the story of the rose of Davida. Occasionally she called upon Joley to supply a detail or confirm a suggestion, but, perceiving that her friend answered truculently, finished the telling herself.

"Oh, Elizabeth," Penny said, "whoever else would do this wonderful work? The young people nowadays—"

Elizabeth finished her sentence: "—must have better things to do. I know they have *happier* things to do, believe me."

"But William says that if it were not for you, some of these strains would have disappeared."

"That's right," said the reverend. "We live in a time of genetic penury. The big flashy hybrids have conquered the world of roses. 'Painted hussies,' I call them."

"But without even cheap perfume," his wife said.

"No more smell than a sheet of notepaper," he said. "We are extremely grateful for your efforts."

"We don't do it for the genetics," Elizabeth said. "We do it for the women who nurtured the flowers in times gone by. And we do it together in sisterly enterprise, Joley and I."

"We know that you trace down the flowers as a team, but you are the one to interpret their . . . language. Is that not correct?"

"Of course it is," Joley said. Her voice was too loud. "I can't do it. I don't have the gift."

"It is not a gift," Elizabeth said sorrowfully. "Not in the usual sense."

"You are not usual. There is only one of you in the world. Never was, never will be. That's why I can't stand to hear you talk about leaving the world. It makes my stomach turn."

"I'm sorry."

"What talk is this about leaving the world?" William asked.

"Only some arrangements I want to make for the future," Elizabeth said. "It is always preferable to be prepared, is it not?"

"It doesn't hurt to be prepared for a future that comes to all."

"A *far* future," Penny said.

Joley crossed to the tray on the spacious library desk and poured more whiskey. She added a few drops of water in afterthought. "No, it's not far. Elizabeth has made up her mind it will be soon."

"Are you ill?" William asked. "Are you getting treatment?"

"When necessary," she said, "but it is not disease. It is nature. I grow old, as do the world and all the flowers."

"I see nothing wrong with being ready," he said. "One never knows the hour and the day."

Joley slumped awkwardly into the armchair, sloshing a dollop from her glass. "Really!"

"I desire to be cremated," Elizabeth said, "and my ashes to be buried in the urn next to my father and mother. There is to be no public service, please." She went on to detail her plans meticulously, dryly. She voiced hope that there might be a memorial service restricted to no more than a dozen friends, at a date no later than one month from her demise. Perhaps William could read appropriate Scripture and then some of the poems they both were partial to—Yeats's "The Secret Rose," perhaps, and Hardy's "The Spell of the Rose," and, most particularly, Dickinson's "Go not too near a House of Rose."

The reverend had produced a leather notepad and was scribbling. He mentioned verses by Rossetti and Herrick. He recited a few lines of the Rossetti before Joley interrupted.

She came to her feet quickly and unsteadily. “No,” she said. Her face was pale. “I will not be a party to this. I will not.”

“What’s wrong, dear?” asked Penny.

Slowly and deliberately, Joley walked to the desk and set down her emptied glass. She turned to face Elizabeth, observing sadly that in this light the silver of her blindness had dulled. The lamp glow caused her eyes to shine yellowish. “You know, don’t you?” she said. “You know when it is going to happen. The rose of that Rathbone woman told you when. I could tell that when we were driving home from the graveyard you knew when.”

Elizabeth did not reply. Her silence darkened the shadows of the library.

“I will not be a party to it,” Joley said again, and left the room with what she hoped was an air of offended dignity, of betrayed friendship.

3

The memorial service was held September 29, three weeks after Elizabeth died, and went off pretty well. Only eleven attended, besides Elizabeth and the Belsons, and it was a simple affair, tearless and dignified. William read from Psalms and the Song of Solomon and then a number of poems. Joley thought the number excessive.

After the comfortless murmurs of consolation, the others departed this small chapel hidden away in an obscure corner of the city, leaving Joley alone in the front pew. On the altar before her stood a small gold cross and a single pale Hyperion lily in a slender silver vase and one burning candle in a pewter holder.

William came to remove the cross and held it in his lap as he sat beside Joley in the pew. “Do you recall how you ran from the room when Penny and I came to visit the last time?”

She nodded.

“No one blamed you for going. We talked about it. Your grief was too much for you. Elizabeth said she never expected to be so deeply mourned. She spoke of you at length. She said many fine things. She certainly didn’t hold you to blame.”

“She wouldn’t.”

"You know what special regard she had for you, what love."

"She left me the house and garden and everything," Joley said. "The money . . . She wanted me never to be afraid again, of Max or anybody else."

"She charged Penny and me to look after you. She feared for you during this difficult time afterward. We were to be stalwart helpmeets, she said. You know the way she talked."

"It *is* difficult. It is very hard."

"Perhaps even more difficult than you know. That power she had of knowing—absorbing—the lives of the women of days past from the flowers they devoted themselves to, well, she was apprehensive it might pass to you."

"Pass—"

"She said you thought of it as a gift, but she did not."

"It was something no one else in the world had."

"Such powers can be burdens, she said. Dangerous ones."

"It must be terrible to know when you are going to die, the day and the hour. That Rathbone woman's rose told her."

"Or maybe her mind and body could not withstand the force of that one last onus of sorrow. Perhaps she just . . . gave way."

"She knew what would happen and she accepted it. She didn't have to. It was almost like a sui—"

"Hush now. You know better than that. Not Elizabeth, ever."

"Why, then?"

"She thought it her duty to rescue to memory women who had died in sorrow," William said, "just as it has been my duty to rescue women who have to live in pain and sorrow."

"Women like me."

"Some of them, yes. . . . But you already know all this."

"Yes. But I don't understand."

He stood, cradling the cross to his chest. "I can see that you want to be alone with your thoughts. Let me impress upon you that Penny and I are here to support you in this bad time and always. If you need help, *when* you need help, you must come to us."

"Thank you," she said, but she did not turn her eyes from the altar with the candle and lily as he went softly up the aisle and out the door of this small rustic stone chapel. When he opened the outer door, she could hear the mutter of traffic on the freeway six blocks west. She had been hearing a subdued murmur she could not identify since she entered here and had ascribed it to traffic. But when she heard that actual sound, it was different.

She sat a long time in the otherwise-deserted chapel, not alone with her thoughts, because she could not form thoughts. She was fixed in a sad, hard trance. She wondered at the arrangement Elizabeth had specified. Why had she chosen a lily instead of the lovely Duchess de Brabant rose, modest and pearly, that grew by Elizabeth's mother's grave in a corner of the churchyard? Why not a *Rosa brunonii,* the Himalayan musk rose that had been her favorite? Elizabeth had valued its fragrance above all others: "Heartrending. A Mozart concert aria." The Hyperion lily possessed a scent so faint as to be almost undetectable.

But now she smelled the musk rose; that fragrance was unmistakable. Its source had to be the lily; nothing else here could produce a floral smell. It grew stronger and to this scent were added the scents of others: *arkansana, gallica, banksiae, helenae, cinnamomea*—all those roses the two of them had discovered and brought away to the garden.

All at once, like a sea surge, the mingled yet separate fragrances filled the room and filled all Joley's spirit and mind. It was overwhelming, this flood, and she felt herself weaken, begin to grow faint, as the voices started to sound. The murmur that had lapped softly at her hearing all afternoon swelled to a music harmonious and discordant, swarming with tints and shades and brightnesses. The voices were those of women no longer living and all the sounds were composed of softer sounds and every smaller sound was a sadness that augmented the great, immortal grief of the chorus, a single chord, within which Joley could nowhere distinguish the voice of Elizabeth.

She was here, though, close by. The lily on the altar began to glow as the figure and spirit of Elizabeth used to glow when a new rose spoke to her. Brighter the lily grew, until it outshone the lilting candle flame.

Now was her *immunity* torn away, so that this brightness was the last thing Joley saw with her eyes before they silvered over with the blindness that was Elizabeth's legacy to her—the gift of understanding, of being able to endure the anguish of those generations of women whose sorrows painted the roses so red, the roses so white, and bestowed upon the flowers a fragrance that outlasts the merely human terms of life to speak lamentation to all the sightless.

CHRISTMAS GIFT!

With all that weight in its bed, the doughty little Dodge pickup ought to have scrambled backward up the slope with ease and aplomb. The grade was not of Everest height nor of Matterhorn steepness. But there was a clutter of loose gravel on the vague tracks and a layer of dust where a drag harrow had scratched across the truck path, and the wheels spun futilely, spewing up a brick-colored haze that got into Jerry's nostrils and made him sneeze. After awhile, Curly Spurling, who was trying to drive and succeeding only in cussing, cut the motor and opened the door lettered with the words MILL FURNITURE CO. and stepped out.

"Is it going to get up the hill?" Jerry asked.

Curly scrawled the dust with the toe of his unelaborate cowboy boot. "I don't see why it wouldn't, but it ain't," he said. Curly was a man who admired machines, fancied he knew them in their logical souls, and held them in cool contempt when they failed his expectations.

"So what do we do now?"

"Well, honey dumpling," Curly said, "there's two possibilities. Either you come up with a hot idea or we try to muscle it. Didn't they teach you how to handle situations like this down at your high school?"

Curly loved to rag Jerry about having graduated before he came up at the beginning of this summer to labor at his uncle's little furniture store over in the gritty paper-mill town of Tipton. "Me, I never got past the fourth," he would say, "and you've got your whole diploma and here we both are, busting our humps for a salary you could cash into a stack of nickels and set on without making a dent in your ass. So, I ask you, where has your fancy schooling got you after all them years?"

Jerry would reply that his schooling was not completed even yet and that when it was all over at last, he expected to have a better plan for making a living than toting sticks of furniture up and down the blue-green hills of western North Carolina. He had several plans, he told Curly, but he wasn't telling anybody what they were. Word would get around and others would beat him to the feed trough.

But he did not have the first inkling how to get this humongous freezer locker out of the pickup truck and then around behind the barn and into the hayloft on that side. This tall barn had been built into the hillside where a gully had crumbled away, and on the east the loft opening was about three feet off the ground and mighty handy for unloading the bales of alfalfa that came from the field spread around the hilltop. But it was not convenient for unloading and storing elephants, battleships, or freezer lockers.

Yet this was where Mr. Ward Carter desired to have his new purchase situated for a while. He had bought it for his wife, Maidey, with a goodish part of the check he received upon the sale of his tobacco crop and he wanted it to be a surprise Christmas gift, the most splendid one he had ever given. They were a childless couple, the Carters, and, without any younguns to spoil, would sometimes maybe spoil each other with an unexpected extravagance. He was buying the freezer at a cut rate because Mill Furniture wanted it out of their building. They needed the floor space for the new models, this one that Carter bought being three years old, a model no longer manufactured. Even so, for the dirt-farming Carter family a freezer locker was a luxury item, and the Mr. designed to wangle the Mrs. into coming around to the barn on Christmas morn and climbing up the ladder from the ground floor and poking her head through the opening in the loft floor and beholding—*Lord-a-mercy, Ward!*—a huge gleaming white freezer locker sitting there among the hay bales, as surprising in this place as a steam yacht in a meadow of red clover.

Well, the boys, as Mill Furniture deliverymen were called—and as they called themselves—were accustomed to the tradition of hiding gifts for customers to unveil on December 25. The custom on Christmas Day in this part of the mountains was to greet any person you saw with the shouted phrase *Christmas Gift!* The one who said it first was owed a gift by the other person. Like many traditions, it entailed scanty logic, since the first person you'd see would almost certainly be a family member who was obliged to gift you anyhow. But customs are huggable entities and usually survive the assaults of common sense.

Surprise of the dramatic moment was most avidly sought after. The humblest gift—a cheap necktie, a plastic hair barrette, even a single grocery-store orange—acquired cachet and achieved festive honor if it could be presented unexpectedly. The necktie might festoon the back of the father's chair at the breakfast table; the barrette would be tucked inside the table napkin; the toes of galoshes were favorite nests for oranges. Ward Carter's desire to surprise his Mrs. was not a radical new fashion, but it did have its novel aspects.

In the first place, today was October 18, one of those Indian summer days when nothing in the landscape hinted at St. Nick and his wingless airborne troop. Scarlet oaks, yellow maples, copper-leaved dogwoods vied to produce the vividest hues. The sun had not put on its winter white, but stood in the blue sky a warm ball of purest gold. Curly and Jerry had sweated freely when loading the freezer onto the truck and now faced the prospect of further and more copious perspiration.

Another matter was the size of the gift. It was one thing to surprise your grandfather with new red suspenders or to embarrass an uncle with some ugly socks, but this freezer locker was six feet long, three wide, and three and one-half tall. It was so massive, the boys couldn't accurately estimate its weight, except for Curly's unscientific description: "Too damn heavy, I swear to God." Three hundred seventy-five pounds would be a probable guess. It was a discontinued model from a manufacturer that would soon go out of business. Manana was the brand name, and Curly grumbled at it. "Manana," he said, rhyming it with banana. "What the hell does that mean?"

Jerry corrected his pronunciation. "It's a Spanish word," he said. "It means 'tomorrow.' "

"Why would they call it something like that?"

"I suppose they mean it's the freezer locker of the future."

"I wish it was a hundred years in the future," Curly said. "Have you come up with any good ideas about getting it into the barn?"

Jerry looked at the pickup, askew on the hillside and appearing to be ready to buck off the cumbrous appliance like a surly pony and then roll free down the hill all the way to Trivet Creek in the cornfield bottomland. He looked at the weathered barn; the roof needed a sheet or two of new tin on this side. He looked at their route around to the back, the gravel and slippery dust, the deep ruts and the weeds. He looked for inspiration and found none. He inspected Curly, whose stocky, muscular figure promised that he'd hold up his end, all right; his frizzly hair still showed streaks of red amid the gray; he was still a strong man, but even so . . . Jerry shook his head.

"Well then, I reckon it's brawn over brain. Too bad Mr. Carter ain't here. If he had a sledge and a willing mule, we could get this done pretty quick."

They took a moment to survey the Carter-less environs. Curly spat. "All right. I reckon we'll just yaw it side to side to get it to the back of the truck. I'll take the front and guide it along and you push from the back."

They climbed into the truck bed, untied the half-inch cotton ropes, shucked off the protective quilts and laid them aside. Jerry squeezed in beside the monster, reached across, and tugged.

It did not budge.

"Lord," he said.

"You know what they insulate these here Tomorrows with?" Curly said. "Sawdust. They cram sawdust down the inside walls. Then when it gets wet from condense, it heavies up worsern lead."

"Sawdust. That's kind of primitive."

"We're about to get a handful of primitive. Give your end a sideways yank. If you can get it to move once, it might start coming."

Jerry followed the older man's instructions and was gratified to feel the locker scrape at least some part of an inch sidewise. Another yank, and it began to move toward him, opening a narrow access behind the cab that he could barely squeeze into. This space wedged him into a cramped, awkward position where he was unable to bend his torso and would have to push while standing straight. But, crooking his knees and pushing with his forearms, he managed to shove the thing forward about two feet, with Curly tugging at the other end and keeping it parallel to the sides of the truck bed.

Now Jerry had a little extra room and was able to stoop slightly and heave with his shoulders and upper arms, though as yet there was insufficient space for leg strength to come into play. He pushed as hard as he could, until he heard a loud *pop* behind him, a sound like a cork extracted from a giant bottle.

"What was that noise?" Curly asked.

"I don't know."

"Was it your backbone comin' apart?"

"Felt more like my tailbone," Jerry said. He squirmed around to try to see. "Uh-oh. I think I busted out the back window in the cab."

"Nothing medical, then."

"Don't think so."

"Let's have a look." Curly hopped off the tailgate and came around to the front. He stuck his head through the side window. "It's all right. You didn't bust the glass, just popped the window out of that rubber gasket."

"I hope it won't cost a fortune to fix," Jerry said. "You might be a rich man, but I need every dime I can scrape."

" 'Rich man'?" Curly said. "Sugarplum, money don't know my name. Tell you what: If I can stick that window back into place, you'll owe me a Dr Pepper and a pack of Nabs at the Bound for Hell Grocery Store."

"Done deal," Jerry said. "Just as soon as we get this freezer into the hayloft."

"Well, that gives me something to look forward to." Curly went back and swung up on the tailgate again.

"Anyhow," Jerry said, "that open window space gives me a little more pushing room."

"Give 'em hell, Tarzan."

Straining every body part, Jerry got the locker to inch forward a little and then a little more, fractions at a time. Going uphill like this, there was no way for the deadweight to pick up momentum. He thought that if a man ever had to push a glacier backward, that job of work would be something about like this one.

But the massy oblong finally did inch forward, until he could feel it begin to tilt toward Curly.

"Hold up!" Curly called. "We got a little problem here."

"What's that?"

"Tailgate."

Jerry left off and went to the back. The tailgate on this little Dodge was a flimsy affair, just a metal shelf attached to the metal sideboards with a small chain on each side. The chains were showing clear signs of strain; the links were stretched. They looked ready to part.

"We're going to have to let it flop," Curly said, "and unload this damn thing straight off the bed. I'll try to lift it up and take the strain off and you unhitch the chains."

"Okay."

The problem with this plan was that there was no room for Curly's hand, or even his fingers, beneath the bottom of the contraption.

"You get in the bed and pull upwards on it and I'll slide my hands under and lift. Then you can hop down and undo the chains."

"That's a guaranteed way for you to lose five fingers."

"I can't afford to lose no fingers," Curly said. "Bill Monroe and the Bluegrass Boys have been after me to join their band and pick the banjo."

"I didn't know you could play any banjo."

"They promised to learn me. Let's try it anyhow, unless you've happened onto that hot idea we been looking for."

So there was Jerry in the truck, trying to lift the freezer by a top corner, with Curly on the ground, getting ready to slide his hands under, when Ward Carter drove up in his variously dented old army jeep. He unfolded his long, lanky body from the seat and got out.

"Howdy, boys," he said. "How come you want to carry that big thing by hand? Why don't you drive around to the back and unload it straight off?"

"Well, Mr. Carter, it's good to see you," Curly said. "We already thought about backing around to the loft, but that just seemed too blame easy."

Carter smiled but did not grin. "That right?"

"Truck won't go up the hill," Jerry said. He was uncertain how Curly's trials at humor might be received. If Mr. Carter didn't catch on, there would be a lot of explaining to do, and the explanation would fall to him. Curly refused—in his phrase—"to chew his cabbage twice." His jokes sometimes left Jerry in awkward situations.

"Won't go?" Carter asked.

"Can't get the proper traction the way the ground is here," Curly said. "So we're going to have to hump it. We've got it to the back of the truck, but now the tailgate is in the way. We're trying to let it down."

"All right," Carter said. He eyed the freezer, the boys, the truck. He closed his eyes and appeared to meditate. "It might seem like we ought to hitch the jeep to the truck and pull her around."

"That ain't a bad notion," Curly said.

"Except I been having a lot of trouble with the engine lately. Might be the block is cracked. That kind of strain would purely kill it."

"I'm grieved to hear," Curly said.

"We ought to be able to hitch my tractor up and jerk her around to the back."

"Another fine idea," Curly said.

"But my tractor is busted and waiting on the factory part."

"That's some gloomy news."

"We might could lower it down onto a pretty good-sized sledge I use to haul tobacco out of the bottom fields with."

"A bright and shining thought," Curly said.

"But Hiram Perkins has my mule Bessie over at his place. He's been pulling stumps in his back field and has borrowed horses and mules from all around."

"That piece of news kind of tops off my sorrows," Curly said.

"Well, I do have a little old J-bar in the jeep. Might be we could raise up my new freezer locker just enough to take the strain off so you could let the tailgate down."

"That would be a help."

While Carter was striding away to find the tool, Curly said in a quiet voice, "I liked his first three notions a lot better."

Jerry seconded his preferences.

Then Carter returned and slipped the little gray crowbar under the object in question just at the edge of the truck bed and raised it slightly. Curly unhitched the tailgate chains and let the tailgate hang. Now the freezer protruded from the truck bed about twelve inches and gave Curly enough free length to grasp both sides at the bottom.

Carter swung his jimmy bar idly by the crook. “That’s going to be sort of hefty, going up the hill,” he said.

Curly nodded. “It ain’t really a two-man job.”

“I’ve been down in my back,” Carter hastened to declare. “I don’t know but what I might have warped a verterbray. Sometimes it works on me so I can’t sleep at night.”

“I’m heartbroke to learn of it. How did you come to hurt your back?”

“Doing something about like what you boys are fixing to do.”

“We’ll get started right now,” Curly said. “I don’t need no more encouragement. Jerry, I’ll pull ’er backwards and you get hold of it just as it slides off the bed. Don’t let it drop.”

Jerry jumped down and trotted to the back. The freezer was moving slowly backward at a slight angle as Curly stepped sideways. Jerry watched for the corner to edge off the bed to grasp it with his left hand. As it kept coming, he ran his right hand along the bottom, ready to catch the other corner. The freezer slid off the bed smoothly enough, but Jerry was not prepared for the dire weight of the thing. He got his right hand around the bottom all right but nearly dropped it when the weight came full on him. He grunted out most of his breath and felt his face heat red from the pressure. His knees trembled.

“Have you got it okay?”

Unable to speak, Jerry nodded, but then he realized Curly couldn’t see him with the bulk between them.

“We’ll go sideways up the hill,” Curly said. “If I try to go backwards, I’ll walk us into a hole. So bring your end around a little and we’ll straighten up.”

Jerry tried to say “All right.”

They started up, both of them struggling for footing. Jerry slid in the powdery clay dust; Curly stumbled in the dusty grass on his side. Still, they made progress, slow and shaky but climbing the grade.

In a minute, Curly said, “Now here comes that little ditch we looked at. Don’t try to step all the way across. Put one foot down in it when I signal and then the other. Then we’ll step up on the other side on a three count.”

This worked pretty well until they had reached almost to the corner of the barn. Then Jerry knew he couldn't handle it any longer. His palms were sweating and the freezer was beginning to slip from his grasp. "Let's let her down and rest a jiffy," he said.

"You sure? Once we set her down, she'll be double hard to get up again."

"I'm sure."

On Curly's count, they bent their knees and lowered it into a patch of pigweed. Jerry staggered over to a grassy tumulus and sat. He looked at his hands, surprised to see he wasn't bleeding under his fingernails. His biceps felt strange with the load off; his forearms and wrists felt weightless, floating.

Curly came to sit beside him and Carter walked over to the freezer and leaned against it. "I hate to make it hard on you boys like this."

"That's all right," Curly said. "We'll get our breath back in a minute. Then we'll stuff her in."

"You might be wondering why I'd want you to go to all this trouble and hardship."

"I was a mite curious," Curly said, "but didn't know whether it might be any business of mine."

"Way it come about was, I was admiring my tobacco after we had cured it good and stripped it off. I swear, boys, that's the prettiest leaf I ever saw in my life. Tips and smokers—maple syrup and gold. That's what I said to Maidey. 'Maple syrup and gold,' I said, 'and see if you don't think so when you go to grading.' So when she and her cousin Bobbie and that other'n, Lilymae they call her, was grading and tying, they said the exact same thing. *Maple syrup and pure gold.* 'Why, I could plumb eat this leaf, mister,' Maidey told me. 'I believe I'll go back to the house and get me a dinner plate.' You ought to heard them girls laugh."

Carter went on to say that they could talk about little else other than the quality of the crop. "Then Maidey hit on an idy that purely surprised me," he said. "I never heard tell of anything like it." She suggested that to give their allotment the best possible presentation to the auction buyers at the warehouse over in Morristown, they ought to flatten the leaves after they were graded. Then she would tie them into the neatest hands you ever saw. That way, the buyers could see that golden honeycomb color. A hand of tobacco wrinkles and darkens as it ages and loses its best looks. But her plan was going to preserve its appearance. She decided she was going to iron it.

"Iron?" Curly said. "What's she mean, iron?"

"With a flatiron," Carter said. Or with three of them, to be exact. Had to be the right temperature, too. If the irons were cold, the leaves wouldn't flatten out; if they were too hot, the tar would ooze and gum up the metal so she couldn't push the irons along.

"Where'd she want to do all this ironing?"

Right there in the kitchen. As soon as the leaf was stripped from the stalks that were taken down from the long pine tier poles in the barn, Maidey graded it into five piles. When she had gathered enough of the top two grades, they laid the leaves in old tobacco-bed canvas and toted them to the kitchen. There she ironed them out and tied them into hands, the neatest and most beautiful hands of tobacco the world has ever seen. Then Carter gathered them and brought them back out to the barn and placed them on the pallets. That had to be done right, too, because Maidey wanted to make sure that her handiwork would be seen to best advantage. In fact, she made him take down two pallets and restack.

"That's a fair day's work, if you ask me," Curly said.

"Boys, I'm telling you," Carter said. "I don't see how she done it, but she did. Ever last top leaf of the crop. Nine hundred pounds."

"Your wife ironed out nine hundred pounds of tobacco?" Jerry said. He was fisting and unfisting his hands to get feeling back. "That's hard to picture."

"And this was right on top of canning season, too, when she'd been working like a dog, day in and day out. You wouldn't think to believe how that woman does, and her not much bigger than a chigger, pert little lady." His voice thickened and his eyes teared.

"Trouble is, them buyers don't take time to stand around and admire a basket of tobacco," Curly said. "They just give it a passing glance and put in their bids and then they're down the line to the next one."

"I tried to tell her. 'Maidey,' I says, 'the buyers won't hardly notice if you do something like that.' And she says to me, 'You wait, Mr. It'll be so pretty, people will stop and stare.' And she was right about that."

"You mean the buyers stopped to admire on it?" Curly asked. "That would be a marvel to the world."

"Not the buyers, no. But the other'ns that brought their crops in." He described how the other farmers and their wives and children crowded up to the Carter space and pointed at the crop and talked and rubbed it gently between their fingers. Some of the women were just plain jealous; you could see that, Carter said. On the other hand, you wouldn't be seeing any of them ironing out a crop of tobacco on smooth oak planks laid across a couple of sawhorses. You wouldn't see any of them eating cold baloney sandwiches for supper while the kitchen was full of tobacco leaf.

"You never would see my Julie Ann doing it," Curly said. "She'd laugh me plumb out of the county if I was to mention such of a thing."

"I couldn't talk Maidey out of it," Carter said. "And you know what was in my mind? The whole time I was watching her iron, I could see her the way she worked in canning season, right there in that same kitchen. How it gets in August—and then this was one of the hottest Septembers we ever had. I heard them say so on the 'Farm Hour' radio. She had that cookstove fired up and the water boiling and she'd sterilized the mason jars and was filling them up with green beans she'd boiled up and tomatoes she'd simmered down and sweet corn she'd blenched. . . . Well, you know how it is in canning time. And she didn't have nobody in to help and of course she won't never let me do nothing in the kitchen. She says she don't trust me with a cookstove." He smiled but then choked up again and wept some, just a little leakage at the eye corners.

"That's what Julie Ann says to me," Curly reported. "But my younger boy, Jules, he's a fair hand to cook. Except for biscuits. His catheads turn out so dry, you could breathe them up your nose like snuff."

"Well, she put in three long weeks at it," Carter said. "We'd have breakfast and I'd go out to the hay field and she'd start in. When I come home at evening, she was still plugging away, sweating like a hog in a wool blanket. Course, she ain't no hog, just a little bit of a thing, like I said. Only thing I could help her do was keep the kindling chopped and the woodpile stacked and then carry in the cans to the storeroom after she laid the rubber on them."

Jerry had never set eyes on Mrs. Carter, but he had watched his grandmother and two of his aunts at the process, and so he pictured Mr. Carter's wife scurrying like a water bug over a pool to the worrisome tasks that canning required.

"So that's when you decided to get her this here freezer locker?" Curly said.

"I heard tell about them," Carter said. "I heard how you can put up stuff now and it'll keep and then you can cook it thawed fresh to go on the table. Mack Owen keeps his deer meat that way, says he butchers it up and anytime he wants a haunch steak just takes it out to thaw and fries it up. Thad Sessoms, him that's the ranger down at Crooked Creek Park, stocks his freezer with trout. Gets him one of these paper milk bottles and cuts off the top and sticks in the fish and fills it with water and into the freezer she goes. It don't have to be trout season if he wants a nice mess of fish with his mustard greens. So I thought I'd get one of these gadgets and save Maidey a whole lot of hard labor. Don't you think her eyes won't pop out when she sees this thing?" He dribbled a few more tears and then chuckled.

"And this is going to be a surprise?"

"Come Christmas morning, I'll coax her out here some way or other. She won't have the least preception what's going on. I'll take her up in the loft and peel the hay bales back and there it'll be. Her eyes will get as big as saucers. I'll holler out *Christmas gift!* She won't know what to say."

"My Julie Ann would have something to say." Curly shook his head. "That's too big of a surprise for her. Something like this, she'd want to talk it over beforehand."

"I'm set on surprising Maidey."

"That being so, I reckon we'd better head this big surprise into the loft." Curly gave Jerry an appraising once-over. "You about ready, sweetness? Reckon we can make it?"

"I reckon," Jerry replied, grateful that Curly had said *we* instead of *you,* admitting that, like Jerry, he was feeling the strain of the task as well.

But the job had not gotten easier. Curly's prediction that it would be much more difficult this time to lift the freezer from the ground proved true. Jerry gave it every bit of strength he could muster and was amazed to find himself standing upright with a good grip on the appliance, both hands. His legs almost buckled at first, but when they started moving along the mostly level space he steadied somewhat.

He couldn't see where they were going. They had to go backward here and it was Curly's job to look over his shoulder. There was a passage to the left, an opening just wide enough to get a tractor and wagon in, and Jerry kept his eyes on his feet, finding the even spots to follow in the wheel tracks. They could travel only a few inches with each step and with each step he felt a rough jarring at the base of his spine. He fancied he heard his spinal disks grinding together. His neck and jaw muscles quivered.

Then Curly stopped. "Here we are," he grunted. "We'll take it easy over to the loft sill and set it down real slow. We'll have to balance it on the edge of the sill and climb in one at a time."

They edged over toward the opening in slow centimeters. To steady himself, Jerry pushed with his hip against the side of the barn as they let the burden down ever so gradually. They made sure it was balanced well enough that one could hold it in place while the other squirmed into the barn loft. If it tipped one way or the other, it would drop and go smash. There would be no way to stop it if it began to fall.

Carter came over to watch their progress and to offer a conjecture. "This next part might be a little teejus."

"How you mean?" Curly asked.

"Well, you've got to get it down from here to the loft floor," he explained. "The sill's about six feet off the floor on the inside."

"The floor?" Curly said. "How come the floor? I thought we'd just lay it on top of these stacked hay bales."

"That wouldn't work out," Carter explained. "That would leave it out in plain sight. Maidey would be bound to see it when she come out this way to look after the chickens or run off younguns that come around to lollygag in the loft. Some of these young couples from the high school come up here to get nekkid. Maidey'll chase them out, but she don't tell on them, even if she knows who they are. Just laughs about it. But what we need to do is set this freezer on the floor and then cover it all up with the bales so she can't know."

"I don't even see the floor," Curly said.

"I expect you'll have to shift the hay so there's a cleared-out space."

"How tall is it stacked?"

"Two bales from under the sill."

"I don't know," Curly said. "Let me think a minute."

Jerry thought, too, and realized that, standing on the floor, he and Curly would have to lift the Great White Burden from the sill at a height over their shoulders. It would not be possible to sustain the weight in that position. The locker would tumble on them, first crushing their skulls and afterward wreaking a lot of other damage they wouldn't mind much at that point. Well, he said to himself, that's the punishment we get for being such good guys. Santa Claus wouldn't go to all this trouble.

"We'll have to step it down," Curly said.

With gray dread, Jerry asked how.

"Have to clear a big space out to the floor. Then we can build it up three bales right below the sill. And then two bales high on all the other sides and then one bale and then at the end we can rest it on the wood."

"That makes sense, I guess," Jerry said.

"When I say *we,* I mean *me,* honeybunch. You're going to have to stand here and keep this freezer balanced where it is now till I get the bales arranged. Don't think about nothing else. If it starts to tip, it's a goner. Won't be no Christmas surprise for Mrs. Ward. But there'll be a mighty big surprise for whatever's down below, because this thing will purely crash through the planks and then it's 'Katie, bar the door,' if you happen to be a mule at the feed trough underneath."

"Ain't nothing down there but some chickens peckin' around," Ward said. "I loaned out my mule Bessie to Perkins to pull stumps. But I sure would hate to have a big hole in my loft."

"I'd hate it, too," Curly said, " 'cause it would sure to God take me with it. But that's the only way I see how. Do you want us to chance it?"

Carter took his time considering. Finally he spoke. "I'll tell you the truth, boys. I've had it in my mind so clear how Maidey's face would look when she catches sight of this handsome new freezer locker, I'd about risk anything." His eyes welled up again and he rubbed them with his wrist.

"That settles it, then," Curly said. "Give me a little time to wrassle them bales around. And you keep it steady, sweet thing. But if it does start to fall, don't try to stop it. You could get pretty good hurt. Just let it go."

"I'll keep her steady," Jerry promised.

Curly straddled the sill, stepped over, and climbed down out of sight.

In a few moments they could hear him flopping the big oblongs of wire-bound hay from one spot to another.

"That man seems to be right fond of you," Carter said to Jerry. "The way he calls you honey pot and sweetie pie and all that."

"That's the way he talks to everybody. Or just about everybody."

"He don't call me sugartit," Carter said.

"If you worked with him hauling furniture, he would. It's just his habit. Doesn't mean anything."

"It's old-timey. I had an uncle over in Red Fork used to talk to people like that. I hadn't heard anybody do it in a long while."

"His people are from over in those parts. I guess it's the way he was brought up."

Curly's struggle with the bales, his thumping them on top of one another, rattled the frame of the barn. Jerry thought maybe he felt the locker begin to wobble and tilt. He clutched it with both hands. The sill was only four inches wide and the freezer was three feet; it was like trying to keep a box of kitchen matches balanced on the edge of a knife blade. He thought that if it started to fall, he'd try to stop it, no matter what. It wasn't so much a matter of preventing damage as of not losing all the dog labor they'd put into the job.

Then there was Curly standing on the top bale in the opening. The sill where the locker perched was ankle-high to him, waist-high to Jerry. When Curly stepped down to the lower stack on his side, the bottom of the locker was just a little higher than his rodeo belt buckle. "I'll hold it steady now and you come on through," he said.

When Jerry got inside, he saw that Curly had arranged the bales in the form of a pre-Columbian temple—homemade Aztec style, as it were. It ascended by the height of one bale at a time to where the freezer sat and there was space on either side for the boys to stand and lift.

"You see how it works?" Curly asked.

"I reckon so."

"You think you can keep your balance on this hay while you're lifting it down?"

Jerry stamped tentatively, jumped up and down. "Yeah, I guess."

"Well, here we go, then. . . . Easy . . . One step at a time."

This perilous experiment worked, to Jerry's amazement and perhaps to Curly's also. Gingerly they felt for the lower bales with their feet; carefully they let down the freezer one step at a time. By now they had achieved a natural rhythm in working together, so that Curly did not need to call a count.

At last the cumbersome oblong sat on the floor of the loft. The long golden light of the afternoon had fled and the amber sunset streaked through the barn-side boards, so that the freezer glowed like ivory lit from inside. It was such an improbable image, this household appliance sitting in eccentric majesty amid the bales of homely hay, that they stood silent to contemplate it.

Then Carter called out to them. "That's mighty fine, boys. Now lay some bales around it and cover it up."

They disposed the hay the way he desired, shoving the bales close so the whiteness would not peep out to alert Maidey Ward that Santa had been busy in her barn loft. Carter directed them to jumble other bales around oddwise, so that they would look "natural like," and they followed his suggestion quickly, anxious to call it a day.

They went down the ladder to the ground floor, shuffled their way through dust and fluttering chickens, and went outside into the gloaming.

Carter came around from behind to meet them. "Boys," he said, "you done an awful fine job. If I'd known it was going to be so much trouble, I wouldn't have asked you to do it. But I don't think Maidey will never find it up there, and it's going to be the surprise of her life. I wish you-all could be here to see her face when she first lays eyes on it. She'll light up like a . . . like a . . . I don't know what."

"Like a Christmas tree?" Curly suggested.

Carter laughed. "That's it," he said. "Like a Christmas tree." He laughed again and then he wept again and brushed away tears with his knuckles.

Curly watched him emote for a space and then said, "If you don't mind my asking, Mr. Carter, what are you going to do with this big Freezer Locker of Tomorrow up there in your hayloft?"

Carter's expression was one of guileless surprise when he replied. "Well now, you know I ain't going to keep it out here in the barn. Where's the convenience in that? It's going to go in the storeroom right next to the kitchen where we keep Maidey's canned goods. I've had the corner picked out in my mind for a long time."

"That's where I'd put it," Curly said. "But how you expect to get it down from there and out to the house?"

"I'm trusting you boys to handle that end of things," Carter said. "Seems to me you've made a fine success of it so far. Boys like you two, they ain't hardly nothing you can't do."

Curly set a leisurely sweet pace rolling the Dodge back over the hill to Mill Furniture in grimy Tipton. It was already 6:30, a half hour past closing time. The blue-violet twilight was darkening to mauve under a low bank of western clouds. The breeze was cool on their necks where it poured through the missing window behind them. They were both "way yonder past tired out," as Curly put it, and they wanted, needed, to feel pride in what they had accomplished, but the rangy farmer's parting remark had dampened their spirits.

"He sure must love his wife an awful lot," Jerry said.

"Mr. Carter, you mean?"

"The way he was crying about her, yeah."

"I thought maybe he was crying about the sorry plight he put me and you into." Curly sighed. "But then he comes out with that last proposition. How are you going to handle that little chore, honey britches? It's a long way from that barn loft out to their house. Hell, it's a long way from the loft to the ground."

"What do you mean? It's my job?"

"Well, you'll be the one left to do it. I'm going to start running from it tomorrow. By Halloween, I'll be in Hawayah. Come Christmas, I'll be shaking hands with Santy Claus at the North Pole. Of course, you can come along with me—unless you'd rather stay here and hump that freezer locker again."

"I can be packed to go in fifteen minutes," Jerry said. "What do folks wear in Hawaii?"

Curly gave him a bland glance. "Somebody told me the women don't hardly wear nothing at all. But I wouldn't get my hopes up too high if I was you."

"Well, Merry Christmas anyhow," Jerry said.

CRÈCHE

Rat was the first to speak. As the stars arced toward midnight and the frosty hills around the farm grew ever more quiet, he had felt the words come into him. It was as if there were a frost in him that the words melted just as the sun would warm the hills at daybreak, turning them from silver to gray-green.

Was he always first? It seemed he might be, so wily and clever he was, but none could remember from one Eve to the next. They did not all begin to speak at once and that was a mercy, for such a clamor might have brought the farmer or his boy down to the big shed and then they would have to fall silent, the words shut up inside them and burning to get free.

This time there was no danger. Cora Kirkman, the farmer's wife, was busy within the house, stashing presents under the little spruce and setting all in order for Christmas Day. The farmer, Joe Robert, and his son, Jess, were in the barn on the slope above, watching anxiously. The prized ewe, Marianna, was lambing perilously out of season. They had brought her into one of the stalls and now sat beside her on milking stools. A kerosene lantern with lowered wick hung on a hook from a joist.

So let it be Rat, then, always first to speak. Yet he was cross because he never could say what he meant to say. Perhaps he would like to sing "Ring Out Ye Crystal Spheres" or "At last our bliss Full and perfect is," but his opening phrase now was "A cold night it is tonight." He muttered it softly, and slyly, like the ending of an obscene story, but that was only his usual way of speaking and signified nothing. Yet he was disappointed. To wait all year every year, from one Eve to the next—and then to begin with a banal remark about the weather . . .

His observation did not overwhelm the assemblage. They regarded him gravely and charitably, as befit the season, but he squirmed with embarrassment. Jackson spared him further anxiety by affirming his statement. The horse lifted his noble head and gazed out of the long open shed into the wide midnight. "It is a hard frost," he said. "Come morning, Mr. Kirkman will be glad of a warm kitchen."

That was not quite the right note, either. Maude gently chided her longtime companion. "Let us not speak of morning, Jackson," she said. "Daylight will come all too soon and then—"

A murmur of agreement ran through the others. Come the dawn and the words would fade from them like the shadows that disappeared from the shed's eastern corner with the sunlight. The hours of speaking were all too brief and only the merciful trance of forgetfulness protected them from a full twelvemonth of yearning. But then perhaps they would not yearn for words; perhaps the midnight feast of them sated until the next feast.

Still there lay the most painful dilemma. If one can speak for only a short time on Christmas Eve, is not one obliged to say something of import? Or if wisdom and philosophy are not ready upon the moment, shouldn't one attempt some flight of rhetoric and flourish an apostrophe or two? Perhaps a poem was in order, if one could only recall the stirrings that spring brought within when daisies and buttercups brightened the turf.

When the words returned, there was no rush of babble, but a hesitant beginning not confined to sound. For when the animals could speak, their silence took on different meanings than when they could not, and they all looked at one another in more communicative ways. Jackson and Maude, calm and patient, took cognizance of all the others, as if making a slow inventory. Rat was under the hay trough, nervously nibbling and glancing all about. His usual foe, Sherlock, the farm cat, seemed not to notice his presence, lifting his orange paw to groom behind his ear. But Rat knew the cat had noted him and Sherlock knew he knew. The two milk cows, Pearl, the Jersey, and Daisy, the Guernsey, stood stolidly chewing cud and taking care to appear insouciant. The tumescence of words within was almost familiar to them, it was so much like milk coming down twice a day. Six hens had perched on the rafters, purring endearments to one another, while Champion, the rooster, alert even in the midnight hour, patrolled the straw-strewn ground below. In the ghostly light of frost and stars, his tail flashed darkly. On the long rafter under the south eave, two pigeons moaned in gladness and now and then sparrows swooped through the space, chattering what seemed nonsense. Trixie, the collie, lay with her head on her forepaws, aware of every sound and motion; little escaped Trixie. She could hear the pig, Ernestine, caroling in her pen some twenty yards down the slope and she saw the lantern glow above in the window of the barn, where Marianna suffered the travail of giving birth.

Rat tried again: "It is like waking up after a long sleep."

Trixie said, "But Rat, you know nothing of long sleep. Your naps are brief and tenuous. Jackson and Maude sleep long and now I sleep longer than I used to, as I grow old. All the others sleep in short spurts, as you do."

"Not Ernestine," said Pigeon One. "In her sty, in the cool mud of August, she will sleep for hours and hours."

"And get the good of it," Pigeon Two said. "See how fat she has become. If I ate and slept as she does, I would drop like a stone when I tried to fly."

"So you would not care to be a pig," said Jackson. "Are you grateful to be what you are?"

"I don't know."

"Yes, you are," said Pigeon One. "Anyone would be grateful to be a pigeon. What is better than to have the freedom of the skies, to coo seductively to a mate, to have food in plenty, and to increase our tribe by admirable magnitude?"

"I don't know," said Two. "I think I might wish—"

At this word, all attention turned toward her. To *wish* was a new thought tonight. They never wished except upon the Eve. One can wish only when there are words to describe things that do not exist. Two could not exist except as a pigeon; to wish to be something else was to describe something that did not exist.

She fell silent, abashed by the pressure of the gazes.

"Please continue," said Jackson, but Two had to be coaxed.

"Well—"

"Yes?"

"Sometimes I wish I had a name," said Two.

"A name?" said One, startled.

A sparrow flew by, chirping an opinion: "Name. Nasty burdensome thing, a name." Another perched nearby: "No name means freedom."

Pigeon One concurred: "A name is a sign of slavish servility. You might as well wear a leg tag as be shackled to a name."

"But look at Jackson and Maude and Trixie and Ernestine and Champion," Two said. "The farmer and his wife take care to feed them regularly and to look after their well-being. Once they confer a name upon you, they will cherish you and treat you with kindly consideration. Is this not so?"

"Not necessarily," said the fourth of the six hens. "The farmer's wife has named me Penny, but she treats me no differently from the rest of our sisterhood."

"She calls me Penny, too," said the second hen. "And me," said the third. "And me," said the first.

The fourth hen replied stiffly, "But that is a case of mistaken identity."

"I have had a name for a long time," Jackson said, "and I do not think it has eased my lot. Plowing, hauling, grazing—these would be my duties whether I went nameless or bore the name of the most regal king."

"If name alleviated one's condition in life, I would be well off," said Trixie, "for I have had three of them. When I was newborn, they called me Fluffball. A young girl thought to make a pleasantry and named me McCollie. When I was traded to Farmer Kirkman, he named me Trixie. None of these was better than any of the others."

"But a name does seem to draw us closer," Maude said.

"To whom?" Jackson asked.

"To humankind."

"I will concede certain advantages in the situation, but perhaps we ought to ask ourselves, my dear, if that is such a great good thing."

"Yes it is," said Daisy, the Guernsey.

"Oh my yes," said Pearl, the Jersey.

"But all of you who make this claim have a vested interest," Rat observed.

"I should not care for the farmer to give me a name. It is not healthy for us to become too familiar with each other."

Pigeon Two, softly, wistfully: "I was only wishing."

"It makes a difference," said the rooster. "Yessiree, an important difference. Now you take me. For good and solid reasons, my name is Champion. All of you applaud my name because you see what I am. But I knew a fellow named Sullivan once and a mighty fine cock he was. He kept his hens in line, yessiree he did. He held at bay the weasel, the serpent, the fox, and every sort of marauder. He would fly at them like a hurricane. But then the farmer's wife took an affectionate fancy to him and began to call him Monsieur Prissy because of a certain style he had developed in striding his patrol. Well, sir, it ruined him; it did indeed. He became finicky about his grain and he started to show favoritism to some few of his hens. He was taking more pride in appearance than in prowess. Then one darkly overcast afternoon a chicken hawk swooped down and, disdaining the fatter, easier prizes, took off this highly conspicuous rooster. If he'd still been called Sullivan, it never would have happened. Never would have happened."

"That's a trap I could never fall into," said Rat. "A name is a sign of bondage. I demand my freedom. Like our friends, the pigeons, I can forage everywhere. The granary of the Earth is open to me. I can range across the total globe without a servile moment."

Then Maude, in a cool tone: "So may we inquire why you hang about this shed and the barn and Ernestine's sty? If the world is open to you, why are you so reluctant to explore it?"

"My dear," Jackson said, "it may be that Rat vaunts himself too gaudily. Perhaps he is not so adept at living independent of mankind as he supposes. It is not easy to survive without the humans."

"We could never do it," said Pearl, the Jersey.

"Oh no, not at all," said Daisy, the Guernsey.

"I believe I have it within me," said Rat, but his tone was meekened now.

"You speak," Trixie said, "as if there were some shame in being closely attached to human beings. But I know them better than do any of you. They have their faults—who does not? But in the main they are a beneficial and beneficent species. Anyone who comes to know them well may learn to think of them as the paragon of animals."

"There is matter for debate in what you say," said the cat, Sherlock. "In fact, there is much to dispute. Are all of us here not perfect in our own ways? Do we not know that we are perfect? I speak of us now as different species and not as separate individuals. Who among us would admit to belonging to an inferior species? And yet man admits his imperfections. He is remorseful about them and prays to have them removed. I would not name man Paragon."

"It is man's modesty that causes him to be ashamed," Trixie said, but the company burst into helpless laughter at this and she took umbrage and rose and turned around three times before lying down again. This was her way of showing displeasure.

They fell silent for a little space and heard Ernestine down in her sty as she lifted her snout starward and sang in an impure but affecting contralto:

"Laetabundus
Exsultet fidelis chorus,
Alleluia."

"That is a happy strain," Jackson said. "Has Ernestine been sampling a wassail bowl?"

Rat said, "From the smell of her slops when I visited earlier, I gathered that Farmer Kirkman emptied into her trough the leftover mash from the home brew he was fermenting."

"Oh my," said Daisy. "I hope her singing does not distress Marianna."

"Oh my word," said Pearl. "I should say. It is no easy job giving birth—especially out of season."

As if to confirm Rat's hypothesis, Ernestine broke into a lusty new carol:

"Bryng us in good ale, and bryng us in good ale!
For our blyssyd lady sak, bryng us in good ale!"

They all tittered, picturing Ernestine down the slope, swilling and singing, making herself merry in the frosty night.

"We giggle," said Sherlock, "but let us consider whether Ernestine does not have a concept superior to ours. All year long we are wordless. Then on the Eve, when words are given, we only debate. Soon we will dispute. Maybe we will squabble. Is it not a higher exercise of speech to sing songs of praise and gratitude and jubilation? Why do we not follow her excelling example?"

"That is exactly what I tried to do at the beginning," Rat said. "I had it in mind to say, 'This is the Month, and this the happy morn Wherein the Son of Heav'n's Eternal King, Of wedded Maid, and Virgin Mother born, Our great redemption from above did bring.' But I could not say these things. They were reluctant to emerge from me. So I made a lame comment about the weather. I was half-ashamed of myself at that moment—and yet I also was not. Can you understand my state of mind?"

"Well, sir," Champion said, "I might suggest that you lacked proper fuel with which to ignite your language. If you had taken a nip or two—nay, I say even a swallow three times—from Ernestine's spiritous aliment, these high-minded phrases would have issued with all address, yessiree. I wouldn't mind a beakerful myself and that is the truth."

"It is not entirely the effects of the mash," Jackson said. "If the heart of our friend were not already full to brimming over, she could not sing so feelingly had she drunk a lake of beer. It is the season, the night, and the hour to carol. It is the one way that we who are not human can pray."

"Now what do you mean by that?" Trixie asked. She was suspicious that her friends here would be all night denigrating and insulting the human species.

"Only that it is not given to us to pray with words," he replied.

"I think, my dear, that you are correct in what you say," Maude affirmed. "During these hours I have all the words I need or desire, yet I feel no impulse to employ them in prayer. I might sing—though not as enthusiastically as Ernestine—but I could not pray in the manner of the humans."

"Are you certain that she is praying?" asked Pigeon One.

"It doesn't sound like the most reverent of orisons," said Pigeon Two.

They listened as Ernestine grew boisterous:

"Bryng us in no browne bred, for that is made of brane,
Nor bryng us in no whyt bred, for therein is no game.
But bryng us in good ale."

"My gracious!" said Pearl.

"Gracious mercy!" Daisy said. "Imagine a lamb being born and hearing this noise as the first it hears in the world." She gave a worried glance toward the barn.

"It might be fitting," Champion said. "Yessiree. Welcome to our earth!"

"We cannot pray with words because we pray with what we are," Jackson explained. "Simply by being ourselves, we express all that we know and feel. We are compact of prayer from muzzle to hindquarters, from beak to tail feathers, from snout to hoof. We need no words."

A sparrow flew in to perch on a rafter and to repeat Jackson's phrase: "Need no, need no, need no." It darted off and was replaced by another, which cocked its head and said, "Words, words, words. Words." Then it, too, flew out into the darkness as if glorying in the nighttime, to which it was unaccustomed. This one night of the year it ignored the shelter of the low-hanging branches of evergreens and slid hither and yon under the naked stars in untrammeled joy.

The cat wondered then what was the point of this so-called benison. "If we cannot use words to pray, what good are they? It is like being given the power of sight and then denied the opportunity of looking upon creation. For we ordinarily express ourselves to our satisfaction, only we do not pray in formal fashion. This is something we ought to be able to do when the gift of words is with us."

"I don't know that we express ourselves so wonderfully well," Maude said. "Time and again I tell the farmer that I am thirsty or overweary or that some strap or buckle galls me. Yet he does not understand. I cannot believe he would ignore me purposely, but I can switch my tail, flap my ears, and shiver my withers a thousand times and he receives no message."

"Oh indeed," Pearl said. "He thinks of the tail as no more than a clumsy flyswatter. He has no concept of it as communication."

"How true!" said Daisy. "He even mistakes the purposes of a kick. He will ascribe it to malice rather than desperation or physical shock. Sometime let his spouse grasp his warm privates with an icy hand and see how he reacts. He will kick like a toad in the maw of a blacksnake. If he had a tail, he would whip it about her three times from the dreadful thrill of that touch."

"I despair of ever making him understand," Jackson said, "and I am not one who gives in to despair."

"Well, I have no difficulty, nosiree bob, none at all," said Champion. "When I bugle reveille, it takes but a short while for the house to rise from slumber, light its lights, and punch up its fires. They comprehend me right enough, yessiree. It is a matter of assertiveness, you understand. It is a matter of being fitted to the mantle of authority."

"But have they never risen at night and lit up the windows without your summons?" asked Sherlock. "And have they never slept through your reveille and risen late?"

Champion retorted, "Rarely."

"It is not wise to disregard the voice of Champion," said one of the Pennies, and the others purled agreement.

"I hate it when they oversleep," Pearl said. "Don't you, Daisy?"

"Oh yes," she said. "That is uncomfortable."

"I have never encountered the least problem," Trixie declared. "I understand their every thought, sometimes even before they recognize them themselves."

"And do they understand completely?" asked the cat.

"Yes," Trixie said.

"Truly now? Each and every time?"

"Yes."

"Really?"

"Well—"

"Well?"

"Maybe not every time."

Sherlock persisted. "So what you said a moment ago is not the truth?"

"Very close to the absolute truth."

"Close, perhaps, but still a fib?"

"A fib!" All the assembly, feather and fur and hide, shouted the word in unison. "Hooray, hurrah! A fib, a fib, a fib!"

"Congratulations!" cried Rat.

"That's the spirit, yessiree!" Champion said.

Jackson spoke gravely: "We must all commend you, Trixie, on your swift mastery of language. Your development has sped far ahead of ours. The pigeon managed to describe something that did not exist when she wished for a name. But you actually denied something that did exist, the fact of a misunderstanding. We all take pride in your accomplishment. Your intelligence must far outshine ours or you could not take such a giant step in so brief a space."

But Sherlock suggested another interpretation: "Perhaps it is Trixie's close attachment to humans that enables her to leap so suddenly to prevarication."

"Perhaps," said Jackson, "but, leaving aside the question of ontogeny, we must consider the range of possibilities she has opened. A fib is but a beginning. We may all be able to progress to the full-fledged lie. The lie direct first, then the bald-faced lie, the black lie, and maybe even the filthy lie—all these may follow. Perhaps by the time morning arrives, we shall have attained to fiction. Wouldn't it be grand if we could invent parables and fables and long, doleful ballads of miserable love and bloody murder? Wouldn't it be marvelous if one of us could tell a story?"

The sudden glimpse of these delicious vistas struck them all dumb for a space. Their silence was blowzily violated by the unsteady voice of Ernestine:

"Make we myrie bothe more and lasse
For now is the tyme of Cristemasse."

Again they all glanced toward the barn, but the lamp glow was undisturbed in the dingy little window.

"I believe I could tell a story," Champion said. "I could make up something about this same Sullivan, the rooster of whom I told you before. Let me see if I cannot." He held himself in such a tense posture, one leg off the ground, that it was easy to know he was concentrating with all his strength. "One day, as Sullivan was patrolling the barnyard, keeping close watch for anything that might betide a danger to his hens, a shadow covered him up. Then it covered the hens, as well. And then—then it covered the whole barnyard. Huge this shadow was, and dark—yessiree, huge and dark indeed." He paused as if for dramatic effect.

The third hen could bear the suspense no longer. "What was it?" she demanded anxiously. "What could cast a shadow so big and dark?"

"It was . . . It was . . ." Champion's voice diminished in volume almost to a whisper. "It was a cloud that drifted across the sun."

Now the silence of the animals told of their deep disappointment. Jackson dispatched the awkward moment diplomatically: "That is not so bad for a first trial. It must be very hard to invent a story and tell it. Human beings do it so often that it looks simple. But it must be a difficult art for them to master."

"I am none so certain they do master it," Trixie said. "I often visit Mr. Kirkman's home and see the bathroom and kitchen and bedrooms, all the rooms. The kitchen is stocked with food; the shelves are filled with cans and jars of tomatoes and corn, oil and beans, bread and fruit—everything to eat. But there is another room where the shelves are stocked with stories. They come already prepared, just like the foodstuffs in jars. They take down these objects called 'books' and stare into them for long periods and then they can tell stories to one another. They don't have to invent stories; stories come to them in containers."

"All right," said Sherlock, "but where do the containers come from? Doesn't someone have to invent the stories that go into them?"

Trixie betrayed her puzzlement: "I never thought about it much. I had a vague feeling that stories were produced by the earth from the earth, like potatoes and okra and squash."

"Perhaps there is a Story Tree on one of the farms nearby," Maude said. "Perhaps the stories are plucked from it like apples and stored in those *books*."

"There is no tree like that anywhere near," said Pigeon One. "We would see it flying over."

Said Two, "We have seen nothing like that."

A sparrow fluttered to the earth floor and pecked among the straws. "No such tree. No such."

"I wonder if it might be possible to construct a story if we all worked together," Jackson said. "Maybe stories are made by communal, rather than by individual, effort. Would we be willing to try? Each of us must contribute something. That would be the first rule."

"What are the other rules?" asked Sherlock.

"I don't know yet. We shall learn them as we go along."

"Hardly a proper way to do things, sir," proclaimed Champion. "Not proper procedure, nosiree."

"If we knew how to begin, that would be a great help," Maude said.

"I can start us," Trixie offered. "I know how stories begin. Many times I have heard Mrs. Kirkman tell stories to her little girl, Mitzi. They always begin in the same way—like this: 'Once upon a time in a kingdom far away . . .' "

"What kind of time is 'once upon'?" demanded Sherlock.

"What is a kingdom?" asked Rat.

"I don't know about the kind of time," Jackson said, "but a kingdom is a domain under the sway of a single ruler whose will is law and whom all subjects must obey."

"I will not inquire what a domain is," Rat said. "I shall go ahead and begin the story. All of you must catch up with it as you can and offer me aid as I go along. Keep your wits nimble. I shall go at a great rate of speed and recount a story of large proportion."

"Let us hear," said Jackson.

"Once upon a time," he said in an unaccustomed formal voice, "in a kingdom far away lived a rat. He was king of this kingdom and all its subjects were under his sway and obedient to his will. They had to do his bidding because he was king of this kingdom. So he ruled them and they were under his sway. And that is the story of the great King Rat."

Another bewildered silence fell and again it was enlivened by the songful Ernestine trolling an ancient verse:

"Nowel, el, el, el, el, el!
I thonke it a mayden everdel."

"I am not able to tell a story," Maude said. "I am too concerned about Marianna. She has been in labor for a long time and must be suffering terribly. I wish we could do something for her."

"That is a highly honorable wish," Jackson said. "It seems to me that most wishes are selfish. Since we have but little time left in which we can make wishes, why don't we all wish in concert for Marianna to deliver safely and without undue pain?"

All the others showed that they assented to this suggestion and again they fell silent for a space. This time, Ernestine did not interrupt it, and some surmised that she had decided to indulge in a light but refreshing doze.

"Very well," Rat said, "but I don't see what was wrong with my story. I took pains to follow the traditional beginning and the concept of a rat as king is not only novel but also a practical plan for better government."

"Well, sir," said Champion, "your narrative lacked interest. I don't mind telling you that right off. It lacked variety of incident; in fact, it lacked any incident at all. And it contained no rooster. That was its most abysmal deficiency."

"And no cows," Daisy said sadly.

"Not one," said Pearl.

"It was not plausible," Sherlock said. "If that kingdom counted any cats as citizens, they would not be ruled by this King Rat. There would be revolution upon the instant."

"There are no cats in that kingdom," Rat said. "It is a utopia."

"Utopias are ruled by great handsome bulls," Pearl said.

"And all the cows are queens," added Daisy.

"Kingdoms are ruled by those who know how to claim authority and to assert it," Champion said. "That means roosters. A common expression like *cock of the walk* does not appear out of thin air. It comes from communal observation and consent. Your rooster is your only natural ruler. I might almost say it is the will of heaven. Yessiree, that's it. The rooster rules by divine right."

All the hens assented. "How true!" they cried. "Well spoken! Incontrovertible! No doubt about it! Divine right!"

Four sparrows zipped in and fluttered in a circle. "Silly silly silly silly," they chanted, and then flew away again. Their shapes were satin shuttlecocks against the graying sky.

Jackson said, "It seems but reasonable that the most reasonable of creatures should rule. To be able to rule requires nicety and firmness of judgment, nobility of presence, patience and calm self-control, and dignity of bearing. All these are ascertainable qualities of the equine race. If this kingdom is not to be a dark, cruel tyranny, it will fall under the command of a horse. I hope that you will concur with my thought, dear Maude."

"It is the wisest of wise thoughts," she said.

"Oh, who wants to be a king anyhow?" said Pigeon Two. "Not I."

"Nor I," said One. "To perch all day on a throne and never to fly. No cockroaches to eat, but only unhealthy sweetmeats. How dreary."

"I know the stories," Trixie said. "I have heard them at Mitzi's bedside many times. The king of this far country is always a human, an old man with three sons, of whom the youngest is the cleverest. Man is the paragon and must be king. Your story, Rat, is an abject failure."

"Oh, what do you know about it?" Rat squealed. "None of you could even make up a story. Not one. You're all a bunch of . . . of . . . of . . ." He was enraged. The word he wanted was not handy. Maybe it was not within him now.

"Miscreants?" Jackson suggested in a kindly tone.

"Dimwits?" said Maude.

"Ignoramuses?" said Sherlock, trying to be helpful.

"I would take it ill, sir, if you were to say cowards," boomed Champion.

"Stupidheads?" the pigeons suggested.

"Pedants?" murmured Trixie.

"No, no, no!" Rat was beside himself. "You can't even get the right word. You're all a bunch of . . . of . . ." At last he found it. "You're all a bunch of goddamned literary critics!"

This stupendous insult should have exploded an Armageddon of enraged clamor, but instead the animals fell silent—all except Ernestine, who, from her sty, loosed a volley of snores tremendous in decibel and epical in magnitude. This sound seemed to escape the notice of Farmer Kirkman and his boy, Jess. They had just stepped out of the milking room of the barn and latched the door behind them. Mr. Kirkman dug a cigarette package from his plaid woolen jacket, lit a Chesterfield with a kitchen match on his thumbnail, and blew a smoke plume with an attitude of victory. Jess lifted the kerosene lamp, raised the shell, and blew out the flame. He grinned at his father. Then they went down toward the farmhouse together.

The hills around had lost some of their silver tinge and were turning gray-green toward the dawning east.

"I believe the lamb is born," Rat said, and these were the last words any of them said for a very long time.

TRADITION

Curly was a good twenty years Jerry's senior and treated his young co-worker as a pupil. It was a viable arrangement: Jerry was from the eastern part of North Carolina and as yet unused to some of the ways of the mountains. He was a good-sized, stout lad, ready and willing to lug and grunt, pick up and haul furniture alongside Curly for the Mill Furniture Co. in Tipton. But Curly felt the young man needed instruction now and again—and so did Jerry.

Curly had tried to explain the custom. "I reckon it's what some people call tradition," he'd said. "Somehow it just don't seem like the Christmastime season unless you go out in the woods and shoot some animal that hadn't got the least idy of doing you any harm. Some people will hunt in the fields for rabbits, but they don't say they're aching to send cute little bunnies to hell. They say they've got to work their dogs to keep them in tone. That way, it sounds like they're doing something useful and necessary. Some people will go squirrel hunting about this time, but the big thing is to go drop a deer, which they think is all right because they're so big."

"How do you mean?" Jerry asked.

"Well, a squirrel is so little, it ain't hardly worth hunting down. You could just set out rat traps, if bagging them was the main thing. And a rabbit is a little varmint, too. But a deer is as big as you are, or bigger, so it is kind of like it's a fair fight."

"Except that the deer doesn't have a gun."

Curly eyed him curiously. "Why would you want to give a deer a rifle? He couldn't hit the side of a hill."

The point was, he went on to explain, that the Mill Co. offered up a cabin and firewood every year the weekend after Thanksgiving for employees who wanted to round up a hunting party. The cabin stood on thickly wooded ridge land over by Arden Creek. It had belonged to old Mr. Henry Mill before he died, and he passed it down to his son, Henry. Old Mr. Henry used to go to the cabin with the men, the "boys" who worked for him, every year; it was like a religious retreat. He never missed a turn until his heart weakened so bad. Henry junior didn't much care for hunting—or maybe his wife didn't care for him to care for it—but he kept the tradition going by allowing employees and their friends and family members the freedom of those woods and the hospitality of that tight little cabin sitting dark-weathered in a clearing bordered by some of the tallest blackberry thicket you'd ever see.

So this year he, Curly, was going with his cousin Marvin Fletcher and some other men. He didn't know all of them, he said, but his thirteen-year-old son, Jules, would not be one of the party. "Jules, he had been nagging at me to go for maybe five year, so I told him he could go next year, which is just what I told him this time last year. But this time he forgot. If he'd had presence of mind to recall what I said, he could've come along, because I'd have to keep my word. I'm trying to get that boy to pay proper attention."

"Have you been out hunting with him yet?" Jerry asked.

"Twicet. One time we went looking for groundhog, but they heard us coming. Might've smelled us, what with them high-top tennis shoes he wears. I make him hose them off about every six months, but that might could cause them to smell worse."

"So, what's the deal with this hunting party?"

"I was wondering if you might like to go along. That would be three, and Woody Johnson wants to go, and I expect old man Anson will hook up with Woody. The old man is pretty spry for going on, I don't know, eighty years maybe. Bud Jason was all set to go and then his mama took ill and had to lie up in the hospital, so him and Maybellene will be looking after her. Bud told this other feller, Max something—I disremember—he could go in his place if the rest of us didn't mind, and I told Bud we didn't. Rackster, that's who. Max Rackster. Bud says he's okay, a little rough-edged, kind of. A war vet, and he served in the South Pacific, so he ought to be all right. If you was to come along, that would be six, and six bunks is all there is in the cabin."

"I don't know," Jerry said. "I don't know about the kind of hunting you do up here in the mountains. And I don't have a rifle. I left my thirty-thirty Marlin back home."

"I can loan you a Winchester I've got extra," Curly said. "It's still pretty new. I traded for it and then found out I liked my old one better and had to buy back at a loss. As for hunting deer, it's about the same everywhere, ain't it?"

"Down east, we use dogs," Jerry said. "I haven't heard anybody talking about their deer hounds since I've been up here."

"Dogs? You don't want to see no dogs around when you're hunting. The deer would scatter into the woods where the daylight don't reach."

Jerry explained that the coastal swamps were crisscrossed with broad paths cut out of the vegetation. The dogs flushed the deer and chased them in the open paths, where the hunters could get clear shots.

Curly shook his head. "No sir, no dogs. They wouldn't do nothing but scare them away. On the south side, the Mill Co. property borders on the national forest, and it ain't legal to hunt in there. You can't go in with a gun unless a wounded deer runs in and you have to chase him down and finish off his suffering. No sir, no dogs. We hunt from blinds built up in trees."

"Like tree houses that kids build?"

"Kinda like, kinda not."

Jerry pictured a square structure with unpainted walls, a cocked red tin roof, and cutout windows with doors that could be closed against the prying gaze of adults. Jerry had never seen such an all-American fantasy edifice, but in the back of his imagination it was complete, lodged in the hospitable forks of an elm like a kite that had searched out the site to land in.

"Sure," he said. "I'd like to come along. What do I have to bring?"

"Something warm to wear," Curly said. "Make certain about that. Arden ridgetop can get as cold as a well digger's ass this time of year. And you being the youngest means you'll get stuck washing most of the dishes—unless you can cook. If you're willing to cook, somebody else gets stuck with them. Somebody else that ain't me, I mean."

"I'm not much of a cook."

"My boy Jules tries his hand at it. He makes a biscuit so dry, you sneeze just to look at it. I think he must put alum in them."

"They're probably better than what I'd make," Jerry said.

"I reckon it's settled, then," Curly said. "We'll head out to the woods Friday evening after work. Just bring your stuff with you to Mill Co. and we'll leave from there and have supper at the cabin. How do you like pork and beans for supper?"

"Just fine."

"How you like 'em for breakfast and dinner and dessert?"

"Just fine."

"Then you're the man to go with us. We thought about calling ourselves the Pork and Beaners, but that got voted down and we decided on something different."

"What was that?"

"Picky Eaters," Curly said. "The idy was, if we can pick it up, we can probably eat it."

"All right," Jerry said.

But the food turned out better than threatened. In fact, except for a half-gallon of coffee that Curly boiled in a gray spatterware pot, this first meal was only warmed up in the oven of the big Rome wood range that, creaking with unaccustomed heat, occupied almost half of the kitchen space. Wives had packed hampers and paper pokes, from which tumbled out in colorful confusion green beans, pickled beets, squares of the thin, crunchy corn bread favored in the mountains, mason jars of iced tea, deviled eggs, slices of country ham pink and salty, tomatoes stewed with onions and okra, and gobbets of fried chicken.

These foodstuffs were laid out in generous array on the checkered oilcloth of the table and the husbands took pains to identify which dishes Elsie and Lilymae and Dinah had contributed. They spoke teasingly of "home cooking," and the weak double entendre was supposed to be lost on Jerry.

There was whiskey too, both bonded and corn, and it was taken in small doses before and during the meal as they carried paper plates around the table, loading them judiciously before going into the other room.

A fire of oak logs green and seasoned snapped and leapt on the river-rock hearth. A couple of sagging cane-bottomed chairs were placed about and the younger men occupied these or sat on the lower racks of the three bunk beds set against the walls. A tall, uncushioned rocking chair was stationed by the hearth and old man Anson took possession with the aplomb of a Baptist minister accepting a bountiful collection plate. He was tall, silver-haired, and quietly assured in manner.

For a while they were silent, occupied with food and with taking stock of one another. They seemed to make up a group congenial enough. Most of them were already friends or fairly close acquaintances. The odd man was Max Rackster, Bud Jason's replacement. He was a skinny, nervous man with thinning red hair and restless hands. His green eyes were over-bright from whiskey and he ate only half of what he had plated before taking it back to the kitchen and raking it into the slop jar. He returned with his tumbler of bourbon and springwater already refilled.

He held the glass aloft in general salute. "Tell you what, boys," he said. "Any feller that don't like whiskey is plumb crazy."

They regarded him in silence for a longish time. Finally, Curly spoke up: "Then I reckon I'm about the sanest man you ever seen." He nodded at Rackster and raised his glass but then set it back down on the floor by his chair without sipping.

His remark made no impression upon Rackster. "It lifts the spirits, good whiskey does," he said. "I get right gloomy sometimes, thinking about things. I was overseas in the big war and I seen many a good man took down. I get to where it preys on my mind."

The others ate steadily, chewing more slowly now, giving Rackster time to air his case. Jerry could feel a new wariness coming over them. They were not judging Rackster, only keeping watch.

But now he fell silent and stared into the fire, taking quick, short sips from his tumbler.

The old man broke the silence. He laid his paper plate on the floor, clean except for a thighbone, took up his quart mason jar of moon, and washed out his mouth with a long draft. When he spoke, his voice was a hoarse whisper that seemed precisely to suit his long-boned frame and white hair, tinged gold with the firelight. “Best not to dwell,” he said.

Rackster roused. “What’s that you say, old-timer?”

Anson put down his jar, wrapped the arm ends of the rocking chair with long thin fingers, and rested a sorrowful gaze on Rackster. He was silent and did not smile.

“Come again?” Rackster said. “I don’t think I quite heard you.”

Curly and Woody Johnson rose to take their soiled plates back to the kitchen. On his way, Curly knelt to remove Anson’s plate, too. To Jerry, their movements seemed a signal, so he rose from where he sat on a lower bunk and went back with them. They raked their leavings into a tall earthenware jar and tossed the paper into a red plastic tub. Although they did not speak, it seemed that they were passing a message.

“What do we do with the garbage?” asked Jerry.

“Burn these plates in the stove,” Curly said, “and tomorrow we’ll dig a pit and bury the garbage, what of it we can’t burn. Are you a pretty good hand with a shovel?”

“I guess.”

“Have to dig down about thirty foot or the bears will come and unearth their breakfast.”

“I try to dig a thirty-foot pit every day,” Jerry said.

“Must be a lot of disappointed bears out your way.”

“They’ll get over it,” Jerry said. “Anyhow, I think you’re funning me about digging a pit.”

When they returned to the others, Rackster was making a point, gesticulating, leaning forward in his rickety straight chair. “I ain’t done a whole lot of deer hunting,” he admitted. “Duck hunting’s my usual. How you fellers go at it don’t make sense to me. You climb up in trees, in them blinds, as you call ’em, and you set there and hope for a clear shot. Seems like you could grow a long white beard just waiting like that. I’d think about getting down on the ground with them. Stalking, the way the Cherokees used to do, back in the day. It don’t feel right, setting in a tree like a owl. That’s sniper tactics.”

Woody Johnson spoke up, his words coming slow. Jerry had noticed that he took his time with everything; he had looked carefully around the cabin after he had arrived in his old Chevy pickup, had closely examined the food before taking a modest plate of corn bread, beans, and stewed tomatoes. "It might be," he said, "that some old-timey Indian might sneak up on a buck, but I'm satisfied I ain't the man to do it." His voice was thick and gave his words a pleasant furry sound.

Curly took his seat. "I ain't that soft-footed, neither."

The old man admitted that it was becoming difficult for him to climb up into the blinds. "I ain't as spry and limber as I used to be, but I wouldn't feel right these days about my chances on the ground."

"We wear these here orange patches," Max said. "They ruin the camouflage, but they ought to keep a man safe."

"If they recognize you in time," Curly said. "But they might shoot first and inspect your colors after you've done flew away to heaven."

"These days," Woody said, "a man on the ground is the same as a deer or bear or anything else. You read about it in the papers all the time, how some poor sumbitch was killed by mistake."

"How do you see any better from up in a tree?" Rackster refilled his glass from the pint bottle sitting by his foot and began sipping without visiting the water pail in the kitchen. "Been many a sniper shot a man on his own side. Without field glasses, you don't see no better. I learned it in the war how if you get down low on the ground, you have your man between you and the light."

"You're game hunting now," Curly said. "The man's what you want to keep away from."

"Yeah. I understand that. I seen too many all shot up. Down there in the South Seas, them Japs . . . I reckon you-all know what I'm talking about."

Curly watched Rackster's hands as he hitched his pant knees and cracked his knuckles and brushed back his sparse hair. "Not me," he replied. "I was too young."

Rackster turned to Anson. "Well, I reckon you remember, old-timer. I hear them say you was in that first big un. They say that was kind of a tough go, for its time."

"Many died," the old man said. His voice, though thin, was steady and calm. "Many fell in battle or lingered on to perish later. Many were wounded with injuries too cruel to describe."

"But you remember."

"If ever I remember, it's because I can't help it," he said. "It's not something to dwell on. I try to turn my mind to other scenes of life."

"But sometimes it comes back, I expect."

"Sometimes."

He doesn't need to remember, Jerry thought. He is old and he has done what he had to do and now he wants to taste his moonshine in peace and sit by the fire. He wants to go out tomorrow morning and sit in a tree and maybe bring down a buck and not ever connect that with firing a weapon in wartime.

"Well, I don't have no tales of combat," Curly said. "But I can tell some pretty good fishing yarns."

"What do you mean by that?"

"Nothing, only I've been trout fishing in places a blacksnake couldn't hardly squeeze through and caught me a brown that like to broke my wrist, and one time I hauled a catfish out at Fontana uglier than—"

"Are you saying I'm a liar?"

"A liar?"

"Are you meaning that I didn't fight in combat and see good men die by my side and dodge them Jap snipers?"

"I was talking about catching fish."

"But you was meaning that what I said didn't amount to no more than some big fish tale. Ain't that right?"

"I only say what I got to say. If I want to say something else, I know how to talk plain."

"Let's hear you talk plain, then."

Curly spoke with mild joviality. "Well, the very first thing I want to find out—"

"Yeah, what's that?"

"—is whether Jerry is going to take our garbage out to that big canister at the farther end of the cabin and then lock down the lid so bears and varmints won't be keeping us awake all night. And while he's out, maybe he could bring back a pail of fresh water from the spring where the trail leads off from the back of the cabin up the hill a little ways. I mentioned it to him before, but he ain't made a lick at it yet."

Jerry stood up. "Sure thing." He stepped into the kitchen, hefted up the slop jar and dumped their leavings into three plies of grocery bags, folded over the top and creased it down. Then he took up the galvanized pail that was a quarter full and went outside. As he poured out the stale water, he could hear the sounds from the front room but couldn't make out what the men were saying. They spoke less loudly than before.

He hadn't thought to slip on his big woolen jacket, and the cold breeze went through his shirt and undershirt as quick as sunlight through a glass curtain. He didn't mind; he was glad to be out of the cabin, where Rackster's presence, and his whiskey breath, had stuffed the space. He felt lighter, almost like a throbbing headache had desisted. He found the garbage canister and dropped the bags in and locked down the big hasp and struck the bolt through. Then he started along the indistinct trail bordered by dead weeds and littered with damp, silent leaves, heading toward the spring.

About thirty yards from the cabin, he found a small basin-shaped pool with two low banks on the sides and a jumble of quartz rocks at the head, down whose fissures the water purled. Someone had cleaned the surface; wet clumps of leaves dotted the edges. A few new ones had drifted in, partially submerged in skim ice. He knelt and parted the ice with a forefinger and leaned and sipped cautiously. It was as cold as frozen steel and pained his front teeth, but it made him feel better, cleaner. Then he dipped the pail in, fending back the oak leaves drifting toward its mouth.

When he stood up, he noticed that the woods, which had been so silent when he exited from the cabin, now whispered with breeze and rattled softly and clicked as twigs and bare branches touched. He thought he heard a rustling amid the duff, as of some nocturnal animal snuffling about, but decided it was an illusion. His presence would make every four-foot go silent.

Now the cold night, which the far, sharp stars made seem even colder, caused him to try to hurry along, but the full pail slowed his pace and he changed it from hand to hand three times before he got back to the porch. Before the door he paused. He had expected to hear voices muffled by the door planking, but the only sounds were those of the restless trees.

When he slid back the bolt and stepped inside, the scene was changed. The men were silent and four of them stood around one of the bunks, looking down. They glanced at Jerry, and Curly motioned him through to the kitchen. As he passed the bunk, he saw that Rackster lay there faceup, his eyes closed, his hands crossed on his chest. He set the pail on the shelf by the stove, slid the aluminum dipper into it, and slipped back.

Anson was breathing heavily and his hands were shaking.

"What happened?" Jerry asked.

"Not much," Curly said.

"It might have been my fault," Anson said. His voice was pitched higher than before. "I ain't supposed to get riled up. The doctor says so. That's the first time I've been real mad at a feller in, I guess, twenty years. It might've been all my fault."

Jerry edged over to look at Rackster's sharp-featured face with its few scattered freckles. Was that a reddish lump on the side of his left jaw? His face was turned away, so that it was hard to tell. Rackster's right hand slid off his chest and the back of it thumped on the floor. Curly picked it up and replaced it, as if he were laying a spoon on a place mat.

"Is Mr. Rackster all right?" Jerry asked.

"He's okay," Curly said. "Just overloaded on the John Barleycorn. Taking him a little naptime. He'll be fine in the morning and won't remember."

"I shouldn't have spoke like I did," Anson said.

"You was just reactin'. Ain't that right, Marvin?"

The stocky Marvin grinned, showing white teeth through a neat triangle of black beard. "Nothing to fret about," he said. "Just a difference of opinion."

"Didn't mean nothing, did it?" Curly asked.

"I couldn't even say what it was all about," Woody Johnson offered.

"I still feel like I should've done different," the old man said. He stepped over to take his seat in the rocker, picked up his jar of shine, then looked at it and set it back down.

"I see you got us some water," Curly said.

"In the kitchen," Jerry said.

"Didn't see no wolves or bears or elks outside?"

"Not a one."

"How cold is it?"

"Witch's titty."

Curly made a sound almost like a little girl when he giggled. "How would you know?"

"It's good and warm in here," Woody said. "You might have a real fight on your hands when you try to drag me out in the morning to face that freezing ridgetop. I can get as close to a warm mattress as lichens on a rock."

"There's a big old twelve-point buck up on the mountain anxious for you to come and shoot him," Curly said. "You wouldn't want to disappoint a poor dumb animal."

"I guess not. I'm just saying I'm hard to roust out sometimes. Like when it's eighty below."

"Maybe we better turn in now," Curly said. "We'll get up more willing when we're plumb sick of sleeping."

"Want to keep this fire going through the night?" Marvin asked.

"Are you going to set up tending it?" Curly said.

"I'll sit up with it for a while," Anson said. "I don't sleep as much as I used to anyhow. A good hearth fire like this puts me to thinking about the old times. I don't think about the war. I think about the good times, the corn shuckings and armory dances and all the hellfire preachers we used to pull rusties on. Seems like the good times don't come around as often anymore."

Woody was stripping down to his faded long johns. "I'm going to have me the best time you ever seen right now." Grasping the rail, he vaulted into the top bunk with surprising ease. "If you want to see some champion sleeping, keep an eye on me." He rolled over to face the wall.

"Up or down?" Curly asked Jerry.

"Up, if you don't mind." He didn't feel capable of imitating Woody's spectacular leap and climbed up the slow way.

"I'll request you not to step in my face on the way down," Curly said.

"Well, looks like I'm the one above Rackster," Marvin said. "I'll try not to step on him."

"Better not get him riled," Curly said. "He's a dangerous man."

Marvin gave his cousin a slow look. "You know, I believe he might be."

Jerry had stripped to his T-shirt and boxers and dark blue socks. He squirmed under the threadbare blanket that covered the thin cotton mattress and marveled at the warmth. The fireplace heat rose to the low ceiling and he felt toasty, thinking how only two feet above him the night held the outdoors in a frosty clutch.

Two ceiling joists slanted down on his left side and the wide boards between them were streaked with veins amber and burgundy. Knot eyes interrupted their flow like eyots in rivers, and this image had a soothing effect.

As he felt his eyes closing, he wondered briefly what had happened in the cabin while he was outside. Had there been a struggle in which Rackster had taken the worst of it? Was the bruise on his jaw the result of a blow? Old Anson had apologized, but he wouldn't have been the one to punch the excitable man. It could have been Curly; neither Marvin nor Woody would do such a thing without Curly's approval. But how had it happened? What had Rackster said to them?

Then his eyes closed and he was aware only of the slight sounds of movement below and the pleasantly acrid tang of wood smoke.

At first he did not know what woke him. There was a loud, sharp roar that seemed to go on for a long time, but when he was fully awake, he realized the noise had been the short report of a rifle. He leaned over the edge of the bunk, to see Rackster sitting on the lower bunk across. He was dressed for outdoors, only lacking his cap and heavy jacket. His .30-06 Remington lay across his knees. Six inches in front of him, a long, clean splinter stuck up from the floor.

"Jesus!" Rackster said. He looked up at Jerry. "Jesus Christ! I was only trying to push the safety forward."

Woody came in from the kitchen and looked first to see if Jerry was all right. "What are you shooting at?" he asked Rackster.

"Nothing. I wasn't shooting."

"It wasn't you?"

"I mean I didn't go to. I was only trying to latch the safety. I must've had my finger on the trigger without realizing. This latch is stiff and my finger slipped."

Curly squeezed through from behind Woody. "Is anybody hurt?"

"No," Rackster said. "My finger slipped. But I was careful where I had the gun pointed."

"That's good. We want to be careful, six of us up here shooting." He addressed Jerry. "You're rising kind of late this morning, ain't you? I figured you'd be up first, boiling coffee and frying bacon. But here you are lying in bed like the lord of the manor."

"What time is it?" Jerry curled down from his bed and began to collect his clothing.

"Near about deer time," Curly said. "Skin into the kitchen and eat you some breakfast. You need to stoke up before going out on this freezing morning. You might want to lay a biscuit in your pocket to take."

He dressed quickly in this room that had cooled and smelled now of stale wood smoke and fresh gun smoke. Rackster, he saw, was examining his rifle as if it were some foreign piece of armament he had never seen before. He was carefully not looking at any of the others.

He went to the wood range. The blue coffeepot stood on one of the back eyes and he filled a tin cup on the table and sweetened the coffee with a dribble of molasses. In the biscuit warmer above the stovetop he found a plate already laid out for him with scrambled eggs and a slab of ham and two biscuits. He wolfed it down, standing before the table and trying to see out the window into the darkness. But he could see only his reflection along with that of the oil lamp. He liked the smell of the kerosene and of the smoky stove and of the dead fire in the other room.

On the table was an unfinished meal: half a biscuit, most of a plate of eggs, half a piece of ham. When Curly called for him to clear the table and hustle along, he said, "Somebody hasn't finished eating yet."

"That's Rackster's plate," Curly replied. "He says he don't feel too hungry. You can rake his plate out."

Jerry tidied up hurriedly and went back in and took from beneath the left-hand bunk the rifle Curly had supplied him. It was snuggled in a brown cloth wrapper. He peeled it out, hefted it, slid back the bolt to make sure the chamber was empty, then rewrapped it. He got his jacket from the peg by the fireplace and shrugged into it. From the stack by Curly's bed, he pocketed two boxes of shells.

"Well, I'm ready."

Curly gave him a slow once-over. "You don't look like no mighty Nimrod to me. Where's your cap?"

"Oh yeah." He filched it from under the bunk blanket and jammed it down over his forehead.

"Nah, you wouldn't want to sleep without your hunting cap. Where's your gloves?"

"Don't have any."

"That's too bad. I wish I'd thought. I could've loaned you."

"I'll be all right."

"Hope so."

The others had gathered around the fireplace and Curly spoke to all of them. "I don't know what you boys had in mind, but I been thinking how we might divide up the territory. Woody and Marvin have hunted here before, so they'll know where I'm talking about. I thought Mr. Anson might go with them out to Soapstone in Marvin's pickup. There's three blinds along that trail and Mr. Anson might like to have the first one. It's just a little ways beyond where the trail forks off to go to Windy Top, and there's been good luck there over the years. Then Woody and Marvin can take the other two trees whichever way they like. How's that suit?"

"Like a coat of paint," Marvin said.

"Tickles me plumb to death," said Woody.

"Well then, me and Jerry and Rackster will go out the other ridge along Windy Top. I'll drive the jeep out to the far blind and drop off Rackster and then, coming back, Jerry can get off at the middle and I'll be back at the first blind right there on Hogback. Is that all right?"

Rackster at the far end, Jerry thought. That ought to put us out of his range.

"Okay," Rackster said. "Whatever you fellers want is hunky-dory."

• • •

Curly followed Marvin's pickup up the steep incline to the ridge back, then turned left and followed the ridgeline while Marvin kept on straight toward his turnoff, about a mile farther. The jeep went bumping along on bare rock for the first part, jolting Jerry and Rackster against each other. Then they went through a stand of trees and the night grew darker and the path was silent over damp leaves. When they broke into the open again, the stars were visible, dancing in the sky as the jeep banged the ruts.

When they reached the turnaround, Curly idled the engine and pointed northwest with his thumb. "You see the trail leading off there through them ferns? You go along for about thirty yards and there's a middling-size poplar off to the left with some board ends tacked into the trunk. Just climb right on up into the blind."

Rackster gave a slight shake of his head but then seemed to think again and nodded. "All right." He pulled up the latch of the flimsy door and straddled out, the rifle in his left hand pointed carefully away from the jeep.

They watched him in the headlights until he waded into the patch of ferns that bordered the trail. Then Curly circled and they headed back. "I wish I knew what that feller is thinking."

"What do you mean?"

"It's kind of like he thinks there's still a war on."

"What's that he was saying about how he didn't like sniper tactics?" Jerry asked. "I didn't understand that."

"Me, neither," Curly said. "But when the wind springs up about dawn, he might be glad to have a little bit of shelter by that tree trunk."

The sky was almost beginning to lighten when Curly let Jerry off. He pointed out the trail at the edge of the road, looked him over again, and said, "I sure do wish you had you some gloves."

"I'll be all right."

"Here," he said, handing Jerry a small ball of butcher's twine.

"What's this for?"

"Your tree's about fifty-sixty yards down and the blind is about twenty feet up. Long time back, some well-meaning damfool went and drove two rail spikes about shoulder-high, but from there on up there ain't no hand-hold but only just branches. If I was you, I'd tie this string to the trigger guard and lay that Winchester on the ground and pull it up after I was settled."

"I'll do that."

"And make sure you're aiming at a deer. If it's a moose, you ain't got no license for it. That temporary hunting license we got you don't cover no mooses."

"All right."

"Or no elephants."

"All right."

He scooted out and stood watching as Curly pulled away. The taillights, one red and the other white, with the glass broken, bobbed up and down across the ruts like harbor buoys. Then he turned and found the trail and began walking.

Soon his eyes accustomed to the lack of light and he went along as quietly as he could. The warmth of the jeep heater began to seep away and he knew the cold was going to be bitter. With the rifle tucked under his left arm, he stuffed his balled hands into the pockets of the heavy green jacket and curled his fingers around the box in each pocket. The smells of the cabin went away from his mind and the smells of the outdoors came to him sharply, odors of frosty mud and packed pine needles. In the spaces between drooping boughs, stars leapt like silver fleas.

The angled boards of the blind against the starlight marked out his tree. It was a poplar about three feet in diameter, and he felt the trunk near his shoulder till he located the handhold spike. It tingled his hand and he thought about gloves and swore silently. From his pants pocket he took the ball of string and tied a square knot to the trigger guard, laid the rifle on the ground, unrolled ten arm's lengths of string, and looped the rest of it around his belt.

He dreaded to grasp the spike but finally pulled himself up with his left hand, reached above and caught the other spike, and went up more easily than he had thought he might, bracing with his boot toes against the trunk. He had to lunge to catch the first branch, but after that the ascent was easier and he clambered onto the six six-inch boards that served as a perch. He rested for a moment, pulling the cold air deep into his lungs and trying not to cough from the shock.

He could see pretty well now and peered over the edge as he drew the rifle up, careful not to foul it on the limbs or bang it against the trunk. Now that he was settling in, he wanted to be quiet, as silent as the starlight. This was an important hour. After he chambered six rounds, he slid his hands into the armpits of his jacket.

Jerry had never killed a deer and was curious why he desired to do so. Curly's cousin Marvin spoke of slaughtering a deer as if the deed were of the utmost urgency. "I been deer hunting more times than they's dimples on a corncob," he told them, "and I ain't never done any good. But this time's my chance; I can just feel it coming. And it ain't going to be no pitiful little muley buck neither, but a big proud rack like the one in Glosson's Barber Shop." When Curly asked him if he would let a little velvet horn go by without potting it, Marvin said, "No sir, I'd shoot it, all right, but I'd be mighty downcast." They had laughed; the yearning in Marvin's voice was genuine.

Jerry thought he would pass up a small deer, and even if he didn't fire his rifle, he wouldn't be disappointed with the experience. The company of the older men, the excitement of the woods, the possibility of bringing down a splendid animal—these were sufficient unto themselves. A trophy would be a sort of bonus, a little like receiving a better-than-expected grade on a math test.

The western horizon of purple-black mountaintops was visible now, though the light was behind him, the gray presilver of foredawn. With the light came wind, a gentle breeze that clattered like tinware the remaining leaves in the treetops. Jerry hunched over, pulling into himself like a heron standing at pond edge. The Winchester that lay on the boards before him seemed to have changed color, and he realized that the barrel and shell chamber had frosted over. Just looking at it made his hands tingle and burn, and he wondered if he could make himself take it up and hold it steady if a worthy deer did happen to show up.

Now he heard sounds. The silence that had cloaked the dark hours gave way to minor rustling and skittering in the dead leaves. Squirrels, he thought, or rats. He peered into the dim area below but could see nothing. Then he thought he saw forms moving but knew that he did not, that his too-eager eyes were sending deceptive messages. The drone of an unseeable airplane sounded far and lonesome, and he pictured the passengers in the sky, drinking coffee and reading newspapers, oblivious to Jerry in a poplar tree a cold mile below them, freezing his butt off.

Then the noises grew louder, a slovenly shuffling through the duff and small pebbles in the trail, and he recognized the sounds as does, ambling along and grazing on ferns and the scattered clumps of grass. He fancied he could hear them crunching their greenery but decided that he was again deceived. He looked intently, stabbing his gaze into the deep shadowy light. He could see nothing. He tried to estimate by sound the number of does below. The sounds had gotten louder and less cautious. Must be five at least, he thought, and then thought, No, only two. Might be only one.

As the light strengthened, so did the wind. Small tears formed in the corners of his eyes, but he did not rub them away, ordering himself to make no unnecessary motions. But the cold was painful to his ears and he had tucked his hands back into his armpits and clenched them. Why couldn't he spot the does? They made racket aplenty. Maybe they were just below him at the base of the tree, but he didn't want to lean over to look.

Then there was a silence, almost eerie in its depth and suddenness. Curly had told him that the largest animals were the quietest. "You take an old yeller buck and he's as big as a toolshed and he won't make no more noise than a pissant in a sand pile." They often followed after the does, he said. "It's almost like they're sending them does out to scout the layout. Course, that's a dumb thing to say, but it's what I've fancied sometimes."

Now he thought he heard the stealthiest of sounds just a little west of the tree and maybe pretty close. He leaned forward and strained to see in the slow brightening. It was time to raise his rifle, but he didn't want to pick up the icy-cold thing until he was sure he could make a shot.

Then he knew he saw a movement out there on the inside edge of the intricate laurel thicket that bordered the clearing. He lifted the Winchester first by its maple shoulder stock with thumb and forefinger, then took up the smooth barrel stock. The string was still attached to the trigger guard and he slipped it back out of the way. His thumb and fingers stuck to the metal as he pushed the safety forward, and he took a deep breath to keep from swearing aloud. The frost melted, freeing his flesh. He peered into the thicket again and brought the muzzle up as slowly and steadily as he could.

There, there now.

It was something shapeless moving through the bushes and he couldn't estimate its size. The color was a little brighter than he expected, a light tan rather than dun. He followed its progress with the sight, thinking this deer was too small and that if he shot it, he would be breaking his promise to himself.

He could not wait much longer. Maybe it would step out of the thicket and he would have a beautiful, clean shot. Maybe it would turn back to safety in the mass of laurels. It had to be young and shy, small as it was.

It stopped moving. Had it nosed him in the tree? He had made no giveaway sound. Perhaps it was leery of the open space and would return to cover. He aimed closely at a spot he calculated would be above the left foreleg, between the neck and the shoulder, and began to squeeze.

He would never know why he didn't fire. He would never be able to say why he had eased his finger off the trigger and thumbed the safety on and laid the rifle gently, soundlessly on the boards.

But he knew why he grew dizzy and almost passed out and why sweat stood out on his forehead and on the back of his neck on this biting cold morning as Max Rackster crawled out of the thicket into the clearing, dragging his rifle with his left hand.

My God.

God damn.

Rackster stood up brusquely, jerked his cap with the red earflaps out of his jacket pocket, and jammed it on his head. He looked quickly to left and right, as if checking whether anyone had observed him.

Jerry's gut clenched and unclenched like a stabbed fist and a sour foretaste of vomitus rose in the back of his throat. He could hear himself breathing, hoarse and ragged, and he closed his eyes. When he opened them at last, he saw that Rackster had found the car path leading down along the ridge and was tracing it back to his appointed blind. He had not seen Jerry. He had seen nothing.

In awhile Jerry had steadied enough to desert his perch. He would be unable to hunt anymore today and probably for a long time to come. Not that game would come close to this area where Rackster had been prowling around on the ground like a lost coonhound.

He checked the string knot and unloaded his rifle and lowered it to the ground, got awkwardly over the edge of the platform, and clambered down the tree, eschewing the use of those icicle-cold spikes and dropping free the last five feet. He could lean the Winchester against the tree and not touch it till midmorning, when Curly returned with the jeep. He could blow into his half-closed fists and plunge them into his jacket and keep them there. He could think how lucky Rackster was, how lucky he himself was.

Goddamn lucky. God damn.

He told Curly what had happened only after the story appeared in the newspaper. The *Tipton Enterprise* had printed the account of Max Rackster's death. They placed it in the sports section, along with a short notice in the obituary section, which informed the world that the testy red-haired man was survived by his wife, two daughters, and three grandchildren. Some unlucky son of a bitch named Whitmire had spotted a small deer in the underbrush, had overcome his buck fever and pulled the trigger twice, killing Max Rackster instantly. Memorial donations were to be sent to the Pole Creek Duck Hunters Association.

"It could have been me," Jerry said. "I might have shot him. I came as close as that." He rubbed thumb and forefinger together.

"What stopped you?"

"I don't know."

Curly smiled wryly. "If I didn't know you better, I might say it was plain good sense."

"No. I was that close."

"Main thing is, you didn't shoot him, and he was begging you to do it. So to speak."

"I read about his family. They're going to have a sad Christmas."

"Yeah. Sad. I know for a fact that Bill Whitmire is tore up about it. I tried to telephone him three times, but the line was busy. Everybody knows it was accidental, but that don't help much."

"I know how I'd feel," Jerry said.

"Well, the best part of your Christmas is over, too."

"How come?"

"You done gave yourself the biggest present you'll ever have just by not pulling the trigger. Think about how it would be, every year people singing carols and talking about Santy Claus and you thinking about having kilt a man. Be the worst day of your life every twenty-fifth."

"It wouldn't be much fun."

"So—Merry Christmas!" Curly said. "And Happy New Year, too, if you don't shoot somebody by then."

"It'll be longer than January before I go hunting again," Jerry said. "It'll be a good little while."

"Don't wait too long or there won't be no deer left. No cows, either. These days, they're shooting everything a rifle can point at."

"They might shoot me."

"Not this year," Curly said. "In this county, the limit on human beings is one per season."

"How come?"

Curly squinted through the dusty windshield at the snow-dusted road ahead. The truck heater was not working today and his breath fogged the glass. "They're saving up the rest of us to make war with."

DUET

I know what I'm supposed to be telling you. I'm supposed to say that I wish for peace everywhere in the world and, true enough, I do. But it's not the kind of thing I've got any special right to say.

I'd rather tell you about Caney Barham, if you didn't mind. I know you never heard of him. He was only just a friend of mine that shot himself, but if I was to try to answer your question with the truth, I would be talking about Caney.

Not on purpose. He was never a man to shoot himself on purpose. It was surely an accident, though they had to guess what took place from the way things were left lying. He was found held upright, tangled in a barbwire fence, with his .22 rifle lying on the ground close by and a shell casing in the chamber. His wife, Frances, found him about seven-thirty on a Thursday evening. What evidence there was pointed to this idea of what took place: That sometime between six and seven, right during twilight, Caney had heard his chickens making a racket and got to thinking some varmint had got in to molest them; and then he'd gone into the bedroom and reached the .22 off the wall and loaded and cocked it and then walked around back to the fence that enclosed the chicken pen; and then, figuring to sneak up on the skunk or king snake or whatever it was, he'd tried to clamber through the fence instead of opening the squeaky gate; and then while he was putting his leg through the strands, the rifle went off and killed him instantly. It had to be instantly because the wire hadn't cut him up the way it would if he had been struggling in agony. The bullet went in under his chin and lodged low in the back of his head.

That's what they told me the county coroner said, and I didn't want to know even that much. I never looked on Caney dead; I never asked a question about the way it must have happened. But you never need to ask; there's always somebody glad to talk about those things.

The first I heard about it was that same night around nine. I'd got home from the sawmill and taken a bite of supper and was putting new strings in my guitar when John Newsome called me on the telephone and told me Caney had shot himself in the head and it looked to be an accident.

I said, "Oh Lord. How is he, John?"

And he said, "He's dead, Kermit. I understand he's passed away."

Then in a little while I said "Oh Lord" again, and "Thank you, John, for calling to tell me." Then I hung up the telephone and went back to messing with the guitar, not getting anything done, my fingers only fussing with it. The idea hadn't really got into my mind yet, you see, and then in a minute or two when it did, I pushed the guitar away from me and sat there on the edge of the bed and moaned out loud. "Oh oh oh."

We were buddies since I could remember. We went to grade school together and to high school, and when we finished with that, we went to the sawmill to drive trucks for old man McCracken. We spent a lot of hours together, even though Caney got married and Frances gave him an awful smart little girl, and I never have married. We fished together and hunted together and many a night he'd come to my house or I'd go to his, and we'd sit till the morning hours shone bright, me picking the guitar and Caney singing along, and us laughing at ourselves till we were near sick of it. We never drank heavy, being moderation men, but we'd sip and carry on and the time eased away.

And now he was dead.

I knew he was dead, but it didn't feel to me like he was gone, and to this day it never has and maybe it never will. Really passed away, I mean, so that I knew I'd never see him again. Maybe because he was so brimful and overflowing with high spirits, a lean brown man with deep brown eyes. When he grinned, easy always, his teeth shone white and his brown eyes lit up like a cat's will glow in the dark. There wasn't nobody didn't like him except a few there's no pleasing ever, the kind that will not like anybody. He was full of devilment, and all of it harmless, as far as I could see—practical jokes that wouldn't hurt a housefly and some silly sayings he was attached to. Like when we were driving the two-ton along and would come to a railroad crossing. "There's been one through here," he would say. "I've found his tracks." Or if he saw a fine-looking young girl walking by, he'd say, "There goes Good Morning Judge and Howdy-do Jailhouse." I can see how these might not be the world's funniest jokes, but when Caney said them, the way he would every time without fail, he'd lean back in the truck seat and laugh like he'd thought them up on the spot.

He wasn't anything wild, just anxious for a good time, and he wouldn't mind a little hardship if he thought a good time might come with it.

Like the time he made the dare. It was one Thursday in early June he said, "Now you and me are going camping this weekend, and all we're going to take with us is our sleeping bags and our shotguns and two shells apiece and six kitchen matches. If we're going to eat anything, that's all we'll have to get it with. And now we'll see what kind of stuff we're made of, old son."

That's what we did.

It didn't turn out all that well, to tell the truth, and I don't know but what I might have been ashamed to tell anybody if it hadn't been for Caney. Because he told everybody and laughed at the tale on us as much as if it was on anybody else. We went up to Blue Meadows, off to the right of Clawhammer Gap, and we tramped those weedy, wet fields from five-thirty in the morning till four-thirty in the afternoon and we saw no game, not a particle, unless you count in butterflies and grasshoppers. I got so hungry, I wanted to suck the moss off the rocks. Then about four-thirty a big old ugly crow came flapping overhead and Caney brought up his shotgun and down it came. Then we both looked at the crow. Then he grinned that grin. "Kermit, old buddy," he said, "it's like I foretold. Going to see what kind of stuff we're made of."

We worked down to the last match before we could get a fire going and we plucked that crow without benefit of water and roasted it on sticks. The meat was as tough and black as a patent-leather shoe, and I won't try to tell you how it tasted, except that a steady diet of it is bound to slow down your worst glutton. Like I say, I wouldn't have told, but when we came back down to the valley, Caney could find no peace till everybody he met heard about us eating crow. I mean, eating crow.

So now I sat there on the edge of the bed and moaned. The sorrow had reached down into me. I didn't cry any tears, but I could feel in my chest and stretching up to the back of my throat a hard something like a bar of iron, so that I couldn't swallow or breathe properly. I sat for a long time, rocking back and forth, with my hands twisted in my lap. When you hear somebody close has died, you act on that sentence, even if you know the blackest sorrow is going to come later.

Memories flashed into my head and I didn't try to keep them away, because I knew I couldn't. Caney bent over his reel, cussing a backlash . . . Caney showing off a brand-new hunting jacket he'd saved up for forever . . . Not drawn-out, put-together thoughts, but little bright pictures. Like when he dipped his finger in a bucket of honey we'd brought from a bee tree and held it out for his little girl, Aline, to lick, stretched up on her tiptoes.

After awhile I started to sort out what I was supposed to be doing. What I wanted to do was nothing but go off to the woods and tramp till some of the pain went away. But I knew that wouldn't be right. There would be people who would want to talk to me and I figured I ought to find out if there was anything I could do for Frances. I didn't relish the prospect of talking to a bunch of people I wouldn't much know. A tragedy fills up a house with strangers. Still and all, there was no way out for me.

I put on a clean shirt and stepped up into my old Dodge pickup—"the Nutbucket," Caney used to name it—and drove to the head of Big Sandy Cove, where the neat little Barham house was. Already the driveway and the shoulders of the narrow gravel road were filled with trucks and cars. I had to park a good fifty yards away and walk up, counting six cars I didn't recognize.

Lights were on in every room but one. In the light from the living room windows I saw Preacher Garvin standing in the front yard under the big red maple. He was wearing a white shirt and tie and he'd had to come a pretty far piece, so I supposed he'd heard about Caney before I did. When I came trudging by, he stopped me.

"Is that you, Kermit Wilson?"

"It's me, Preacher."

"Come here, son, a minute."

I went and he put his hand on my shoulder and struck up talking in a hushy voice. He had chewing gum in his mouth, and there's nothing strange about that, but it hit me odd right then, the way piddling things will do in such a time, and I kept staring at the way his mouth worked and not much attending what he said. Then I pieced it out that he was telling me the story of what had happened, all the way from the rifle on the bedroom wall to the arrival of the sheriff, who had to come out to any gunshot wound, and then the one doctor in our county, who was also the coroner. Then he told me about having to send a car over to Caney Creek to tell his mother because she didn't have a telephone, and I hadn't recollected till now that Caney had been named after the place he was born and how he used to say jokes about that, too.

Then Preacher Garvin took his hat off and stood back and gave me that straight-on look that ministers have got down pat. "You boys were pretty close, weren't you?"

"Yes, sir," I said. "We were close."

"An awful shame," he said. "Young man like Caney, all his life ahead of him."

"Yes, sir."

"In the midst of life, we are in death."

And what can you say to that? I know it's the way preachers have to talk, but I never know how to act when they do. So I just shook his hand and walked on up into the house.

The living room was crowded but quiet. It was mostly women in there, the elder women who always come when somebody is taken, sitting without moving except now and again to pull their shawls tighter around their shoulders, though the room was boiling already. The three men present looked mighty uncomfortable, and I nodded to them. I didn't see Frances; one of the ladies told me she was lying down in the back bedroom, that the doctor had given her a sedative. The little girl, Aline, had been sent to her aunt Margaret's house down in Little Sandy and would be staying there till the funeral on Saturday. I started to ask how come they knew so soon the time of the funeral, but didn't. They'd been through this so many times, they knew everything needful to know.

Aunt Prudie Swann asked me if I wanted anything to eat, but I reckoned not. “You could drink some fresh coffee, then, couldn’t you?”

But I wasn’t going to let her make me take anything. “No, ma’am,” I said. “It wouldn’t set well.”

I stepped out the door onto the porch and stood there in the shadow, breathing deep. The living room had nigh overpowered me with the worn-down hooked rug and the family pictures on the end tables and the blue-and-yellow picture of Jesus on the wall and the old record player in the corner that would sometimes go and sometimes wouldn’t. Too many nights Caney and I had talked and sung in that room, and the hard feeling in my chest grew harder, and I had to get out.

I stood in a patch of darkness and lit a Camel and pulled at it and realized that this was the first cigarette in a long time that wasn’t a habit only, but a comfort. I tried to think what worldly good I was doing here, with Frances and Aline not around, nor anybody else that Caney and I’d had much truck with. I decided I make an awful poor social mourner and flipped my butt into the yard and went down the steps, ready to head home.

Preacher Garvin stopped me again. “Not leaving us, are you, Kermit?”

“I guess so. I don’t see what I can do here.”

“Yes. These things are most in the hands of the womenfolk. How are they bearing up in the house?”

“All right, I reckon. The doc has got Frances lying down to rest.”

“That’s good. I guess you know we’ll be having the services on Saturday afternoon in the church.”

“All right.”

He stepped closer and lowered his voice. “I was thinking something over, Kermit. You and Caney used to like to get together and make music, didn’t you?”

“Yes, sir, we did.” Those words made me flinch, *used to.*

“I was thinking it might be fitting for you to give the opening hymns for the service. I know it would be a hardship, but would you be willing to sing?”

I took a deep breath. This was the first thing that had come up that I could do for Caney, but I didn't know if I could get through a song, with him lying by me in his coffin. "Preacher Garvin," I said, "I can give you maybe one hymn. Never in this world could I sing two."

"One is all right," he said. "One is just fine. What would you care to sing? Didn't Caney have some hymn he held special? One that would be proper for a funeral service?"

"We liked a whole lot of hymn tunes," I said. "I don't know which would be the right one for his laying-away."

"All right. You think on it and call me tomorrow."

"Yes, sir."

I went along and got into my pickup and drove away. It occurred to me I might drive the thirty miles over to Plemmonsville to the Ace High Grill, where Caney and I used to go now and then to drink six bottles of beer and hear Mac Wiseman or Don Reno on the jukebox. But that would just make me feel more lonely. Everything I thought of made me feel bad.

I drove home. I went into the bedroom and took up the guitar, and this time I strung it. I tuned it, twisting the keys, testing the strings over and over. I got it in perfect tune before I went to sleep.

Friday, I laid out of work. I didn't want to see the people we worked with every day, I didn't want to hear what they'd be saying, and I did not want to answer questions. Seeing I wasn't part of Caney's family, old man McCracken might well dock my pay. Well, let him. He'd done it before and I didn't starve. Maybe I never wanted to work again.

I put on my red wool shirt and my hunting boots and warmed up a cup of day-old coffee and drank it while cleaning my twelve-gauge. Then I got into my tan jacket and found my cap and went out. I didn't carry any shells; the heart wasn't in me to be killing. I just wanted the gun solid in my hands as I walked along.

It was the early April season, with the air crisp and cool and the sky scrubbed blue. The first minute I set foot in Colter's Grove, I felt better. I liked the pine needles springy underfoot and the smell of trees and the sunlight coming through in rags and the silence everywhere about, the silence I could feel on my skin at first. I walked a long time, not following a true path, just keeping my feet where they would make the least noise. After half an hour, it looked like I was headed toward Ember Mountain, and I figured I could climb it if I desired, setting one foot before the other and feeling no strain, not today.

When I came to Burning Creek at the foot, I decided not to climb. I knelt and cupped up three mouthfuls of water in my hand and then sat on a rock on the creek bank with my shotgun across my knees. There I sat for the longest time. The comfort to me here was the sound of the water rolling over the stones. That's a clean sound to listen to for hours, always the same but never exactly the same one minute to the next. A sound going on forever, but with little changes inside it that never exactly repeat. You can make it louder or softer while you listen, just by the way you concentrate. If a music group, especially one with a good banjo or mandolin, could capture some of this creek sound and get it right, they would be famous and folks would come from anywhere to hear them. There are musicians who can make sounds of every kind, the wind in the treetops and freight trains picking up speed and fox hunts on the mountaintop, but I never heard anyone try to get the creek sound down.

I sat and listened. Little by little, the hard iron went out of my sadness. All night I'd had bad dreams I couldn't remember except they left my mind dark, and now that darkness lightened. I wasn't reconciled and I surely was not happy, but I didn't have that cold, bitter taste in my throat. I'd come out to the place of purest sadness, sad but free and floating, sad but natural-feeling. It was fitting and proper how I felt now, and I knew for the first time I'd be able to sing and it wouldn't unman me with Caney lying by.

I sat awhile longer and then got up and walked home. The sun was higher now and the day was getting warm.

In the house, I stowed my shotgun and hung up my jacket and cap and unlaced my boots partway. Then I went into the front room and dialed Preacher Garvin. His wife answered and then went off to fetch him.

"Hello?"

"Hello, Preacher. This is Kermit Wilson."

"Yes, all right. How you doing, son?"

"Okay, I reckon. A little better than I was."

"That's right," he said. "Good. The Lord disposes. He giveth and He taketh away."

"Yes, sir."

"What can I do for you, Kermit?"

"Well, I believe I've decided I can sing at the funeral all right."

"That's fine. That's mighty fine. Have you decided what number?"

"Yes, sir. That is, I've got one I know will be all right, but about the other one, I don't think you'll be pleased."

"What is it?"

"One hymn that he liked awful well was 'Peace in the Valley.' And it's a good song for baritone and I believe I can handle it."

"Fine," he said. "Be hard to think of one more suited to this time of trial."

"The other one, I kind of doubt," I said. "It was his favorite song and that's the reason I want to sing it. He never got enough of it. We might sing it five times in a night now and then."

"Which one are you talking about?"

"'Roll in My Sweet Baby's Arms.'"

"No."

"I know it's not a hymn tune."

"And you know well enough already you can't sing that. You're talking about a secular song."

"It was the one he liked the best."

"I wouldn't mind stretching it some if you wanted to do a good old-time church shout, something like that. But the one you're talking about you can't sing in church."

"It's the one he'd want to hear."

"There's other people to think about. Caney's kinfolks and Frances and her kin and the church members."

"Caney Barham," I said. "He's the one I'm studying on right now."

He didn't answer right away, then said, "Well, I don't see how. There might be one way to work it out, but seeing as how you're one of the pall-bearers—"

"Not me. I'm not going to be a one to put him in the ground."

"I didn't know that. I just naturally had you down on the list."

"I think John Newsome would take my place."

"John's already one. But maybe if we could find another'n, you might could sing your song afterward. Not as part of a Christian funeral service, no sir, but if you wanted to sing it at the grave site after the service is over and the last prayer is prayed, I wouldn't be able to stop you. It looks like you're bound and determined."

"Yes, sir."

"Then that's the way it'll be. I'll pass the word in private so if anybody wants to stay on, they can. But I can't announce it in church and I can't stay myself."

"Ever how you like, Preacher," I said. "I'm not anxious for people to stay on."

"All right, then," he said. "Now at the service you'll be singing first, after Juney McClain stops playing the piano for people to come in by. And that's all the arrangements we need to make, you and me. See you tomorrow at two o'clock."

"Yes sir," I said, and we hung up.

I arrived early at the church and parked around back. I didn't want to have to shake hands. I wanted to keep to myself until I started singing. There was a momentful thing inside of me, something important not to disturb, and I had to keep it like that or I would never be able to bring off what I was setting out to do in the necessary way.

So I went through the side door into the little anteroom beside the choir stall and unpacked my guitar and tested the tuning. Then I did nothing but sit and wait. I had dressed in fresh tan cotton pants and a white shirt and my dark brown suit jacket and a blue necktie, and this was the closest thing to a full dress outfit that I had. If I'd had one, I would have put on an Opry singer's outfit, with piping and copper buttons and a big cowboy hat; that's the kind of rig Caney would appreciate. But back then, I'd never seen one of these outfits in person.

I heard Juney McClain start playing the piano, soft and slow and out of rhythm, like always, and I could hear the scuffle and whisper of people sliding into the pews. Then Preacher Garvin came in and stopped and adjusted his black string tie and said, "You doing all right, Kermit?"

"Yes, sir."

"That's fine. You just follow me out. I'll go to the podium, and when Juney stops playing, I'll give you a nod. After you're finished, you turn around and go sit in the choir stall and I'll start the service."

"All right."

I followed him out, gazing at his heels till I got where I was supposed to stand. When I looked up at the congregation, I was fearful I'd never get it done. I caught a glimpse of Frances and Aline and Caney's mother on my left-hand side and heard the mumbles and sobs and whimpers and I cut my eyes away and wouldn't look that way again. I knew almost everybody else out there, but I didn't look on their faces.

There was one fellow I didn't know, somebody I'd never laid eyes on before. He was dressed in a dark expensive-looking suit and seated in one of the back pews. He leaned forward, with his hands draped over the empty pew in front of him, and on one wrist was a shiny watch and the sun gleamed on it, making a silver patch, burning white. I decided that while I was singing, I would rest my eyes on the gleam of it.

I looked at Preacher Garvin and he nodded and I began.

Now "Peace in the Valley" is not a tricky song to sing and, like I'd said, a good song for the baritone voice. But being easy is what makes it hard, because you're likely to want to throw your voice around and fancy it up. I'd made up my mind to treat it right, to make it clear and strong and simple. I wanted to hit the notes as telling as a clock striking.

And when I started, that momentful thing I'd been feeling since the day before at the foot of Ember Mountain took hold of me. My whole body was at ease and my voice came out in a way I'd never heard before. It was like it wasn't my voice, but another person's, someone standing at my right-hand side and singing away unconcerned while I accompanied him on the guitar. I didn't understand what was happening, but I thought, Probably this is the last time. Maybe I'll never sing again after today.

When I had finished, I turned and walked to the choir stall, unstrapping as I went. I laid the guitar down as easy as I could on the varnished oak seat, because the church had gone as quiet as the midnight sky. Even the sobbing and whimpering had hushed.

A long time, it seemed to me, passed before Preacher Garvin said, "Thank you, Brother Kermit, for that fine rendition, just mighty fine."

Those were his last words I heard, and not even one from the funeral service. I sat there pondering the days gone by forever and how I'd come to sing the way I did, and then once more Caney Barham alive and the things we used to say and do. I believed that if he heard me sing "Peace in the Valley," he liked the way I did it and was soothed.

The time came at last when the service was over and the casket was to be carried out to the little graveyard beside the church. The bearers shouldered it and the family followed them, moaning now again and crying, and then the rest of the people. I waited in the anteroom, tuning the strings again and watching through the window till I saw the procession had got through the gate. Then I went out and followed, keeping well behind.

From the grave, too, I kept my distance. They set the casket down and Preacher Garvin read prayers I couldn't hear and then they lowered Caney into the deep red ground and sprinkled dirt on him by the handful. Finally the preacher led away the family and five or six others. They didn't look at me standing over to the side as they went by. They were pretending I was not there.

But a lot of people stayed, and when I walked up to the grave and the mound of loamy clay, they stepped back and spread out a little. I was surprised, because I hadn't expected anybody to linger on. Even the stranger with the shiny wristwatch was there; he had a square black leather case hanging by a strap from his shoulder, and I took it to be some kind of radio or camera. I thought maybe I ought to say something to explain that I meant no sin and no shame, that I was only singing my buddy a onetime last memorial song.

It was a warm day, the sky as blue as ever you'll see, and a warm, light breeze over the slopes. I didn't look at anybody this time, but watched the tops of the pines at the graveyard border, where they swung in the wind and dipped.

"Where were you last Saturday night
While I was lying in jail?
Walking the streets with another man.
I had no one to go my bail."

And whatever had been with me when I sang in the church house was with me still, the calm, strong voice of the one that had stood by my side.

Now while I was playing and singing so fast and hard, I recognized what it was. It was my own sadness, which had come out of my body and taken a shape apart from me. It was the ghost of the way things used to be, given to me to make it a little easier to keep on going down the road. I'd been wrong about it in the church house, because it wasn't going to go away. It was my own sorrow and would always be with me and I could call it to come whenever I wanted to sing. A ghost and my companion.

"Ain't going to work on the railroad,
Ain't going to work on the farm.
I'll hang around the shack
Till the mail train comes back
And roll in my sweet baby's arms."

When I finished, it seemed to me I'd finished with a great many things. Maybe I could sing like that whenever I wanted, and maybe I would never sing again. I didn't care. A slow, wide feeling of peace settled in me like snow on a new-turned field; I didn't want anything to disturb it.

None of the people said anything, not even to one another. They started away, and I waited for them to go, keeping my distance. Then I headed back to the church to pick up my guitar case.

But there at the gate, the stranger with the shiny wristwatch and the black leather carrying case stopped me. "That was mighty fine singing," he said. "I don't know when I've been so impressed. You've got a good voice, just fine."

"Thank you," I said, and tried to push on by him.

"Wait a minute." He stepped over to block my path. "My name is Ramey Bucke," he said, "and I'm a country-music promoter from Nashville, Tennessee. So when I tell somebody they've got a good voice, it means something. I don't travel up and down this country just for my health. You've got a good, big, old-fashioned voice and there might be some things we could do with it if you got the right kind of material and some good handling and all."

"Much obliged," I said. "But I don't believe there's anything I need right now." I tried again to get past him.

"Just a minute," he said. "I was standing so far back there at the grave that I'm not sure if I taped your song too well." He held out toward me a little wire-covered tube connected with a black cord to the carrying case. That was the first microphone I ever saw.

I looked down at it and then looked up at him, square in the face. "Mister," I told him, "if you don't get that fancy little machine out of the way, I'll bust it to a thousand pieces."

He stood aside then, and that was the end of it.

But of course that was not the end and only the beginning. If that was the end, you wouldn't be here, right?

I'm begging your pardon now for giving such an almighty long answer to a short and simple question. I know what I'm supposed to say. Ramey Bucke—who is my agent these days—told me last night that a woman from a music newspaper would be here this morning to interview me. So we tried to figure out some questions you might be asking, and sure enough you hit on one: If I could have one single wish to come true, what would it be? Right over there in that desk drawer is a sheet of paper with the answer he wanted me to say: I wish for peace everywhere in the world.

It's a good answer, I guess, but tremendous ambitious for a Horton County guitar picker. If you really did want to know, I'll tell you.

I wish I had never come to this damn crazy town of Nashville, with its blinking lights and yellow-haired women and trashy money people. I wish I'd never heard myself coming out of a radio speaker or in a nightclub with no air or squeezed down on a record player. I wish I was back at the head of Big Sandy Cove in the Carolina hills at Caney Barham's house, me and him singing "Brokenhearted Lover" or any other old-time song you'd care to mention, and laughing till we were red in the face. Or if it couldn't be that way, if it happened that he was fated to die, then I wish I was on a grassy bald on the southern side of Ember Mountain, singing into the wind and the blue daylight, because nowhere else on earth could he ever hear me now.

CHILDREN OF STRIKERS

They were walking, the twelve-year-old girl and the younger bleached-looking boy, by the edge of the black chemical river. A dreadful stink rose off the waters, but they scarcely noticed it, scuffling along in the hard saw grass among the stones. It was a dim day, rain threatening, and the girl's dun face and dark eyes looked even darker than usual. The boy trailed some little distance behind her and would stop now and again and shade his eyes and look upstream and down. But there was no more reason for him to look about than there was for him to shade his eyes.

Occasionally the girl would bend down and look at something that caught her eye—a scrap of tin, a bit of drowned dirty cloth, jetsam thrown up from the river that poured through the paper factory above and then by the mill settlement behind them. This, "Fiberville," was a quadruple row of dingy little bungalows, and it was where the two of them lived. In the girl's dark face was something harsh and tired, as if she had foretold all her life and found it joyless.

Now she reached down and plucked something off a blackened wale of sand. She glanced at it briefly and thrust it into the pocket of her thin green sweater.

The boy had seen. He caught up with her and demanded to have a look.

"Look at what?" she asked.

"What you found, let me see it."

"It ain't nothing you'd care about."

"How do you know what I care? Let me have a look."

She turned to face him, gazed directly into his sallow, annoying face, those milky blue eyes. "I ain't going to let you," she said.

He gave her a stare, then turned aside and spat. "Well then, it ain't nothing."

"That's right." She walked on and he kept behind her. But she knew he was gauging his chances, considering when to run and snatch it out of her pocket. When she heard his footsteps coming sneaky-fast, she wheeled and, without taking aim, delivered him such a ringing slap that his eyes watered and his face flushed.

"Goddamn you," he said, but he didn't cry.

"I've told you to keep your hands away from me. I told you I wouldn't say it again."

"You ain't so much," he said. "I seen better." But his voice, though resentful, was not bitter.

They walked on a space and she began to relent. "It's a foot," she said.

"What you mean? What kind of foot?"

"It's a baby's foot."

"No!" He glared at her. "I ain't believing that."

"You can believe just whatever little thing you want to."

"I ain't believing you found no baby's foot. Let me see it."

"No."

"Well then, you ain't got nothing. . . . How big is it?"

"It's real tiny."

"Gaw," he said. It had seized his imagination. "Somebody probably kilt it."

"Might be."

"They must have kilt it and cut it up in little bits and throwed it in the river." He was wild with the thought of it. "It was some girl got knocked up and her boyfriend made her do it."

She shrugged.

"Ain't that awful to think about? A poor little baby . . . Come on and show it to me. I got to see that baby foot."

"What'll you give me?"

They marched along and he struck a mournful air. "Nothing," he said at last. "I ain't got nothing to give."

She stopped and looked at him, surveyed him head to toe with a weary satisfaction. "No, I guess you ain't," she said. "You ain't got a thing."

"Well then, what you got? Nothing but a poor little dead baby's foot which I don't believe you've got anyhow."

Slowly she reached into her pocket and produced it, held it toward him in her open palm, and he leaned forward, breathless, peering. He shivered, almost imperceptibly. Then his face clouded and his eyes grew brighter and he slapped her hand. The foot jumped out of her hand and fell among the grasses.

"That ain't nothing. It's a doll, it's just a doll baby's foot."

She could tell that he was disappointed, but feeling smug, too, because, after all, he had caught her in the expectable lie. "I never told you it was real." She stooped and retrieved it. It lay pink and soiled in her soiled palm: bulbous foot and ankle, little toes like beads of water. It looked too small and too separate from the rest of the world to be anything at all.

He took it from her. "I knowed it wasn't no real baby." He became thoughtful, turning it in his fingers. "Hey, look at this."

"I don't see nothing."

He held the tubular stub of it toward her. "Look how smooth it's been cut off. It's been cut with a knife."

She touched it, and the amputation was as smooth as the mouth of a Pepsi bottle. "What's that got to do with anything?"

It had gotten darker now, drawing on toward the supper hour. Fiberville grew gloomier behind them, though most of the lights were on in the kitchens of the houses.

"Means that somebody went and cut it on purpose. . . ." Another flushed fantasy overcame him. "Say, what if it was a crazy man? What if it was a man practicing up before he went and kilt a real baby?"

"It's just some little kid messing around," she said.

"Ain't no kid would have a knife like that." He ran his thumb over the edge of the cut. "Had to be a real *sharp* knife. Or an ax. Maybe it was a meat chopper."

"Kid might get a knife anywhere."

He shook his head firmly. "No. Look how even it is and ain't hacked up. Kid would rag it up. A man went and done it, being real careful."

At last she nodded assent. Now at the same moment they turned and looked up the riverbank into Fiberville, the squat, darkening houses where the fathers and mothers and older sons now wore strained, strange faces. The men didn't shave every day now and the women cried sometimes. They had all turned into strangers, and among them at night in the houses were real strangers from far-off places saying hard, wild sentences and often shouting and banging tabletops. In the overheated rooms, both the light and the shadows loomed with an unguessable violence.

BON TON

1

When Harris T. Bonforth appeared at the reception desk, Walt and Belmont were startled. They had previously decided that the person who had reserved a room three months ago, back in mid-April, was the same Harris T. Bonforth who had placed the intriguing advertisement in Friday's *Gallinton Bugler,* the town's weekly newspaper. But both cousins had pictured him, without discussing the topic, as a shortish figure, probably bearded, with a whiff of charlatanry emanating from a seedy tweed jacket. Instead, he was a tall African-American, handsome, dignified, and mellifluously soft-spoken. Walt took pleasure in his voice. He was dressed in a red turtleneck, dark green slacks, and was jacketless. He had the poise of a scratch golfer.

Walt and Monty often shared fancies and premonitions. They had been thrown upon each other's company since childhood and had shared their present business venture for the past seven years. They thought so much alike that they did not think they thought alike.

Yet they were different, too. Walt was the younger by about eighteen months and the more impulsive of the two—the more "artistic," Monty would claim, with more than a hint of admiration in his tone. Walt was the chef; he enjoyed assembling and serving the breakfasts that the B and B establishment they had named Waltmon Inn was proud to offer. Monty was the more precise, furnishing the hard head necessary for business.

He doted on Walt's ambition to make the inn a quality hostel, though he recognized that his cousin had only a partial grasp of what was needed to make his idea a reality. To state the case in its mildest terms: Walt was fuzzy-minded.

And sometimes his artistic side got the better of him, Monty thought. For instance, he held in high disfavor Walt's peculiar phrase for his ideal. "Bon ton," Walt would say, nasalizing the words in so thorough and high-schoolish a manner that they sounded like a Jersey heifer's attempt at human communication. Monty feared and detested every foreign tongue, especially the Gallic, but he understood Walt's intention. This was not always so. Walt's mind was a nervous, agile entity that leapt about the landscape of reference like a camel cricket. His acuities, as well as his dizzy delusions, were so swift that he sometimes left himself behind, a natty figure dimly descried through the mists of misapprehension.

Originally they were members of the boisterous Blanton clan, a family prominent in this part of eastern North Carolina and handsomely self-satisfied. They had separated themselves from the rest of the tribe when they were teenagers, and one of the more bumptious of the Blantons had stigmatized them as sissy boys. Walt resented this insolence to the point of physical protest, and it was whispered that the scattering of his brains was the result of powerful and frequent knocks to his noggin by his inartistic kinsman. This ungenerous treatment had served to bond Monty and Walt.

While Monty was signing Bonforth in, Walt removed, not entirely surreptitiously, the newspaper laid out on the counter and turned to the quarter-page ad:

HARRIS T. BONFORTH

DO YOU HAVE SOMETHING TO TELL ME?

THURSDAY, FRIDAY 9–12, 1–5

WALTMON INN

GALLINTON, NC

1-800-TELLALL

Bonforth appeared to take no notice. He only raised his slow, warm gaze to Monty after signing the registration card and saying that he would like to keep the bill on his Visa card. Monty assented and inquired how many nights their guest would be staying.

"Tonight and the two following, just as I reserved. You would know that from the newspaper." His voice, mellow as a knife-ready cantaloupe, inspired trust.

Monty informed him that room 27 was upstairs in this building, at the opposite end of the hall, and asked if he required assistance with his luggage. He did not, but said that he was gratified to learn that breakfast would be served from seven till nine-thirty in the adjoining house. "I understand that your breakfasts have a strong reputation."

"Walt puts them together," Monty said, "and people seem to like them. Can we assist you in any other way?"

"I hope you won't find it a nuisance," Bonforth said, "that I will be welcoming a number of visitors to my room. There will be no loud disturbances or trouble of any sort. Your other guests will not be inconvenienced."

"I'm sure it will be all right. You don't look the sort for rough parties."

"I avoid parties."

"May I ask what sort of work you engage in?"

"You saw my advertisement. It is a reminder to those people who may wish to talk with me."

"I understand," Monty said, having not an inkling. But his question had already ventured beyond his customary limits of propriety, had almost distressed the bon ton Walt said they must maintain. He heard his cousin clear his throat and knew it for a sign of disapproval. But this was not consistent: Sometimes Walt was the politer of the two; sometimes he was downright insensitive.

Bonforth turned down the offer of a tour of the room and a second offer of luggage assistance. He carried only a single suitcase of forest green leather, dignified and expensive. He accepted the room key with its bulky crystal doorknob attachment amusedly and ascended the stairs with a steady tread.

The cousins listened, silent till he climbed out of earshot. Then Walt said, "Monty, what were you thinking of? Asking Mr. Bonforth—"

"I don't know what came over me. It just slipped out. With this fellow, it seemed to be all right—like he wouldn't mind."

"He didn't seem to mind. But I thought I'd keel right over. I embarrass easily." Walt brushed a lock of silver hair from his forehead and tugged his vest down to meet his belt. He was proud of his vests and his silver hair. Monty's hair was a sprinkled gray.

"No you don't," Monty said. "You're never embarrassed."

"Yes I am. I was just now."

"That's the exception that proves the rule."

"And after all, you didn't find out what he does."

"True," Monty said. "Let's look at the ad again."

Walt retrieved it and they studied, but it informed them no more fully than before. "Do you have something to tell me?" Walt read. He looked at Monty. "Well, you had something to *ask* him, but—"

"Enough. Please."

Walt tugged his earlobe. "Is he some sort of spiritual adviser, like a palm reader?" He was recalling Sister Zandella and Madame Topaz. Gallinton was a sleepy, sun-drenched town of eight thousand placid souls, yet it boasted two females who proclaimed their powers of prophecy and clairvoyance on untidily lettered signs posted out by Highway 427. Walt had always been curious, but never curious enough to rap on their doors.

Monty thumbed his red suspender straps out and snapped them back upon his well-padded chest. "What does Mr. B. expect to be told?"

"I don't know."

Then it was four-thirty and other guests arrived. There were but two parties today besides Bonforth, a family of four traveling toward Savannah and a honeymoon couple. The children of the family, a boy of about twelve and a girl about ten, were lively. This quartet was consigned to the adjoining house, where quarters were larger than those in this venerable Victorian dwelling with its tall ceilings and narrow hallways. Walt was the better hand with children, so he led the family across, helped them with their luggage and a battered stack of board games, showed them the bath arrangements, and exhibited the daintily handsome Episcopal church outside the east window. "Eighteen thirty-seven," he said with unconcealed pride, disappointed that the structure drew only cursory glances from the parents, who were occupied with commanding their offspring not to assassinate each other.

The honeymooners did not arrive until six. They looked both exhausted and exhilarated, softly tipsy maybe, and were preternaturally quiet. They seemed almost sad, or so Monty imagined. It had been thought prudent to place them upstairs rather than in the house where the children were lodged. "We don't want to discourage a young couple," Walt had said, and Monty had replied, "You impudent thing." It took but fifteen minutes to settle the pair; they seemed to long for sleep.

Then Bonforth made his second appearance, descending the stairs silently. He warned the cousins that their comfy small lobby might become a little crowded on the morrow. "I regret the bother," he said, "but there's not much I can do about it. I can guarantee they won't cause any trouble. But some always show up early. When they arrive early, they just have to hang around. I'm strict about time. My appointments never run over, but there's no way to control the early birds."

"What size crowds are we talking about?" Monty asked.

"Not crowds. Two or three at most, early on. Later in the day, they thin out."

"No problem. Will they have any special needs?"

"They'll just sit around and wait. Leaf through your magazines, stare into space. You know how people behave in lobbies."

"We could offer coffee," Walt said. "They could chat with one another and get acquainted."

"They won't chat," Bonforth said.

"I wish we had more parking space," Walt said.

"It's sufficient. Some of them will probably just walk over."

"So your . . . guests will be from around here?"

"From Gallinton or close by, almost all."

"Then we'll know who they are. We'll recognize them," Walt said.

"You'll know some of them, I'm sure. You may be able to recognize them."

"If I know them, I'm bound to recognize them."

"Perhaps."

"We'll do everything we can to be of service," Walt said. "For dinner, would you like information about area restaurants? I can recommend three nice places. Easy drives."

"I thank you, but I've already made dinner arrangements. In fact, I'm going out now and will return later tonight." He pulled his room key from the pocket of his tan blazer. "I'll keep the key with me so I won't have to bother you when I come in."

"Be glad to keep it for you at the desk."

"I don't think I'll lose it," Bonforth said. He tapped the crystal knob to swing it back and forth.

"That's one reason we attached those pendants. Monty and I were determined to have real keys that turn in the locks. Those plastic card thingies are so tacky. Don't you prefer a real key that fits and turns?"

Bonforth agreed that this was the more elegant option. He gave a look around before saying, "You have a nice place. Has it been in your family?"

Monty beamed and spoke of his darling aunt Miriam and how her property came to him and how he talked Walt into the B and B idea and they waited until the Tramble property next door was available, so they could have two houses and enough space. "But, wouldn't you know, after Walt had signed on, he got cold feet. He wanted to back out, and we'd already signed for the Tramble place. I told him, 'Walt, the time to back out was *before*.' I finally got him to come around."

Walt shook his head. "It wasn't like that. Not exactly."

"It was precisely like that. And I think it's turned out rather well, don't you, Mr. Bonforth?"

"Yes indeed."

"Of course, they don't match up well. This house was built in 1892; the one next door only dates back to the 1920s. We're not sure of the year. We keep meaning to find out."

"Both are very nice."

"Well, I've just rattled on, haven't I? I should be asking if your room is all right. Did you find the alarm clock by the bed? And the TV channel guide? We've had cable installed. Walt and I like the nature shows and the cooking shows."

"I don't like that Portagee fellow," Walt said. "All those fools cheering for garlic."

Bonforth said, "I have everything I could possibly need."

"We have a turn-down service," Walt said. "All hours."

"I'll see you later, then," said Bonforth, and gave his key pendant a waggle before restoring it to his pocket. He stepped noiselessly to the door and paused on the wide front porch to inspect the front garden and then stepped down into the pea-gravel front walk.

Walt said, "Monty—"

His cousin grinned ruefully and tugged at his red braces. "Sorry about that. I really did give him an earful. I don't usually chatter that way, do I?"

"No."

"I just rambled on and on."

"You like him. I could tell that."

"He seems a likable sort. He seemed interested."

"I couldn't tell if he was interested or just polite, the way you jabbered at him. It's not like you, Monty."

2

Bonforth was early to breakfast the next morning. He took OJ and coffee, two bacon strips, a sausage patty, and Walt's famous French toast. "It's not really famous," the silver-haired host confessed. "Folks brag on it, so I took to calling it famous. A joke."

"It's tasty," Bonforth said. "I'm sure fame is just around the corner." He announced that he was going for a constitutional, and Walt suggested that he visit the graveyard with its interesting stones.

The tall man nodded and departed. When he returned in forty-five minutes, he did not say whether he had paid his respects to the dead or not. Monty hailed him from behind the desk and told him that someone had telephoned for him and would call back later. Bonforth seemed annoyed. He looked at the clock. Eight-ten. "Too early," he said, and went upstairs.

At eight-thirty, a man entered and asked if Harris T. Bonforth was in residence. Monty told him that Bonforth was in room 27 upstairs. The man nodded, glanced at his wristwatch, and took a seat on the maple deck sofa in the middle of the room. He sat straight, hands on knees, and stared into the space before him as if it were a TV screen lurid with melodrama.

Monty would describe him as the most ordinary-looking person he had ever seen. In his late thirties, with nondescript brown hair, of medium height, and dressed in a green sport shirt and khaki trousers, he was the type of figure you think you recognize but can't place immediately. If you wished to hide from the FBI, you would try to look like this man.

At five minutes till nine, the porch door opened to admit a different sort of personage, an older black gentleman of commanding presence and graceful bearing. He wore a light woolen three-piece suit with a heavy gold watch chain. The frames of his rimless spectacles were gold. He advanced with stately tread to the desk and asked in a rich, deep voice, "Mr. Bonforth?"

"Room twenty-seven."

He turned then to survey the room, took in the other gentleman, who sat unmoved, and looked away, as if he'd seen what he expected to see. Then he took a chair and opened the *Newsweek* he had been carrying, but did not read it.

At nine, the ordinary fellow did not look at the clock, but stood suddenly, his movement jerky, as if it surprised him to stand, then marched stiffly to the stairway. There he paused and looked upward before climbing slowly, as if counting the risers one by one.

At nine-fifteen, the Savannah-bound family began checking out. This business occupied a good fifteen minutes, as Billie Jane tried to fend off her brother's pinches and one of the valises flew open. The unremarkable man made his way through the confusion and was out the door before Monty could get a good impression of his state. Had he been trembling and white-faced, or was that a silly fancy?

Now the computer began making ominous chirping sounds, and as Monty turned his attention to it, the grave black gentleman mounted the stairs and was on the landing before he turned around, escaping Monty's attempt at close observation. He had promised Walt to see all and report.

At nine-fifty, a woman entered, gave Walt a quick and sneaky glance. She went to the east window to look out into the garden with its hostas and daylilies and late-blooming white azaleas. Her face was turned away, purposely, it seemed. She wore a light lime housedress, over which she had drawn a red leather coat that had no business in its company. A wig she wore, too, the color of strawberry Kool Aid, and it was perched on her head as if she'd clapped it on while fleeing a house fire.

Monty felt that he knew her and would recognize her if only she would turn so he could see her face. He called out across the lobby space, "Can I be of service, miss?" She shook her averted head and continued to stare out.

Now quit of his breakfast duties, Walt came in from the back and started to say something, but a swift warning glance from Monty silenced him. Monty nodded his head at the woman and Walt peered at her closely, widened his eyes in wonderment, and peered again. He moved close to Monty to whisper.

But then the grave black gentleman came down, and Monty was struck by the differences in the man. His step was lighter than before and his grave manner partly abated. His bearing was still dignified, but it seemed that a burden had been lifted from him. Monty watched him closely as he went out the front door, abandoning his *Newsweek* on the coffee table.

"Sir, you forgot your magazine," Walt said.

The fellow gave a dismissive wave of his hand and strode away into the bright morning.

"Did you see what I saw?" Walt asked.

"Yes, he left his *Newsweek*."

"No. The woman in the weird wig. She just went up the stairs."

"I saw her before."

"She was quite a sight."

"I couldn't see her face."

"You didn't recognize Mamie Barnhart?"

"No!"

"Yes."

"Dressed like that? She kept hiding her face from me."

"I don't wonder."

"Are you sure? I thought it was somebody familiar, but I wouldn't have said Mamie."

"I'll swear on Bibles."

"What in the world is she—"

"How about the others?"

Monty admitted that he had been distracted, but he did try to describe the changes he thought he had discovered in the grave black man. He had little success. Walt made confusion of mind his vocation and subtleties muddled him irremediably.

"How do you mean, he walked lighter?"

"Like folks say, 'a weight off my shoulders.' You understand?"

"Maybe. Like, for example, if he had told a terrible secret he had been keeping? Something he had to get off his chest?"

"Maybe."

"And Mamie Barnhart—"

"I wouldn't have believed it. It wouldn't be anything bad, of course. Not really. Mamie's a fine woman."

Walt nodded but said, "Still, she *is* married to Howie. Everybody knows about Howie."

"Maybe everybody but Mamie," Monty said.

"But what would Bonforth—"

"I don't know."

Walt shrugged. "It's too deep for me," he said. "Have our honeymooners showed up yet?"

"No."

"They've missed breakfast. I told them, no breakfast after nine-thirty."

"They won't mind."

On the stroke of ten, Mamie Barnhart marched down the stairs with a gladsome spring in her step. Her red coat was draped over her left shoulder and she twirled the garish wig round and round by a lock of its nylon hair. She addressed them perkily: "Good morning, boys. See you in church." At the door, she paused to let in a short Hispanic man. Then she exited.

Monty was thunderstruck but had no time to reflect as the swarthy small man with the toothbrush mustache came to the desk and said, "Señor Bonforth?"

"Room twenty-seven," the cousins chorused. He wheeled and jittered away upstairs, possessed by an energy he could barely contain. They could hear that on the stairs above the landing he was taking two at a time.

They turned to each other. Monty made an attempt. "Well—" he said, but then fell silent. Walt shrugged.

"You're real sure it was Mamie," Monty said.

"So are you. You saw her carrying that wig."

"Yes, but what in the world—"

Walt waited a long time before advancing a careful philosophical proposition. "Human curiosity," he said, "is a powerful force."

Monty waited a longer time before replying. "Yes."

In a while, Walt said, "A person can't help wondering."

Long pause. "Yes." And Monty tugged at his red suspenders.

They looked at each other, wondering, and were relieved when this portentous moment was interrupted by the advent of the sleepy-looking but carefully brushed bridegroom, who came to say that the clock had stopped in room 21 and he and Eunice had overslept. Any chance of a late breakfast?

Monty informed him that after nine-thirty the meal was impossible. His tone was regretfully respectful and he recommended the Tick-Tock on the east side of Gallinton, Highway 427, where they served breakfast till eleven-thirty.

Eunice came down just in time to hear that this diner served hot biscuits, strong coffee, fresh brown eggs, and country ham. She grasped her husband's hand and playfully dragged him toward the parking lot.

While this was taking place, the small Hispanic man rattled down the stairs, flitted through the lobby, and bumped into the Reverend Edgar Waller, who was entering. The Reverend Waller was the revered minister of the starchily respectable First Baptist Church of Gallinton, boasting a congregation of no fewer than 780 souls, of whom more than half were active members. He came to the reception desk, shook hands with the cousins, and asked warmly after their health and welfare. Satisfied that they were still Episcopalians, he told them without hesitation or embarrassment that he had an appointment with Mr. Harris Bonforth. Having learned the room number, he shook hands again, besought the blessing of the Deity upon Monty's gray and Walt's silver, and took the stairs with manly forthrightness.

There was a small roller stool below the mail slots and Monty went to it and sat heavily. Walt would have said that he tottered to it, but Walt did not see, having collapsed over the desk with his face in his hands. The cousins held these postures for a while, unable to speak.

Finally, Walt straightened and declared, "That tears it."

"What do you mean?"

"Everything I've been thinking, every idea I've come up with, has been exploded."

"What were you thinking?"

"You first."

A sigh, then Walt said, "I am beginning to think the unthinkable."

"How? When?"

"How is the closet at the end of the hall. When is noon."

"In that closet you can hear what they say in twenty-seven, but you can't see."

"Don't need to. One of us would work the desk and keep a list of his visitors and the other would be in that closet storeroom listening. Then we would compare notes."

"You sound like you are going to do it. Walt, this is creepy."

"Not me—us. It has to be both of us. And, yes, it's creepy. But don't we have a right to know what's going on in our own business establishment?"

"I don't know."

"What if it's something illegal?"

"Like what?"

"Well . . . drugs, maybe."

"The Reverend Waller? Give me a break."

"Something is going on. Maybe not illegal, just . . . illicit."

"Or fattening," Monty said. "You're just looking for an excuse."

"If it were illegal, we could be liable. Lawyers. Courtrooms. Newspaper headlines."

"And anyhow, there's not enough room in that closet. We keep piling stuff in there and never sorting it out."

"That's why I suggested noontime. While Bonforth is out to lunch, we can clean out a space. It won't take long."

"No," Monty said. "This is stupid."

"Just natural curiosity," Walt said.

"Voyeurism. You're turning into Norman Bates."

"Who?"

"In the scary movie—with the shower and all. Alfred Hitchcock."

"This is real life. . . . I'll make space for one of us. Then you decide if you want to get involved."

"If I know you're doing it, I'm already involved."

"So?"

"I'll have to sleep on it."

"Tomorrow? That's a long time off."

"Tomorrow or never," Monty said, and the debate might have continued in this vein if the Reverend Waller had not now come waveringly down the stairs. He flourished a large white handkerchief at the cousins and then wiped the back of his neck. He lumbered to the wicker chair by the coffee table and lowered himself with tender carefulness.

"Are you all right, Reverend?" Monty asked. "You seem distressed."

The minister twisted his damp handkerchief and requested a glass of water.

"Of course." Walt hurried to the kitchen. When he returned, the reverend had recovered his composure. He accepted the glass gratefully and drained it.

"Are you all right?"

"Yes, I am, Walt. Just need a moment to catch my breath."

"I hope there's nothing bad."

"Bad? No. But sometimes a person doesn't realize just what kind of burden he has been carrying."

"There have been people going up all morning. Monty and I have been wondering what it's all about."

"You don't know?" He handed the glass back. "I had assumed that since Mr. Bonforth chose the Waltmon Inn, he'd tell you."

"Not a word," said Monty.

"Not the first syllable," said Walt.

The Reverend Waller rose to his full imposing height and spoke with calm seriousness. "If he hasn't said, then I don't feel I'm at liberty to speak about it. You understand. I don't wish to be secretive, but I don't feel it's my place to say."

"We're sure it can't be anything bad. Anything illegal or like that."

But the minister did not respond to the sally and only repeated that it was not his place to divulge. With that, he shook Walt's hand, waved casually at Monty behind the counter, and was out the door into the glorious day that had developed from the pretty morning. They watched as he trudged down the front walk and nodded to the girl making her way to the porch.

When the girl came into the lobby, Walt guessed her age at fourteen or so and thought he could almost say who she was. He would be certain to know her parents. She exhibited a teenager's awkward shyness when inquiring about Bonforth, and Monty divulged number 27 with ill-concealed reluctance. A professional bachelor, he was sharply concerned about the welfare of the young, feeling that too many of them were not looked after as they should be. "Are you going to be okay, honey?" he asked. "Let us know if we can help."

"I'm fine, thank you."

"I just thought I'd ask."

When the girl had made her way to the second floor, Monty said, "All right, Walt, you can count me in." He shook his head sadly.

"Are you sure?"

"That young girl . . ."

"We'll have to work fast," Walt said. "That storeroom is a mess and we've only got an hour at the most."

"We've been meaning to clean it up for a long time. I wish we had."

"There are other problems, too. Whoever is in there can hear pretty well what's going on in twenty-seven, but he won't be able to see anything."

"Maybe we could—"

"No," said Walt. "We won't be boring any holes. That would be disgusting."

"Yes, but it's such a highly unusual—"

"*Weird* is the word. . . . And it's going to be awfully warm in there, and whoever is in there is trapped until Bonforth leaves for dinner. There's no way to get in and out without making noise. It will be stuffy, and that is another solid reason not to fart."

"That bears thinking out," Monty said. "Four hours in a stuffy little hole in the dark. That room isn't wired. . . ."

When the girl came down, she appeared to be sound and happy, unharmed in any way. Whatever had transpired in 27, she had taken it in stride, and Monty was relieved. Then when Bonforth came down, he was calm and casual, though perhaps a little tired. He greeted his hosts and asked about telephone messages. He seemed gratified when Monty told him there had been no calls.

Upon his departure, the cousins raced upstairs, flung open the door to the closet, and began chucking things into cardboard boxes—broken lamps, rickety wicker tables, worn-out throw rugs, musty drapes, and other discards. They piled the boxes in the hallway and took them down the stairs and out back into the garage.

The need for haste made the job harder. They sweated and swore and found their tempers unimproved by the return of the honeymooners, who asked pointed questions about their activity. Walt fobbed them off till they ran out of patience.

"You know," said the male, "sometimes a big breakfast makes me sleepy. I think I'll turn in for a little nap."

Eunice giggled and asked if they might have the turn-down service. "We had a long day yesterday," she said.

Walt reddened but acquiesced and trotted to the end of the hall to freshen the bed of 21 and straighten the room. His departure left Monty struggling with a big box of nonmatching crockery and glassware. He balanced it against his sloping belly, strained down the steps, and did not drop it until he reached the lobby. Luckily, the box did not burst, so he hoisted it again and puffed his way out to the garage, clacking and clinking with every step.

On his way back, he stopped in the kitchen and got a chrome dinette chair. This he situated in the storeroom and then helped Monty lug the last object, a smelly old living room carpet, to the garage. He told Monty the honeymooners had retired.

Now the spying arrangement was complete. They washed up at the kitchen sink, restored their clothing with fitful tugs, and then looked at each other with mournful expressions.

Monty said, "Walt, are we really going to—"

Walt said, "I'm beginning to have—"

"Cold feet. Me, too. But—"

"Maybe we'd better think again before—"

The counter bell summoned them to the lobby. At the reception desk stood a dark-complexioned gentleman who sported a bristly mustache and a tightly wound blue turban. His dress otherwise was a tweed suit of an English cut. "Good day," he said in an East Indian accent. "I am inquiring if this is the Waltmon Inn of Gallinton, North Carolina."

The cousins acknowledged the fact.

"Then I am wondering if such a person as Mr. Harris T. Bonforth has ensconced himself herein."

Monty so affirmed, though he was uncertain that *ensconced* was entirely accurate.

"And he is absent now but will return at one o'clock?"

"Yes," Walt said. He glanced at his watch. "Five minutes from now."

"Perhaps I may then await with some certitude his arrival in this space?"

They nodded and the Indian gentleman nodded back. He emitted a rather pleasant aura of cinnamon and clove. "I will now sit," he announced, and did so, choosing the wicker rocker by the coffee table.

At this point, the gazes the cousins exchanged were decisive. They may as well have said aloud, "Yes, we will carry through our odious plan. We will spy upon these people, learn whatever we can, discuss them endlessly when alone together, and never feel the least twinge of compunction."

Bonforth came in at two minutes past the hour, greeted Walt and Monty with a smile, and went upstairs. The Indian fellow sat for another three minutes before following. They watched him ascend out of sight.

Then Walt blurted, "I believe she does know."

"Know what?"

"About Howie."

"Who?"

"Mamie Barnhart."

"For God's sake, Walt," Monty said. "Can't you— Don't you ever—"

"What?"

"I give up," Monty said.

3

The difficulties that Monty faced in this dinky little storeroom were more considerable than he had imagined. He could not lock the door from inside; there was a small brass thumb latch outside. If anyone opened it, he would be discovered sitting here, caught shamefaced, and probably liable for a volley of lawsuits. The air was like a warm, damp towel, noisome and stale, and his nerves were at an abrading pitch. Already he regretted entering into this unholy covenant and knew that he would sit in the dark all afternoon, upbraiding himself for a fool.

But the dialogue he was going to hear would dissipate his boredom. He had thought to bring a penlight and now he turned it upon his Bulova.

He could hear room 27 just fine. He heard the smart little rap at the door, heard Bonforth rise to greet his visitor, heard her quick manner of seating herself in the straight chair by the foot of the bed. He heard the two of them begin an animated conversation that promised much but revealed nothing.

Bonforth and the woman had chosen to communicate in French.

"*En français*" was about all he was able to gather. What little store of the language he had ever possessed was rust-eaten *jusqu'à l'os* and the very sound of the tongue always made his flesh creep. He sat in the dinette chair with its sticky plastic seat for an eternity of twenty-five minutes, understanding at last only two words—when they said to each other "Au revoir."

My God, he thought. He reflected on the callers who had come and gone. Would he spend the entire afternoon eavesdropping on the gibber of Hindi, the crackle of Croatian, the growl of German, the ululation of Urdu? He hated above all things that Bonforth must be a crackerjack linguist.

He was immensely relieved to find that the next caller, a male probably of middle age, spoke not only English but good ole southern at that. But his happiness disappeared after greetings were exchanged and the narrative began. Soon all prospect of relief vanished, to be replaced by utter disbelief and listless boredom. The boredom changed to mounting horror when the next guest showed up, a lady in her forties or fifties, who gave Bonforth no opportunity to question or respond, but poured forth her mind in a breathless deluge.

When she stopped and departed, Monty sighed, thinking he must now have heard the worst of it. But when the next visitor, an elderly fellow with an irritating tenor voice, began, he almost screamed. He flashed his watch again and saw that he had another fifty minutes still to endure. He sat clutching his elbows to his sides.

When at last the dinner hour arrived and Bonforth left his room, Monty discovered that he could not move. The ordeal had been too dreadful. He required two black minutes to recover, and when Walt came to turn the latch and rescue him, he was white-faced and trembling.

He stood in the hall, dazed by the light, and found that he had lost the power of speech. He mutely followed as Walt led him downstairs and seated him on the deck sofa in the lobby. Alarmed by Monty's pallor, Walt brought him a glass of cognac and the stricken man gulped it gratefully, though it went against his rule of taking no alcohol before seven.

Finally, Walt said, "Well?" and Monty shook his head pitiably and said, "It's no use asking."

"As bad as that?"

"Worse."

"In what way?"

"I can't describe it."

"Is it illegal?"

"No."

"Could you hear what they said?"

"All too clearly."

"I made notes on who they are. First, there was a fashionable young lady with a foreign accent; then came a peanut farmer from South Carolina or somewhere, and then—"

"Don't bother," Monty said. "I have them pictured pretty well."

"In that case—"

"No. Maybe later. But I will tell you there is no point in your sitting in that vile little hole tomorrow morning, listening to—"

"To what?"

"To people who—"

"People who what?"

"People like us," he said. "People like you and me. I learned more than I can ever put in words, Walt."

"Is it blackmail or something like that?"

"No."

"Then it can't be too bad."

"It is."

"But what—"

"If I understood what was going on, I'd draw a picture for you. Maybe you could understand. But if you go into that suffocating closet and eavesdrop, you may come out a blubbing, cross-eyed, drooling mental ruin. If you do it, don't blame me, because I'm telling you, *don't.*"

"When did I ever blame you? Anyhow, if you could stand it, I'm sure I could."

"But you're—"

"What?"

"Sensitive."

"I wish you'd stop calling me that. I'm just as strong as you are."

"You're going to do it, then? In spite of everything I say?"

"I have every right to know what you do."

"Well, you've been warned . . ."

"And I thank you for your concern. We have a busy day tomorrow at the front desk. Can you handle it?"

"Better than you can handle that closet."

"We'll see."

So it was settled, with Walt marching up the stairs with the determination of Pickett at Gettysburg while Bonforth was out for his constitutional. Monty manned his reception post with a distracted air, expecting the worst.

When Bonforth came in, he glanced at Monty fleetingly, but the gray-haired innkeeper thought he saw a gleam of suspicion in the man's eye. No, he decided, that was just guilt feeling. His one clear thought was that he wished he had never heard of Harris T. Bonforth.

He was glad to have duties to keep him busy. Foremost among these, he thought, was the log he was to keep on the arrivals. So he noted the red-haired lad with the thick brogue and the seedy fellow he recognized as the local bail bondsman. Then there was a nervous young lady with gothic makeup, but before she could mount the steps, the bondsman came lumbering down to report to Monty that there was a lot of commotion, just a terrible racket inside a closet next to room 27.

Monty bounded upstairs, to find that Bonforth had opened the closet door and was supporting Walt as he staggered out.

"Are you all right?" Monty asked.

Walt looked at him unseeingly. His hands were shaking.

"Can I be of help?" Bonforth asked.

"No, it'll be all right," Monty said. "Walt suffers from a touch of claustrophobia. He must have gotten himself locked in."

This obvious lie did not disturb Bonforth's demeanor. "Maybe a glass of spirits might help, if you have some in the house."

"Thank you. That's a good idea." Monty shoved the closet door closed hastily, hoping Bonforth had not seen the dinette chair in its position. He put his arm around Walt's shoulder and guided him toward the stairway. "Don't worry," he said. "He'll be all right. He's had these spells before."

"If you say so," Bonforth said, and returned to 27, closing the door firmly.

Monty hustled Walt through the lobby and into the back bedroom, settled him on the bed, knelt, and pulled off his shoes. "Lie back," he said. "Relax. Bonforth's suggestion was sound." He hurried into the kitchen, found a snifter and the cognac, and forced a healthy dose upon his cousin.

"Oh Monty," Walt said.

"I warned you, didn't I?"

Walt lay back and stared at the ceiling. "Elvis Presley scuppernong pie," he whispered.

"I know," Monty said. "Try to rest. Take a little nap, if you can. There's someone at the desk, but I'll be back in a jiffy." He did not wait for a response, but left Walt communing with the comfortless ceiling. When he finished checking out the honeymoon couple at the desk, he picked up the morning mail that had been delivered to the desk and looked through it. The new *Gallinton Bugler* was in the batch. He paged through it, tucked it under his arm, and went back to Walt.

Color had returned to Walt's cheeks and the quantity of cognac in the bottle had decreased. But the liquor had not restored Walt completely. His expression was mournful and his tone was pitiable when he said, "Oh Monty, I had no idea."

"Neither did I."

"Stole three quarters from the Sunday collection plate—"

"Hush now. It's bad enough we spied. We shouldn't pass on what we heard—not even to each other."

"Why not? It's all so—"

"Yes, I know. And I think I've figured it out—part of it at least."

Walt gave him an admiring stare. "What is it, then?"

"Secrets."

"Yes, I understood that much, for Chrissakes, but secrets like these—"

"Are not theirs."

"Say again."

"These are secondhand secrets. . . . Walt, how many times has someone said to you, 'I'll tell you something if you promise not to tell another living soul'?"

"Lots of times."

"How many times have you said the same thing to somebody?"

"I don't know. Not that many."

"Lots. Lots and lots."

"If you say so."

"I say so because everybody does, everybody. And how many times were these important secrets? How many times did they involve crimes or misdemeanors or conspiracy or anything like that?"

"I couldn't say."

Monty tapped Walt's foot with the folded *Bugler.* "Never."

"Never?"

"Almost never. Every time someone says that to you, the secret they reveal is some trivial, half-assed, chickenshit bit of information that isn't worth the breath it wastes."

"Like what?"

"Well, suppose I said, 'I'll tell you a secret if you promise not to tell anyone else ever,' and you said, 'Okay, I won't,' and then I told you Bobo Braintree doesn't change his socks but every three weeks."

"Who is Bobo Braintree?"

"Nobody. I just made him up as an example."

"He sounds real."

"He's not. I was trying to explain—"

"It stands to reason," Walt said, "that if a guy is named Bobo Braintree, he wouldn't wear fresh socks. With a name like that, there wouldn't be any point in it."

"Forget Bobo. He's just a figment. Anybody named Bobo Braintree wouldn't own socks. My point is that when people extract that solemn promise from you never to breathe the secret to another soul, what they tell you will burden you with some piece of lint that is not worth knowing in the first place."

"So?"

"So then you're stuck with it. You don't want to know it, but you can't pass it on. It just lodges in your mind like a tennis ball stuck in a gutter pipe. It's like those Christmas ties we get from Aunt Sudie."

"Or the fruitcakes from Aunt Miriam. We have at least eight out in the freezer."

"Then these dumb-ass secrets build up like steam in a boiler. Sooner or later you have to tell somebody or you'll explode."

"Even if it's really nothing."

"Especially."

"Let's say your sister let you have her recipe for Elvis Presley scuppernong pie, which was rumored to be one of his favorites. You would never in your life make such a dish, but your sister has told you the secret recipe. Would that count as a secret you don't want to possess and need to pass on?"

"Oh yes."

"Well, what you do is make your usual crust and bake it blind for fifteen minutes. Meanwhile, take your three cups of peeled grapes and push them through—"

"You're not supposed to tell me. Why do you think they call Bonforth? Because he won't blab it around. They've told this one person whose job it is to listen and he moves on to another town and probably never will return to Gallinton and he takes all these pocket-lint secrets with him, and he takes away the one you've been carrying around in your head, cursing the evil day that Baby Jocko ever told it to you."

"Who is Baby Jocko?"

"Nobody. Just a name I made up. You understand what I'm saying about the burden of Bonforth, don't you? He is the repository for the pointless secrets that build up in your head. He provides a relief valve."

"Is he any kin to Bobo? The names kind of sound alike."

"Bobo who?"

"Bobo Braintree, that guy who never changes his socks."

"Yes, Bobo Braintree and Baby Jocko are kin, in the sense that neither of them is real. They're just names I made up to try to explain to you my theory about Bonforth and that cuckoo, utterly idiotic crap we found ourselves listening to in that ghastly closet. . . . We ought to nail that closet door shut with railroad spikes."

"Why?"

"To stop us from ever spying again."

"Don't need to nail it shut," Walt said. "I've learned my lesson. What Harold Massey does with his toenail clippings is enough to—"

"Please. I don't want to hear. We're not supposed to know."

Walt sat on the edge of the bed, speaking in a tone of profound conviction. "It would be different if the secrets were valid. If they were about embezzlement or forgery or incest or murder, I could stand it. I could keep my mouth shut. It would be a point of honor. But this moronic, dust-bunny, chipped-paint junk will drive me crazy if I can't get rid of it. How does Bonforth listen to this stuff day in and day out and keep his sanity?"

"It's his vocation. He saw a need for someone to do what he does. Nobody else does—or ever will."

"Why don't these people go to a psychiatrist or psychologist or a priest or minister?"

"Would you?"

"Well . . . no. I would feel I was supposed to tell a priest or a psychiatrist something important, some dark secret that might destroy others as well as myself. I wouldn't bother a minister with this flea dirt."

"And besides, you had given your word not to tell."

"Yet here I am, spilling the beans to Bonforth."

"You finally had to tell *somebody.* The secret is not worth keeping, but you gave your word. It drives you nutty, like an itch you can't scratch—

right between your shoulder blades. Then you see an ad in the paper: 'Do you have something to tell me?' Harris T. Bonforth to the rescue. You see that he is going to be at the Waltmon Inn in Gallinton. As soon as you see the ad, you know what it means. You're going to make a pilgrimage and get off your chest how Jimmy Peru saw Madeleine Ecuador pinch three quarters from the church collection plate on Easter Sunday, 1993."

"It wasn't Jimmy Peru and Madeleine Ecuador. It was Byron Jones who saw Helen Parker."

"You shouldn't have told me. I'm not supposed to know."

"You knew already. You only got the names wrong."

"It was a coincidence. I didn't know about Helen Parker."

"You must have heard."

"I heard it when one of Bonforth's visitors told him in room twenty-seven." Monty unrolled the *Bugler* and turned to the back pages. "Byron never told *me*."

"But you got the date right."

"That's a coincidence, too. I'm aghast to hear that Helen stole money."

"She was just nine years old."

"See—that's a secret not worth knowing."

"I wish I didn't," Walt said.

"Me, too. . . . Look. Here is the new Bonforth ad. It's the same as before, except he is going to be at the Wander Inn in Eberle on Monday and Tuesday."

Walt sighed. "And people will flock to room twenty-seven or whatever and tell all the ratty little secrets that bug them?"

"Yes."

"How come he doesn't charge for this service? Nobody mentioned paying him while I was listening."

"They've already paid by credit card. It's a subscription service. You give your card number and the lady runs it through and offers you a time slot."

"How do you know?"

"I called the number." Monty held the page up: 1-800-TELLALL.

"Who answered?"

"A woman. She sounded like she might be his wife."

"How did she sound?"

"Sad. Weary."

Walt nodded. "I believe it. What a life."

"I'll tell you what," Monty said. "This Bonforth is a stronger man than I am."

"Or me. . . . Harlow Massey's toenail clippings. God help us."

"Let me have a taste of brandy," Monty suggested. Walt handed him the snifter and he tipped in a heroic dose.

"I dread to check Bonforth out when he leaves," Walt said. "I'm ashamed to stand in front of him."

Monty set his glass down. "You'll have to do it, though. And I'll tell you something else: If you ever say the words *bon ton* again, I'll strangle you with a dog leash. The Waltmon no longer has any right to that description. Just look at us."

"All right. But what are we going to do?"

They looked at each other for a long time.

"It's forty-five miles to Eberle," Monty said at last. "We can't both be absent from the inn. Do you want off Monday or Tuesday?"

"I'll wait till Tuesday," Walt said. "Maybe I'll feel less guilty by then."

And now they looked quickly away, as if fearing that they might read each other's dread secret—that Walt might see that Monty was going to tell him that Billy Joe Tyson reported to him in third grade that he saw Nelda Willets eat a booger from her very own nose, and that Monty might discover that Walt, in his wonderful Walt-like way, was going to reveal to Harris T. Bonforth what he had learned about the disgusting footwear habits of Bobo Braintree.

THE LODGER

1

We better understand Robert Ackley's character and temperament when we recall that he referred to the presence that had recently usurped so large a part of his mind as the Lodger. He was a great admirer of Alfred Hitchcock's movies and his assiduity in pursuing his interests had led him to read the novel from which the film was adapted, though with a dash of disappointment. He found the story clumsily cobbled together.

His judgment was generally trustworthy because he read a great deal. Poe's familiar phrase describes the tenor of his book list—"many a quaint and curious volume of forgotten lore"—and he had lifelong opportunity to trace down arcane interests because he was a librarian at Bryan University in Plattsborough, North Carolina. His daily ongoing task in these years was to transfer titles from the card catalogue into the computer; the twentieth century had waited until its final decade to overtake Bryan University.

And to overtake Robert Ackley also. He was not altogether willing to be a modern person, even though he was still in his early thirties, sound of body and mind (until these latter nine days at least), wholesome in his appetites, wryly humorous in disposition. He was a slight man with dark hair cut straight across his forehead, a gauzy swatch of mustache, and bright, inquisitive eyes as black as licorice. Not exactly prepossessing, we might say, but those lively eyes often attracted the notice of females, in whom Robert took a pleasant and, with one exception, casual interest.

Bryan University was not one of the largest, and its library, the David Shelton Greene Library, included only some two million volumes. In these days, that number may fairly be described as a modest one, yet six zeros with an integer compose an obese magnitude when it comes to counting books. It is hard to be convinced that human beings have ever known or needed to know two million different ideas. There were surely enough *curious* volumes among the ones he recatalogued to keep Ackley's lazy connoisseurship fastidious. He decided early on that he would have to forgo reading such intriguing delights as a three-volume history of Burmese marriage customs, a soi-disant "Tantric" interpretation of the Kabbalah, a duodecimo treatise on the engineering feats of the Mongols, and the newly discovered translation of the *Satyricon* by Sir Richard Burton.

Even so, the shelves and tables and chairs and floors of his snug three-room apartment on Granby Street were stacked, strewn, and scattered with all sorts of titles that Ackley turned up in the catalogue, books that had aroused no attention other than his own in years, pages that had not felt the pressure of human gaze since their first publication. There must have been a good 150 of these, and if we are constrained to choose one title to serve as an index to Ackley's taste and to represent the multitude of these books, we might single out Annie Francé-Harrar's *Die Tragödie des Paracelsus,* published by Seifert in 1924 at Stuttgart.

He was a dilettante—as we see. For the Francé-Harrar opus is reckoned by those who are renowned in judging such things as being of little value as science, history, drama, or poetry. Even for Ackley, its main attraction was that it was obscure, for though he did profess an interest in alchemy and some other occult sciences, he had only opened the volume in the middle, jogged along with one finger in his German dictionary, and then laid it aside, perhaps to look into it more closely later on, perhaps to return it to the library with the regretful conviction that life is devastatingly *brevis* and a mastery of German excruciatingly *longa.*

The book that afflicted him, the book that brought on the advent of the Lodger, was not a striking volume in the least. It was poetry and as slender as those collections usually are. Its salient features, according to

Ackley's judgment, were that it had been privately published in Asheville, North Carolina, in 1934, and that it had been written by Lyman Scoresby. It was entitled *Chants of a Wander-Star.*

In light of later developments, we might make a lame joke by saying that Lyman Scoresby was hardly a name to conjure with. It is true that his name is but barely known to scholars of American literature and nowhere appears in the anthologies or histories and that he never even supplied subject matter for journal articles. A lonesome footnote in one book review or another mentions him, usually in parentheses, and to trace his name in literary history is rather like trying to outline the flight of a firefly on the far side of a nocturnal lake. There are occasional gleams at random points but little hint of coherent pattern.

He attracted Robert Ackley's notice because he had once been associated with that strange group of artists and writers who had gathered in Cleveland in the 1920s: Samuel Loveman, the poet, and William Sommer, the painter, the artist and architect William Lescaze, Hart Crane and his philosopher friend Sterling Croydon, the stage designer Richard Rychtarik and his wife, Charlotte, the accomplished pianist. There were others, too. H. P. Lovecraft, though not a resident of Cleveland, was once a visitor among them, as was the blind mathematical theorist who called himself "Dormouse," and the taciturn, ever patient observer of the group, the book designer E. Warburton, to whose later casual memoir, *Songsters in a Flock,* we owe our knowledge of his friends.

They were never formally organized, being too anarchical, and so they never gave their group a name. And after the baffling disappearance of Sterling Croydon in 1923, these artists and thinkers scattered themselves across America, keeping so far apart from one another that it seemed their conscious plan to do so. But intermittently for the three years earlier, they had met and rejoiced in mutual company.

E. Warburton implies in his account that it was the poet Lyman Scoresby who acquainted this homegrown Cleveland avant-garde with the use of drugs. Scoresby was a mysterious figure to them, a vagabond who claimed to have extensive knowledge of such things as European movements in painting, of the group of decadent poets currently raising bourgeois eyebrows in San Francisco, of the sexual practices of Lafcadio Hearn, of the most abstruse Oriental philosophies. He had written and published at his own expense a sonnet sequence, *Spindrift Twilights,* which Hart Crane had praised as being "pretty unusual, after all—at least not the usual wagonload of horseshit."

But even for the redoubtable Crane, Scoresby's personal habits were too bizarre to permit a close friendship to develop. Scoresby as a general practice engorged a number of obscure and poisonous-smelling drugs at once, draped himself in a diaphanous silk robe shoulder to toe, and sat for hours on a scrap of Ispahan carpet in his apartment bedroom, chanting incomprehensible phrases, incantations in no known language. Crane enjoyed Scoresby's drugs, the cocaine and the various cannabis derivatives, but could not endure the man himself, considering him a poseur. "As phony as a glass eye on a bulldog," he said.

In artistic terms at least, the description seemed accurate. There was nothing original about such poems as "Meditation of the Lycanthrope," "Etude in Puce and Nacre," and "Secret Glances." The sonnet beginning "Though vile thy kisses drawn am I to thee" was easy material for one of Hart Crane's obscene parodies, one that he improvised at a party while being so hilariously inebriated, he did not notice Scoresby's presence in the room. Scoresby's reaction to the incident is not recorded, but it is likely that he simply shrugged it off.

As far as Robert Ackley could discern—at a distance of some sixty years—that weary, sardonic, careless shrug had characterized Scoresby's attitude toward life. Though he had died (according to fairly reliable rumor) in Buenos Aires in 1945, he wrote to the end the kind of verse which was already fading from fashion when the century began. Lines rubbly with semiprecious stones—agate, onyx, beryl, and the like; quatrains fetid with head-aching perfumes and incenses; sonnets that mentioned but did not describe "unspeakable desires," "sable impurities," "unnameable caresses," and so forth. All this was Scoresby's stock-in-trade, the images he lived for, the phrases he died amid.

What gave Scoresby the confidence to shrug life off like a lightly dozing sleeper brushing away a fly was his steady conviction that he was immortal. So reports Warburton in his *Songsters* account. The names of Guillaume Apollinaire, T. S. Eliot, Arthur Symons, J.-J. Fleury, and the others would blaze in the firmament like ruptured stars but then, like those same stars, would fade and disperse to filmy rags. The name of

Lyman Scoresby, the name that soulless injustice had treated as a mere tattered ghost during his earthly years, would come to life again and burn with a strong and steady light.

But it took a long time for Robert Ackley to understand that the life Scoresby was trying to assume was Ackley's own. The struggle began when he woke one morning with a strong craving for nicotine. He had once been a smoker for a short time, but that had been seven years ago, and when he decided to jettison the habit, he was able to do so without fuss or fret. But now he felt such strong desire for a cigarette to accompany his customary single cup of Maxwell House, he tried to think why. There had been a dream, one of those vivid morning dreams that occur when the mind is on the edge of wakefulness. There had been tobacco smoke in it and . . . water. There had been water in it. When he pondered the fact of the water, a word came to his mouth and he said it aloud: "Hookah." Then he smiled and nodded; he recalled reading Lyman Scoresby's poem just before he dropped asleep. "The Hookah" was the opening poem in *Chants of a Wander-Star.*

He fetched the volume from his bedside table to his breakfast bar, perched himself on a stool with his coffee, and read through the poem with desultory curiosity. In the cool morning light, it seemed even less interesting than before.

Strange visions in the smoke are gliding
Like dusky isles in eastern seas
Where foreign constellations sliding
Suggest most ancient memories!

The latter seven stanzas bore out the lack of promise displayed in this first one. Ackley found it vapid entirely.

But his severe judgment did not quell his yearning for tobacco, and all day long he had to keep pushing this desire to the back of his mind. The result was a deafening headache and so he stopped by Keeler's Drug Store on his way home and picked up a package of Old Golds. He was startled by the expense; when last he smoked, cigarettes had cost fifty cents a package.

In his apartment, he did not light up immediately, but began to rummage through the clothes in his closet for a piece of apparel he could not at first put a name to. Vexed at a palpable absence, vexed with himself, he plopped into his one armchair, smoked the cigarette he resented, and tried to understand what was wrong.

What had he been seeking in his closet?

He smoked down to the filter before it came to him that he had been trying to find his smoking jacket. He gasped at this revelation, then giggled. He had never owned a smoking jacket. At work, he wore a jacket and tie and blue jeans and his only concern about fashion otherwise was to ascertain that he didn't wear a T-shirt with an offensive slogan. To Robert Ackley, a smoking jacket was as alien a garment as fuzzy pink bedroom slippers. Especially bizarre was the sort of jacket of which he had received an image: a burgundy velvet creation with scarlet silk lapels and wide cuffs and a gold cord sash.

Good Lord, he thought. What in the world has gotten into me?

He determined to puzzle it out. He went into the kitchen, took a Budweiser from the fridge, popped it, and came back into the living room. Abruptly, he rose again from the armchair and after a moment's searching returned with a glass. That was odd enough, for he was used to sipping from the can, but when he poured it, a scrap of poetry flashed into his head: *liqueur jaune qui fait suer.* Where had he ever heard that? And how had he memorized it? His French was not even as good as his pitiable German.

The one clue he had to the distress of this day was Lyman Scoresby. He had thumbed about in *Chants of a Wander-Star* last night in bed and wondered about the career of that marginal versifier—born out of his proper time and now remembered by Ackley in an era even less congenial. He got the book from where it sat by his cold coffee cup on the breakfast bar and riffled through it. There must have been one particular poem that had brought on his restless sleep, his flustered day.

But all of Scoresby's strophes were so vague and pastel that they misted into one another. Ackley could not remember whether he had drowsed off over "Assignation at Midnight" or "Vampire Kisses" or "The Wine of the Unforgotten" or "Violet Eyes." Still he persisted. He did not want to take up smoking again and he was determined to suppress savagely any budding passion for velvet smoking jackets.

The centerpiece of *Chants* was a longish effort entitled "The Incantation." It was divided into four parts, of which the first was comprehensible enough and conventional enough, too, a poet's ordinary boast that his work shall outlive marble and bronze. The remaining sections surpassed Scoresby's usual vagueness. Part II began with these lines:

> Sylphs of elements aethereal,
> In all contiguous shades and properties,
> Numinous and nominal, employ
> To every corner of the universe.
>
> Might and power and ebon puissance
> In service to thy servant proud and humble,
> His willing spirit joining to your strength
> Infernal, and his soul to subterranean
> Dis indentured and the compact signed
> Eternally in blood, eternally,
> Indissolubly bound, admixtured, mingled.

Mere blather, mere daft natter.

But then Ackley thought he noticed something and took a closer look. Sure enough: His half-forgotten knowledge of Latin had picked out an acrostic. The initial letters of the lines spelled it out: *Sint mihi dei Acherontii propitii! Ignei, aerii, aquatici, spiritus salvete! Orientis Princeps Beelzebub*, etc.

Etc.

Etc.: It was a classic invocation for the appearance of Beelzebub, or Mephistopheles, or Satan—what's in a name? Scoresby had designed his poem to call up the Prince of Darkness by whatever cognomen he might care to be hailed.

Supposing that notion to be true, for what purpose might he have done so?

Well, for the same reason that any weak-minded, ne'er-do-well poetaster would sign to such a stupid, ruinous association—to ensure the longevity of his work.

But in Scoresby's case, the terms of the contract must have been a little different; he must have secured an agreement for the reanimation of his spirit in the mind and body of another person, someone who would be living after he died, someone sympathetic to his poetic ambitions and exotic doctrines. He would enter this victim—whom he had to count upon as being more or less willing—and through his or her agency begin a campaign to rescue his stanzas from oblivion. Only a poet or an utter idiot would be willing to strike such a bargain, giving up as hostage his immortal soul.

Yet Scoresby might have had reason to consider himself lucky. Are poets not known almost universally as a puling, equivocal, and feeble race of beings? Over the millennia, some hundreds or even thousands of them must have called upon the Tyrant of Shades to pocket their souls and preserve their phrases and had been rejected by the infernal regent. Perhaps the Evil One felt momentary pity for a mankind long burdened with verses, or perhaps he knew that these spirits were already forfeit to him for other, more lurid, reasons. Or maybe he considered these particular souls too dingy and cheapjack to be worth the collecting.

But for some reason he must have appeared to Scoresby and taken an interest in his proposal.

Robert Ackley regarded this strain of thought rather as if he were reading a detective story and trying to discover the author's solution. Or like someone trying to diagnose and repair an ailing kitchen appliance. For though he probably did not truly believe in Satan, his powers and dominion, he did not entirely disbelieve, either. In this matter, as in so many others, he was strongly neutral.

So the situation presented itself to him in pragmatic terms: The spirit of the dead poet Lyman Scoresby had been summoned by Ackley's reading of "The Incantation" to take over the young librarian in order to work his posthumous stratagem. It was as if he were a bright new duplex apartment infested by a ghost. The task at hand was simply to get rid of this unwelcome lodger, to drive him away.

Then occurred the incident that removed the problem from the provenance of the suppositional. A voice spoke in Ackley's mind, cool and unmistakable. Its timbre was very like that of Vincent Price in a sinister role—unctuous but soaked in sarcasm. And the voice said:

Drive me away! What makes you think you can do so, you pustulant, inconsequential little turd?

2

With these words began the struggle of Robert Ackley for his life. It was not epic in proportion nor cosmic in its philosophic terms, but for the young man it was in deadly earnest. His mettle and his cunning were tested thoroughly. And so was his temper. The moment he heard those first two sentences in his mind, he no longer thought of Lyman Scoresby as the Lodger, but as the Squatter, and he determined to evict the dead poet, even if it meant standing against Satan and all his legions.

Scoresby broke into these valiant ambitions. "As for Satan," he said, "that notion is all putrid claptrap. The simple acrostic is present merely as a red herring to draw attention away from the truly effective mechanism of the poem. There are other, more complex anagrams in the lines that spell out in letter symbols Sterling Croydon's mathematical formulae for the manipulation of temporal-spatial emplacement. It is science, not hoodoo."

"That is valuable information to have," Ackley said.

"Not for you," replied Scoresby. "I have observed your mind at extremely close range for three days now and a more muddled swamp of puerility and incoherence would be impossible to discover. There is no way you could comprehend the information. You possess no strength of character, no sense of purpose, no true love of learning, no aptitude for luxury, no capacity for logic, no taste in literature."

"No taste in literature? You say that to someone so deeply engrossed in *Chants of a Wander-Star*?"

Ackley's attempt at sarcasm made no impression upon Scoresby. "I would almost prefer to be devoured by hogs than to be read by Robert Ackley. I watched your perusal of 'Evanescent Crepuscule.' You caught not the least glimmer of even one of its beauties. There is a delicate nimbus of nuance about every line of that sonnet, yet you worked through it like a groom mucking out a stable. You have no ear for assonance, no eye for filigree. A poet must clout you with a brickbat to catch your attention."

"Well then, if I'm such unpromising material, who don't you go take over someone else's mind?"

Dark bitterness suffused Scoresby's reply. "Since my death, you are the first to look into my poems. The only one! Can you comprehend that? I was Hart Crane's unacknowledged mentor, his greatest influence. I talked with Emile Verhaeren in a café in Bruges all one rainy September afternoon, learning the secret of his music. My long correspondence with George Sterling is lost now, but it changed the whole complexion of his work. It was from me that J.-J. Fleury purloined that famous line, '*Bateau des rêves, blessé par la lune!*' Yet fifty years have passed since anyone so much as opened the *Chants,* and here I am, called by my 'Incantation' from that zone of silent oblivion to greet my savior—a tin-eared, slovenly, tasteless little nincompoop in tennis sneakers!"

Ackley was so addled by the acridity of this outburst that he could only ask, "What's wrong with sneakers?"

"They are called Nikes, for God's sake! Can even that ham-handed irony be lost upon you?"

"No," Ackley said. Then: "Yes." Then: "I don't know."

Scoresby continued in a tone resonant with barely suppressed malevolence. "But I do not despair. The situation seems impossible. It is not that I must make a silk purse from a sow's ear; it is more like having to fashion a Venus de Milo from a lump of wet cow dung. But I believe that I can persevere and triumph."

"You'll have to do it without my help," Ackley said. "So far, you haven't given me any reason to be happy with our relationship."

"Oh, but I shall," Scoresby said. "I have a multitude of gifts to confer. I am privy to confidences you cannot yet imagine. I know things about life and love and literature that talented poets would kill to learn. The greatest part of my knowledge lies far beyond the tiny purview of your acquaintance."

"Maybe you know a lot of stuff I don't care to know."

"Once you glimpse the vistas I can provide, once you taste the arcane knowledge I have acquired, you will find my outlook irresistible."

This prediction turned out to be lacking in accuracy. Ackley discovered that his attraction to literary obscurities was never so powerful as he had believed. Scoresby related encounters with poets and writers from nations that had long disappeared from the maps, but Ackley responded lukewarmly at best. He had heard of hardly any of these scribblers; sometimes he had not even heard of the cities they inhabited. Now and again some famous spot would turn up, Café Les Deux Magots or the Catalán or the Café Royal or The Fabulous Pickwick—but the writers with whom Scoresby had conversed, argued, and brought to heel in those legendary rooms were unknown to Ackley.

"It is no use trying to educate you," Scoresby said, his tone pallid with disappointment. "The completely ignorant are ineducable. Knowledge has to find some little niche to serve as a toehold. But you—you are a blank page."

"I am a more widely read fellow than almost anybody else you could have latched on to," Ackley said.

"So you say. And yet you know nothing of Montalini's ballet, *Schisma,* or the cycle of Onotrio's poems that suggested it."

"No."

"You never heard of Henri Dollé's scandalous novel, *Les Liaisons Scabreuses.*"

"No."

"You never even heard of that legendary literary review from the Four Oaks group in Texas, *Hashish Cayuse.*"

"Never."

"I have returned too soon," Scoresby said. "I have arrived in a new dark age, when literature and art and music are unknown. I suppose the most able minds of your generation are preoccupied with television wrestling shows and roller derby."

"Well—not the *very* most."

"I despair of ever intriguing your intellectual curiosity or your aesthetic sensibility. You have neither." The tone of his words sharpened then and Ackley heard a hint of threat. "But there are other means to my ends."

"What are you referring to?"

"You'll understand. Soon."

But Ackley did not at first understand; he only began to experience jittery days and excited sleep. His mind was distracted and his body incapable of repose. When he sat, he twiddled his fingers, and when he stood, he twisted in his shoes. His condition was just as it had been during the day he had been plagued by a craving for cigarettes. He knew that he desired something, that Scoresby had worked upon his sleeping mind to produce this powerful wanting in him, but he could not say what it was that he desired.

He knew that when he was asleep, he was almost defenseless, that the vengeful poet could exacerbate his nerves dreadfully. Yet clear understanding did away with the artificial desire as neatly as light devours shadow. As soon as Ackley comprehended that Scoresby had planted in his psyche an artificial need for tobacco, he threw away those cigarettes and had not craved them since.

Of course, as soon as Ackley figured out the process, Scoresby, inhabiting his mind, also knew. Therefore, Scoresby was producing in him a strong craving for something or other but would not say what, because when Ackley knew the object of his enforced desire, he would be able to disregard that desire.

So he only grew more anxious and more wildly nervous. Scoresby operated in his mind at night and was silent when he was awake. When his colleagues at the library remarked upon the state of his nerves, Ackley replied that he was trying to give up coffee. He had decided from the beginning that he could speak frankly to no one about the truth of his situation. They would neither believe nor understand.

So he tried to figure out what Scoresby was causing him to desire by analyzing the sensations he felt. It was something liquid, probably a liquor of some sort, and he detected in his mouth the faint anticipatory taste of licorice and in his soft palate the strong odor of gymnasium floors.

The latter olfactory clue was tantalizing, and when he tried to put it together with what he knew of Scoresby's life and personality, he at first drew a blank. Only the chance mention of Pablo Picasso's name in a newspaper article reminded him: *The Absinthe Drinker.* Scoresby was trying to work up in his host a thirst for absinthe.

Ackley sat in his armchair and laughed aloud, and when he did so, the voice, which had not spoken in actual words for two days, returned. Scoresby's tone was sour and disappointed. "I do not find this situation amusing."

"Oh, come on," Ackley said. "Absinthe. You've got to be kidding. In the first place, it's been illegal for decades. And in the *real* first place, this is America. We don't do absinthe here. I know that you know better. What the hell are you up to?"

"I'm only trying to make myself comfortable. I find that I am forced to inhabit, as it were, a shabby suite of rooms in a particularly seedy hotel. I am only trying to furnish the locus with a few civilized amenities."

"Well, you can stop trying to get me hooked on all the vices you used to enjoy. I've got enough of my own, thank you."

"Your boast is pointless," Scoresby replied. "You worry about having three beers instead of two in the evening. You fear you'll become overweight. You fret endlessly about something called cholesterol and what it will do to your system. Can you possibly conceive how humiliating it is for me to be trapped in the psyche of a man who worries about the inner walls of his arteries? Do you realize what disgusting images are thrown at me when you think about eating a hamburger sandwich?"

"I hadn't thought," Ackley said. "I hadn't known you could see my subconscious thoughts so clearly." He fell silent under force of a presentiment. "Oh my God. That means you can see into my sexual fantasies, too."

"Let us please not go into this subject. The whole matter is stomach-wrenching."

"Well, you're a dirty old man by vocation. I expect you're voyeur enough to be turned on."

"*Turned on*. The mechanical nature of your metaphor gives you away completely. Do you realize that you are in process of falling in love with a female soccer coach? That your most daring fantasy involves this woman and a trampoline? Have you happened to notice that this *athlete* has freckles?"

"I think they're cute," Ackley said.

"Cute? Cute! This conversation is nauseating. A soccer coach . . . Oh, this is hell, nor are we out of it."

"Well," said Ackley, "I regret that my sex life fails to thrill you."

"It isn't even sex, not in the true sense—and I'm not convinced it's a life, either."

"I'm sure you have better ideas."

"I believe so," the poet said, and there began to take shape in Ackley's mind a face and afterward a figure. Cold blue eyes, and a complexion fair and unblemished, a careless lock of ash-blond hair falling over a low forehead, and a full and petulant mouth that hinted at cruelty. This face looked over a naked white shoulder, and then the figure turned slowly, presenting itself full length.

"Not my type, I'm afraid," said Ackley. "An Etonian, I presume?"

"He is the Love that Dare Not Speak Its Name. You would know him at first as a mere wanton, but after you became intimate, you would find unsuspected shadows in his character, surprising profundities."

"No, I wouldn't."

"You would be taught," Scoresby promised. "You need to realize that each of the appetites can be developed into a wild excess of poetic inspiration and dark correspondences and revelatory hours of ecstasy."

"I've got no interest in playing with boys, whether they can speak their names or not." Ackley's voice was firm. "I'm not interested in burning incense or smoking hashish or buying a lot of haberdashery in mauve and olive. You've got the wrong guy, that's all. I am never going to change the way you want me to."

"You spend half your life in sleep," Scoresby said. "That's when I work my will. We have a long way to go together, you and I."

3

The next afternoon, Ackley began his counteroffensive. In the supermarket, he bought a case of beer, economy-size packages of potato chips, Fritos, and fried pork rinds. For reading matter, he picked up a *TV Guide* and a tabloid newspaper that informed him that Elvis was an angel sent down by Saint Peter to serve as an example of what can happen with drug abuse. He had been taught to sing in heaven.

Ackley had planned a full evening for himself and his Squatter. He ate most of the junk food, got squidgy on twelve cans of Budweiser, and sat through a loud television session in which a hairy wrestler in silver lamé trunks and cape promised dire revenge upon his personal nemesis, a surly chap who was billed as the Eviscerator but who found the pronunciation of his sobriquet a tricky proposition.

There Ackley sat in his armchair, munching, guzzling, and stunned, while his brain cells committed suicide. After an hour he switched over to a political talk show; its format seemed identical to the wrestling show, blustering bellowers trading insults. He then watched four sitcoms in a row, foreseeing the punch lines and mouthing them along with the actors. Finally he turned to the C-SPAN channel and watched the public workings of the government. This spectacle seemed to combine all the qualities of the programming he had watched earlier: hysteria, predictability, illogic, swagger, decibel abuse, and hollow threats. Two hours he spent with the Senate before he went to bed, convinced that he must have dealt his Squatter a telling blow, perhaps a fatal one.

He had certainly dealt sorely with himself. He woke with a dull red headache, grainy eyes, a tongue as shaggy as an angora goat, and a painful bladder. He tended his urgencies as best he could and hoped that this coming day would not be molested by those unsettling nonspecific yearnings with which Scoresby had been attacking him. Maybe he had crippled the poet's powers.

"What a dolt you are," the voice said. "Do you think I could find mere simpleminded vulgarity threatening? Do you not understand that poets early in their lives develop armor to protect themselves from the babble of mass idiocy? You'll have to try harder than that, my dear philistine. If you can. For I believe that such a regimen as you have experimented with will be harder on you than on me."

Ackley, heavy-headed and with trembling hands, could only agree with his adversary. It was a trial to get coffee made this morning, and after he had poured a cup and added his skim milk, he could not bear to taste it. He left it standing on the breakfast bar and went off to work bloated and crapulous.

His condition was such that he could not even attempt to formulate a new plan of attack and he was resigned to the idea that Scoresby would punish his sleep again tonight, worming some silly craving deeper into his psyche, undermining his strength continuously.

He knew that he had to hit the poet swiftly and forcefully, but his tenderest spot, his overweening vanity, seemed impossible to reach. It was too bad that *Spindrift Twilights* and *Chants of a Wander-Star* had been so thoroughly ignored by critics. If they had not been, Ackley could read Scoresby's unfavorable notices again and again until the plummy scribbler shriveled to a prune.

His aesthetic sensibilities seemed also immune. The temperament that could withstand an evening of World Championship Wrestling and *The National Enquirer* could take every brutal punishment.

But perhaps that choice of poisons had been mistaken; perhaps it was not popular vulgarity that would debilitate Scoresby, but an entirely different aesthetic philosophy.

At work, he raided the library shelves and brought home a boxful of poetry books of widely different sorts. He took them from the box immediately after clearing away his frugal supper and stacked them by his faithful armchair—which he had begun to think of as his "command post." Here he laid out poets beatnik, bleatnik, and fruitnik; propaganda poets of every persuasion, Marxist, feminist, environmentalist, animal rightist, animal leftist, fetishist, capitalist, elitist, antielitist, pacifist, militarist, pessimist, and even optimist; poets heterosexual, homosexual, bisexual, pansexual, neutered, and undecided; poets advocating revolutions in Haiti, Mongolia, Chile, Bosnia, France, Canada, the Solomon Islands, Nebraska, and Antarctica; poets for and against, beneath and above, behind and beyond; cowboy poets and poets playing Indian; regional poets and universal poets; poets pragmatic or mystic or merely helpless; love poets and hate poets and indifferent poets; poets who wrote in nonstop blocks of print and others who brought out books filled with blank pages.

Ackley served himself soda water on the rocks and gritted his teeth and began. The first book he picked up was called *Bustin' on the Brazos* and the poem he turned to was "Old Red":

Well, they said Old Red was a helluva horse
But me and the boys didn't feel no remorse
And my nerve didn't flag

When I roped that nag
And swore I'd ride him to hell or worse!

This poet was named Willie "Tex" Brannigan and he was powerful partial to exclamation points.

After twenty pages or so, Ackley began to feel saddle-sore, so he switched to a chapbook of wild typography called *Werewolf Amoco Sutra* by someone who signed himself "Loper." This poet had raised the art of poetry to pure interjection; his lines were composed of transliterated animal cries: "Woooaugh! Rrrr! Wuhwuhwoo! Ahaaagh!" and so on. Now and then he would return to the minor theme announced in his title and interpolate a phrase like "Next gas 100 mi." and "unleaded" and "high-test." Loper's lines were hard to concentrate on, Ackley found, and when he tried to read them aloud, he couldn't stop giggling.

Next up was Gerald Greyforth and his *Autobiography Regarded as a Species of Refracted Flourish.* Reading the poem called "Weeds" (in which weeds were not mentioned), Ackley could not decide whether Greyforth had visited the Alps or not. Those mountains were often named but never described, yet it seemed at least possible that some sort of sexual encounter had taken place among three people on skis. But it was not clear how Titian, Thelonious Monk, and the elephant were involved. Ackley became impatient and flipped over to a poem called "Lenox Avenue: 2:43 p. m., 1948 or '72."

I said did you see Lady Day was she really
and Frank said Pardon me in that way he used to
and nobody knew they would die then
because after all he was Frank and she was
Lady Day and how it all happened was beyond
the taxis and the glare and Lenox even out to
124th St.

Greyforth seemed to have trouble concentrating on his subject matter and his way of muttering lines on the page made Ackley feel apprehensive and ashamed, as if he were overhearing some penurious, deranged, homeless person in the street and had no way to give aid.

He found no relief in the next effort, either, a book-length poem called *Squall.* It was about "demon-headed hipsters" and incestuous impulses and unfortunate gustatory experiences. Ackley turned from skimming the middle of the poem back to the opening lines, then snapped the book shut. If this poet really had seen the best minds of his generation, it was obvious that none of them had spoken to him.

And so on through the night till 2:00 A.M., Robert Ackley ran the gauntlet of contemporary poetry, feeling more and more dislocated with every page he turned. When he rose on the morrow, he still felt dislocated; he was light-headed and forgetful and divined that some part of his morning was missing, though he had kept to his usual routine. Then he realized that the presence of Lyman Scoresby was in some measure diminished in him. He could feel that the poet was still there—it was a sensation like standing in front of an open refrigerator—but he knew he must be on the right track. Scoresby had suffered a palpable hit. Ackley wished that he knew which book had wreaked the largest amount of damage so that he could seek out that bard's collected works and deliver his Squatter a destroying barrage.

But such a tactic might not work. It was possible that Scoresby could develop an immunity to the ravages of contemporary poetry. Ackley had known two persons in his life who claimed not only to read the stuff frequently but even to enjoy it. Now that he had given a long evening to the experience, he did not know whether to admire his friends' fortitude or to doubt their veracity. Still, he would take no chances; he would move on to the next stage of his plan, escalating the ferocity of his attack.

It was the weekend, two days of promised October sunshine that Ackley would ordinarily have spent cycling or playing softball or fishing at Platt Lake. But his task lay before him and he felt, carrying another boxful of books home from the library on this cozy Friday evening, that he had amassed the armament necessary to make this onslaught on Scoresby the final one.

He took pains to set a nourishing table: a small steak, baked potato, green salad, and a thawed slab of apple pie. He ate at his kitchen table, lonesome and somber, sipping iced tea and trying to clear his mind. When he felt sufficiently prepared, he marched to his command post, kicked his way through the volumes of poetry, cleared a space for the book box, and set it down beside him. He leaned back in the armchair, closed his eyes, and breathed deeply. He paused for a long, dramatic moment, summoning his powers. Then he plunged his hand into the box and took out the first volume he touched.

It was Rhoda Taylor-Smythe-Bernstein's *Shakespeare and Other Crimes Against Women* and it lived up to the promise of its title. This scholar held more grudges against the male animal than she had names for. Ackley learned, to his surprise, that the high regard Elizabethan male poets avowed for their sovereign was a plot to put all womankind on a pedestal, thus making the gender more vulnerable to attack. He was astonished to read that the practice of using boys in female roles was a conspiracy designed to keep women away from the stage and therefore less important in the later history of Elizabethan literature. But this eager savant did not stint her praise of Francis Bacon, after first advancing the thesis that the prim philosopher was a transvestite lesbian.

Ackley's consciousness had been raised by these pages to such a towering height that he experienced a brief attack of vertigo. So he put aside Taylor-Smythe-Bernstein's latter chronicle of the acts of the martyrs and took up an English translation of Guillaume Aride's famous *Of Syntactology.* Plunging into it at reckless speed, he soon mired and turned back to the title page to assure himself that he was indeed reading English and not some *bêche-de-mer* that combined English, French, and all the classical languages. "The *poikonos,*" he read, "represents neither time nor place, person nor thing, vegetable nor mineral; neither a speech particle or a nonparticle of incipient *discours;* neither a consummation nor indifference; neither the primal state nor any state dependent upon sense aporia *hors de soi en soi* in either of its possible tendencies to *l'exergue* or *le propre.*"

This was it, the real stuff—the kind of writing Ackley had heard rumors of but had never peered into. He didn't understand it, of course, but then, he had not expected to. It was renowned for its silliness, pomposity, disdain for common intelligence, and especially for its barbarous macaronic cacophony of sounds, which might drive the ghost of Scoresby out of both minds—his mind and the poet's own. He counted most of all upon the versifier's hatred of bad French.

Ackley acquitted himself against Aride with honor. When his attention slid around the text like a live escargot evading a diner's fork, he would begin reading aloud. When he came to paragraphs impossible to pronounce, he would place his fingertip upon each word as he went along and murmur the syllables slowly. Sometimes he found himself reduced to spelling the individual words letter by letter. He was valiant; he was determined; he was confident of victory.

No fewer than sixty-six pages of *Of Syntactology* were gotten through in this way, and Ackley felt that he had earned some refreshment. He visited the bathroom and the kitchen, replenishing his iced tea, then rested a moment and took from the box his next blind choice, Natterjee-Renaud's *Despotic Signifiers and the Baylonian Antireactionary Episteme.* He started the first paragraph with a soldierly resolve but finished its perusal in white-faced alarm:

> Aride's post-signifying regime of subjectification struggles with an after-image of the regime of significance in the figure of some (absent) guarantor and guarantee of stable meaning, its only resource and solace being the delusions of individual subjectivity. Desire is either blocked, as by the meaninglessness of existence in the Sartrean "Absurd," bouncing off the blank wall onto the desolate subject; or surrendered, as in the Lacanian metonymy of desire for the lost object, falling into the black hole of tragic subjectivity.

Robert Ackley closed the book slowly. Sweat filmed his forehead and he stared in sheer terror into the space before him. Surely he must be mistaken in his impression. He opened the volume again, turned over fifty pages, and once more began to read:

> Lacan would say we are subjectified in language as a signifying system from which the signified has dropped out as the unapproachable Real, or we are subjectified in the Symbolic Order in which we are immediately divided and condemned by desire to slip along the two poles of language (metaphor-condensation and metonymy-displacement) in the chain of signification.

This time he let the book fall from his fingers. He leaned back in his armchair, rested his head on the cushion, and closed his eyes. It was no mistake. *He actually understood the sentence he had just read.* He was not able to paraphrase it; perhaps, like the sounds of static heard during a radio transmission, it was unparaphrasable. Yet it made sense to him; it spoke to him with an authority that had no need for logic or even for communication in the normal sense of the word. There was an overmastering posture native to these words. In some implicit but undeniable fashion, and despite the froufrou of qualification and professorial persnickitiness, this sentence snapped an arm's-length salute, clicked its heels smartly, and barked *Heil!*

Slowly and tentatively, Ackley began to search his mind for the presence of Scoresby. But he was only making sure of his conclusions, for he felt he already knew the truth. The poet had been driven off, never to return. He was free at last.

While he felt relief at this knowledge—it was rather like entering a newly fumigated house—he also felt let down, a bit disappointed. He had been so distracted by Scoresby's presence and then later so intent on driving him away that he had not noticed how much the struggle had taken out of him. He was exhausted; he felt darkly displaced. He knew he was a very different person from the one he had been before.

He returned to the bathroom and rinsed his face with cold water and looked into the mirror. He saw that he *had* changed, and as he observed his features and attempted to study what had taken place, a sentence popped whole and unbidden into his mind, as if it had been spoken in his ear: "This signifying object (the face) is characterized by mere *relative* deterritorialization, for though its physicality is posited as a typological genome, its *différence* can be endlessly reproduced by other mirrors, as in any capitalist mass-production signification web."

There are worse things than being haunted by ghosts. Scoresby had posed a threat to the integrity and sanity of his unwilling host. Yet it was Ackley's own defense that did him in.

Almost all of us have succeeded in exorcising the poet from ourselves and we are forever afterward different persons than we imagined we could be. But the doom that came in later years to Robert Ackley was so terrible that Nature drew a merciful veil over his mind, causing him to imagine that he enjoyed his new situation and that he served some useful purpose in the scheme of things. He observed this fact but could not comprehend its truth: He had become the leading theorist of the neo-post-postmodernist generation. His first volume, *The Spirit Killeth: The Compromised Signifier in the "Forgotten Poems" of Lyman Scoresby,* is reckoned a classic of its kind.

MANKIND JOURNEYS THROUGH FORESTS OF SYMBOLS

1

There was a dream, and a big gaudy thing it was, too, and for six hours it had been blocking Highway 51 between Turkey Knob and Ember Forks. The deputies came out to have a look-see, tall tobacco-chewing mountain boys, and they stood and scratched their armpits and made highly unscientific observations like "Well, I be dog, Hank," and "Ain't that something, Bill," and so on, you can just imagine. Finally, Sheriff Balsam arrived with his twenty years of law-enforcement experience, but he, too, seemed at a loss.

The dream would measure about two stories tall and two hundred yards wide and it lay lengthwise on the highway for a distance of at least two miles. It was thick and goofy, its consistency something like cotton candy. Its predominant color was chartreuse, but this color was interlaced with coiling threads of bright scarlet and yellow and suffused in some areas with cloudy masses of mauve and ocher. It had first been reported about seven o'clock in the morning, but it had probably appeared earlier. Traffic was light on that stretch.

Sheriff Balsam observed that it would be a problem. No dream of such scale and density had been reported before in North Carolina, and this one looked to be difficult. Balsam had never dealt much with dreams, and there was a lot *to* this one. It was opaque and complex; you could see it working within itself like corn-whiskey mash in a copper cooker.

Balsam and the boys set up blinking barricades down the highway, detouring the traffic onto a circuitous gravel road, and then there was nothing to do but wait. The theory was that when the dreamer woke, the dream would go away, disappear like a five-dollar bill in a poker game. And who could afford to lie in bed all day dreaming? Balsam and Hank and Bill returned to the sheriff's office in the Osgood County courthouse to busy themselves with lost dogs and traffic citations.

But by lunchtime, the telephone began ringing and didn't let up. Folks were irate. Whose dream was it out there on the highway and what, by God, was Balsam going to do about it? "I voted for you last time, Elmo Balsam," said the vexed farmwife.

"I was the only one running, Ora Mae," Balsam said.

Finally he left the receiver off the hook and looked over at Hank and Bill, who were sharing a newspaper and a spittoon. "Boys," he said, "looks like we got bigger trouble than we thought."

"Yup," says Hank, and Bill says, "Looks like."

Balsam said, "What if whoever is dreaming that damn thing is drugged?"

Now there was a thought. Crazed drug freaks everywhere these days. Just think of that high school over there with its chemistry class. Hank and Bill thought of the high school and shook their heads mournfully. *These days anymore, you just don't know.*

"Might be awhile before he comes out of it. And it could be even worse."

Worse brightened their interest considerably. They looked at Balsam in mute wonder.

"He might could be in a *coma*. Might be weeks and months. Might be years."

They looked at one another.

"I think we ought to get an expert up here from the state office." Balsam said. He looked the number up and paused with his finger in the dial. "What do you boys think?"

Whew, Lordy, the state office. Bill thought it over and said, "Yup," but you could tell he considered it an extraordinary step to take. Bill was the slow and earnest thinker. Hank, the ebullient enthusiast, was intoxicated by every whim that sailed down the pike.

They watched, astonished, as Balsam spoke into the telephone. They realized it was the state office on the other end of the line.

Balsam hung up and told them that the state office had already dispatched an expert; he ought to have been here by now. Seemed that a farmer flying over in his Cessna had spotted the dream and radioed the Highway Patrol and they'd gotten in touch with the state office. The state office had said a lot of other things to Balsam that they would, of course, regret saying later on, so he wouldn't repeat all that. But they were to keep an eye out for this expert—Dr. Litmouse, his name was—who ought to have been here by now.

Just at that precise moment, a state patrol car pulled up in front of the sheriff's office, blue light twirling, siren whining. Two men entered. One was only a patrolman, but it was easy to see the other was an expert, the genuine article. His pinstriped gray suit was too large for him, as if he'd wandered into someone else's clothing by accident. He had but a paucity of hair and what there was, was white and frazzly. The thick lenses of his spectacles so magnified his eyes, they looked like they were pasted on the glass. He was carrying a quart mason jar of brownish liquid.

"I'm Dr. Litmouse," he said. "I hope I'm not late."

Balsam rose with unaccustomed alacrity and shook his hand. Introductions all around.

"I guess you're anxious to get out on Fifty-one and see about that dream," the sheriff said. "We'll drive you out."

"Kind of you," Litmouse said. "I wonder if you have a safe place where I might put this." He held up his quart jar.

"Sure thing, Doc. What is it?"

"I suppose you might call it a kind of secret formula," the expert said.

Balsam gave the muddy liquid an uneasy look. "We'll put it in the safe. . . . No, better put it in the filing cabinet," he said, recalling that he'd forgotten the combination to the safe. It wasn't needed; Balsam and Hank and Bill were not often entrusted with secret formulae.

"Fine."

Balsam and Litmouse got into one car, Hank and Bill into another, and the patrolman followed them. Dr. Litmouse seemed preoccupied, saying not a word the whole trip. This guy wouldn't look like much if you saw him just anywhere, Balsam thought, but once you knew he was an expert . . . That was what Science would do for you. Balsam began to regret that he wasted his evenings watching championship wrestling on TV instead of reading chemistry books.

When they arrived at the famous dream, they found a little girl, a towhead about eight years old, standing just this side of it. She wore jeans and a blouse and was popping bubble gum.

Balsam hollered at her. "Hey, little girl. You get back away from that thing."

She snapped a bubble. "There's already three cars drove in there."

"Good Lord," he said. "Didn't they see the detour sign?"

"Sure they did," she said. "Drove right around it."

"They must be crazy."

"They didn't look crazy."

"Well, you stand back now."

Dr. Litmouse had already begun to examine the dream. He paced back about fifteen feet and surveyed it from there, then walked over and stared closely, like a man peeking through a keyhole. He pulled his earlobe, pushed his glasses up on the bridge of his nose. "Bring me my case out of the car, please," he said.

Hank fetched it.

"What do you think, Doc?" the sheriff asked.

"I'm not quite sure," he said. He set the case on the ground and squatted to open it. It was a large square box of black leather, lined with blue plush. Inside were flasks and bottles and test tubes, forceps, big hypodermics, clamps, and other unrecognizable stainless-steel instruments. He took out a two-liter beaker and a pair of shiny clamps and went back. He inserted the clamps gently into the surface of the dream and gave them a slight twist and slowly withdrew. A hand-sized blob of it came away like a greenish cobweb, trailing filmy rags. The expert stuffed this blob into the beaker and held it up against the sunlight to judge whatever he was judging. He shook his head.

From his vest pocket he took a book of papers like cigarette papers except that they were blue and pink. He blew on them and tore out one of each color. He lowered the blue paper down into the dream blob and took it out and looked. Obviously dissatisfied, he threw it to the ground. Then he tried the pink paper.

Bill nudged Hank. *Damn, boy, look at him go.*

The stooped gray expert held the beaker to his face and sniffed—carefully. Then, very gingerly, he put his finger into it. When he brought his finger out, it was tinted pale green and dream threads clung to it. They watched, muscles tensed, as he put his finger into his mouth.

Almost immediately, a fearful transformation came over the scientist. He trembled from head to toe in his too-large suit, like a butterfly trying to shed its cocoon. His eyes rolled crazily and blinked back, showing the wild whites. His voice was high and thin and visionary when he cried out:

"La Nature est un temple où de vivants piliers
Laissent parfois sortir de confuses paroles;
L'homme y passe à travers des forêts de symboles
Qui l'observent avec des regards familiers."

Then he keeled over flat on the ground, unconscious.

Balsam sprang into action. "Hank, Bill! Pick that man up and bring him over here. Hurry up. And stay away from that stuff, whatever it is."

Hank and Bill deposited Dr. Litmouse at the sheriff's feet and he knelt to examine him. The doctor's eyelids quivered and he began to breathe more regularly, regaining his senses. He sat up and rubbed his face with both hands.

"You okay, Doc?" Balsam asked.

"I'll be all right in a moment," he said. He put his head between his knees and breathed deeply.

"You took a bad turn there. Had us all worried," Balsam said. "What is that stuff, anyhow?"

Dr. Litmouse rose and brushed ineffectually at his baggy suit. "It's a more serious problem than we thought. The mass we have to deal with here is not a dream, but something rather more permanent. Unless we can think of a solution."

"What is it, then?"

"I hate to tell you," Dr. Litmouse said, "but I believe it's a Symbolist poem. I'd stake my professional reputation that it's a Symbolist poem."

"You don't say," Balsam said.

Hank nudged Bill with his shoulder. *Damn-a-mighty, boy. Symbolist poem. You ever see the beat?*

The little girl came over to stare at Dr. Litmouse and to pop a bubble at him. "What's the matter with you? she asked. "You act like you're falling down drunk."

2

Dusk had come to the mountains like a sewing machine crawling over an operating table, and Dr. Litmouse and Hank and Bill and Balsam were back in the sheriff's office. Balsam sat at his desk, the telephone receiver still off the hook. Bill and Hank had resumed their corner chairs. The three lawmen were listening to the scientist's explanation.

"Basically it's the same problem as a dream, so it's mostly out of our hands. Somebody within a fifty-mile radius is ripe to write a Symbolist poem but hasn't gotten around to it yet. As soon as she or he does, then it will go away, just as the usual dream obstructions vanish when the dreamers wake." He took off his glasses and polished them with his handkerchief. His eyes looked as little and bare as shirt buttons and made the others feel queasy. They were glad when he replaced his spectacles.

"It's worse than a dream, though, because we may be dealing with a subconscious poet. It may be that this person never writes poems in the normal course of his life. If this poem originated in the mind of someone who never thinks of writing, then I'm afraid your highway detour will have to be more or less permanent."

"Damn," Balsam said. He leaned back in his swivel chair. "What do you mean, 'more or less'?"

"Death," replied the expert.

"Say what, Doc?"

"If it doesn't belong to a practicing poet, you may be stuck with it until the originator dies."

"Damn," Balsam said. "And there ain't nothing we can do? Nothing at all?"

"In Europe they've been heavily afflicted, but in America we've been lucky," Dr. Litmouse said. "The largest American Symbolist obstruction is in California, and is, I would estimate, about twice the size of this one. Fortunately, it's at the bottom of a canyon in Whittier National Park and no real inconvenience. But it's been there, Sheriff Balsam, for fifteen years."

Hank and Bill exchanged glances. *Fifteen years, boy.*

Balsam said, "Doc, we can't leave that thing there fifteen years. That's an important road."

"I sympathize, but I don't know what can be done."

The sheriff picked up a ballpoint pen and began clicking it. "Well, let's see. . . . There it is, and if somebody writes it down on paper, it'll go away."

"Correct."

"What we got to do then is get folks around here started writing poems. Maybe we'll hit on the right person."

"How will you do that?"

He bit the pen. "I don't know. . . . Bill, Hank—you boys got any bright ideas?"

They shook their heads sorrowfully. Bill spat; Hank spat.

"Say, Doc," Balsam said, "you tested this here, uh, poem. Did you get any notion what it was about?"

"Very difficult to say. It affects the nervous system powerfully, sending the victim into a sort of trance. Coming out of it, I have only confused impressions. I would say the poem is informed by tenuous allusion, strong synesthesia, and a wide array of hermetic symbols. But it was quite confusing, and I could gather no details, no specifics."

"That's too bad," the sheriff said. "I was hoping we could track it down. Because if it was about Natural Bridge, say, and we could find somebody who had been visiting up to Virginia . . ."

"It's a Symbolist poem, Sheriff," Dr. Litmouse said. "Doesn't have to be autobiographical in the least. In this case, we're probably dealing with archetypes."

Hank winked at Bill. *Them ole archetypes. We better watch out, boy.*

"Well, what we got to do then is just get as many people as we can out there writing poems. Community effort. Maybe we'll luck out."

"How?" asked Dr. Litmouse.

He clicked his ballpoint furiously. He got a sheet of department stationery and began printing tall, uncertain letters. The other three watched in suspense, breathing unevenly. When he finished, Balsam picked up the paper and held it at arm's length to read. His lips moved slightly. Then he showed them his work. "What do you think?" he asked.

The SHERIFF'S DEPARTMENT
of OSGOOD COUNTY
in cooperation with the
NORTH CAROLINA STATE HIGHWAY DEPARTMENT
announces
A POETRY CONTEST
$50 FIRST PRIZE
Send entries to SHERIFF ELMO BALSAM
OSGOOD COUNTY COURTHOUSE
EMBER FORKS, NC 26816

SYMBOLISM PREFERRED!!!

"I suppose it's worth a try," Dr. Litmouse said, but he sounded dubious.

3

Then opened the beneficent heavens and verses rained upon the embattled keepers of the law.

Sheriff Balsam kept his equanimity. He had posted Collins, Dr. Litmouse's escort patrolman, out at the site to keep an eye on the dream and report to the office. Collins radioed in every half hour that there was no change.

The other four sat in the office, reading sheaf after sheaf of manuscript. Dr. Litmouse held each page by a corner, regarding every poem as if it were some new species of maggot. Balsam turned pages mechanically; his eyes looked tired. Hank and Bill read ponderously, chewing their plugs as if they were digging graves.

Balsam glanced up. "Anything look promising?"

"These are just all Spring and Mother," Hank said. He sounded aggrieved.

"How about you, Bill?" the sheriff asked.

"Kinda boring," he said. "Spring and Mother and all. But there was one—"

"What about it?"

"I thought it had something, but it didn't work out."

"Let's see it." Balsam squinted and read aloud. "'The bluebird in our firethorn tree / Fills the merry day with glee. . . .' Aw, come on, Bill. This ain't the kind of thing we're looking for."

"Yeah. I know." He chewed. "But I was thinking if maybe it went different—"

"Different how?"

"Like if it wasn't no bluebird and glee and stuff. Like if it started off 'The squalid eagle in the thornfire,' maybe we'd be on the right track."

Balsam gave him a steady gaze. "How you say that?"

"Say what?"

"Squiggly eagle in the bush?"

"I was trying to think how it *might* go. 'The squalid eagle in the thornfire. . . .' I guess I've got the whole wrong idea."

They looked at him with fierce interest.

Balsam turned to the expert. "What do you think, Doc?"

Dr. Litmouse nodded slowly. "It's worth a try. Why not?"

A sputter of static came from the radio on the sheriff's desk and then the tinny voice of the patrolman. "Collins here, out at the site. You there, Sheriff Balsam?"

Balsam leaned and flipped a switch. "Right here," he said. "Anything happening out your way?"

"I think maybe I saw some movement. Top of it got a little ragged, like maybe the wind took hold of it."

"When was this?"

"Just a minute ago. Nothing happening now, though."

"Stay right there and keep watch," the sheriff ordered. "I'll send some help." He cut the switch and stood up and took his keys out of his pocket.

"Doc," he said, "you drive my car and radio back when you get there. When we hear from you, we'll start working with Bill here."

"Work with me how?" Bill's brow furrowed plaintively.

The sheriff led Bill to the desk and seated him. He crowded papers out of the way and got a fresh sheet and two pencils and laid them before the deputy. "You ever wrote any poems, Bill?"

He looked down at his big wrists. "Not much," he said.

"Have you?"

His face and neck were scarlet. "Used to try one every once in awhile."

"I never knowed that!" Hank exclaimed. "Boss, I swear he never told me nothing about it!"

"You're going to write one now, Bill," Balsam said.

"What do you want me to write?" He picked up a pencil as if it were loaded and cocked.

"Write it down about that squirrelly eagle."

Bill wrote, sticking the tip of his tongue out of the corner of his mouth. "Now what?" he asked.

"Just go on from there," the sheriff ordered.

"I don't know nothing that comes next."

"You just settle down and see if it doesn't come to you."

"Come on, old hoss, you can do it!" Hank shouted.

Bill closed his eyes. His lips twitched. He opened his eyes and shook his head.

"Anything we can get to help you?" the sheriff asked.

He thought. "Well, maybe, uh, maybe I could use a glass of wine."

"Wine!" Hank was thunderstruck, but at a glance from Balsam recovered himself. "Damn right, good buddy. What you want? T-Bird? Wild Irish Rose? Mad Dog?"

"Like maybe a pretty good Burgundy," Bill said firmly.

"Hank, you zip down to the supermarket and see if they got any Burgundy wine," the sheriff said. Hank started for the door, but Balsam halted him. "No. Hell. Wait. Get this boy the best champagne they got. Don't spare the horses."

"Damn right," Hank said, and went out.

Again the radio rattled and spoke. "Sheriff Balsam, this is Dr. Litmouse. I'm in place out here at the site. We're ready to begin when you are."

Balsam switched on and said, "We're ready to go. We'll keep each other posted. . . . No, wait. Bill's going to be concentrating pretty heavy in here. Maybe we ought to stay off the radio for a while."

"Quite sensible," Dr. Litmouse said. "We'll wait for your call."

"Fine." The sheriff switched off and turned to Bill. "Don't worry about a thing," he said. "You just go on and write down your poem. Won't nobody disturb you."

"I don't know if I can," Bill said.

"Look here, Bill," Balsam said, "you're a deputy sheriff of Osgood County. I don't have to remind you what a responsibility that is. Sometimes the job is dirty and dangerous, but you knew that when you put on the badge. I never expect to see you back off from the job, boy. Never."

Bill swallowed hard. "Do the best I can," he said.

"Okay, then. I'll be right over here in the corner. Anything you need, just holler. Don't forget we're all behind you one hundred percent." Balsam sat in a corner chair and pretended to read a sheaf of poems.

Bill lifted a pencil and laid it down again. He closed his eyes. His neck and shoulder muscles bunched and veins stood out on his temples. He breathed slow and harsh and a film of sweat covered his forehead.

He picked up a pencil and began to write, poking the tip of his tongue out of the corner of his mouth.

Hank came in with a bottle of champagne. He started to speak, but Balsam silenced him with a gesture. Hank looked at Bill with an expression of tender commiseration. He gave the bottle to the sheriff, who took it into the washroom and worked the cork out and poured a tumblerful of the wine and took it to Bill, setting it gently on the desk.

Bill didn't notice. He scratched out old words and wrote in new ones. In awhile he drained the water glass without appearing to realize he'd done it. The expression on his face was startling to look upon.

Balsam and Hank sat watching Bill and glancing at each other. Time seemed to stop.

Bill wrote and rewrote, grunting. At last, with a savage, anguished cry, he flung down the pencil and buried his face in his hands. When he turned to Hank and Balsam, his face was ashen and his brown hair had turned gray. "That's all," he said. "I can't do any more. I can't."

They took his arms and half-dragged him to his usual chair in the corner. "See how he is, Hank. We can have an ambulance here in five minutes."

"I'll be all right," Bill said.

Balsam went to the radio. "Hey, Doc, are you there? How's it look?"

The excitement of the scientist was unmistakable. "It's all gone, Sheriff Balsam. Disappeared. You've done a fine job back there."

"All cleared up?"

"Well, there are a few scattered patches, but the highway is clear. We can probably get rid of the leftovers if Bill wants to correct his meter and line breaks."

"Hell with that," Balsam said. "Bill has done enough for one day. You boys come on in." He clicked off and turned to his deputies.

Hank was punching Bill's shoulder and wrestling him about. "You hear that? You done it, old hoss! By damn, you done it!"

Bill smiled weakly and tried to look modest.

"We ought to celebrate," the sheriff said. "What say we finish off this here champagne?"

When Dr. Litmouse and Patrolman Collins came in, they all switched to the confiscated corn whiskey Balsam kept in his bottom drawer. They poured a couple of farewell drinks and talked happily. Dr. Litmouse promised to turn in a glowing report about the sheriff and his deputies to the state office. They shook hands and the other two departed. Patrolman Collins cut in the siren for a couple of blocks.

They listened, and then Balsam was struck by a memory. "Oh hell," he said.

"What's the matter?" Hank asked.

"The secret formula," he said. "The doc forgot his secret formula." He took it out of the filing cabinet and set it on his desk. They regarded it with apprehension.

"What do you reckon that stuff does?" Hank asked.

"I don't know," Balsam said.

"Well, hell," Bill said, "let's find out." He unscrewed the lid and stuck his finger into the liquid and tasted it.

Hank and the sheriff eyed each other. It was clear now that Bill had the courage of tigers; he was afraid of nothing.

"What is it?" the sheriff asked.

Bill licked his lips. "Barbecue sauce," he said. He thought for a moment, tasting. "With about a cup and a half of Château Beychevelle '78."

ANCESTORS

Harry and Lydie were enduring their third ancestor and finding it a rum go. Not that they were surprised—the first two ancestors had also proved to be enervating specimens—and now they regretted the hour they had joined the Ancestor Program of the Living History Series. Sitting at dinner, fed up with Wade Wordmore, Harry decided to return this curious creature to his congressman, Doy Collingwood, at his local office over in Raleigh, North Carolina.

They were goaded into joining the program by that most destructive of all human urges, the desire for self-improvement. When, as part of the celebration of the 150th anniversary of the Civil War, the U.S. Archives and History Division called Harry Beacham and told him that he had no fewer than three ancestors who had fought in the great conflict and asked if he'd be interested in meeting these personages, he replied that yes, he would love to meet them.

What southerner wouldn't say that?

It is also in the southern manner to take the marvels of modern technology for granted. The crisp impersonal female voice in the telephone receiver explained that from the merest microscopic section of bone, computers could dredge out of the past not only the physical lineaments of the person whom the bone once held perpendicular but the personality traits, too, down to the last little tic and stammer. In their own house, Harry and Lydie could engage with three flesh-and-blood examples of history come to life. Of course, it really wasn't flesh, only a sort of protein putty, but it was real blood, right enough. It was pig blood: That was a biochemical necessity.

"Can they talk?" Harry asked, and was assured that they spoke, remembered their former lives in sharp detail, and even told jokes—rather faded ones, of course. They also ate, slept, and shaved, were human in every way. "That is the departmental motto," the voice said. "Engineering Humanity for Historic Purpose."

He asked casually about the cost, and she stated it, and he was pleased but still desired to think just a few days before deciding whether to subscribe to the program.

"That will not be necessary," said the voice. "The arrangements have already been taken care of and your first ancestor is on his way to you. The Archives and History Division of the United States Department of Reality is certain that you will find real satisfaction in your personal encounters with living history. Thank you and good day, Mr. Butcher."

"Wait a minute," Harry said. "My name is Beacham." But the connection was cut, and when he tried to call back, he was shunted from one office to another and put on hold so often and so long that he gave up in disgust.

So then, as far as Harry was concerned, all bets were off. He was a Beacham and no Butcher and proud of it, and if some artificial entity from the Archives Division showed up at his door, he would send the fellow packing.

But he didn't have to do that. Lieutenant Aldershot's papers were in apple-pie order when he presented them with a sharp salute to Lydie. She met him at the front door and was immediately taken with this swarthy brown-eyed man in his butternut uniform and broad-brimmed hat. A battered leather-bound trunk sat on the walk behind him.

"Oh, you must be the ancestor they sent," she said.

"Lieutenant Edward Aldershot of the Northern Virginia reporting as ordered, ma'am."

Confused, Lydie colored prettily and looked up and down the lane to see if any of her neighbors here in the Shining Acres development were observing her exotic visitor. She took the papers he proffered, started to open them, but paused with her fingers on the knotted ribbon and said, "Oh, do come in," and stepped back into the foyer. The lieutenant moved forward briskly, removing his hat just before he stepped over the threshold. "Honey," she called. "Harry, honey. Our ancestor is here."

He came downstairs in no welcoming frame of mind but then stood silent and wide-eyed before Aldershot, who snapped him a classy, respectful salute and declared his name and the name of his army. "I believe the lady will be kind enough to present my papers, sir."

But Harry and Lydie only stood gaping until the lieutenant gestured toward the packet in Lydie's hands. She gave it to Harry, blushing again, and Harry said in a rather stiff tone, trying to hide his astonishment, "Ah yes. Of course . . . Your papers . . . Of course."

And for a wonder, they were all correct. Here was the letter from History identifying Aldershot and congratulating the Beachams on the opportunity of enjoying his company for three weeks and telling them what a valuable experience they were in for. Then there was Aldershot's birth certificate and a very sketchy outline of his military career and then a family tree, in which Harry was relieved to discover not a single Butcher. It was all Beachams and Lawsons and Hollinses and Bredvolds and Aldershots and Harpers as far as the eye could see, all the way to the beginning of the nineteenth century.

"This looks fine," Harry said. "We're glad to have you as one of us."

"I'm proud to hear you say so, sir," the lieutenant said, and tore off another healthy salute,

"You needn't be so formal," Harry told him. You don't have to salute me or call me sir. We're just friends here."

"That's very kind of you. I'm afraid it might take me a little time to adjust, sir."

"You'll fit right in," Lydie said. "I'm sure you will."

"Thank you, ma'am," said Aldershot. "I do take tobacco and a little whiskey now and then. I hope you won't mind."

"Oh no. If that's what you did—I mean, if that's what you're used to, please feel free." A bashful woman, she blushed once more. She had almost said: "If that's what you did when you were alive." "Harry, you can bring in the lieutenant's trunk, if you don't mind."

• • •

The Confederate officer had too modestly described his pleasures. He did not take tobacco; he engorged it, sawing off with his case knife tarry knuckles of the stuff from a twist he carried in his trouser pocket and chewing belligerently, like a man marching against an opposing brigade. He was a well pump of tobacco juice, spitting inaccurately not only at the champagne bucket and other utensils the Beachams supplied him as spittoons but at any other handy vessel that offered a concavity. The sofa suffered and the rugs, the tablecloths, the lieutenant's bedding and his clothing. His shirts came off worst.

In fact, his whole appearance deteriorated rapidly and ruinously. In three days, he no longer wore his handsome butternut, but had changed into the more familiar uniform of Confederate gray, a uniform which seemed to grow shabbier even as the Beachams gazed upon it. His sprightly black mustache, which Lydie had fancied as complementing his dark eyes so handsomely, became first ragged, then shaggy. He would neglect to shave for four days running, and he began to smell of sweat and stale underwear and whiskey.

For he had also understated the power of his thirst. On the first night and always afterward, he never strayed far from the jug and, when not actually pouring from it, would cast amorous glances in its direction. He drank George Dickel neat or sometimes with sugar water and praised the quality of the bourbon in ardent terms, saying, for example, "If we'd a-had a little more of this at Chancellorsville, it would've been a different story." Liquor seemed to affect him little, however; he never lost control of his motor reflexes or slurred his speech.

Yet the quality of his address had changed since that sunny first moment with the Beachams. It was no more "Yes, sir" and "No, sir" to Harry, but "our friend Harry here" and "old buddy" and "old hoss." He still addressed Lydie as "ma'am," but when talking indirectly, he would refer to her as "our mighty *fine* little female of the house." He was never rude or impolite, but his formal manner slipped into an easy camaraderie and then sagged into a careless intimacy. His social graces frayed at about the same rate as his gray uniform, which by the end of the second week was positively tattered.

The lieutenant, though, had not been ordered to the Beacham residence as a dancing master, but as a representative of History, which, as the largest division of the Department of Reality, shared much of its parent organization's proud anatomy. And of Living History, Lieutenant Aldershot offered a spectacular cornucopia. The outline of his career that came with him from the government agency barely hinted at the range and length of his fighting experience. He had fought at Vicksburg, Fredericksburg, and Gettysburg; he had survived Shiloh, Antietam, and Richmond; he had shown conspicuous bravery at Manassas, Rich Mountain, Williamsburg, and Cedar Mountain; he had won commendations from Zollicoffer, Beauregard, Johnston, Kirby Smith, Jackson, and Robert E. Lee. The latter commander he referred to as "General Bobby" and described him as "the finest southern gentleman who ever whupped his enemy."

Harry's knowledge of history was by no means as profound as his enthusiasm for it, and he had not found time before Aldershot's arrival to bone up on the battles and campaigns that had occurred a century and a half earlier. Even so, the exploits of the ambeer-spattered and strongly watered lieutenant began to overstretch Harry's credulity. In order to be on all the battlefields he remembered, Aldershot must have spent most of the war on the backs of two dozen swift mounts, and to survive the carnage he had witnessed, he must have kept busy a fretting cohort of guardian angels. Any soldier of such courage, coolness, intelligence, and resourcefulness must have left his name in letters of red blaze in the history books, but Harry could not recall hearing of Aldershot. Of course, it had been some seven years since he had looked at the histories; perhaps he had only forgotten.

For in many ways, it was hard to disbelieve the soldier's accounts, he was so particular in detail and so vivid in expression. When telling of some incident that displayed one man's valor or another's timidity, he became brightly animated, and then heated, and would squirm in his chair at the table, sputtering tobacco and gulping bourbon, his eyes wild and bloodshot. He rocked back and forth in the chair as if he were in the saddle, leaping the brushy hurdles at the Battle of Fallen Timber. He broke two chairs that way, and his host supplied him a steel-frame lawn chair brought in from the garage.

He was vivid and particular most of all in his accounts of bloodshed. Although he spoke only plain language, as he averred a soldier should, he so impressed Harry's imagination and Lydie's trepidation that they felt extremely close to the great conflict. In Aldershot's bourbonish sentences they heard the bugles at daybreak, the creaking of munitions wagons, the crack of rifles and bellow of cannon, the horses screaming in pain and terror. They saw the fields clouded over with gun smoke and the hilltop campfires at night and the restless shuffle of pickets on the sunset perimeters. They could smell corn parching for coffee and mud waist-deep and the stink of latrines and the worse stink of gangrene in the hospital tents.

The lieutenant's accounts of battle progressed from bloody to chilling to gruesome, and the closeness with which he detailed blows and wounds and killing made the *Iliad* seem vague and pallid. He appeared to take a certain relish in demonstrating on his own body where a minié ball had gone into a comrade and where it came out and what raw mischief it had caused during its journey. He spoke of shattered teeth and splintered bone and eyes gouged out. When he began to describe the surgeries and amputations, dwelling at great length on the mound of removed body parts at the Fredericksburg field hospital, Lydie pleaded with him to spare her.

"Please," she said, "perhaps we needn't hear all this part." Her eyes were large and teary in her whitened face and her voice trembled.

"Uh, yes," Harry said. "I think Lydie has a point. Maybe we can skip a few of the gorier details now and then." He, too, was obviously shaken by what he had heard.

"Well now," Aldershot said, "of course I didn't mean to alarm our mighty fine little female of the house. I hope you'll forgive a plainspoken soldier, ma'am, one who never learned the orator's art. You're a brave un in my book, for there's many a refined southern lady who will faint when she hears the true story of things. Especially when I tell how it is to be gut-shot."

"Please, Lieutenant," Lydie said. She took three sips of her chardonnay, recovering her composure pretty quickly, but looking with dismay at her plate of stewed pork.

"How about you?" Harry asked. "Were you ever wounded?"

"Me?" Aldershot snorted. "No, not me. I was always one too many for them bluebellies, not that they didn't try plenty hard."

• • •

This discussion took place at the end of the second week. At first, Aldershot had referred to his ancient opponents as "the enemy" and then changed his term to "the Northern intruder." In the second week, though, it was "bluebellies" every time, and in the third week, it was "them goddamn treacherous Yankee bastards," to which epithet he always appended a parenthetical apology to Lydie: "—saving your presence, ma'am."

Even that small gesture toward the observance of chivalry seemed to cost him some effort. In the third week, the weary Confederate appeared to have aged a decade; his clothes were now only threads and patches, his mustache a straggly bristle, his eyes discolored and dispirited, and his speech disjoined, exhausted, and crumbling. It was clear that remembering had taken too much out of him, that he had tired himself almost past endurance. He had cut down on his tobacco intake, as if the exercise of a chaw drew off too much strength, and had increased his frequency of imbibing whiskey, although this spiritous surplus did not enliven his demeanor.

On the eve of his departure, Lieutenant Aldershot begged off telling of the destruction of Atlanta and gave only the most cursory sketch of the surrender at Appomattox. For the first time in three weeks, he retired early to bed.

The next morning, he came down late and took only coffee for his breakfast. He had dragged his leather-bound trunk to the front door and stood with his foot propped on it as he bade the Beachams farewell. Gravely they shook hands. When he spoke to Lydie, Aldershot held his hat over his heart. "Ma'am, your hospitality has been most generous and not something a plain soldier will forget."

Lydie took his hand. She blushed, feeling that she ought to curtsey but not knowing how.

He looked straight into Harry's eyes. "So long, old hoss," he said. "It's been mighty fine for me here."

"We've been honored," Harry said. "Believe me."

Then the government van arrived and the driver came to load Aldershot's trunk, and they shook hands once more and the lieutenant departed. As they watched him trudging down the front walk, Harry and Lydie were struck silent by the mournful figure he presented, his shoulders slumped, his head thrust forward, and his step a defeated shuffle.

When he mounted to the van cab and rode away without waving or looking back, a feeling of deep sadness descended upon them, so that they stood for a minute or two holding each other for comfort and looking into the bright, empty morning.

Finally, Harry closed the door and turned away. "I don't know about you," he said, "but I feel tired. Tired in my bones."

"Me, too," Lydie said. "And I've got to get this house cleaned up. There's tobacco spit everywhere. Everything in the house is splattered."

"I feel like we just lost the war."

"Well, honey, that's exactly what happened."

"I'll tell you what I'm going to do—if it's all right with you, I mean. I'm going to call these government History people and tell them not to send the other ancestors. I'm utterly exhausted. I can't imagine how I'd feel after two more visitors like the lieutenant."

"Do it now," she said.

Harry got on the telephone and dialed a list of bureaucratic numbers, only to find that each and every one gave off a busy signal for hours on end. His E-mails were acknowledged and that was the sole response.

So on Monday morning at ten-thirty on the dot, Pvt. William Harper presented himself at the front door and handed his papers to Lydie with a shy bow. His was a diffident gray uniform that had seen better days, but it was clean and tidy. He was accompanied by no trunk; only a modest, neatly turned bedroll lay at his feet. "Ma'am, I believe you are expecting me?" he said.

Her first impulse was to send him away immediately, but the van must have departed already, since it was nowhere in sight, and anyway, her second stronger impulse was to invite him into the house and feed him. Lieutenant Aldershot must have been in his early forties—though he had looked to be sixty years old when he left—but Private Harper could hardly have been out of his teens.

He offered her his papers and gave her what he obviously hoped was a winning smile, but he was so young and clear-eyed and shy that his expression was more apprehensive than cordial.

Lydie was childless and her heart went out to him entirely. She took the packet without looking at it, staring almost tenderly upon Harper, with his big bright blue eyes and rosy complexion, in which the light fuzz was evidence of an infrequent encounter with the razor. He was a slight young man, slender and well formed and with hands as long-fingered and delicate as a pianist's. He seemed troubled by her stare and shifted restlessly in his boots.

"Ma'am," he asked, "have I come to the right house? Maybe I'm supposed to be somewhere else."

"No," said Lydie, "you come right in. This is the place for you."

"I wouldn't want to be a burden," the private said. "Those government people said that you had invited me to come here. I wouldn't want to impose on you."

"We're glad to have you. Don't worry about a thing."

He looked all about him, wonder-struck. "You belong to a mighty grand place. It's hard for me to get used to the houses and everything that people have."

"We feel lucky," Lydie said. "Lots of people are not so well-off." Then, seeing that he could formulate no reply, she stooped and picked up his bedroll. "Please do come on in. I was just getting ready to make some fresh coffee. You'd like that, wouldn't you?"

"Yes, ma'am."

In the kitchen, Private Harper sat at a table and watched moonily every step and gesture Lydie made. His nervousness was subsiding, but he seemed a long way from being at ease. She took care to smile warmly and speak softly, but it was apparent to her from Harper's worshipful gaze that she had already conquered the young man's heart. When she set the coffee before him with the cream pitcher and sugar bowl alongside, he didn't glance down, looking instead into her face.

"Now, Private Harper," she said, "drink your coffee. And would you like something to eat? I can make a sandwich, or maybe there's a piece of chocolate cake left. You like chocolate cake, don't you?"

"No, ma'am. Just the coffee is all I need to wake me up. I was feeling a little bit tired."

"Of course you are," she said. "You can finish your coffee and I'll show you to your room and you can get some sleep."

"You're awful kind, ma'am. I won't say no to that."

• • •

When the private was tucked away, Lydie telephoned her spouse at his place of business, Harry's Hot-Hit Vidrents, to tell him the news.

He was not happy. "Oh, Lydie," he said. "You were supposed to send him back where he came from. That was what we agreed on."

"I just couldn't," she said. "He's so young. And he was tired out. He's already asleep."

"But we agreed. Don't you remember? We agreed to send him packing."

"Wait till you meet him. Then send him away. If you can do it, it will be all right with me."

And, having met the young man, Harry could no more order him gone than Lydie. Harper was so innocent and willing and open-faced that Harry could only feel sympathy for him when he saw what puppy eyes the young man made at his wife. He offered him a drink—Aldershot had overlooked a half bottle of Dickel in a lower cabinet—and was not surprised when the lad refused.

"I promised my mother, sir, before I went off to war."

"I see," Harry said, and reflected gravely on the difference between the lieutenant and the private. "But in the army, that must have been a hard promise to keep."

"Oh, no, sir. Not when I promised my mother. And to tell the truth, I don't have much taste for liquor."

He did accept a cup of tea, spooning into it as much sugar as would dissolve, and was profusely grateful.

Harry then readied himself with a gin and tonic for another stiff dose of history. "I suppose you must have fought in lots of battles," he said.

Private Harper shook his head sadly. "Only two battles, sir."

"Which were those?"

"Well, I fought at Bethel, sir, and then we were sent down toward Richmond."

"You were at Manassas?" These were place-names that Aldershot had deeply imprinted on the Beacham memory.

"Yes, sir."

"And what was that like?"

"Well, sir . . ." For the first time, Private Harper lifted his eyes and looked directly into Harry's face. His boyish countenance was a study in apologetic confusion as he steadied his teacup on his knee and said, "Well, sir, if you don't mind, I'd rather not talk 'bout that."

"You don't want to talk about Manassas?" Harry asked. Then his surprise disappeared with the force of his realization: Manassas would have been where Private Harper had died.

"I don't like to talk about the war at all, sir."

"I see."

"I know I'm supposed to, but I just can't seem to make myself do it. It opens old wounds."

"That's quite all right. Where are you from originally?"

"Salem, Virginia," Private Harper said. "We had a farm right outside town. I miss that place a great deal."

"I'm sure you do."

"I miss my folks, too, sir. Something terrible." And he went on to talk about his life before the war, and his story was so idyllic and engaging that Harry called Lydie from the kitchen to hear it.

The private spoke rhapsodically of such ordinary tasks as planting corn, shoeing horses, repairing wagons, cutting hay, milking cows, and so forth. His face glowed even friendlier as he spoke of these matters, and as he warmed to his stories, his shyness melted and his language became almost lyrical.

He was the only male in a female family, his father having died when Billy was about eleven. He allowed that his mother and three sisters had rather doted on him, but it was obvious to the Beachams that he had no real idea how much they doted. He had not been required to join the army; he had done so only out of a sense of duty and from a fear of the shame he might feel later if he did not join. He had supposed that the colored men attached to the family, Jupiter and Peter—who were not thought of as being slaves—would look after the ladies and take care of the farm. But shortly after Billy went away to war, these two had slipped off and were not heard of again. He had been in process of applying for permission to return home when the Battle of Manassas befell him.

He seemed to remember mornings fondly, and summer mornings most fondly. To wake up to the smell of ham and coffee and biscuits and grits, to look off the front porch into the dew-shiny fields and to see the little creek in the bottom winking with a gleam through the bushes—well, these sights made him feel that Paradise might be something of a letdown when finally at last he disembarked upon that lucent shore. The haze blue mountains offered deer and partridge, possum and quail, and Billy loved to take his bay mare, Cleopatra, and his father's old long-barreled rifle and hunt on those slopes from morn till midnight.

About that mare, he was rapturous. "If I told you how smart Cleo was, and some of the things I've known her to do, you'd think I was straying from the truth," he said. "But I'm not. She really is the best horse in the world, the smartest and the gentlest. Not that she doesn't have a lot of spirit. Why, I believe she has more courage than a bear, but she's as gentle with children as a mammy. And she's the best hunter I know of, bar none."

The Beachams smiled, trying vainly to imagine that Private Harper would deliberately stray from the truth; but it was clear that in regard to his horse, his infatuation might fetch him out of the strait path of accuracy without his ever being aware. It seemed that Cleopatra knew where game was to be found up there in the hills and, when given her head, would unerringly seek out the best cover from which to shoot deer and fowl of every sort. There never was a horse like her for woodlore. Harry felt his credulity strained when Harper mentioned that she could sniff out trout in the river and would carry her master to the sweetest fishing holes. And Lydie left unspoken her reservations about Billy's account of Cleo's stamping out a fire and thus saving the Harper farmhouse and the lives of the four of them.

A skeptical expression must have crossed her face, though, because Billy looked at her imploringly and said, "Oh, it's true, I assure you it is. You can ask Julie or Annie or my mother. They'll tell you it's gospel truth." Lydie realized then that she must keep her emotions out of her face, that Billy Harper always forgot that his family was sealed away in time past and that he was an orphan in a world of strangers.

He forgot himself so thoroughly when he spoke that his unhappy situation appeared to escape his memory. Yet something was troubling him. As the days went by, he grew restless and his soft volubility began to wane. Toward the end of the second week, not even questions about Cleopatra could alleviate his distractedness.

On Monday of the third week, he spoke his mind. "I know you-all want to hear about the war," he said glumly. "And I know that's what I'm supposed to be telling you. It's just that I can't bear to open up those wounds again. I guess I'd better try, though, since that's what I'm sent here to do."

"You're not supposed to do anything that you don't want to," Harry said. "We haven't been notified that you are required to talk about the war. In fact, we haven't been notified of anything much. I wish I could get a phone call through to those History people. Or that they would answer my E-mails."

"That's right," Lydie said. "I'm tired of hearing about that ugly old war. I'd much rather hear about your mother and your sisters and the farm."

All the reassurances would not lighten Billy's darkened spirits. The more they spoke soothing words, the gloomier he became, and they could see that he was steeling himself to broach the subject and they became anxious about him, for his nervousness increased as his determination grew.

When he began to talk, after supper on his third Wednesday, he was desperate. His hands trembled and he kept his eyes trained on the beige patch of living room carpet in front of his armchair and he spoke in a low mutter. His sentences were jumbled and hard to understand. He was sweating.

"There were onlookers up on the ridges," he said. "We were down in the bottom fields at Manassas when McDowell brought his troops around. We could see them up there—the spectators, I mean—and I borrowed Jed's glass and took a look, and they were drinking wine and laughing and there were ladies in their carriages, and younguns, too, setting off firecrackers. So when I handed him the glass back, I said, 'I don't believe it's going to be a fight, not with the society people looking on; I expect that McDowell and General Bee will parley.' And he said, 'No, it'll be a fight, Billy. Can't neither side back off now; we're in too close on each other. McDowell will have to fight here right outside of Washington because Lincoln himself might be up there on a hilltop watching.' But I didn't believe him. I never thought we'd fight that day."

He paused and licked his lips and asked for a glass of water. Lydie brought it from the kitchen, ice cubes tinkling, and told the private with meaningful tenderness that he did not need to continue his story.

Harper took the glass and sipped, appearing not to hear her words. He kept his eyes downcast and began again. "At nine in the morning, it was already warm and we knew we'd be feeling the heat, and then with no warning it started up. Sergeant Roper hadn't no more than told us to brace ourselves because there appeared to be more Yankees here than ants in an anthill when we saw gun smoke off to our left, a little decline there, and heard the shots, and in that very first volley Jed fell down with a ball in the middle of his chest, but before he hit the ground, he took another in his shoulder that near about tore his left arm off. I didn't have the least idea any of them was close enough to get a shot at us. I laid down by Jed and took him in my arms but couldn't do nothing, and they made me let him lay and start fighting."

His face had been flushed and sweaty but now was sugar white and drenched. His eyes were dark circles, and when he raised them for the first time, caught up as he was in his memories, he seemed not to see Lydie or Harry or anything around him. He was sweating so profusely that his uniform was darkening—that was what Lydie thought at first, but then she rose to clutch Harry's arm. Blood was dripping from Harper's sleeve over his wrist and onto the rug.

"So I got on one knee to see what I could and brought my rifle up, but I didn't know what to do. I could tell they were all around us because my comrades were firing in every direction, but I couldn't spot anything, so much smoke and dust. I saw some muzzle blazes on my right and thought I might shoot, but then maybe that was one of our lines over there. I was a pretty good marksman to go a-hunting, but in a battle I couldn't figure out where to aim."

His voice had sunk almost to a whisper, and his tunic and the chair he sat in were soaking with blood. Harry remembered that it would be pig blood and not human, but he was horrified all the same—more disturbed, perhaps, than if it had been Harry's own blood. He looked quickly at Lydie and then rushed to her aid. He knew now what Billy Harper had meant when he'd said that to talk about the war opened old wounds.

He took his wife by the arm and drew her toward the bedroom. She went along without a murmur, her face drawn and blanched. He could feel all her body trembling. He helped her to lie down and told her to keep still, not to move; he would take care of everything, he said. It was going to be all right.

But when he returned to the living room, Harper was lying facedown on the floor. He had tumbled out of his chair and lay motionless in a thick, smelly puddle of brownish blood. Harry knelt to examine him and it was obvious that he was gone, literally drained of life.

Harry telephoned for an ambulance and sat down to think what to tell the medics when they arrived. Perhaps they wouldn't accept Private Harper; perhaps they wouldn't regard him as a real human being. To whom could he turn for assistance in that case? He knew better than to call Archives and History; the last time he had called those numbers, a recorded voice had informed him that they had all been disconnected. Now he was trying to reach, by E-mail and telephone and fax machine, his congressman, Representative Doy Collingwood, but so far had received no reply.

When the ambulance came, though, the young paramedics understood the situation immediately and seemed to find it routine. The fellow with the blond-red mustache—he looked like a teenager, Harry thought ruefully—only glanced at the inert figure on the rug before asking, "Civil War?"

"Yes," Harry said. "My God, it was awful. My wife is almost hysterical. This is just terrible."

The fellow nodded. "We get them like this all the time. Faulty parts and sloppy workmanship. Made in China, probably. Sometimes we get four calls a week like this."

"Can't something be done?"

"Have you tried to get in touch with Ark and Hiss?"

"With who?"

"The Archives and History Division . . . in Washington." He saw Harry's expression. "Never mind, I know. Tell you what, though. I'd better have a look to see if your wife is okay. Where is she?"

Harry showed him into the bedroom and stood by while he ministered to Lydie. She murmured her gratitude but kept her eyes closed. The young medic gave her some pills and went with Harry back to the living room. "She'll be all right," he said. "Probably have a couple of rough nights."

The driver had already laid down a stretcher and rolled Harper's body over onto it. His eyes were open and a dreadful change had come to his face, a change that was more than death and worse, a change that made Private Harper look as if he'd never been human—in this life or in any other.

Harry had to look away. "My God," he said.

"Pretty awful, isn't it?" The medic's response was cheerful, matter-of-fact. "Shoddy stuff, these Ark and Hiss lackeys. But there's some good salvage there, more than you'd think by looking at it."

"What did you call him?" Harry asked. "Lucky?"

"Lackey. It's a nickname. A simulacrum from the Division of Archives and History. Your tax dollars at work, know what I mean?" He handed Harry a clipboard and a pen. "Sign here," he said, turning a page. "And here. And here. And here. And here. And here. And here. And here."

The paramedic had predicted rough nights for Lydie, but she suffered bad days as well and took to her bed. She kept the shades drawn and the lights low and tuned to chamber music on the vidcube. Harry gave his shop over to the attentions of two assistants and stayed home with his wife, preparing her scanty meals and consoling her and monitoring the installation of the new carpet and choosing a new chair for the living room. Lydie would probably hate the chocolate-colored wing-back he'd bought, but that was all right. She could exchange it when she was up and around.

He planned to stay home with her for a week or two—for as long as it took to make certain the government was sending to the Beacham household no more lackeys. Harry pronounced the word with an angry clack: *lackeys.* He made it sound as harsh and gracklelike as possible, but there was no satisfaction in it.

He was so infuriated and felt so impotent that he even began to wish a new specimen might turn up, just so he could send it away with a message for the people who had dispatched it. He prepared several speeches in his mind, each more savage than the last, each more heartfelt and more eloquent.

He never got to deliver any of them, even though the expected third visitor did, after all, show, a week later than had been stipulated. But he didn't announce himself, didn't knock at the door and present his papers as Aldershot and Harper had done. He just stood in the front yard with his back turned toward the house and gazed at the houses opposite and at the children riding bicycles and chasing balls along the asphalt lanes of Shining Acres. Often he would look at the sky, at the puffy cloud masses scooting along, and he would take off his big gray hat with the floppy brim and shade his eyes with his hand.

This hat was not of Confederate gray, but of a lighter, mineral color, nearly the same gray as the man's clothing. Nor was his attire military; he wore cotton trousers held up by a broad leather belt and a soft woolen shirt with an open collar. When he removed his hat, shining gray locks fell past his ears and the sunlight imparted to this mass of silver a whitish halo effect. He turned around to look at the Beacham house, and Harry saw that he wore a glorious gray beard, clean and bright and patriarchal, and that his eyes were clear and warm.

Even from where Harry stood, the man's gaze was remarkable: calm and trusting and unworried and soothing. When he replaced his hat, Harry recognized his gesture as easy and graceful, neither sweeping nor constrained. There was a natural ease about his figure that put Harry's mind at rest. He would still send him away, of course he would, but Harry began to soften the speech he had planned to make, to modify its ferocity and to sweeten a little its bitterness.

But when had this fellow arrived? How long had he been standing there, observing the world from his casual viewing point, with his little gray knapsack lying carelessly on the lawn? He might have been there for hours; nothing in his manner would ever indicate impatience.

Harry opened the door and called. "Hey you," he said. "Hey you, standing in my yard."

The man turned slowly, presenting his whole figure, as if he wished to be taken in from crown to shoe sole, to be examined for what he was as a physical being. "I am Wade Wordmore," he proclaimed in a voice full of gentle strength. "I have come a great distance, overstepping time and space. I am the Visitor who has been sent."

"Yeah, that's right," Harry said. "The government sent you, right? The History people? They sent you to the Beacham residence, right?"

"That is correct in some measure," said Wade Wordmore, "but I believe there is more to it than that."

"Well, go away," Harry said. "We don't want you. We've had enough—" He didn't finish the sentence he had planned to say; he found that he could not look into Wordmore's gaze and say, "We've had enough of you goddamn lackeys to last us a lifetime."

Laccckkkkeys.

"Gladly I go where I am wanted and unwanted," Wordmore said. "The world is my home, in it I am free to loaf and meditate, every particle is as interesting to me as every other particle, the faces of men and women gladden me as I journey."

"I don't mean for you to wander around like a stray dog," Harry said. "I mean go back where you came from. Go back to the government."

"But what to me are governments?" the gray man replied. "I, Wade Wordmore, American, untrammeled by boundaries, unfixed as to station, and at my ease in all climes and latitudes, answer to no laws save those of my perfect nature (for I know I am perfect, how can a man tall and in pure health be not perfect?), and am powerful to pass any border."

Here was a stumper. Harry had foreseen that Ark & Hiss would send another defective simulacrum, but he had not imagined being put in charge of a bona fide, grade-A, blue-ribbon lunatic. It was clear from Wordmore's manner as he stooped to take up his knapsack and sling it upon his shoulder that he was willing to stroll out into a century he knew nothing about, utterly careless about what would happen to him for good or ill. And beyond this privileged residential suburb, Wordmore's adventures would be mostly ill; his strange aspect and wild mode of speech would mark him an easy victim to chicanery and violence alike.

"Oh, for God's sake," Harry said. There was no help for it. "For God's sake, come in the house."

As Wordmore stepped over the threshold, he removed his floppy hat. But this gesture of deference only served to underscore a casual preeminence of presence; he entered Harry's house as if he belonged there not as a guest but as by right of ownership. "I am most grateful to you and to everyone else in the house. White or black, Chinaman or lascar or Hottentot, they are all equal to me and I bid them good day."

"We're fresh out of those. There's no one here but me and my wife, Lydie. She's not feeling well and she's not going to be pleased that I let you come in. I'll have some tall explaining to do."

But Lydie stood already in the hall doorway. She had drawn a bright floral wrapper around her nightgown, yet the cheerful colors only caused her face to look paler and her eyes more darkly encircled. Her hair was unmade and she appeared feverish. "Oh Harry," she said softly, wearily.

"Honey, I—"

"Among the strong, I am strongest," Wordmore said in a resonant, steady voice that quieted almost to a whisper. "Among the weak, I am gentlest." He tucked his knapsack under his left arm and went to Lydie and took her hand and drew her forward as if he were leading her onto a ballroom floor. He placed her in the new chocolate-colored wing-back chair and smiled upon her benevolently and gave her the full benefit of that gray-eyed gaze so enormous with sympathy.

She responded with a tremulous smile and then leaned back and closed her eyes. "I hope you will be nice to us," she said in a voice as small as the throbbing of a faraway cricket. "We've never harmed anybody, Harry and I. We just wanted to know about his ancestors who fought in the Civil War. I guess that wasn't such a good idea."

"You know," Harry said, "our genealogy papers from the government don't show any Wordmores in our family. Are you sure you're related to me?"

"Each man is my brother, every woman my sister," Wordmore stated. "To all I belong equally, disregarding none. In every household I am welcome, being full of health and goodwill and bearing peaceful tidings for all gathered there."

At these words, Lydie opened her eyes, then blinked them rapidly several times. Then she gave Harry one of the most reproachful glances one spouse ever turned upon another.

In a moment, though, she closed her eyes again and nestled into the wing-back. Harry could see that she was relaxing, her breathing slowed now and regular. Wordmore emitted a powerful physical aura, an almost visible emanation of peaceful, healthful ease. Harry wondered if the man might have served as a physician in the war. Certainly his presence was having a salubrious effect upon Lydie, and Harry decided it would be all right to have Wordmore around for a few hours longer. If he was a madman, he was harmless.

"Can I offer you a drink?" Harry asked. "We still have some bourbon left over from an earlier ancestor."

"I drink only pure water from the spring gushing forth," Wordmore replied. "My food is ever of the plainest and most wholesome."

"Tap water is all we've got," Harry said.

"I will take what you offer, I am pleased at every hospitality." He turned his attention to Lydie, placing his delicate freckled hand on her forehead. "You will soon be strong again," he told her. "Rest now and remember the summer days of your youth, the cows lowing at the pasture gate and the thrush singing in the thicket and the haywain rolling over the pebbled road with the boys lying in the hay, their arms in friendship disposed around one another."

Lydie smiled ruefully. "I can't remember anything like that," she said. "I grew up in Chicago. It was mostly traffic and street gangs fighting with knives."

"Remember, then, your mother," Wordmore said. "Remember her loving smile as over your bed she leant, stroking your hair and murmuring a melody sweet and ancient. Remember her in the kitchen as the steam rose around her and the smell of bread baking and the fruits of the season stewed and sugared, their thick juices oozing."

Lydie opened her eyes and sat forward. "Well, actually," she explained, "my parents divorced when I was five and I didn't see much of either of them after that. Only on holidays, when one of them might visit my convent school."

He was not to be discouraged. "Remember the days of Christmas, then, when you and your comrade girls, tender and loving, waited for the gladsome step in the foyer—"

"It's all right," Lydie said firmly. "Really, I don't need to remember anything. I feel much better. I really do."

Harry returned with the water and looked curiously at the duo. "What's been going on?" he asked. "What are you two talking about?"

"Mr. Wordmore has been curing me of my ills," Lydie said.

The gray man nodded placidly, even a little smugly. "It is a gift that I have, allotted me graciously at my birth, as it was given to you and you, freely offered to all." He sipped his water.

"To me?" Harry asked. "I don't think I've got any healing powers. Business is my line. I own a little video-rental shop."

"Business, too, is pleasant," Wordmore said. "The accountant weary, arranging his figures at end of day, his eyeshade pulled over his furrowed brow and the lamplight golden on the clean-ruled page, and the manager of stores, the keeper of inventories, his bunched iron keys jangling on his manly thigh—"

"Well, it's not quite like that," Harry said. "I can see what you're getting at, though. You think business is okay, the free enterprise system and all."

"All trades and occupations are equal and worthy, the fisherman gathering in his nets fold on fold, and the hog drover with his long staff and his boots caked with fine, delicious muck, and the finder of broken sewers and the emptier of privies—"

"Yes, yes," Harry said, interrupting. "You mean that it's a good thing everybody has a job to do."

Wordmore smiled warmly and took another sip of water.

"Maybe it's time we thought about making dinner," Harry said. "I'm not a bad cook. I'm sure Lydie would rather stay and talk to you while I rustle up something to eat."

"Oh no!" she exclaimed. "That would never do. I feel fine. I'll go right in and start on it."

"I wish you wouldn't," Harry said. "You ought to be resting."

"Honey," said Lydie with unmistakable determination, "you're going to be the one to stay here and talk to Mr. Wordmore, I don't care how much I have to cook."

"My food is ever the plainest," Wordmore intoned. "The brown loaf hearty from the oven, its aromas rising, and the cool water from the mountain spring gushed forth—"

"Right," said Lydie. "I think I understand."

• • •

They knew pretty well what to expect at dinner, and Wordmore didn't surprise, drinking sparely and nibbling vegetables and discoursing in voluminous rolling periods upon any subject that was brought up—except that he never managed to light precisely upon the topic at hand, only somewhere in the scattered vicinity. Yet it was soothing to listen to him: His sentences, which at first were so warm and sympathetic and filled with humane feeling and calm loving-kindness, lost their intimacy after awhile. They seemed to become as impersonal and distant as some large sound of nature: the muffled roar of a far-off waterfall or wind in the mountaintop balsams or sea waves lapping at a pebbled beach. His unpausing talk was not irritating, because his goodwill was unmistakable; neither was it boring, because the Beachams soon learned not to listen to it for content and took an absentminded pleasure in the sound. Harry thought of it as a verbal Muzak and wondered how Wordmore had been perceived by his contemporaries. They must have found him as strange an example of humankind as Harry and Lydie did.

On the other hand, they must have gotten on well with him. He'd make a good neighbor, surely, because he never had a bad word for anyone. He had no bad words at all, not a smidgen of disapproval for anything. If potatoes were mentioned, Wordmore would go a long way in praise of potatoes; it if was bunions, they, too, were champion elements of the universe, indispensable. Housefly or horsefly, rhododendron or rattlesnake, Messiah or mosquito—they all held a high place in the gray man's esteem; to him, the world was a better place for containing any and all of them.

He went on so placidly in this vein that Harry couldn't resist testing the limits of his benignity. "Tell me, Mr. Wordmore—"

"Among each and every I am familiar, the old and the young call me by my First-Name," Wordmore said. "The children climb on my lap and push their hands into my beard, laughing."

"Sure, all right. Wade. Tell me, Wade, what was the worst thing you ever saw? The most terrible?"

"Equally terrible and awesome in every part is the world, the lightnings that jab the antipodes, the pismire in its—"

"I mean personally," Harry explained. "What's the worst thing that ever happened to you?"

He fell silent and meditated. His voice, when he spoke, was heavy and sorrowful. "It was the Great Conflict," he said, "where I ministered to the spirits of the beautiful young men who lay wounded and sick and dying, the chests all bloody-broken and—"

"Harry!" Lydie cried. "I won't listen to this."

"That's all right," said Harry quickly. "We don't need to hear that part, Wade. I was only wondering what kinds of things you might think were wrong. Bad, I mean."

"Bad I will not say, though it was terrible, the young men so fair and handsome that I wished them hale again and whole that we might walk to the meadows together and there show our love, the Divine Nimbus around our bodies playing—"

"Whoa," said Harry.

"Are you gay?" Lydie asked. She leaned forward, her interest warmly aroused. "I didn't think there used to be gay people. In Civil War times, I mean."

"My spirits are buoyant always; with the breeze lifting, my mind happy and at ease, a deep gaiety overtakes my soul when I behold a bullfrog or termite—"

"No. She means—well, *gay*," Harry said. "Are you homosexual?"

"To me, sex, the Divine Nimbus, every creatures exhales and I partake willingly, my soul gladly joining, my body locked in embrace with All, my—"

"All?" Harry and Lydie spoke in unison.

Wordmore nodded. "All, yes All, sportively I tender my—"

"Does this include the bullfrog and the termite?" Harry asked.

"Yes," Wordmore said without hesitation. "Why should every creature not enjoy my manliness? Whole and hearty, I am Wade Wordmore, American, liking the termite equally with the—"

"Wade, my friend," Harry said, "you old-time fellows sure do give us modern people something to think about. I'd like you to meet my congressman and give him the benefit of your ideas. Tomorrow I'm going to drive you over to the state capital and introduce you. How would you like that?" He slipped Lydie a happy wink.

"The orators and statesmen are ever my camaradoes," Wordmore said. "I descry them on the high platform, the pennons of America in the wind around them flying, their lungs intaking the air, and the words outpouring."

"It's a date, then," Harry said. "Pack your knapsack for a long stay. I intend for you and him to become fast friends."

But when they arrived in Raleigh the next day and Harry drove around toward Representative Collingwood's headquarters, he found the streets blocked with cars honking and banging fenders and red-faced policemen trying to create some sort of order and pattern. The sidewalks were jammed with pedestrians, most of them dressed in the uniform of the Confederate States of America.

Lackeys.

"My God," Harry said. He could not have imagined that so many people had subscribed to the Ancestor Program, that so many simulacra had been produced. Looking at the people who were obviously not lackeys, he saw written on their faces weariness, exasperation, sorrow, horror, guilt, and cruel determination—all the feelings he and Lydie had experienced for the past weeks, the feeling he now felt piercingly with Wordmore sitting beside him, babbling on about the Beautiful Traffic Tangles of America.

Finally a channel opened and he rolled forward, to be stopped by a tired policeman.

Harry thumbed his window down and the officer leaned in.

"May I see who is with you, sir?"

"This is Wade Wordmore," Harry said. "You'd find it hard to understand how glad he is to meet you."

"I am Wade Wordmore," said the graybeard, "and glad of your company, admiring much the constable as he goes his rounds—"

"I'm pleased that you like company," the policeman said. "You're going to have plenty of it." He turned his bleared gaze on Harry. "We're shifting all traffic to the football stadium parking lot, sir, and we're asking everyone to escort their ancestors onto the field."

"Is everybody bringing them in?"

"Yes, sir, almost everyone. Seems like everybody ran out of patience at the same time. They've been coming in like this for three days now."

"I can believe it," Harry said. "What is the History Division going to do with them all?"

"There is no longer a History Division," the policeman said. "In fact, we just got word awhile ago that the government has shut down the whole Reality Department."

"They shut down Reality? Why did they do that?"

"They took a poll," the policeman replied. "Nobody wanted it."

"Good Lord," Harry said, "What is going to happen?"

"I don't know, sir, but I'm afraid I'll have to ask you to move along."

"Okay, all right," Harry said. He drove on a few yards, then stopped and called back: "I've got an idea. Why don't we ship all these lackeys north to the Union states? They're the ones who killed them in the first place."

"I'm afraid those states have the same problem we do," the policeman said. "Please, sir, do move along. There will be someone at the stadium to give you instructions."

"Okay. Thanks." He rolled the window up and edged the car forward.

Wordmore had fallen silent, looking in openmouthed wonder at all the cars and the Confederate soldiers streaming by and mothers and children white-faced and weeping and dogs barking and policemen blowing whistles and waving their arms.

"You know," Harry said, "I just never thought about the Yankees wanting to meet *their* ancestors, but of course they would. It's a natural curiosity. I guess it must have seemed like a good idea to bring all this history back to life, but now look. What are we going to do now?" The van in front of him moved and Harry inched forward.

"The history of the nation I see instantly before me, as on a plain rolling to the mountains majestic, like a river rolling, the beautiful young men in their uniforms with faces scarce fuzzed with beard—"

But Harry was not listening. His hands tightened on the steering wheel until the knuckles went purple and white. "My God," he said. "We've got all our soldiers back again and the Yankees have got theirs back. War is inevitable. I believe we're going to fight the whole Civil War over again. I'll be damned if I don't."

"—the beautiful young men falling in battle amid smoke of cannon and the sky louring over, the mothers weeping at night and the sweethearts weeping—"

"Oh shut up, Wordmore. I know how terrible it is. It's too horrible to think about." Then he remembered Lieutenant Aldershot and Private Harper and a gritty, tight, wry little smile crossed his face. "Bluebellies," Harry said. "This time we'll fix them."

JANUARY

This wasn't as long ago as it seems. My sister was three years old and she was following me to the barn. It was very cold. When the wind blew, it hurt, but there was not much wind. It hurt, too, when I walked fast, the cold air cutting my lungs as I breathed more deeply, and so I walked slowly.

Step for step behind, my sister whimpered. She wore only a little dress with puffy sleeves smothered in a thin blue sweater. She had long blond curls, and I thought they were brittle because it was so cold and might splinter on her shoulders like golden icicles. It was late dusk and the moon was yellow, bulgy and low over the hills of the pasture, a soft handful of butter.

There were men in the barn I had never seen. They sat on sacks of crushed corn and cottonseed meal in the dimness. They looked mute and solid. Someone said, "That's a little girl behind him."

One of the men rose and approached slowly. He was tall, and his gray eyes came toward me in the dusk. His hair was blond but not as yellow as my sister's.

"Where you from, boy?" he asked.

"Home."

"Is that your sister?"

"Yes. She's Sandra. My name is James."

"Don't she have something more than that to wear?"

"I told her not to come with me."

"You better strike out," he said. "She'll freeze to death out here."

" 'Strike out'?"

"You better light out for home." He rubbed his big wrists. "Hurry up and go on before she freezes to death."

"Come on," I told her. She was still whimpering. Her hands were scarlet, smaller and fatter than mine. I touched her hand with my finger and it felt like paper. There were small tears in her eyes, but her face was scared, not crying.

I started back. The rocks upon the road were cold. Once, I didn't hear her whimpering, and I looked and she was sitting in the road. In the dim light she looked far away. I went to her and took her elbows and made her stand up. "Come on," I said, "you'll freeze to death."

We went on, but then she saw a great log beside the road, and went to it and sat. She had stopped whimpering, but her eyes had become larger. They seemed as large as eggs. "Please come on," I said. "You'll freeze to death out here."

She looked up at me. I pulled at her. Her wrists felt glassy under my fingers. "What are you doing?" I cried. "Why won't you come on? You'll freeze to death." I couldn't move her. It terrified me because I thought she had frozen to the log.

It had got darker and the moon was larger.

I jerked her again and again, but she didn't get up. Nothing moved in her face. Two small tears were yet at the corner of each eye. She looked queer, stonelike, under the moonlight, and I thought something terrible had happened to her.

"What are you doing to her? Why don't you leave her alone?"

My father suddenly appeared behind me, huge and black in the moonlight. He, too, had a small tear in each eye. He was breathing heavily in a big jacket. White plumes of breath bannered in the air.

"What makes you hurt her? What gets into you?

She raised her arms, and he gathered her to his jacket, holding her in both arms as in a nest. She knotted herself against his chest, curling spontaneously.

He turned his back toward the moon and strode. Sometimes I had to trot to keep up, and I continued in this limping pace until we reached home.

"Open the door," my father said hoarsely.

My mother stood waiting inside and looked through my head at my sister, red in my father's arms. "What happened?" she asked. Her mouth thinned.

I went to the brown stove and put my hand flat against its side, and it seemed a long time before its heat burned me. My face began to tickle.

"What were they doing?"

I walked to the window and looked at the moon huge and yellow behind the skinny maple branches. A dim spot emerged from the windowpane as I breathed, and as I stood there it got larger and larger, like a gray flower unfolding, until it obscured the total moon.